WHAT ONCE WAS TRUE

THE ROBINSWOOD STORY - BOOK 1

JEAN GRAINGER

GOLD HARP MEDIA

CHAPTER 1

obinswood, Co Waterford, 1940
'Well, if you want to be the big man, going off to fly planes for the British, don't let me stop you.' Kate knew she probably sounded petulant, but Sam was being so annoying.

He grinned at her, the sun dazzling behind him. He looked so much older than twenty-one in his RAF uniform, and Kate hated the way he made her feel like a stupid kid.

'Kate, I *am* British,' he replied, delighted to annoy her. It was always like this—him teasing her, and her quick temper rising to it every time.

'And what about Robinswood? And all your responsibilities as the new Lord Kenefick? None of that matters anymore, I suppose? I know you are all caught up in the war and going off to be a pilot, but what about us? What about your home? Now that your father is gone, God rest him, you can't just up and leave this whole estate, the house, all the people who work here, who rely on Robinswood for their livelihoods.' She had to try to get through to him.

They walked through the orchard as they had done since they were children. The big old house up on the hill to the east of them might have looked imposing or intimidating to others, but to Kate

1

and Sam, it was just home. And, indeed, it was a beautiful house. Four floors and a basement, built in 1770 of cut limestone with red sandstone edging, with a huge front door accessed by fifteen granite steps. Verdant green lawns stretched to the ha-ha, the sunken fence used to keep the deer and cattle off the perfect grass, and beneath the bank was rich farmland, acres of it, dotted here and there with belts of trees. The winding avenue up from the village was two miles long.

Kate often admired the paintings in the long gallery of hunt balls and parties at Robinswood years ago. It was where the landed gentry had come to play, in and around the house and estate. Of course, that sort of thing no longer happened, but in its heyday, the house was one of the finest in Munster.

Kate automatically pulled weeds from the strawberry beds as she had been taught to do since she was small. Her father was the estate manager and her mother the housekeeper, so she and her sisters had scampered all over every inch of that house, just as Sam and his older sister, Lillian, did.

Sam opened the orchard door, resting his hand for a moment on the warm stone wall facing west - it absorbed the evening sun. When Kate was a child, and several gardeners worked on the estate, glass houses were built against the wall, full of grapes and lemons and pears. But no more. Old Danny O'Leary did all the gardening now, and it was all he could do to keep the grass down. Only the hardiest of fruit grew now. Sam led her down the path to the old stone bridge over the river that ran through Robinswood. On one side of the bridge was an ornamental pond with a huge marble statue of a kingfisher in the middle, and the water's surface was covered with lily pads. Kate loved it there. It was where they'd had all their serious chats over the years.

He said nothing until they were both sitting on the bridge, feet dangling over the edge, the water slowly flowing from the pond into the stream below them.

'Look, Kate, I know.' Sam's tone was no longer teasing. 'I don't want to go - well, that's not true. I do, I want to fly, be a pilot, and of course we have to defeat Hitler. It simply must be done, and we are

2

the generation to do it. My father's generation saw them off the last time, but now it's our turn.'

Kate could hear the excitement in his voice, no matter how hard he tried to sound regretful.

'But you're Irish, for God's sake, in every way that matters. I know you were born there and went to school, and you're Protestant, and the title and all of that, but you grew up here. This is your home. I just can't believe you're going to walk away from...well, from everything.' She coloured. What she could never say was how she hated the thought of him leaving her.

'No more Keneficks at Robinswood? Your family have lived in Robinswood for centuries. It's just...well, it's just wrong.'

His voice softened, and he turned to face her.

'If there was any other option, some way of keeping things going here, I'd take it, I swear I would. But there isn't. The debts my father left are beyond even what Mummy knew, and she knew a lot. He gambled almost everything. Patches of land, the artwork, antiques, horses... He never really let on how bad things were. You know what he was like—all parties and whiskey and off to the races. He didn't want to face the truth.

'And now that it's all mine, well, I've been over it with my mother, and there's no other way. We'll rent the land to Charlie Warren and close up the house. We'll sell the rest of the furniture, china, silver—everything that we can, and that will have to be used to pay the debts. Nobody in their right mind would buy Robinswood. The house is too big, and it needs a fortune spent on it to even make it waterproof. You know yourself all about the damp and everything. I hate to do it, Kate, I really do, but there's no other way. I'm going to talk to Warren, though, to make sure you girls and Dermot and Isabella are looked after. He'll probably keep your father on; he can't manage four hundred extra acres on his own, and nobody knows Robinswood like Dermot Murphy, my father always said that.'

Kate swallowed. 'When Daddy hears about—'

Sam interrupted her.'Kate, please,' Sam interrupted her. 'Let me try to sort everything out first. Don't say anything to your family until I can make sure they are provided for. Please, there's no point in worrying everyone unnecessarily. Promise me?' He lifted her face with his finger to look straight into her eyes.

She sighed.

'Please, Kate, just let me deal with it.' He gazed at her, and she melted inside.

'Fine,' she said gruffly to hide her embarrassment.

'Thanks. I'll sort this out for your family.' He looked around, taking in the beautiful vista of the trees, the babbling brook, and the glimpses of the azure Atlantic in the distance. 'I'm heartbroken, but we'll have to ship out. It's the only way.'

'There's always another way,' Kate muttered, though she was only parroting something she'd heard in a film. She'd had no idea things were so bad. Daddy and Mammy were appalled at how much land Austin, Sam's father, had given up, and while her father was excellent at his job, she knew he was being expected to do more and more with less and less money. She and her sisters, and her mother too, were taking on so much more work. Half of the household staff had been let go, and many of the farmhands were no longer full-time. No matter what Dermot did, he couldn't work with nothing.

'Look, Kate, my mother is so fed up at this stage,' Sam went on. 'Lillian is swanning around in London, not a care in the world except where her next bottle of champagne is coming from, while Mother is trying to keep my father's creditors at bay. And now that I'm going back to England as well… Well, she's had enough. But I'm going to make sure you and your family are taken care of, I promise.

'To be totally honest, she'd been trying to tell me for ages, but I didn't want to hear it. My father always said to ignore her, she was always fussing or worrying about something, and that seemed by far the easiest option. But now that he's gone and all of this falls to me, I've come to realise I should have listened to her a long time ago. Maybe if I had, I could have averted this mess before it went beyond saving. But I didn't, and here we are.'

Kate turned to look at his profile as he stared despondently into the river below. She knew he loved Robinswood and this wasn't easy for him, but surely there was something less drastic that could be done? She couldn't bear the idea of him leaving—maybe even forever.

He'd always been handsome, even as a boy, but in his RAF blues, and his curls Brylcreemed back under his hat, he was just irresistible. Of course, she would die if he ever realised how she felt about him. He saw her as a tomboy, the servants' child. Sure, she was a girl who could beat him at arm-wrestling and was not afraid of anything, but that was all he saw. Her love of Sam, and that's what it was, pure love, took her by surprise.

She was seventeen, and while she knew she wasn't very worldly, she knew how she felt about Sam Kenefick. Growing up in the dullest village on earth - Kilthomand, County Waterford - so far, her life experience went from Robinswood, to their farmhouse on the estate, to the school in the village. Someone like him, who had been to boarding school in England and regularly went to Dublin or Galway or even over to London, and now was joining the RAF... No wonder he saw her as a provincial nobody.

'You can't promise that, Sam. Nobody can. If Charlie Warren takes over Robinswood it will be up to him who he hires. He won't take instructions from you or your mother. And what about Mammy? She's a housekeeper, but Charlie Warren's wife runs their house. So she's going to be out of a job as well, all because you want to play war games with the Germans, defending a country you're not even from. No, we Murphys will have to take care of ourselves.'

She'd hoped to see a spark of something in his eyes. At night, she dreamed that he realised she wasn't some ragamuffin servant child but the great love of his life. But so far, there had been no indication of that.

'Well, I hear Aisling is going to be alright anyway. Isn't she doing a line with Sean Lacey? She'll do well there, getting her feet under the table of the draper's only son?' He nudged her to show he was joking, but Kate was suddenly angry and defensive.

'You don't know what you're talking about! My sister is not trying to get her feet under anyone's table. Aisling isn't like that. She would never go out with someone just because he had money. It shows how little you know about real life here in Kilthomand. Maybe it is better if you take off for your precious England.' Kate jumped up and stalked off the bridge. 'So go on off, Sam, and to be honest, I couldn't care less if I never see you again!'

She stormed off, seething all the way home. She was so upset at Sam leaving tomorrow for God knew how long—maybe he would never come back—and then how dare he say that about Aisling? She was by far the nicest of the three Murphy sisters, two years older than Kate and two years younger than Eve, and she was in love with Sean Lacey. Even if nobody in the Murphy family thought Sean was good enough for Aisling—he was a bit of a Mammy's boy and really boring with it—Aisling really liked him.

When she let herself in to their house, everyone was out. The clock ticked loudly on the dresser as it had done for as long as she could remember. She loved their home, though technically it belonged to the Keneficks. It was as part of Dermot's package that they got to live there, but they saw it as theirs. In fact, Kate didn't think any of the Keneficks had ever stepped inside the door.

In lots of ways, it was so much nicer than the big house. It was cosy and warm and always smelled of baking or fresh laundry. It had a large kitchen where everything happened, with a huge AGA stove for keeping the whole house warm. There was a parlour as well, but it was north facing and always felt cold so they hardly ever used it. There were three bedrooms and a bathroom upstairs, but the three girls shared a room, and the spare room was full of stuff. Mammy was a meticulous housekeeper, and the place was always neat and tidy, but that one room was full of clothes that didn't fit, old coats, toys, and all manner of other rubbish she should really have thrown out but had yet to get around to. The girls were happy sharing anyway. They had three single beds in a huge sunny bedroom that overlooked the river on one side, and on the other, you could see as far as the ocean. Her parents had the back bedroom.

Kate checked the cake tin, and sure enough, there was an apple tart inside. Kate could eat anything she wanted and never gain an ounce of weight. It drove her sister Eve mad because she had to watch her figure, though Kate thought she was imagining the fat. She went to the larder, spooned the cream off the top of the milk, and poured it on her apple tart. She always ate when she was upset. She never understood those ones in the films fading away to nothing when the hero goes off with someone else. She was the total opposite.

Mammy would be still up at Robinswood, cooking and cleaning, and Daddy would be out milking for another hour at least. Eve was helping him, because yet another farmhand had been let go, and Aisling was gone into the village for some groceries, hoping to bump into dreary Sean, no doubt.

So Kate went up to their bedroom and threw herself on the bed. Only then did she allow herself to cry. She really didn't want Robinswood to change. It was all she knew; her whole family relied on it for everything. But that wasn't the main cause of her tears.

What if some German shot Sam's plane down? What if he got killed and the last thing she ever said to him was that she didn't care? Maybe she should go back and apologise. He was leaving tomorrow morning.

But she couldn't. She'd have to go up to the house, and though it wasn't ever said outright, she knew Lady Kenefick would not be in favour of their friendship, so they'd always kept it under her radar. She was such a snob, Kate couldn't stand her, but neither her father nor her mother allowed any talk like that in the house.

She cried into her pillow. Even Eve and Ais wouldn't understand. They'd think she was off her head to be setting her cap at Samuel Kenefick. She probably was, too.

CHAPTER 2

'Mammy will murder you if she sees you with that,' Eve warned Kate, who was busy pulling all sorts of faces in the mirror to spread the tiny amount of scarlet lipstick on her generous lips. She was testing it out in the hope of being allowed to go to the dance.

'Where'd you get it, anyway?' Eve flopped down on the middle bed.

'It's Aisling's, but don't breathe a word or she'll go mad. Old Lady Kenefick gave it to her, said it was almost gone anyway. But sure that old bat is half blind—there's loads left.'

'Kate, don't say that about the mistress, you know full well she's only in her fifties and she is remarkably well preserved at that. I do wish she'd employ some more young lads for the milking, though. I'm exhausted from it.' Eve sighed and examined her cracked and broken nails.

'Well, she's like a briar since her precious Sam is gone off to single-handedly finish off Hitler,' Kate muttered. 'Not that he ever did much farming anyway, but still. The workforce situation is getting ridiculous. Daddy is shattered; he nearly bit the head off me earlier when I mentioned about the dance in the hall on Friday night.'

Eve smiled at her sister's indignation.

'Not that there's going to be any point anyway. There'll probably be nobody even half decent left to dance with anyway. All the good-looking fellas are gone over to England—Sam Kenefick, Douglas Radcliffe, Daniel Burgoyne...'

'All the Protestants, you mean.' Eve grinned. 'There's plenty of local lads who are still here. Sure, can't you dance with them?'

'Ah, Eve, you're as bad as Aisling, in love with that clown, Sean Lacey. She is so much better than him, I just don't see what she sees in him. I met him in the village earlier, and he hardly was able to string a sentence together.'

'You probably scare him.' Eve winked. 'There's some nice lads still left. What about the O'Learys? Or Damien Keane, he's always smiling at you at Mass?'

'Damien Keane is a child; sure, he was a class below me in the national school. And as for the O'Learys, all they care about is heifers and silage, and they'd bore you to tears. The only hope would be a gang would come out from Dungarvan; otherwise, we're stuck with the local eejits here with their dung-encrusted boots trampling the toes off you and thinking if they buy you a bottle of lemonade they'll get a grope in the bushes on the way home. Sam is so lucky to be away from this place. Imagine what it's like in England compared to here? I was reading that there's going to be Americans over there soon, and dances every night, and everyone in uniforms. It sounds fabulous, doesn't it?'

Eve threw her eyes heavenward. Kate was full of the romance of the war. It was all over the newspapers, every single day, and Mr deValera was full of how it is nothing to do with us and we're a neutral country and all of that. Eve was sick of it already, and it was only just started. She hoped it was going to be over quicker than the Great War. They said the last time that it was all going to be finished by Christmas, but it dragged on for four years. Chamberlain had done his best to avoid a war coming so soon after the last one, but Hitler wasn't going to be stopped, it would seem.

Most of the local Protestants were gone, but then, they felt more English than Irish. Kate had expressed a wish to join them as the family walked home last Friday night after Mass. Mammy and Daddy had nearly gone cracked when she said it.

'Would you have a hair of sense, you foolish girl?' Daddy said unusually sharply. He usually indulged Kate's mad notions. 'The British have sent more than enough young Irish men to their deaths that last time out. At least this time, deValera is keeping us out of it, and out of it we'll stay. Now, I'll have no more talk of such rubbish. Join up indeed, and go over there and fight their war for them? No chance. Churchill and Hitler can be scrapping away to suit themselves —'tis one of them, two of them, as far as I'm concerned. But I'll tell you this: no child of mine will have anything to do with it. Do I make myself clear?'

'Yes, Daddy.' Kate had been despondent, and Eve squeezed her arm. She was the youngest, and she was a divil for a bit of adventure. Eve could hardly blame her; life these days wasn't exactly exciting. The same dull routine of housework and farmwork, day after day. They were expected to pitch in even more now as staff were let go.

'Come on, let's go down and have a cup of cocoa to warm us up.' Eve dragged her weary body off the bed with a sigh. 'I'm fit to collapse, but I'm freezing. Let's get a heat up downstairs and then get into bed.'

Kate looked down ruefully at her chapped hands as she got up to follow Eve downstairs.

'I'm wrecked, too. I swear Mammy was finding smears on purpose,' Kate grumbled. 'I polished the fire irons about fifty times, but still, it wasn't good enough. And anyway, it's all going to be sold and the house closed up, so why on earth is she on a cleaning frenzy? She had Sheila Hanratty and Jenny Glavin helping poor Ais to clean the flipping windows. Four floors and only three of them to do it, and all of this before Aisling went to visit drippy Sean and his scald of a mother. And Lady Muck then swanning around as if she's loaded when the whole parish knows she hasn't one shilling to rub off the other.'

'If Mammy or Daddy hears you talking like that, you'll be for it,' Eve warned. Since they were small girls, their parents had drilled into them the need to keep a respectful distance from the family of the house and estate they served.

'I know, I know, but I'm only telling you, Eve. Sure, I can tell you anything; you're like the grave, Mammy says.'

Eve gave a hoot of laughter.

'Oh yes, Kate, I'm like a grave all right.' She winked and pushed the door open into the big warm kitchen. 'Aisling should be back soon.'

'And we'll have to hear all the fascinating details of Mrs Lacey's latest hymn for the choir.' Kate sighed dramatically.

'Ah, Kate, don't be mean. You know Aisling was all excited to be invited to Laceys for her tea. I know he's a bit of an eejit, but she's mad about him, so try to be nice, all right?' Eve shivered and pulled the old brown flannel dressing gown around her. It had been left behind by one of the guests after the Robinswood New Year's Eve Ball two years ago, and even though it was a man's dressing gown, Eve loved how cosy it was.

Their parents were still out, so Eve set some milk to heat on the stove and Kate went to the larder for the cocoa.

'I'll be absolutely gushing, I promise. Though why our Aisling, who is gorgeous and could have anyone she wants, is considering shackling herself to the monosyllabic Sean Lacey and his warbling screecher of a mother, I will never know.' Kate shook her head theatrically, and Eve giggled. 'He's not even good-looking. Not like Sam!'

Eve swiped at her and rolled her eyes.

'You better not let anyone hear you going on like that about Samuel Kenefick, miss.'

Despite the years between Kate and Eve, they were very close. And even though the little sister was incorrigible, she had a way of making everyone see the funny side of things. For example, Mrs Lacey ran the choir with an iron fist, and even poor old Father Hartigan was afraid of her, so nobody challenged her. That's why the devout of Kilthomand had to endure her ear-splitting version of *How Great Thou Art* every Sunday, trying not to wince as she almost reached the high notes. Her only child, Sean, was her pride and joy, so the invitation extended to Aisling was a very significant event.

Eve went on to admonish her youngest sister,

'And anyway, Sean is nice.' Eve poured the hot milk into two mugs and stirred in the cocoa. 'He's just a bit shy. But Aisling says he's very chatty with her, so that's all that matters.'

'I'll never understand it.' Kate shook her head and took her cup to the old armchair beside the stove. 'There's a whole world out there beyond this place, and yet she's hitching her wagon to Kilthomand's bachelor boy. I'll tell you something for nothing—I definitely don't want to go with any of the fellas from around here. Sure, where would that lead? Only to a life that never ventures beyond the parish of Kilthomand for your whole life? Not for me, Eve, no way. I'm going to travel the world and have adventures and give scandal wherever I go by keeping bad company and drinking gin.'

Eve laughed out loud at her little sister. She really was a character.

Kate drew attention wherever she went with her unruly black curls. She looked like a painting Eve had seen one time of a gypsy girl, all dark hair and flashing eyes. She was tiny, barely five feet, with a handspan waist that Eve could only dream of. And Kate knew full well the effect she had. Men found her delightful, and women thought she was flighty. Both were right.

There was no mistaking her and Aisling as sisters. Aisling was taller, and her hair was straight but the same jet-black. And she had the same voluptuous curves and dark-blue eyes—almost navy blue. They both took after their mother, who always told them they got their looks from their grandfather, who had been a Spanish sailor who fell in love with an Irish woman in the west of Ireland when he was delivering wine. The story went that he couldn't bear to leave her, so he settled in County Galway and they raised a huge family, Isabella being the youngest. When people questioned her exotic name, their mother explained she was named after her father's mother, who pined away in Granada for her only boy, who would never leave Ireland.

Eve caught a glimpse of herself in the mirror over the dresser and sighed. To be fair, the brown dressing gown and beige bedsocks probably didn't do much to improve the situation, but she definitely was more like her father's side. Tall and well built, strong from all the manual labour, with copper-coloured hair that was neither curly like Kate's nor shiny and straight like Aisling's but just kind of wavy with a mind of its own. Her hazel eyes were set wide apart, and a sprinkling of freckles dusted her nose. She didn't take the sun, unlike her sisters and mother, who in the summer were the colour of conkers. She felt so dowdy beside them and was sure that where looks were concerned, she'd really drawn the short straw.

Aisling burst in the door. It was unusual for the three girls to be at home alone, but their mother had gone to settle Mrs Kenefick in for the night and Daddy was out looking for poachers. Someone was helping themselves to rabbits and pheasants off the estate, and he was determined to find out who it was.

'Well, how was the big occasion?' Kate delivered the last word in a high-pitched warble that had her sisters giggling.

'Stop!' Aisling took off her coat and hung it up behind the door. 'She was grand. Not exactly welcome-to-the-family, but fine. Poor Sean was mortified, though, with her going on and on about how he was top of his class in school, and all the hurling medals he won, and how he was basically the best person for four counties. Poor fella nearly died. He kept trying to change the subject, but she's determined, you'd have to give her that. I had to see his certificates and medals and everything. That house is like a shrine to him. He was disgraced.'

'So did he walk you home?' Kate asked slyly, nudging Eve.

'He did, and that's as much as I'm telling you because you are obsessed with sins of the flesh, and 'tis down on your knees you should be, praying for your own black soul instead of worrying about what two respectable young people get up to on a perfectly innocent walk home. Now, is there any more cocoa going? I'm perished.' Aisling winked at Eve behind Kate's back.

'A chance to be obsessed with sins of the flesh with someone would be a fine thing,' Kate responded, not realising her father had entered the kitchen behind her. Eve smiled as she made her sister a drink.

Dermot Murphy looked suitably horrified at the conversation going on between his daughters.

He opened his mouth to say something but closed it again. He once tried to be an authoritarian, but with three opinionated daughters and a spirited wife, he had long since accepted his fate.

'Don't worry, Daddy, we're only messing,' Kate said when she spotted him. 'Sure, nobody around here is up to anything, only working and sleeping.' She smiled sweetly and kissed her father on the cheek.

CHAPTER 3

*L*ady Violet Kenefick gazed in dissatisfaction at her reflection in the harsh winter morning light and sighed. Old age really was most dispiriting. At fifty-five, everything sagged so badly, which was quite unfair when she'd taken such care of her skin in her youth. Her hair was thinning, but she just couldn't bear to cut it. She'd worn it long all her life, though nobody ever saw it these days, since she'd kept it in a low bun on the nape of her neck for decades now. Her once glittering blue eyes had dulled, and the svelte figure of her youth had become that of a thin middle-aged woman.

She gazed miserably at the pile of bills Isabella had delivered to her room with her breakfast tray. She didn't need to open them; she knew already how dire the situation was. They owed money everywhere.

Since Austin had died, she really did find the running of the estate a real bother. She'd never realised how much he did, she admitted to herself. Of course, Samuel, being his only son, inherited everything, but it was up to her to look after it all now that he was so busy with the RAF. She felt regret at forcing him to face the reality of their situation, but they'd had no other option.

Up to the day Austin had died, she'd assumed his days were spent in examination of the racing form and walking the land. At night, they would have a preprandial aperitif together in the small sitting room; the large one took forever to heat up, so they'd left it closed up, apart from over Christmas, when they entertained. They'd discuss the trivialities of the day, or at least she would—who was ill, who was courting, what the news of the village was—and Austin would half listen and half read the paper, always muttering something at the appropriate pauses.

When he died in his bed, aged seventy-four, she had been sad, of course, but she'd had no idea how much she would miss him. He was more like an old faithful dog than a husband in many ways. They'd not shared any intimacy since Samuel was born, and that was over twenty-one years ago now. Nonetheless, they rubbed along nicely together. Violet found being a widow really was trying, and to find herself a *penniless* widow, well, that was really the final straw. She found any vaguely fond memories she had of her husband were being eroded with each new bill. He really had driven them to the edge of destitution. He'd never pretended things were any other way, but she'd been sure he had something put away.

He hadn't.

She rose from her dressing table and stood at the window of her bedroom. The draught immediately caused her to draw her cardigan more tightly around her. The timbers were rotten, but there was no money for such repairs as might add to the Robinswood's creature comforts. The estate was run well enough by Dermot Murphy and his family, and his wife Isabella really could work marvels on the limited household budget. But, no matter how good they were they were not miracle workers. She could kill Austin for leaving her in this mess, if the irritating old fool were not already dead.

THE KENEFICKS WERE a military family first and foremost, and Austin had given quite a good show in the Great War. Battle was in the Kenefick blood, he was fond of saying. There was a cabinet full of medals in the drawing room to prove this, not that Violet ever looked at them. Samuel loved them, however, and could name each one, and which of his ancestors won it.

The news of just how bad things were had come as a shock to Samuel. Violet had tried before to raise the issues of their ever-dwindling funds, but Austin was alive then, and he and the children teased her for making an unnecessary fuss. It was the running joke: here's Mummy, getting all het up again. But Samuel was under no illusions now. She took no pleasure in being right; it had hurt her to see the pain on her darling boy's face when he realised his title, his family seat, everything was about to go. Some support from her daughter at this difficult time would have been welcome, but of course, Lillian didn't give a fiddler's, so long as the funds kept coming. The new reality would mean a drastic readjustment for all three of them. They were used to things being a certain way all their lives, and they'd imagined it would go on like that forever.

Violet glanced at the dark patch on the wall where the portrait of the former Lord and Lady Kenefick once hung. It had been sent for auction, though whoever would want a painting of the less than glamorous elder Keneficks hanging on their wall, she couldn't fathom. The idea of Austin's father glowering with his hairy eyebrows and handlebar moustache or his timid little wife looking anxious in a stranger's house was bizarre. But if it raised some much-needed funds, who was Violet to question it?

Archibald Kenefick, Austin's father, had made a fortune when stationed out in India in the glorious Edwardian era because he had fingers in many pies. That was back when there was real money to be made, before the foolish and ungrateful native people started agitating and demanding to leave the empire. Really, it was most ignorant, the same thing here in Ireland; people really were a mystery. But, despite the fortune he'd been amassing, old Archibald had despised India and the heat and the flies, so he'd retired back to his estate here in Waterford, leaving the whole operation in the very incapable hands of his son. His utterly silent wife, Delia, Austin's mother, followed like the little lamb she was.

Archibald grumbled often enough about his son being a wastrel and good for nothing, but he could stick the heat no longer, and so Austin was left in India allegedly managing the business but in reality going to parties, hunting, having clothes made, and generally enjoying himself.

It wasn't entirely Austin's doing, she had to admit. Perhaps she should have intervened, though in what way, she couldn't imagine. Their home in Shimla had been sumptuous, but then lots of people worked for them, so living a less grand life would have hurt those in their employ. And the Indians were notoriously tricky when it came to business. They didn't dare try to hoodwink grumpy old Archibald, but Austin signed things without even glancing at the contents and gave all power to the manager.

She sighed. Those were the days; she had been so happy then. They'd both lived life to the full, enjoying all the exotic world of the British Raj had to offer and making absolutely no provision for the future.

She left the window and returned to her writing bureau, a beautiful wedding gift from her parents. She rifled through the buff-coloured envelopes until she came to a cream one, and immediately she recognised her daughter's writing. She'd better open it, she supposed, though she had a fair idea of its contents. She slit the top with the beautifully carved knife, part of a set given as an anniversary gift from the Farleigh-Bowes, and unfolded the single sheet therein.

Dear Mummy,

Apologies for the brevity of the note, but I really am at my wits' end. I desperately need an injection of funds. I simply cannot continue like this, it is so humiliating. Hector's deplorable girlfriend even made a catty remark last night at bridge about people outstaying their welcome. I simply have to get a little flat of my own. Chelsea, Kensington, even Bayswater, anywhere (within reason, obviously). It's not a matter of want Mummy, more need. Sam, at least, can stay at the base, but I am virtually destitute.

Your daughter, (in case you'd forgotten)

L

Violet folded the letter and placed it back in the envelope. She dreaded the conversation when she told Lillian the truth. She had hoped Samuel might meet up with her in London, tell her himself; after all, it was his estate now. But he and Lillian had little in common and didn't seek each other out. Violet sifted through the letters again, hoping for perhaps something more cheerful from Samuel, but there was nothing. His last visit was a flying one. He'd been back at the RAF base at Biggin Hill for weeks now, and she'd only had one short note.

VIOLET LIFTED the debutante picture of her daughter she kept on her desk. It was taken five years ago, and she was still not married. Violet sighed. Lillian was passably beautiful, but utterly and completely useless. She had no skills whatsoever, was not especially bright or gifted with any creative ability, and seemed to think that money grew on trees. Her father had spoiled her of course, able to refuse her nothing.

He never let on to the children how bad things actually were, managing instead to sell off a few heirlooms and horses and the like to keep afloat. But now there was nothing left but the house and its contents—minus the more valuable pieces—and most of the estate. Alarmingly, he had gambled several parcels of land as well, so Robinswood had shrunk considerably, to add to their woes.

Lillian's face beamed out of the photo, and Violet smiled. She could not berate her daughter too much. She herself was more or less the same when she was a young woman, except she'd had the good sense to snap up a husband. Lillian was not lacking in admirers, but she seemed to have an aversion to settling down. She was as skittish as a mule and could settle to nothing, including a boyfriend. At least when Violet moved to London, she could keep a closer eye on her, encourage friendships with the sons of her titled friends, and hope-fully get her married off and installed as mistress of some lovely seat in the home counties as soon as possible. It would be nice to see more of her. She was a good sort really, just, well, useless.

. . .

She thought back once again to the glorious days when she was a girl in Shimla. Austin used to tease her when he caught her wearing what he called her 'India face.' Something about her memories of that time softened her, but the reality of dreary Ireland always brought her back to earth with a bang.

Her father had been transferred from London to oversee the packaging and exportation of tea, and Violet remembered the excitement when he came home and told her and her sister they were moving to the other side of the world. Mother had been horrified and hated every second of their exile, but Violet and her sister Agatha simply adored it. A lifestyle that their father's generous enough salary could simply have never afforded in England became their norm.

Long days passed, days of tennis parties and dances at the Viceregal Lodge. It was there she met Austin in the long, happy summer of 1908, and they married in 1910. They'd had the most glorious wedding, in Shimla. She'd never wanted to leave. Servants, dressmakers, endless days spent in frivolous diversion—they'd had no idea how their idyllic life was about to change.

But change, it did.

The war came, and Austin went off to fight. Her father was recalled to London, and he took his wife and his unmarried daughter Agatha with him. Violet thought she could stay on in India alone; after all, she was a married woman and knew absolutely everybody. But Austin firmly said no, and so she was dispatched, unceremoniously, from their beautiful villa in Shimla, in the foothills of the Himalayas, to his parents' draughty, crumbling old pile here in County Waterford.

Oh, how she despised damp, cold, inhospitable Ireland! The Irish were so different from the Indians. Mostly, the Indians were grateful, saw the significant benefits that British rule of their country brought —but not here. Here, all they wanted to do was get rid of every last Briton, by fair means or foul. Finding herself expecting Lillian, and later Samuel, compounded her sense of being stuck.

It was during The Troubles—that's what they called it when the Irish Republican Army wreaked terror on the people, burning houses and attacking policemen. Back in the twenties, so many of the neighbouring families who lived in houses like Robinswood even had to leave for a while. Everything they were was a symbol of the hated occupation of Ireland by British encroachers. At least that was how the natives saw it. Austin and his parents refused to go, however, much to Violet's horror. She would have loved to go back to England. She didn't like Ireland, not from the very first day she set foot in this infernal country. She tried to tell Austin they should leave, if only to keep their children safe, but he scoffed.

'We'll be fine. Nothing to worry about for us. We know the right people.' He refused to elaborate, but she always got the impression that Austin sympathised somewhat with the Irish.

Eventually, things settled down. There had been all sorts of nonsense, but Ireland got the freedom she apparently so desperately wanted, and life returned to normal. The two old Keneficks died in due course, Archibald as curmudgeonly as always, and Delia silently, as she had lived. Violet and Austin then assumed the titles of Lord and Lady Kenefick of Robinswood.

And now, here she was, alone.

'A fine estate,' Austin would often remark as she surveyed his land from the breakfast-room window, cup of Darjeeling in hand. Typical Austin, fond of saying things but not such an expert at actual action.

He was a lazy man, she knew it. He liked the Lord of the Manor lifestyle, but he did not enjoy any work as such. He attended every race meeting in Ireland and was one of those men known by everyone. A real hail fellow well met, Austin could charm the birds from the trees, but when Violet or Dermot Murphy tried to talk to him about the state of the books, the yields and all of that, Austin just tuned out. Violet, while she thought Dermot far too proud for a servant, was grateful for his efforts at getting Austin to see sense. But all her husband ever did was clap Dermot on the back, saying, 'I have every faith in you, Murphy, old boy.'

Dwelling on what Austin should or should not have done to turn Robinswood into what could have been a very profitable business was a fruitless exercise at this juncture. Austin was gone, and that was that, though she would have wrung his neck if she'd had the chance. Samuel was in the RAF, having passed out of the Royal Air Force College at Cranwell with flying colours rather than going to Sandhurst as his ancestors had done. Samuel was a natural-born flier and well on the way to a glittering RAF career. Austin would have been so proud to see his boy in his RAF blues. War came too soon for Violet, and she couldn't bear to think of her darling boy flying over enemy territory, but Samuel couldn't get at the Germans fast enough. And burdening him with details of monies owed seemed, well, unpatriotic.

'Well, damn you, Austin,' Violet muttered crossly.

The aroma of baking bread wafted up from the kitchen. Isabella was preparing the meal for this evening, though it hardly seemed worth the effort just for one. Still, she laid the table in the dining room each evening, and there, Violet sat alone.

Not for too much longer, at least. Charlie Warren, a neighbouring farmer, was going to lease the land, and Samuel had reluctantly agreed they should sell off what was left of the antiques, paintings, china and glass, and all the rest of it, and shut the house. Nobody would buy it even if Samuel could have borne to sell it. Whether or not the place would ever reopen was anybody's guess, but they could live off the proceeds and the rent of the land combined. Not the lavish life Violet had come to expect, but they would survive.

Once she relocated to London, a dealer was taking all the house contents, and Violet assumed the land would be farmed as it always had been. Charlie Warren was a recalcitrant man, but she imagined he would keep the Murphys on, or Dermot at least. He couldn't think he would manage Robinswood all alone, surely. What with the war on, food production in Ireland was booming. In the right hands, Robinswood could be very profitable, and Dermot Murphy knew the place like the back of his hand. They'd been loyal and good servants, and their house was part of the arrangement. But Samuel had said Warren was noncommittal when he mentioned them when he went over there before he left. He'd been really worried about the Murphys, but she'd assured her son it would be fine, Charlie Warren was just like that.

An agent had sent her some brochures of houses for rent in London. Being a tenant didn't appeal particularly, but it would suffice in the short term, until everything was sorted out.

For a while, she'd considered relocating back to Shimla. It was where she'd been happiest, after all. But the war had put paid to that plan. No, at least for the time being, there was nothing for it but to move to London and then retire and live the life of a gentlewoman.

Telling the Murphys was another matter.

CHAPTER 4

$\mathcal{K}$ate was driving her mother to distraction.

'But it's only in the village hall, Mammy! What on earth could happen to me in the village hall in Kilthomand? It's not exactly New York City now is it? Please, Mam, I'll do everything you want me to do next week, and I won't even complain about the flippin' chickens, even though they make me want to vomit. Aisling and Eve can come with me. Please...'

Isabella knew her youngest daughter could be relentless when it came to things like this, and she wished Dermot would come home soon. Though she was the more authoritarian of the two, Isabella knew her husband would back her, and Kate had been mithering at her about the dance all day. She was at breaking point. Ever since Sam Kenefick had left for England two months ago, Kate had been impossible. Isabella knew her youngest daughter well and could tell she was besotted with the new Lord Kenefick, but that would get her nowhere. And Isabella knew full well Kate only wanted to go to the dance so she could write to him about it later and try to make him jealous. Still, maybe letting her go to the dance was a good idea; she might meet someone more suitable. But Dermot would have to be convinced. In the meantime, she would maintain a strong opposition.

'Kate.' Isabella stood and faced her daughter squarely. 'Aisling doesn't want to go to the dance, because Sean Lacey isn't going, and Eve has no more interest in dances than the man on the moon. Your sisters have never gone to the village dance, and I don't see why it's such a big thing for you. There is no way on God's green earth your father is going to allow you down there with all the old batchelors of the parish, and every parish for miles around, to be ogling you. You are a lovely girl, Kate, and some day you'll meet a nice lad, but in the meantime—'

'AND HOW IN the name of God am I to meet this nice fella if all I see is the inside of the chicken coop every day of my life?' Kate interrupted. 'Would you mind telling me that? Because, Mammy, the only things inhabiting that stinky coop are chickens! I just want to go for an excuse to get dressed up, and just for the craic, you know? Life is so boring here, the same hard work day in, day out, with nothing to look forward to. And now that Sam is gone, well, I've no friends, Mam. None of us do. We just need to be young and have a bit of fun now and again. The people in Kilthomand see us as part of the Keneficks, and the Keneficks only see us as the servants. We've always kept ourselves to ourselves, and that's fine. Me and Eve and Ais are best friends anyway. I'm not looking for a boyfriend or anything; I just want to have a dance and a laugh. Is that too much to ask for?'

Isabella suddenly felt sorry for her lively, fun-loving daughter. She was heartbroken after Sam, and she was right, their lives were very humdrum. Aisling was all about Sean, and Eve didn't seem to mind— she was kind of a practical girl, like her father, just getting on with things—but Kate was a live wire, and life in Robinswood was very dull. Isabella loved all her daughters for different reasons. Eve was so steady, so generous and responsible, and Aisling was sweet tempered and always saw the best in people. But her youngest child held a special place in her heart.

Isabella smiled at her. Kate was very funny when she was riled. Her dark eyes flashed, and her curly hair escaped in coils from her ponytail. She'd have no shortage of admirers, but her father really believed her much too young to be thinking about romance.

Aisling came in the back door with a bucket of pig's blood, set it down on the floor, and rubbed her hands where the handle was cutting into her skin.

'Urrggh!' Kate exploded. 'That is revolting! Honestly, I'll marry anyone who is not a farmer. Farms disgust me.'

Aisling grinned. 'You won't be saying that next week when we've made the black puddings and we're frying up rings of it in dripping for your breakfast. You'll forget quick enough what the pudding is made of.'

Aisling heaved the bucket up again and landed it in the pantry. 'Sean says he's amazed how I'm not one bit squeamish,' she called from the pantry, and Kate rolled her eyes at her mother. 'He said he thought all girls were afraid of mice and didn't like to get their hands dirty.'

'More gripping stories from the life and times of Sean Lacey, the most boring boy in Kilthomand, and that's saying something,' Kate muttered.

Isabella swiped her with the tea towel she was using to dry the delph.

'Don't be mean,' her mother warned, a smile playing on her lips.

'Honestly,' Aisling went on as she entered the kitchen once more, oblivious to Kate's remarks, 'I don't think he knows anything about girls at all. Mrs Lacey runs a very tight ship, I'd say, no girls allowed past the threshold, so it really was nice of him to invite me to come for my tea, wasn't it?'

Isabella nodded cautiously. Secretly, she agreed with Kate, and she would not have chosen Sean Lacey for her lovely, sunny daughter. He was all right, she supposed, but not near nice enough for Aisling, and the fact that his mother was such a tartar didn't help. The Laceys owned the draper's shop in Kilthomand, and even though it was a small little shop, Noreen Lacey behaved as if it was Switzers above in Dublin she had. So Isabella had been surprised when she heard Aisling had been invited to the Lacey house; she would have thought Noreen would have set her sights higher than the daughter of the manager on Robinswood estate for her one precious son. Still, he was harmless enough, she thought. Both she and Dermot only hoped he would make Aisling happy.

'It certainly was nice of him.' Isabella said nothing else.

'Don't mind about all of that.' Kate was off again. 'Aisling, please come to the dance on Saturday. Mammy says I can't go because you and Eve aren't going.'

'That is *not* what I said, Kate Murphy, and well you know it. I said you were not allowed because you are too young, and even if your sisters were going, which they're not, you'd be staying at home. So trying to convince Aisling is a total waste of time. Now, peel those potatoes while I do the carrots and parsnips, and if I hear one more word about that blinking dance, I'll murder you with my own bare hands, do you hear me?'

Kate was sullen. It was absolutely ridiculous. She was virtually an adult—she'd be eighteen in July—and still she was treated like a child by everyone, including Sam, even though he was only four years older than her. She dug the eyes out of the potatoes with venom. As she gazed out the kitchen window onto the yard and across the triangular field, her eyes settled on Robinswood. How she wished he was still there, that she could run over after dinner and they could sit on the bridge and talk like they always did. She hated that he'd left on a bad note. She'd written, but every letter ended up in the bin. She didn't even know how his meeting with Charlie Warren had gone. She wondered if Daddy had spoken to him yet? She hated knowing something her family didn't, but Sam was right—better get everything sorted out and then tell them, rather than everyone going off half-cocked with only a bit of the story.

Robinswood without the Keneficks was so hard to imagine.

It wasn't a mansion, not like the ones you'd see in books, like ones they had over in England, but it was a big house all the same. Before Lord Kenefick had died, they used to have dances there, and hunt balls, and Kate remembered sneaking down the back stairs and watching all the dancing from the balcony above the ballroom.

Carriages would come crunching down the driveway, and all the gentry from Waterford and Cork and Tipperary would come in all their finery. There were loads of staff in those days, and even more brought in for the night, and Lillian and Samuel would be all dressed up as well. It all looked so glamorous, and Kate remembered thinking how on earth could there be anywhere more exciting than Robinswood? How times had changed.

Violet Kenefick was all right, Kate supposed; she always gave each of them a ten bob note at Christmas, but she was a bit posh and spoke in a very lah-di-dah way, which was ridiculous considering she'd lived most of her life in Kilthomand. She didn't know Kate and Sam were good friends, and she would have had a stroke if she did. Kate wondered where Sam was now. It was hard to imagine him in an aeroplane, and she got a thrill of excitement every time she tried to picture him. She used to spend the spring counting down the days to the summer holidays, when Sam would come home from boarding school in England. He loved to hear about her family and often remarked how different it was from his own.

Lady Violet and Lord Kenefick had separate bedrooms, which had bewildered Kate as a child. Her mammy and daddy had a big feather bed that had room not just for them but for Eve and Aisling and her too, so she wondered why Lord and Lady Kenefick needed a bed and a bedroom each.

'Maybe the Lord snores so Lady Kenefick couldn't sleep,' Mammy suggested years ago, knowing that fobbing Kate off never worked.

'Does Daddy snore?' she'd asked.

'Never, he's totally perfect in every way.' Mammy winked at Daddy, and he grinned from behind the paper. They were always joking around like that.

Kate gazed up at the sky and thought about Sam as she peeled the spuds. He got to have all the fun, and here she was, stuck here. The sound of conversation outside in the yard interrupted her reverie.

Peering out the window, she saw Eve come around the corner from the stables, and behind her was a man Kate had never seen before. Strangers were rare at Robinswood these days, so curiosity dispelled her dark mood.

They entered the house through the back kitchen door, so he mustn't be anyone very important, Kate surmised. As she turned to meet the visitor, he took his cap off and smiled. He was very good-looking in that country way, not like Samuel Kenefick and all his RAF friends, but they were out of this world. This lad had dark hair that fell in front of his eyes when he took his cap off, and he had the most piercing blue eyes. He was slight but muscular and had a gorgeous smile. She flashed him one of her best grins—she'd been practicing in the mirror. Isabella shot her a warning glance and turned her attention to Eve and the visitor.

'Mammy, is Daddy about?' Eve asked. 'This is Jack O'Neill. He's working over for the Warrens, and he was wondering if he could borrow the plough tomorrow for the day because theirs hit a rock and buckled, and Teddy Leary's forge is shut because he's gone to his cousin's funeral in Wexford.'

'Sorry for interrupting your work, ma'am,' the lad addressed Isabella politely. 'I wouldn't ask, only we're badly stuck.'

She smiled.

'That's not a Waterford accent?'

'No, Mrs Murphy, I'm from Cork, but I'm working here.'

'Well, Jack, my husband is above at the house, but I'd say it will be fine if it's only for a day. He's busy with repairing the fences that came down in the storm last week, so he won't get to ploughing for a while, I'd imagine. Take it away. Eve will show you where it is. Have you a way of bringing it back?'

'Thank you very much, ma'am, that's very kind of you. I have indeed. I've the donkey and cart outside, if the cursed animal is still there. A more cantankerous creature you couldn't meet. I'll have it back to you either late tomorrow evening or first thing Friday morning.'

'That's fine, Jack.'

Before he could go and walk out of their kitchen forever, Kate piped up,

'If you're new here, you should go to the dance in the village hall on Saturday. Everyone is going. You'll get to meet everyone.'

Jack smiled slowly. 'I'm not much of a dancer then, Miss...'

'Kate. Kate Murphy.'

'Miss Kate, two left feet I'm afraid.' He turned to go.

'Well, you don't have to dance. You could just...mingle.' Kate smiled coquettishly, and her mother shot her another glance to say *enough with your carry-on*. If her father saw her flirting like that, he would not see the funny side.

Jack was anxious not to give offense to either mother or daughter, so he did the wise thing and beat a hasty retreat. Eve led him around to the shed, where they kept the plough.

'Here, I'll help you to drag it out,' Eve offered. 'It's a ferocious weight.'

'Not at all. 'Tis good enough of ye to lend it to us without you having to put your back out dragging it.' Jack bent to lift the metal plough and failed to budge it.

Eve leaned on the doorjamb of the shed and smiled.

'My father has a kind of trolley cart over there. He kind of shunts it onto that, and then he can pull it out on the wheels. But it will take two.' She went to get the low platform on wheels her father had made for just such jobs.

'I'll never live this down, that a girl had to help me lift it,' Jack said between gasps as they heaved the heavy plough onto the trolley.

'Oh sure, the whole place will have the story by the morning, I'll make sure of it,' she teased him.

With much huffing and puffing, they managed to drag the trolley out to where the donkey waited.

'So, Miss Farmer of the Year, any thoughts on how we get the blasted thing up on the back of the cart?' Jack stood with his hands on his hips, breathing heavily from the exertion, surveying the scene. The plough was beside the cart, but they would need to hoist it up a good four feet to get it onto the back of it.

'There's a hoist over there. We use it for lifting the farrowing

30

crates. If we could drag the trolley over and then line the cart up alongside, we might be able to do it?'

Jack shook his head in amazement as he removed his jacket. The effort of lifting and dragging the heavy plough had soaked his shirt, and it clung to his muscular back.

'You're much more than just a pretty face,' he remarked, and then immediately reddened. He wasn't one of those lads who was always trying to charm women, obviously.

Eve was embarrassed as well, but secretly pleased he thought she was pretty, even if he was just repeating an old phrase. Aisling and Kate were the ones all the lads watched when they went up to receive Communion at Mass every Sunday. They drew everyone's attention because they were so exotic-looking.

She said nothing, but together they dragged the trolley over to the hoist, then Jack went back for the donkey, who stubbornly refused to budge an inch.

'Move, you stupid beast,' Jack muttered, pulling on the headcollar. But the donkey refused to move.

Eve strolled over and smiled.

'He's not helping you today?'

'This animal doesn't help me any day, he's neither use nor ornament. 'Tis like he's determined to make a total eejit of me. I'd swear he knows, does it on purpose. I can't lead nor drive him. And he'll do whatever the other lads want, no bother, a more obliging creature you'd never see, but he has some kind of a set against me.'

'Did you ever beat him?' Eve asked cautiously. She loved animals, and even though Robinswood was a working farm, and animals were slaughtered, she tried to be kind to all creatures while they lived.

'No, I did not, tempting though that might be. I couldn't hurt him. I think he knows that too. He smells that I'm too soft or something.' Jack chuckled. 'You must think I'm a right clown.'

'No, I don't—' Before she could go on, the donkey stepped forward and started nuzzling her pockets. She reached into her coat and pulled out an apple she'd brought as a snack to eat when she went up looking for lambs on the ridge this morning and had forgotten about.

31

She offered the apple to the donkey, and docile as a lamb, he walked slowly across the yard after it, right to the hoist. Once they were lined up, Eve gave him the fruit, which he crunched noisily.

Jack shook his head again. 'Well, that traitorous creature! I know when I'm outdone, Miss Murphy.' He grinned, and Eve felt herself smile.

Together, they pulled the ropes on the hoist and managed to get the plough up on the cart. The donkey gave a start at the sudden weight, but he soon settled.

Jack made sure the plough was tied down with a rope and went around to the donkey's head once more.

He rested his hands on his thighs and looked straight into the donkey's face.

'Now, Donkey, one man to another, will you please not disgrace me even further in front of this lovely girl? Be a good donkey now, and we'll walk home nice and slowly, and I'll have a lovely bit of hay for you and even a turnip if you're on your best behaviour. Have we a deal?'

Eve laughed out loud.

'You're as daft as the donkey!'

He nodded. 'Probably, Miss Murphy, very probably.'

'It's Eve, by the way. There are three Miss Murphys, so you'd better call me Eve.'

'Eve, what a lovely name. It's nice to meet you, Eve, and thanks for all your help. I couldn't have done it without you.'

'You're right about that. Goodbye so.' She grinned and turned to go back to the house.

'Goodbye, Eve. I'll be back with the plough and my trusty steed here tomorrow evening. I hope I'll see you then?'

She turned. 'You will, I suppose.'

Eve tried not to skip back home.

CHAPTER 5

*V*iolet had been holding off until she heard from Christie's, the auction house in Dublin she'd contacted with a view to selling off the contents of Robinswood. They came back reasonably quickly with a guide price, and while it wasn't spectacular by anyone's standards, it was a sum which would, when combined with the rent of the land, allow her, Samuel, and Lillian to live, just about.

She glanced around the room. There were tell-tale pale patches on the peacock-blue walls where paintings had once hung, and the furniture was faded and worn with age, but there were things dating back years and years and quite a few nice pieces. Funnily enough, she felt no sadness at parting with them. She always saw them as belonging to Austin's family.

She felt rather like the house herself these days—old, pointless, and neglected beyond retrieval. She most likely wouldn't even bother to take much of the stuff that remained for her new house, wherever that might be. Let the *nouveau riche* squabble over the Royal Doulton dinner services and the Waterford Crystal decanters and show it all off in their ghastly new houses. That sort of thing would sell, the auctioneer had assured her, but the furniture was the issue. Most of it was too big and cumbersome for a normal sized house. Heirlooms from a bygone age.

She would ask Lillian and Samuel if there were any specific things they wanted brought over to England, but they would have to be small. Shipping was going to be difficult and costly, even more so now because of the war.

In general, she tried not to think about it and avoided the newspaper and wireless. She remembered when Austin was at the front, during the last war. She hadn't worried about him. Something had told her he would be fine, and he would return and they would have a family. But the thought of Samuel up in the sky, only the thin metal of an aeroplane between her boy and Hitler's bullets and bombs, filled her with a dark dread. Part of her wanted to stay away from the war, but a stronger part felt, irrationally, she knew, that if she was on English soil once more, gazing up at English skies, she could, in some way, protect Samuel.

The Irish prime minister—though they didn't call him that, they used some ridiculous Irish word for him that was virtually unpronounceable—was behaving despicably in his refusal to move on the subject of Irish neutrality. And what is more, the people of Ireland seemed to be thrilled about it. Jolly bad show, she thought. Of course, there were issues, between the Irish and the British, that was bound to be the case after so many years of uneasy living together over here, but surely, they could rise above these petty squabbles and do what was right. Put their shoulders to the wheel, as it were, and join the war effort. But it would seem not.

She wondered what Dermot Murphy thought about it all. He never discussed politics, either Irish or British, but she supposed someone in his position, working for Lord Kenefick, could have been a target back in The Troubles, so perhaps that's why he remained tight-lipped. Austin had mentioned cases he'd heard of, in 1920 and 1921, when things were very bad, where people who worked for the Anglo-Irish gentry, as her class were called, were penalised by the thugs in the IRA. Their fellow Irishmen, harassed and often attacked simply for earning a wage to support their families. She wondered if

Dermot Murphy ever experienced anything like that. If he did, he'd never mentioned it. He'd always been loyal and hardworking. If only the man were a little more deferential, he would be fine.

She stood up once more and watched as he crossed the yard. She would have to tell him the truth. He and his family would have to leave Robinswood. The only hope would be if he were to have better luck with Charlie Warren than Samuel. After all, the Irish tended to stick together. She did feel bad, but one has to do what is best for one's own family, she reassured herself. She rapped on the window, and he looked up. She beckoned him into the house.

SHE WAS DREADING this conversation but the sooner it was over the better. 'Ah, Dermot, come in. Have a seat, won't you?'

'I'll stand, if you don't mind, m'lady. I'm fairly dirty.' Dermot stood on the timber floor, refusing to step onto the rug.

She watched him for a moment, noticing him properly for the first time in ages. She realised that she'd seen Dermot Murphy virtually every day of her life for over twenty-six years and yet she had never actually seen him. She thought he was in his forties, late forties probably, and he had reddish brown hair, still quite full and wavy and combed back off his face. He was tall, with a slim, muscular build, and she now realised how much Eve was like her father. They both had that handsome, solid presence about them. The younger two were Isabella through and through, much more European-looking than Irish, but Dermot and indeed his eldest daughter, Eve, were very striking.

'No, please, sit, it doesn't matter about that.' Violet could not say what she needed to if he was all the way over at the door.

'Very well.' Dermot walked in and sat opposite her, as he'd presumably done so often with Austin over the years. Austin had been so much better at dealing with the staff. He was Irish, after all, she supposed, and he just seemed to be able to connect with them in a way that eluded her. And, of course, he was a man, so they could talk about men's things, whatever they might be. Horses and dogs and matters of that nature, she imagined. She had never actually had a conversation longer than ten seconds with Dermot Murphy in her life. Still, she'd just have to do her best.

She took a deep breath.

'Dermot, you know how much you and Isabella and the girls mean to me, to the whole family, and indeed to Robinswood itself, I am sure, but I'm afraid I have some news that you may find somewhat discomforting.' She paused. It was going to be considerably more than discomforting to potentially lose their home and their livelihood in one fell swoop. She would have liked to have been able to give them a better settlement, help them set up again elsewhere, or at least a guarantee that Warren would keep them on, but she couldn't.

Dermot waited. He was unnervingly calm. He was one of those people who did not feel the need to fill awkward silences. You could never truly know what he was thinking. He was always perfectly polite, but something about him had always intimidated Violet slightly. She dismissed the thought as absurd. She was the lady of the house, and he was the gamekeeper, groundsman, and, yes, he had a myriad of other responsibilities, but still, he worked for her. She had to keep telling herself that. He was her inferior, not the other way round.

'Well, the fact of the matter is, the estate has been running at quite a considerable loss for many years now. Due in no way to your excellent management, I hasten to add. But it is the case nonetheless that as a property, and indeed, a business, Robinswood has run up what are, frankly, insurmountable debts.' She tried to keep her hands on the desk in front of her, but she found herself twisting her handkerchief, a most irritating habit she'd been unable to shake off since her childhood.

Again, Dermot just sat there.

'I know. I did try several times to speak to Lord Kenefick on the matter.' His tone was gentle but firm.

'Yes. Indeed, you did. As did I. But, well, we are where we are. Which leaves me, really, with no other option, but to, ah...close the house and rent the land, I'm afraid.'

The silence hung heavily between them in the drawing room. Violet wished he would say something. She knew he wouldn't rant or plead, but he must surely react in some way.

Really, the man was infuriating.

She could hear Austin's voice in her head: 'Well, you hardly expect him to dig you out of the hole you've made for yourself, do you, old girl?'

Her husband had found Dermot to be an intriguing kind of man; she just found him strange.

When he said nothing, she went on laboriously. 'And so, Charlie Warren will rent the land, and the contents of the house will go up for auction in Dublin in April. I will, at that stage, vacate the house, and I hope to purchase a smaller house in England. Much smaller, actually. Though, with everything so uncertain with the war, well, we shall see.'

She didn't intend for the conversation to go in the direction of her future plans—she'd decided earlier that it would be insensitive—but in the vacuum created by the infuriating man's stubborn silence, she'd just blurted it out.

'And am I expected to vacate our family home at that stage as well?' His words were like stones falling on the carpeted floor.

'Well, Dermot, we did ask. Samuel made specific enquiries regarding your future with Mr Warren, but he was noncommittal. Perhaps if you meet with him yourself? Samuel also did ask that he take into consideration your service to the family and your extensive knowledge of the estate, but as I said, he wouldn't be drawn.' Violet knew she was sounding pathetic, but she didn't know what else to say.

'Right.' Dermot's voice betrayed no emotion.

'Of course, once the sale of the contents goes through, I will be able to make some small financial settlement on you, in respect of the fine service you and your family have shown. I wish I was in a position to give you more, but as I mentioned, there are many debts and—'

'Do you know when in April? Early, late?'

. . .

VIOLET NOTICED it was the first time he'd ever addressed her without reference to her title. He usually said *m'lady* or *ma'am*. But he was bound to be upset, so she tried not to bristle.

'No, Dermot, not yet, but I assure you once I have word, I will make you aware of the date with all haste.'

Either way, it was February now. That only left two months at the outside.

He nodded and stood. He said nothing, simply walked out the door, leaving it open behind him.

Violet stood at the window, a little bit back in case he turned and looked up, as he strode down the driveway.

CHAPTER 6

*I*sabella watched her husband as he ate his dinner silently. He wasn't the most talkative man in the world at the best of times, but something was wrong, she knew it. The girls were chatting animatedly as usual as they tucked into the stew that was heavy on carrots and spuds but very light on meat. They'd been self-sufficient for so long, and ate very well as a result, but since Robinswood was no longer producing its own food, they were reliant on shop-bought produce, and that needed to be paid for.

Lord Kenefick had managed somehow to keep the place limping along, but since he'd died, the cracks really were showing. Things hadn't been prosperous since his father, the old Lord Kenefick, was alive, but Austin used to get a lucky break on the horses now and again, or some wealthy old relative would 'pop their clogs just in time to keep the wolf from the door,' as he was fond of saying.

Isabella missed him around; he was a charming old goat. Not beyond flirty remarks or trying for a squeeze now and again, but basically harmless. She never told Dermot that, of course, and Austin was perfectly well behaved when her husband was around, because Lord or no, if Dermot thought Austin was making free with his wife, the old lad would find himself knocked into next week.

Isabella would never forget the time they were back in Galway, visiting family, when this fella she used to know vaguely as a girl decided to try his luck at a local dance they'd gone to with her cousins. They were not long married, and Isabella pointed out her wedding ring politely and assumed it would be enough to deter him, but this eejit had too much porter on board, so after she politely declined, he made a grab for her to get up to dance.

She then told him firmly that she was waiting for her husband, and he called her a not-very-nice name. The next thing he knew, he was on the flat of his back in the middle of the dance hall with Dermot standing over him, silent but unashamed. She smiled a little at the memory. Of course, she admonished Dermot for fighting and making a show of them, but secretly, she was pleased. Dermot loved her and the girls with such depth and sincerity. He didn't say much, but he didn't need to. They had a connection that went much deeper than words. She caught his eye over the dinner table and gave him a smile. He'd tell her what was bothering him tonight in bed; that's when they did all their talking.

Isabella was drawn back to the girls' conversation.

'So is Jack going to the dance? He might if he thought you were going, Eve.' Kate winked at Aisling, who giggled, and Eve blushed.

'He told you he's not a dancer, Kate, and anyway, what difference would it make to me if he went to the dance or not, for goodness sake?' Eve looked flustered.

'Well, you're not getting any younger, Evie darling, and you don't want to be left on the shelf, now do you?' Kate laughed. ''Tis high time you were looking around to see what's on offer. He seemed nice. A bit rough around the edges, obviously, from all that rough work, but not too bad.'

Aisling helped herself to another ladleful of stew. 'Jack is a hard worker, just like us.'

Kate sighed. 'I wonder how Sam Kenefick is getting on over in England?'

Eve gave her a warning glance; their parents would not like her mooning over the heir to Robinswood. She wanted to put Kate off even thinking about Sam in those terms, and though it seemed cruel in the short term, there was no future in it.

'I'm sure he's grand. Sure, he's of the officer class; they don't send them out to do the fighting at all. They decide who does what from behind a desk, and the poor lads with no rank get to risk their lives. Just you watch, he'll be all dolled up in his RAF uniform, and he'll marry some lady or heiress, and she'll come back here and he'll use her money to fix the place up. I bet that's what will happen, and Lady K will be able to sleep easy in her bed without the wind whistling around her ears from the draughts.'

Kate swallowed. Nobody in the family knew the truth.

There would be no rich wife for Sam coming with her money to fix the place up. For the millionth time, she wondered if Lady Kenefick had spoken to Daddy. If he didn't say something soon, she would have to tell him what she knew. She felt so disloyal, but she'd promised Sam she would stay quiet, and anyway, maybe he would sort it out with Charlie Warren. She nailed a smile onto her face so as not to betray the anxiety she felt and steered the conversation back into safer waters.

'Maybe he will, and maybe he won't. Anyway, in the meantime, what are we to do? Sit at home, knitting, when there's a perfectly good dance on in the village hall tomorrow, and it coming down with men looking for wives. Three spinster daughters, Daddy. I'm surprised you're not hunting us down to the dance yourself to see would we snare three rich farmers for ourselves.'

Dermot swallowed the last mouthful of stew.

'That was lovely, Bella, thank you.' He gave her one of his special smiles, the rare ones meant especially for his wife. Then he turned to his daughters.

'And I know I will probably regret asking this, but why are you not going to this blasted dance if it's going to be so wonderful?'

'Because your wife won't allow us,' Kate said with a frown.

Dermot glanced at Isabella, who gave an almost imperceptible shake of her head.

'Well, she's the boss, so if Mammy says no, then no it is. Now, clear

41

away here, you three. I'm going for a smoke. Will you come with me, Bella? 'Tis a bit chilly, I know, but you can take my big jacket if you like?'

Something in his request told Isabella that it wasn't just company for a stroll on a chilly February evening he wanted. They needed to talk, clearly, and getting five seconds' peace in that house was close to impossible.

'Right so, my boots are by the door there.'

Dermot helped her into her wellingtons. There had been a lot of rain, and the ground was soaking.

Isabella slipped her hand into her husband's as they crossed the yard, and he put both his and her hands into his coat pocket. Such displays of affection were not often seen around Kilthomand, and she knew it elicited whispers when Dermot held her hand going up to Mass, or the odd time they went to the pictures. But neither of them cared in the slightest. Dermot was his own man, always had been, and she loved that about him.

When the IRA were burning all the big houses during the War of Independence back in 1920, so many Protestant land owners went back to England for safety. Dermot was warned by a loudmouth after the mart in Dungarvan to have nothing more to do with the Keneficks. The local IRA were all right, but this man came from Cork. He was starting to throw his weight about, and eventually he came up and challenged Dermot. Called him all the names going, including a traitor to his country, for working for the Keneficks, the symbol of British rule in Ireland. Dermot had taken him aside and in one or two sentences told him to check his facts before he showed up out of the blue, making accusations.

Isabella knew her husband had been involved with the IRA. Gun running, attacks on police barracks, and keeping men of the Flying Columns safe in their house or in the Keneficks' barns was part of life back then. She remembered when Eve was only a baby, Dermot waking her to take Eve out of bed so some man could hide in the base of the cot. Eve was put back on top once he was settled in, and when the auxiliaries came round on a house-to-house search, all they saw was a sleeping baby. Dermot was always above reproach, being so loyal to the Keneficks; the British assumed he wouldn't dream of going against them. But he was a proud Irishman, and he did what needed to be done for his country.

That was a dark time, and Isabella was glad it was all over. The carry-on in Europe, on the other hand, was getting worse with each passing day. It seemed hard to believe it wouldn't touch them here in Ireland, despite Mr deValera's assurances.

They walked through the yard behind the house in companionable silence, as Dermot smoked a cigarette. He'd tell her whatever he had to tell her in his own time.

The stables were empty now, apart from Titan, the old cart horse. All the rest of the horses had been sold. The sheep were still there, munching away, but the cattle were dwindling. Austin had moved from the lucrative dairy herd to beef, because it was easier and less work, but the estate badly missed the monthly milk payment from the creamery.

'Herself called me in today, Bella.' He kept walking but pulled her closer to him. 'She's closing up the house, renting the land.'

'What?' Isabella felt like she'd been punched in the stomach. She knew things were bad, but they'd been bad before and something always saved the day—or someone. She just assumed the same thing would happen again.

'She can't do that, can she, Der? Sure, it's not just our jobs, it's our home too. Is she evicting us?' Isabella tried to keep her tears in check.

He stopped and turned to face her. He took her hand and gently led her to a small stone wall, where he sat and drew her onto his knee.

'She's renting the land to Charlie Warren. She asked him to keep us on, but I doubt he will.'

Isabella clung to the slight hope.

'He might, though. I mean, he can't run his own place and Robinswood as well. He's going to need someone, and you're the best person for it.'

'I know, but I just don't think he will. I'll certainly talk to him, but don't get your hopes up.' Dermot sighed heavily.

'But, Der, if he says no, where will we go? I mean, there's nothing around here. Kenefick's is the biggest farm for miles, and everyone else farms their own land.' The IRA had driven most of the gentry out in the twenties, and they hadn't come back... She was trying not to panic, but it was hard.

'Look, something will turn up. I promise you. I'm thinking, though, about the girls. Whatever hope we might have of getting something, together, hopefully in a big house again, we won't have much hope with the three lassies in tow.'

Isabella looked up at him. This was breaking his heart. She hated to hear the pain in his voice.

'Maybe we should let them go to the dance, Bella. Husbands with farms is exactly what they'll need now.'

Before it was a running joke in the house—Dermot bemoaning how he'd never get such girls as theirs off his hands because of them being so troublesome. But now there was no hint of a joke.

Isabella couldn't bear the thought of being separated from her daughters. 'Maybe they could get jobs, near us somewhere?'

'Let's see what comes up. There is something else, though, another way of getting money.' He spoke quietly, though there was nobody but them for at least a mile.

'Go on,' she said, though she didn't like the sound of it.

'I could apply for a pension from the government.'

Isabella didn't understand.

'A pension for what?'

'An IRA pension. The government give them out in respect of military services to the state during the War of Independence. I never wanted the money before, and anyway, the Keneficks would have probably sacked me on the spot if they found out what went on during those days. But, well, now, I've nothing to lose.'

'And they give you money for that now, after all these years?' Isabella was deep in thought. 'What would you have to do to get it?'

'Someone senior would have to vouch for you, I think, verify that you really did what you say you did.'

'And you could get someone to do that?' She shivered; with the weak sun setting there was a biting breeze.

'Yes, I don't think it would be a problem. I'd ask Oskar if he was here, but there are plenty of others who made it who knew me back then. So will I do it? It will finish us with the Keneficks and their like for good, but maybe that's a good thing. It's not much money, the pension, but it would be enough to keep us going for a bit anyway, until I found another job.'

He opened his big coat and put his arms around her waist, drawing her close to him, wrapping his coat around her. She rested her head on his chest.

'If you think it's a good idea, I suppose you should. I'm just worried, about us, about the girls, the future...'

He rested his chin on her head, his arms holding her tightly.

'Don't worry, Bella, I'll look after us, and I'll mind the girls too. Please, don't worry.'

So close against her husband, feeling his heart beat against her ear, the working-man smell of him, she knew somehow they would be all right.

CHAPTER 7

'Eve!'

Eve looked up from the metal bathtub in the pantry where she was rinsing the sheets.

'Eve, he's here! Oh for God sake, look at the cut of you! Here, take off that old apron and tidy yourself up a bit.' Kate was fussing around her.

Eve knew perfectly well who she meant, but she pretended she didn't.

'Who's here? Oh, Kate, get off me!' She swatted her sister as Kate tried to tame Eve's copper waves.

'Jack, you clown,' Kate gushed. 'As if you weren't waiting for him all morning! I saw you looking out that window about a thousand times since breakfast.'

Eve reddened.

'See? I knew it!' Kate crowed victoriously. 'Now, for the love of God, will you tidy yourself up and go out and say hello and not be all sweaty and mad looking?'

Eve took down her ponytail and shook out her copper curls. She splashed cold water on her face and straightened her cardigan and dress. Kate almost shoved Eve out the door into the yard, where Jack was thanking her father for the loan of the plough.

Eve felt awkward, standing in the doorway. She couldn't just go up and join them, or say something funny like Kate could. She tried to go back inside, but Kate was blocking the door, and now Aisling had appeared from upstairs and was in on it too.

'Oh, Eve, he's lovely looking. No wonder you like him.' Aisling strained to see over Kate's head as the youngest sister determinedly barred Eve from getting in.

'I don't—well, he's grand, but he's... He's just delivering back the plough and... Oh for God's sake, let me back in this second, Kate, I'm warning you!'

Kate refused to budge.

Eve turned around, deciding she'd leave altogether if they wouldn't let her back in. She turned to go down the lane.

But Daddy called her over. 'What's this I hear about my daughter being strong enough to lift the plough? Well, Evie, if I knew you could do that, I wouldn't have been pulling and dragging the bloody thing myself all these years.'

She went to join him and Jack, and Dermot gave her a quick squeeze with one arm.

'We did it together.' The words came out crossly, which wasn't her intention, but she was flustered.

'So I've been hearing.' Her father smiled gently. 'Anyway, Jack, 'twas nice to meet you, and thanks for dropping it back. There was no need to be in such a rush, but sure maybe there was more bringing you back here than the need to return a plough.' He grinned at Eve and winked.

Eve could have strangled her father. She was absolutely mortified as Jack looked down at his boots.

'Right, I think Bella is looking for me, so I'll leave ye to it.' And her father strolled off whistling, his hands in his pockets.

Eve wanted the ground to open and swallow her up. All the easiness of the previous day was gone, and she could not think of one sensible thing to say.

She was twenty-two but had no experience talking to men really. There were lads that worked on the farm, coming into the kitchen for dinner at harvest time or when they were lambing or calving, but she just helped her mother to serve up the food and passed the time of day with them. Then there were the corner boys gathered after Mass on Sundays, and she knew Aisling and Kate got a lot of admiring glances, but Mammy and Daddy were always with them so nobody ever approached them. The only male she really knew was Sam Kenefick, but he was a Protestant, and rich, and everything she wasn't, so he hardly counted.

'So, ah... The donkey sends his regards.' Jack smiled shyly.

'Did you not bring him today?' Eve was glad the conversation was going again; the silence had been excruciating.

'No, the boss said I could take the cart horse instead. She's a very nice old mare who does what I ask and doesn't try to kick me or stamp on my feet.'

'Well, that must be a relief, I suppose.' Eve wished she could think of something wittier to say. If she were Kate, she'd have had him hanging on her every word by now.

'Eve, em... Remember your sister was saying about the dance, tonight in the village hall?' Jack was looking down at his feet again.

'She talks about nothing else. She has the whole house driven half cracked with it.' Eve wondered if Jack was going to ask about Kate, if she was going or something. Her stomach churned.

'Well, I was wondering, if...if you were going, or if you wanted to go maybe, then I could take you?' He was looking straight at her now, hopeful and unsure.

Eve swallowed and could feel her face redden. He was asking *her* out, not Kate.

'I...I'd have to check, but I...I would like to go,' she managed to get out.

'Really?' he sounded incredulous. 'W-Well, I'll come over around seven, will I? And if you can go, then great, and if not, well...I'll just go back.'

'Or you could go anyway?' Eve blurted, and immediately regretted

48

it. Why would she be encouraging him to go alone, and the whole parish there full of girls looking for someone more interesting than the same old eejits that had been knocking around for years?

'Well, I'm not much of a dancer, I told you that yesterday, but I'd love to take you out, so if you can't go, I won't go.' He smiled, and her heart gave a little leap.

'I'll go. Mammy and Daddy won't mind, but I'll probably have my sister with me. Is that all right?' Eve knew they would never let her go without at least Aisling. They would probably still refuse to allow Kate—she was only seventeen—and a part of Eve hoped they would. Kate done up would turn any man's head, and she didn't want Jack distracted by her younger sister, much as she loved her. Aisling wouldn't dream of flirting, and besides, she was besotted with Sean Lacey. Kate, however, could do or say anything.

'Grand, I'll be the envy of the place arriving with the three best-looking girls in Kilthomand.' Jack was delighted and seemed more confident than he had a moment ago.

'Well, two of the best-looking girls, anyhow.' Eve grinned. 'And their sister.'

'What?'

'Well, it's just, Aisling and Kate, they're usually the ones everyone looks at...' Eve was blushing now to the roots of her hair. Why did she start this?

'You're not serious, are you?' Jack put his head to one side, and his eyes held hers.

'Ah, I was just joking. I just meant my two sisters are the good-looking ones. They have Mammy's Spanish blood. But I'm more like Daddy's side, big and brawny and—'

'I think you are the nicest-looking girl I've ever seen in my whole life, Eve Murphy, and if you'll go to the dance with me, I'll be the proudest man in Ireland.'

There was something so sincere, so honest in that sentence, that years later, Eve would pinpoint it as the exact moment she fell in love with Jack O'Neill.

* * *

Isabella and Dermot watched the exchange from the kitchen window.

'He seems all right, I suppose.' Isabella wasn't convinced anyone was good enough for her girls.

'He's a grand lad. I knew his father, Mick O'Neill, back in the day. He and I and Oskar were friends at one time. He used to do some work for the Warrens as well; him and a few other Cork lads came to work there seasonally. He was a kind of travelling odd-job man. Very nice fella he was too.'

Dermot thought back to those days, him and Oskar, his closest friend, taking all sorts of risks to rid their country of the British. It seemed like a lifetime ago now. It surprised him that he hadn't thought of his old friend for years.

Isabella turned; something in Dermot's voice suggested he wasn't telling her everything. 'Was? Is he dead?'

'He is. He was shot by the Free State army in 1923.' Dermot spoke quietly so neither Kate nor Aisling would hear if they were to walk in. 'He went against the treaty, but loads of them did in Cork. He saw Collins as a traitor and hated everything the Treaty represented. His beliefs, wrong as they were, made him take arms against his own friends, men he'd fought alongside. But that's how things were in those days.'

'Had he other children?' Isabella asked.

'I don't think so, but I can't remember, to be honest. I just remember hearing he was gone. I was kind of out of it by then, but Oskar wasn't, so he told me about it. Apparently, Mick had been ordered to stop in the street by the Free Staters, and he refused, so he was shot. Sure, that lad out there could only have been five or six at the time.'

'Oskar Metz,' Isabella said. 'I was only thinking about him the other day, when they were on about Germany on the radio. I wonder what he's doing? 'Tis hard to imagine him all the way over there now. Anyway, back to this Jack lad, he's not involved in anything now, is he? I don't want Eve mixed up in anything like that.'

'Sure, there's nothing going on for him to be involved with. She'll be grand, and the way things are going, it would be good to have at least one of them settled.'

Isabella did not like that answer, and her face showed it. The idea that the only reason young Jack O'Neill wasn't plotting against the British or the Anglo-Irish gentry was because there was nothing going on did not fill her with confidence. Especially because it wasn't true.

'Nothing going on, indeed,' she snapped. Isabella was not going to be fobbed off. 'Tell that to Henry Somerville, who was shot in West Cork by the IRA for recruiting young fellas into the British army. And what about the raid on the army barracks' guns above in Dublin last Christmas? What did the IRA want all those guns for if they're gone away? Dermot, the IRA are alive and well, and you know it as much as I do. This war is great news for them—the same old ideas again—Britain's difficulty is Ireland's opportunity and all of that? God knows what they've planned, but it won't be good anyway, that's for sure.'

Dermot put his big hands on her shoulders and looked down into her face,

'Yerra, anyone with a hair of sense has realised those days are over now. 'Tis only a few simpletons and diehards are left, trying to keep it going. Young Jack out there isn't involved in anything, I'm sure of it.'

'Hmm.' Isabella wasn't so sure. Feelings were still running high in the country. The name had only just officially changed to Ireland, after being 'the United Kingdom of Great Britain and Ireland' for eight centuries. And though it was essentially independent, it had yet to become a full republic. If Jack's father was so involved with the Irregulars that the Free Staters shot him in the street, then was it likely his son wanted nothing to do with it?'

'I wonder is Oskar in the German army?' Dermot mused.

'Well, sure if he is, he's one age to you, so he's either in it fairly high up or not at all. I hope he's not. Funnily enough, I never think of him as German. I mean, I know his father was and all of that, but he was more like his mother and growing up here and everything, he was

Irish. Remember the nights he came back here, and Eve was only small and he'd be around the floor with her on his back?' Isabella smiled at the memory of the blue-eyed blond lad who was always full of fun and games despite the seriousness of the situation.

'I do,' Dermot said. 'I remember him well. He saved my life.' Dermot gave her a swift kiss on the cheek and shrugged into his jacket once more; he had to meet the dealer who was buying the remaining cattle.

Isabella remembered the blue-eyed blond lad, always full of fun and games despite the seriousness of the situation. He gave her a swift kiss on the cheek and shrugged into his jacket once more, he had to meet the dealer who was buying the remaining cattle. As Eve walked back into the kitchen, the girls came running downstairs.

'Well?' Kate was fit to burst. 'What happened?'

Aisling was excited for her older sister, too. 'Did he ask you out?'

'He asked me to go to the dance tonight,' Eve said shyly, unused to being the centre of attention.

'Oh my God! That's absolutely stupendous.' Everything was stupendous with Kate these days, since she'd heard it in a film.

Kate looked at her mother and immediately launched her attack. She spotted her chance, and she took it. 'You're not going to try to stop her now, are you? Jack is after asking Eve to the dance, and sure, she can't go alone! I mean, we don't know who this fella is—he could be a criminal, for all we know. No, the only safe thing is for me and Aisling to go with her.'

Kate was suddenly on her knees on the kitchen floor, theatrically begging her mother. 'Ah, Mammy, please, please say yes! Daddy wants us to go, but he's only waiting on you. We're all only waiting on you.'

Isabella ignored her and addressed Aisling. 'Do you want to go?'

Aisling looked down at her youngest sister, and over at Eve. 'I don't, really. Sean isn't going, so I wasn't going to. It might not be right, like if Mrs Lacey heard I was out dancing and poor Sean at home doing the books for the shop...' Aisling was torn; she didn't want to let Kate and Eve down, but the wrath of Mrs Lacey was a formidable force. 'I suppose I could go with you, Eve, but I'd hate if Mrs Lacey—'

'Ah, for the love of all the saints in heaven, Aisling, ye're not even walking out properly, and already he's deciding what you can and can't do!' Kate was fit to explode.

'Kate,' her mother warned. 'Enough.'

'Fine, fine! Look, Sean's grand, the finest in the world if you're into that sort of thing, but what Sean Lacey and his mother should have to do with whether I—I mean, *we*—get to go to the dance tonight is a total mystery. We are free agents, fine single girls, out and about in the metropolis of Kilthomand of a night...'

'All right, all right. If Aisling will go, ye can all go. You'd try the patience of a saint, do you know that, Kate Murphy?' Isabella could hardly get the words out as her youngest daughter smothered her in hugs and kisses. 'Honestly, I don't know where you were got; that kind of carry-on is from your father's side anyway. None of our crowd went on like you!' She pulled away from her daughter.

'But Daddy will be collecting you, do you hear me? On the dot of eleven! And unless you want him disgracing ye by going into the dance hall in his pyjamas and escorting ye out, ye'll be outside and ready to go, is that clear?'

"Ah, Mam, sure, Jack is taking Eve, can't he walk us home?' Kate asked. 'And that way there won't be any hanky-panky between the two of them, with me and Aisling keeping a close eye.'

'There won't be any hanky-panky either way, not with *any* of my daughters,' Dermot said as he came back in from the yard to overhear the end of the conversation. 'And it's not Eve I'm worried about.' He kicked off his boots and sat beside the fire.

'Chance would be a fine thing, Daddy. Sure, all the single fellas around here are so old 'tis down on their knees they should be, praying for a happy death.' Kate grinned as she scampered up the stairs to get ready, and her mother and sisters couldn't help but laugh.

CHAPTER 8

*D*ermot walked purposefully up to the Warrens' front door. He would rather have done anything else, but his family needed to come first, so he would humble himself if needs be.

A young servant girl opened the door, and Dermot removed his cap.

'Hello, miss, I was wondering if Mr Warren was at home?' He spoke gently, and some of the suspicion left her eyes. Men calling at eight o'clock at night wasn't the norm.

'He's out in the yard, sir. His horse is lame, and he's checking on her.' She seemed uncertain.

'Oh, right. I'm Dermot Murphy from Robinswood beyond; I'll just stroll out to him so. Sorry for disturbing you.'

He put his cap back on and turned towards the stables.

Warren was in a stall with a mare, fixing a poultice to her fetlock.

'Evening, Charlie,' Dermot said over the half door.

Warren looked up. He said nothing but continued attending to his horse. When he was sure the poultice was secure and the mare settled, he emerged from the stall and went to a big old sink in the corner of the yard to wash his hands, still saying nothing. Dermot just stood there.

Drying his hands on a rough grey towel, Charlie Warren walked back to where Dermot stood.

'I wondered if you'd come. I thought you wouldn't, to be honest. You must be desperate.'

Warren was the same age as Dermot and had done well for himself, but he looked older. He was bald and heavy with a red nose from taking too much whiskey at night.

'I'll come straight to the point,' Dermot said. 'Will you keep us on when you take over Robinswood?' He tried to keep any emotion out of his voice.

Charlie gave a cynical bark of a laugh.

'Well, you've some neck, I'll give you that much, Murphy.' He stared at him, his small eyes never leaving Dermot's face.

'I HAVE A FAMILY, and our house is part of the job, as you know,' Dermot explained. 'I was hoping we might be able to leave the past where it belongs. I'm a good manager, I work hard, and I know that place inside out. You can't run the two hundred and eighty acres there and here as well, not on your own. You'll need someone.' Dermot didn't want to beg, and he wouldn't, but this was so important.

'I will. That's true. But that person sure as hell won't be you.' Warren injected resentment into every word.

'Did you seriously think you could just walk up to my door and ask me for a job? That everything you did, everything that happened would be forgotten? Memories run deep around here, Dermot, you should know that. We were supposed to be comrades. We fought alongside each other, you, me, Oskar Metz, Mick O'Neill, all of us. 'Twas we that got the Brits out of here, not them up in Dublin with their suits and their treaties. *We* did it. And we were supposed to be loyal to each other. It was all we had.

'But you bailed out. You got sick of it and had to go home to your missus and your babies. When I was arrested for the raid on the barracks, and I never said one word about who my accomplices were, they pulled out my fingernails, they beat me to within an inch of my life, Dermot, but I never said a bloody word. And what did I get in return? You walking away, sick of violence! Ha! We were all sick of it, Dermot, did you never understand that? We were all sick to the back teeth of it, but that bloody treaty, that traitorous document, you defended it. You, and all those like you, hadn't the balls for the fight, and ye left us to it.

'You went back to your cushy number playing lord of the manor with that eejit Austin Kenefick. And not only that, ye Free Staters and ye're army paid for with the King's shilling, ye turned ye're guns on us. Oskar left for Germany, and poor old Mick was shot in the back, shot while he walked down the street in his own city, by your crowd. I have his young fella working here now, a lad that grew up without his father.' Charlie shook his head. 'The Free State army threw me in jail again after we lost touch, and do you know what? The Brits taught ye well, all you so-called men who turned their backs on their brothers in arms. Your lot tortured and terrorised us every bit as efficiently as the Black and Tans before them, the good little puppets doing what England told them to do. I could have told that old fool Kenefick plenty of times, and I was tempted, I can tell you, to explain what his golden boy was really up to. But I didn't. I saved your skin, Dermot Murphy, and in return, you turned your back on me.'

Dermot lit up a cigarette. This conversation had to happen. It was just twenty years too late.

'Charlie, I know that's how it looked. But I swear to you, I thought the treaty was the best option. I still do. We gave our youth, so many of our friends and comrades lying in wet ditches, taking potshots at them, them rounding us up... And then Collins mobilised us. Turned us into a proper army, and you're right, 'twas us that drove them out, and we paid a very high price for it. We all did things—*I* did things, that keep me awake at night. And I know you never squealed. If you had, they would have come after me, Isabella, the baby—well, God alone knows. And I never thanked you. And I should have. I'm sorry.

'But when Collins got that deal in '21, it wasn't perfect, of course it wasn't, it still isn't—but I thought it was the best we could do. And it was a step on the right road. A free state wasn't a republic, what we were fighting for, but it was a start. You accuse me of joining the Free Staters, but I did not. I just left the whole bloody thing behind me. Oskar, too. He took off for Germany because he'd had enough. And maybe ye were stronger, the likes of you and Mick, who kept going, rejected the Treaty, fighting the bloody civil war, but I had no stomach for it, and that's the truth.'

Charlie Warren stood squarely in front of his old comrade.

'We were brothers in arms, friends even. There was a time when I would have trusted you with my life, but you let me down, you let us all down, and so now, there's no going back. You sided with the enemy, and that's all there is to it. So I won't be hiring you. In fact, I want you and your family off that land and out of that house on the day I sign the lease, and if I never see you again, it will be too soon.'

Charlie turned on his heel and walked back to the house.

* * *

THE DANCE WAS in full swing as the three Murphy girls entered, followed by Jack O'Neill. They had never attended the monthly dance before, and nobody had ever seen Jack, so there was a marked reduction in noise as people…didn't *stare* exactly, but there were definitely a few nudges and questioning glances.

Eve knew from school that many of the families in the village thought the Murphys had ideas above their station. They thought Dermot and Isabella working for the Kenefick made them look down on their neighbours, which simply wasn't true. Mammy was in charge of hiring and sometimes firing the domestic staff for the house, and Daddy did the same for the yard. People were inevitably going to be offended over the years—local slackers getting their marching orders or others not being hired in the first place—so they just kept themselves to themselves. They went to Mass and got the bit of shopping they needed from the village shop just like everyone else, but Daddy didn't go to the pub and Mammy never gossiped in Kelly's grocers or after Mass on a Sunday.

Eve, Kate, and Aisling stood by the wall, Kate suddenly far less confident than she'd been at home, and Aisling anxiously scanning the room for anyone connected with the Laceys. The band were good, and Eve recognised one or two of them as locals. They were playing sets mostly, and the hall was full of groups of men and women facing each other and dancing the steps they'd learned as children—The Siege of Ennis, The Walls of Limerick. Father MacIntyre was taking a quick walk round to make sure nothing untoward was going on. He was very nice and had a word for everyone.

He stopped right in front of Eve.

'I didn't think you and your sisters were much for going to dances, Eve?' His round face smiled gently.

'It's our first one, Father,' Eve answered politely. Jack was gone to get them some tea, and she hoped he wouldn't return until the priest moved on to someone else. She wouldn't like him to think she was courting.

'Right, well, enjoy yourselves, and don't be falling in with some of the less devout members of the congregation,' he murmured, glancing over at the table where Mrs McCarthy and her son Jim, who was a bit slow, were serving tea. To the left of the table were the same group of men who waited outside Mass every Sunday. They'd all been to Keogh's pub before the dance and were distinctly glassy-eyed.

'Thank you, Father, we won't.' Eve wished he'd go; Jack had just got the tea and was on his way back. Thankfully, Mr O'Leary, who was taking the money at the door, was beckoning the priest over, ready to hand over the takings from the dance.

Fr MacIntyre moved on, glad to get his money and leave.

Eve sighed with relief and then turned her attention to Jack, who was balancing three cups of tea and three buns as the crowd danced around him. Amazingly, he managed it.

He handed a cup and a bun to each of the girls.

'Did you not want one?' Eve asked. She'd wanted to pay for her own, but Jack had insisted, not just in getting them tea and cake but also paying the two-shilling entrance fee for all four of them.

'No, I could only carry three cups at a time.' He grinned, and his black hair flopped over his forehead in what Eve thought was a most endearing way. She longed to reach up and smooth it back, but she didn't dare.

As soon as Father MacIntyre made his exit, the music changed. The sedate sets with nobody touching or dancing too vigorously were replaced by a waltz. Jack looked down at her.

'Will you dance?' He put his hand out, and Eve placed her teacup on the ledge that ran around the hall. She caught a quick glance of her sisters - Aisling smiling encouragingly and Kate pulling faces.

Jack took her hand and led her to the middle of the dance hall. She'd danced with Daddy often in the kitchen and was able to waltz, but suddenly she forgot all the steps.

'I'm sorry if I stand on your toes,' she said with a smile.

'I'm used to it after the donkey.' He chuckled 'Anyway, I'll probably do the same to you. How about we keep the fancy footwork to a minimum and spare both of us hobbling around next week?'

She giggled and tried not to gasp as Jack slid his arm around her waist and held her hand with his other one. He drew her close to him, but not so close as to be improper, and she placed her hand on his shoulder.

'I've a confession to make,' he whispered in her ear as they moved gingerly in time to the music.

'What's that?' Eve looked alarmed. What on earth was he going to admit to?

'I've never danced with a girl before. In fact, I've never taken a girl out before, so if I do something wrong, you might let me know?'

Immediately, she relaxed. 'Well, I wouldn't know if you do, because I've never been to a dance before either, and I'm a novice in the romance stakes as well. So we're well met.'

She felt the rumble of his laugh in his chest, and he held her a little closer. She wished the song would go on forever. Who knew Mort Kingston and his ceili band could play 'Somewhere Over the Rainbow'? She only knew it because she and the girls had gone as a rare treat to the cinema in Dungarvan for Kate's birthday last month to see The Wizard of Oz.

As the last notes of 'Why oh why can't I?' filled the small hall, Jack made no effort to release her. She noticed other couples around them for the first time. Some were politely leaving the dance floor, but others, like her and Jack, remained, her eyes never leaving his.

'Now.' Mort's voice seemed to break the magic spell. 'Since there seems to be a great take-up for the modern music, I'll give ye one more before we go back to the sets. How about this one?'

The opening bars of *'Begin the Beguine'* started everyone off again, and Eve felt like she and Jack were the only ones in the room. She looked up into his face and smiled.

'You're lovely,' he murmured in her ear.

She smiled bigger. Mammy had helped her alter an old green dress of hers, and the girls had said it looked great with her hair. She was afraid her bust was too pronounced, and she'd had to stop her mother from cinching the waist in even more, much to the hilarity of her sisters. She'd worn a little lipstick and some rouge and a pair of shoes that Lillian had left at Robinswood and Lady Kenefick had given to Mammy. They were lovely, black patent leather with a high heel, and though they were a bit too tight, Eve felt very glamorous in them so she endured the pain.

Kate and Aisling looked stunning as usual, both curvy and petite; Eve towered over both of them. Kate was in a red dress and Aisling in cream. With their dark eyes and jet-black hair, they turned every head in the hall. But Jack was looking at her.

'You're lovely yourself,' she replied, wondering if it was the done thing for a lady to return a compliment like that. But she didn't care. Jack *was* lovely. He looked even better out of his working clothes, and tonight, she'd nearly had to catch her breath when she saw him in his dark trousers, freshly ironed shirt, and pinstriped waistcoat. His dark hair flopped over his eyes, and she longed to trace her fingers over the delicate bones of his face. Up close as she was now, she could see the individual freckles on the bridge of his nose and the compelling blue of his eyes. He smelled of soap and cologne, and she never wanted to let him go.

Eventually, the traditional set dancing music started up again, and they joined in. Kate was in high demand, but of Aisling, there was no sign. Eve looked around the packed hall. She could have joined a different group for the first dance, so Eve wasn't worried. Rows and rows of people filled the hall. Unlike the slower waltz, everyone got up to dance The Siege of Ennis. She'd see her sister soon enough as they danced under the arms of the row facing them at the end of each set.

When she was finally facing Kate, she asked,

'Is Aisling dancing? I can't see her.'

Kate shrugged and looked around but was definitely more interested in the young man who'd asked her up.

'She might be in the toilet?' she suggested.

Eve turned to Jack. 'I might just check where Aisling is; I can't see her.' She was reluctant to let go of his hand, but she needed to find her sister.

Jack nodded, and the moment she let him go, Bernadette Conlan swooped in and took her place with a smug smile. Eve had once had a run-in with her in school, when Bernadette was bullying one of the girls from the orphanage out the Dublin road. Eve stood up for the girl and came off the worst. The Conlans were notorious, and ever since, they'd avoided each other.

So Eve was delighted to see Jack make a face behind Bernadette's back and mouth, 'Hurry back.'

Eve weaved her way through the crowd to the back door that led to the outside toilets. All three were occupied, and there was a long queue. She passed several women who were waiting.

'Hey, Miss Murphy, there's people waiting, you know.' It was Judy Power, Bernadette's best friend.

'I'm just looking for my sister,' Eve said with dignity.

Someone tapped her on the shoulder. It was Doreen Casey; her brother worked at Robinswood.

'She's in the middle one. I think she's a bit upset,' she murmured, so the whole gathering didn't hear.

Eve nodded her thanks. This was so unlike Aisling.

She tapped on the door and whispered, 'Aisling, are you in there? It's me. Can you come out?'

The queue watched in total silence; this was all very exciting. The Murphys, who didn't mix, were now the centre of a scene in the toilets of the dance hall. The whole village would get a week of gossip out of this titbit.

Eve heard the bolt slide, and the door opened. Aisling emerged, her face red and puffy from crying. She grabbed Eve's arm, and together, they walked through the gathered girls out into the yard behind the hall. There was some activity up against the wall, and they realised this was where the courting couples went.

Eve half dragged Aisling away, and eventually, they'd walked around the building to the front. The music was spilling out, but the world away from the dance hall was in darkness. The measures since the war had broken out meant there was to be no lights visible, but people didn't take much notice. The Germans were looking for England, and there were plenty of lights there. They'd hardly be bothered dropping a bomb on one little light in County Waterford. Kate had once joked that it might be a blessing if they did.

'Aisling, what happened? Did someone hurt you?' Eve was imagining one of the men making a grab for her or something.

'Oh, Eve, did you not see? When you were dancing with Jack?' Aisling was trying to hold back the tears.

'See what? What are you on about, Ais?' Eve knew that no matter what had been going on, she wouldn't have seen anything except Jack.

'Sean!' Aisling wailed. 'He wasn't at home doing the books; he was dancing with Eleanor Conlan, Bernadette's sister. And when I went up to him, he got all embarrassed, and she basically made a total holy show of me in front of everyone, saying everybody knew she was doing a line with Sean and that I was only sniffing around like a poor foolish calf. And everyone was laughing at me, and then Eleanor said the Conlons have a farm and everything, so why would Sean want anything to do with a nobody like me?'

The whole tale came out in one breath, and when she finished, Aisling just dissolved into tears of heartbreak and humiliation.

'And Sean Lacey?' Eve asked. 'What did he have to say for himself?'

She could feel her temper rising. How dare he? Aisling was worth fifty of the snivelling little mammy's boy.

'Poor Sean was mortified. Father MacIntyre even heard it! He'd come back in to the dance for something. He didn't know where to look.' Aisling was defending him to the last.

Eve wanted to shake her sister, to make her see what a creep he was, but now was not the time.

'AND WHERE WAS Kate during all of this?' Eve was furious with herself; she should have been taking better care of her sister, not gazing up at Jack. But she'd thought Aisling and Kate were together.

'She went outside for a cigarette with Dr Ryan's son home from university,' Aisling said, forgetting in her distress to protect her little sister's recently acquired smoking habit.

'Right. Stay there.' Eve left Aisling sitting on the wall and marched back into the dance hall. She'd never been so angry. She would deal with Kate later, but how dare he, that pathetic excuse for a man, Sean Lacey, humiliate her sister like that? And as for that Conlon one...

The band had taken a break, and there they were, the two of them in the middle of a huge group, and Eleanor all over Sean like a rash.

'Excuse me, Sean Lacey.' Eve tapped him on the shoulder, and he spun around. The gathering stopped their conversations, all eyes on Eve.

Before he had a chance to open his mouth, she laid into him.

'Who the hell do you think you are? You have been trying your best to court my sister these past months, inviting her here, there, and everywhere, and even begging her to go to tea with your mother. And even though none of us liked you, Aisling is kind, so she went, and then you have the nerve to humiliate her like this, with this'—Eve pointed at Eleanor—'this *yoke*, when you and everyone else here knows that Aisling is worth ten of her.' She stepped closer to him, her face inches from his.

'Listen carefully to me, Sean Lacey, with your poky little shop, thinking you're better than everyone else. My sister had no real interest in you, but she was too nice to say it. The idea that the likes of you could get a girl like Aisling Murphy, well, it's a joke. She was only being kind, and you threw her good nature back in her face. You're pathetic. So see what your adoring mammy makes of this one'—she cocked her thumb in Eleanor's direction once again—'who, by the way, was up against the wall outside with Johnny O'Brien not twenty minutes ago, just so you know you're not the only pig feeding at that trough.'

Eleanor was like a goldfish, her mouth opening and closing, but she couldn't actually say anything.

Johnny O'Brien turned to the rest of his drunken cronies and belted one of them on the arm. In full earshot of everyone, he announced, 'I told ya I got a go off her, didn't I? And ye wouldn't believe me! So who's lying now?'

At some point, Jack and Kate had appeared behind her as the whole of Kilthomand witnessed this amazing scene.

Sean stood wordless, his face puce, and the Conlan sisters were absolutely savage.

'Well, I suppose we'll go home so,' Jack announced with a grin, and, offering an arm each to Eve and Kate, they waltzed triumphantly out the door.

CHAPTER 9

*I*sabella was gone up, and Dermot was just waiting up for the girls. He'd have been happy to walk down, and Isabella wanted him to, but Jack O'Neill was a good lad and Dermot didn't want to be undermining him by going down to the village to collect the girls like they were in national school.

He looked around the warm cosy kitchen and sighed. Soon, they'd have to tell the girls they'd have to leave the only home they'd ever known. He'd tried everything, used all the contacts he could think of, but there was no work to be had anywhere. He wished he had some good news, some hope to give them along with the news of their eviction, but it would be public knowledge soon and he couldn't risk them hearing it from someone else. He took the clock from the mantelpiece and wound it as he did every night.

He cursed his own shortsightedness. He should have at least tried to buy a house when things were all right and he had a good wage coming in, but the house with the job was big and comfortable and there never seemed any need. He'd foolishly thought the Keneficks would stay in Robinswood forever. Now, faced not just with unemployment, but with homelessness as well, he pitched from deep despair to determined optimism.

He wasn't past it yet. He was fifty years old, and fit and strong. He was a good farm manager and handyman, able to turn his hand to most things. Surely he'd get work. Getting work was one thing, though; finding a house for his family was quite another.

The days of the big houses were almost gone. The Anglo-Irish gentry had been driven out in The Troubles. And those that remained, their fortunes were depleting by the year. Most of them had made their money in the glory days of the British Empire, but that was crumbling before their eyes like a sandcastle as the tide came in.

He hadn't yet made an application for an IRA pension. He was definitely entitled to one, and while the sums involved weren't huge, it would probably tide them over. The problem was, if the Keneficks or any of the other landed gentry got wind of his past, he could forget getting a job on any of the remaining estates. Even though most of them who had returned once the country was stable were sympathetic, at least nominally, to the Irish cause, they'd suffered badly at the hands of the IRA—their houses burned, their property destroyed, people injured and even killed. So whatever chance he had of getting work *without* his republican past being common knowledge, he would have absolutely none with it.

He'd have to talk to Violet Kenefick again, see if there was any way she could put in a word with any of the other families. Maybe they could get something similar somewhere else. He'd got on better with Austin than Violet, as she'd never really liked Ireland. He always found her to be a bit haughty, and she looked down on Isabella, which drove him mad. He wished his wife didn't have to kowtow to the likes of her. And Violet Kenefick had passed on her distaste for the country to her daughter, but young Sam was more like Austin. Dermot knew he would be devastated, but like his father, he obviously didn't want to know until it was too late. Dermot hadn't seen him the last time he was back, a flying visit before he was deployed, but at least he'd tried with Charlie Warren, for all the good it did. Sam was a good lad, and Dermot hoped he'd survive the war, though it seemed unlikely.

He was deep in thought when he heard the girls come across the yard. He got up to open the door, but they burst through. In astonishment, he took in the scene: Aisling, eyes puffy and face tear-stained, Eve and Kate fuming, and Jack bringing up the rear.

'Aisling, are you all right? Did something happen?' Dermot looked at Jack for a more measured response; his daughters were in no fit state.

Isabella appeared at the kitchen door, in her dressing gown and slippers.

'What on earth... Aisling, what's wrong? What happened?'

Eve recounted the whole story, which involved Sean Lacey and Eleanor Conlan.

'I can't ever show my face again, I'm so embarrassed,' Aisling sobbed, her mother's arms around her.

'I'm leaving Kilthomand, I mean it, I can't be here—'

'Well, if you're hightailing it out of here, I'll be going with you,' Kate began. 'Honestly, this is such a horrible village, everyone stuck in everyone else's business all the time. I know you imagine we'll all be here forever, but honestly, Daddy, it's too much...'

Dermot looked at Isabella. It wasn't ideal, but they had to be told.

"Sit down, the three of you. We need to talk about this.'

'Maybe I should go...' Jack began. He didn't want to intrude on a family matter.

'Well, you'll know the story soon enough, Jack, so you might as well stay and have a cup of tea anyway.' Dermot sighed. This was going to be a difficult conversation, and perhaps having an outsider there would curb the worst of the inevitable histrionics.

'Right, well, I'll make myself useful so,' Jack said and went to fill the kettle.

'What story?' Eve asked. Big, dramatic pronouncements were not her father's style at all.

Dermot sat at the table, and Isabella sat right beside him. He loved so many things about his wife, but this was the reason he would do anything for her—she was loyalty personified. He was never alone; no matter what, she was one hundred percent in his corner.

'Right, well,' Dermot began, 'Lady Kenefick called me in to tell me that she is leaving. The estate is to be rented out, the house closed up, and the contents sold. It means we'll have to leave Robinswood. She only called me in yesterday to tell me, and to be honest, I had no idea things were so bad. I knew they were on thin ice, but Austin always managed something. However, this time, it's not going to happen. Maybe we should talk to the neighbours more.' He tried a small grin, but the stony faces of his three daughters told him his joke had fallen flat.

'But we have two months to find somewhere,' he went on, 'so at least there's that. And I'm a highly skilled man'—his smile was met at least by Eve—'so we'll be grand. Absolutely fine. It's just a matter of finding something else.'

He sensed the girls weren't falling for his optimism, so he was relieved to hear Isabella pitch in.

'Your dad is right. Sure, with so many joining up to go and fight in the war, there's loads of work around the place. We just need to find something. And we're all trained and well able to work, so we'll be fine. Honestly, we're not worried, and neither should you three be.'

Dermot watched in amazement as their mother's words of reassurance calmed them. They believed it when it came from her. He got up and went to help Jack make the tea, the level of chatter from the table allowing them a chance to talk.

''Tis bad luck, I'm sorry to hear it, Mr Murphy. This is a great setup you have here.' Jack was putting cups on a tray.

'Dermot, please. And I know, sure, 'tis a bit of a disaster to be honest, but I don't want the girls to know. I'll find something. I'm not worried about getting a job, but relocating the entire family is a whole other matter.'

'Well, I'll ask around,' Jack promised, 'back at home, as well, in Cork. You never know. I'm actually going home this weekend, to see my mam. It's her birthday, and I'm an only child.'

Dermot stopped and looked at him.

'I knew your father.'

A flicker of recognition crossed Jack's face. When a man of Dermot's age said that to him, and it had happened before, it meant only one thing. That they were comrades in arms.

'Did you? I only barely remember him, to be honest, but Mam misses him still.'

'Does she get a pension?'

'No, she never applied. She hated the Free Staters as much as he did, still does, so she wouldn't take their money even if they offered it. She is doing all right, though; she has her own little house, and she works in a shop in town.' Dermot could tell from the way he spoke about her that Jack loved her and was fiercely protective.

'She must not have been best pleased to hear you were going over the county bounds for work then?' Dermot asked as he took a cut of brown cake and some butter and jam from the larder.

'No, she wasn't, but I like working outside. I couldn't be stuck in an office or a shop, so I have to go where the work is. Charlie Warren remembered my father, so when I asked for work, he gave it to me.'

Jack stopped. 'I suppose you wouldn't work for him, would you?'

Dermot sighed. 'I'd work for anyone who would give me a job and a house and that's the truth, but Charlie and I, well, you might as well know, we took different sides after the Treaty, and he hates me for it.'

Silently, Jack processed it. If Dermot had taken a different side to Charlie Warren, then he'd clearly taken a different side from Jack's father too. Dermot hoped it wouldn't affect the boy's relationship with Eve.

He needn't have worried. Jack smiled. 'Those were complicated times. Something will turn up, and as I said, I'll keep an ear out.' He carried the tray over to the table.

The girls had calmed down, and they were discussing where they might like to go. Dermot threw his wife a look of gratitude.

* * *

An hour later, Jack stood up. 'Lads, I better go and let ye get to bed. These ladies need their beauty sleep.' He winked.

'I'll walk you out,' Eve said shyly, praying her parents wouldn't object. Kate cast a sly glance in her direction, but nobody else even noticed.

The night was clear and starlit but biting cold. Eve had grabbed her coat from behind the door, but the cold was stinging her face.

'You'll perish walking home,' Eve said. ''Tis three miles to Warren's.'

'Yerra, I'll run, and I'll keep warm. 'Twill do me good. I play hurling at home, so I'd be training all the time, and if I go back unfit, the trainer will murder me.'

The thought of Jack going back to Cork when the setting of the crops was all done filled Eve with dread.

'How long more will you be here before you have to go back?' she asked, trying to make her voice sound light and not reflect the sadness she felt. She shivered involuntarily.

Jack took off his overcoat, leaving him in just his waistcoat and shirt, and put it around her.

'Not at all, I'm grand—' she began to protest, but Jack put his finger to her lips.

'I want to look after you,' he said quietly. 'I know you're tough out, and well able to look after yourself but... I just... Well, I'd like to be involved.'

She looked up at him and moved into the circle of his arms. She felt his arms go around her waist inside his big coat, and as he did, she felt her arms snake up around his neck. He bent his head until his lips met hers. They kissed for ages, and the cold, the stars, her family in the house only yards away, just ceased to exist. Jack occupied every part of her—her mind, her heart, her body.

Eventually, he pulled away with a groan.

'I better go, before your father comes out and puts the run on me with a shotgun.' His grin melted her heart.

'Will I see you tomorrow?' She knew it sounded needy, and Kate would no doubt tell her to play it cooler, but she didn't care.

'You will, if you would like to,' he said. 'I'll come over after work. Maybe if I get here before it gets dark, we could go for a walk or something?'

'I'd love that.' Eve smiled and leaned up to kiss him quickly once more.

He turned to go and then turned back, grabbing her hand.

'Just to be clear, because tonight's festivities between your sister and that eejit Sean Lacey seemed to be caused by a giant misunderstanding, are we courting now, like, are you my girlfriend?'

Eve laughed. 'Do you want me to be?'

'More than anything I've ever wanted before.' All the joking was gone, and he was totally sincere.

'Well then, yes, Jack O'Neill from Cork, I am your girlfriend.'

Jack pulled her into his embrace once more and kissed her passionately. Eve felt her head swim as she hugged him closer to her, never wanting to let go.

'I'll see you tomorrow, Eve,' he whispered in her ear. 'I can't wait. Charlie Warren will never see a field ploughed so fast in the morning.' And then he was gone, running down the lane into the dark night.

CHAPTER 10

*B*y the time she came back in, the whole family were gone to bed. Eve crept into the bedroom, trying not to disturb her sisters, but as she slipped her nightie over her head, they both sat up.

'Well?' Kate was not going to rest until she got all the details. 'You went in behind the byre wall so we couldn't see what was going on, you miserable old spoilsport.' She thumped her sister playfully on the arm.

'Are you OK, Aisling?' Eve asked, ignoring Kate.

'Yes, mortified and humiliated in front of the whole place, dumped by Sean Lacey for Eleanor Conlon, of all people, and now about to be evicted, but generally, yes, I'd say things were just wonderful.' The rueful smile on Aisling's face belied the words. Suddenly, the funny side of the night dawned on her.

'But it was nearly worth it to see Bernadette's face when you rounded on them, Eve. You were magnificent.' Kate smiled in admiration of her older sister. 'Honestly, Ais, if anyone was mortified, it was that pair, not you. She even told Sean that Eleanor was up against the wall outside with manky old Johnny O'Brien, who stinks so much even Mossy in the post office serves him before others just to get him out.'

'Did you really say that?' Aisling was wide-eyed.

'I did, and it's true. I saw them when I was dragging you out of the toilets. See what Mrs Lacey makes of that.' Eve grinned.

'Just so you know you're not the only pig feeding at that trough,' Kate quoted. 'That's what she said to Sean! I swear, Ais, it was gold. I thought Bernadette Conlan was going to inflate like a bullfrog, and the sister looking mortified, it was so funny.'

Despite the drama of the night, the three girls proceeded to disintegrate into fits of giggles.

Eventually, when the laughing subsided, Eve wiped her eyes.

'So, go on, was there kissing?' Kate asked her, and Aisling raised her eyebrow questioningly.

'Fine, and this is all you're getting: there was some kissing.'

'Oooh, you're so lucky, Eve! He's gorgeous, and not just like around here kind of good-looking, but like Jimmy Stewart in *Mr Smith Goes to Washington*. Remember we saw that, and I was swooning for weeks after? Well, I think Jack is better looking than Jimmy Stewart,' Kate gushed. 'And he's not from here, he's from Cork! Honestly, we'll wither into old maids if we stay around here. It's actually a good thing we're losing this place, I think. At least we'll get away from Kilthomand.'

'And since I can never walk down the street again, you're probably right.' Aisling sighed.

'We should start thinking about the future though, seriously.' Kate was practical. 'We won't be able to stay together, so we should make plans.'

'You mean we all split up?' Eve hated that idea.

'Well, come on, Eve, who is going to employ five people in one go? Nobody. And there is so much else to life anyway than skivvying and farming for someone else. There's a whole big world out there, just waiting to be explored. I mean, why don't you look for something in Cork? That way you'll be near Mr Dreamy,' Kate teased her. 'Unless of course he's another love rat like Sean Lacey, who isn't even good-looking…'

Aisling's face fell.

'Ah, Ais, come on, you know what I mean. He's a total grunter, and his handshake is as wet as an otter's pocket—I hate that in a person. You're as well off without him—'

'I know, I know, but—'

Eve interjected before the conversation descended into more tears. Kate was absolutely right, Jack and Sean were both male but that was where the similarity ended.

'He asked me to be his girlfriend,' Eve announced, interjecting before the conversation descended into more tears. Kate was absolutely right—Jack and Sean were both male, but that was where the similarity ended.

'HE DID NOT!' Kate was all agog. 'Like, just asked you straight out, will you be my girlfriend?'

'More or less. He said he didn't want any misunderstanding and wanted to know if we were courting now, and I said we were and that was that.'

'Imagine, Eve! You might marry him, and then you'd be Mrs O'Neill, not just Eve Murphy anymore.'

'It's a bit early for that,' Eve chided. 'We've only gone out once. But he's coming over tomorrow after work.' She tried to keep the excitement out of her voice but failed.

Kate threw herself back on her bed.

'I wonder where Sam is now?' she sighed.

'Not this again.' Aisling had heard her sister mooning about Samuel Kenefick since the day he turned up in his RAF uniform. 'Honestly, Kate, you're so easily impressed. He was under your nose here all your life, and then he puts a uniform on, a British uniform I might add, and suddenly you're all gooey over him. Honestly, he's just the same annoying Sam he always was, chasing us with frogs and throwing snowballs at us.'

'Ah, but he's not, Aisling! He's a pilot, flying against the nasty old Germans, being all brave and manly...' She sighed again.

'You don't know one single German,' Eve snapped as she got into bed. She'd always been the most political of the three. 'They could be the finest people on earth, for all we know. The Brits are telling us they're so bad, but have you forgotten your history? They said the same and worse about us, so you won't find me charging to attack any poor old German who's never done me an ounce of harm, not like the Brits.'

She loved her country and was always the one encouraging their father to tell them stories about the Rising back in 1916 and the War of Independence that was on when Eve was a baby. She'd asked her father if he'd fought in the war, and he'd denied it, but as an adult, she wasn't so sure. She had nothing concrete, but something about him, about the way he spoke about it, made her think there was more to his story than he let on.

'Not to mention the tiny insignificant fact that he's a big posh Protestant, and it would be a mortal sin for you to have anything romantic to do with him,' Aisling went on. Thankfully, Aisling backed Eve up in trying to discourage Kate in her ideas. Aisling knew Kate was in love with Sam—not just some silly crush, but she really loved him, and always had—but Kate would never let anyone else see just how lonely she was for him, nor how worried she was. 'So don't go getting mad notions, little sister. Samuel Kenefick is not for the likes of you. I told you before, he'll marry some horsey-faced one with tons of money over in England, that's what they all do in the end. Sure, look at old Austin; he loved Robinswood and was kind of Irish, in as much as that class can be, but he still went to his own kind for a wife.'

Kate lay back and closed her eyes.

'Hmmm... The thing is though, I am not horsey, I am lovely, and its 1940, not 1840. Sam will see that when he comes home, and that, Aisling, will be that. Rubbish like class and nationality don't matter anymore. I don't give two hoots about sins, and anyway, with all due sensitivity and everything, you're hardly an expert at picking men, are you?'

'Kate, don't be mean,' Eve admonished. She loved chatting with her sisters, and despite the teasing, they were very close, but tonight, she'd have loved it if they'd just fall asleep. She wanted to be alone with her thoughts, to process the events of the night. It seemed like a lifetime ago they were in this bedroom getting ready for the dance. So much had happened—they'd lost their home and their livelihood, she'd stood up to the Conlans, Sean had showed his true colours, and then, Jack.

Eve wondered if she would marry him. Jack was her first boyfriend, and she was his first girlfriend; maybe that sort of love didn't last, but she thought it would. The family liked him, even Daddy, and she'd always thought any lad coming to court one of the Murphy girls would have his work cut out to impress their father. Even more amazing, Mammy liked him too, and she didn't think anyone was good enough for them.

Eventually, her sisters stopped bickering and went to sleep. Eve opened the curtains, lay on her back, and gazed out the window at the stars shining in the sky, and hoped Jack was home safely. She tried to picture him running along the dark road to Warren's. Was he there yet? Was he lying in bed? Was he thinking about her? These unfamiliar feelings were both exhilarating and frightening. When Jack had kissed her, she'd felt stirrings in her body she'd never felt before, and the force of it had taken her by surprise.

Beside her, Aisling and Kate slept quietly, and Eve wondered what the future held for them all. Robinswood was all they'd ever known; it was their home, and they had clambered all over every inch of it. They knew the Keneficks' big house as well as their own; they'd polished its floors and dusted its ornaments since they were small. It was impossible to imagine leaving it all behind.

Eve also worried about her father and where he would find work. He was well got here on the Kenefick estate, but he was always saying the era of the big house and all the surrounding locals working there was well and truly over. Ireland was a different place to what it was a generation earlier.

It was independent, a republic for the first time in eight hundred years of British subjugation, and while it was a good thing, of course it was, all that had once seemed certain was in a state of flux. Sure, farmers were working their own land, now that Mr deValera had managed to take the land back from English landlords and return it to the rightful owners, the people of Ireland. But that meant smaller holdings, families working them, and no place for the managers of big estates like Robinswood. Her father was strong and well able to work, but if a farmer was to take a man on, surely he'd take someone young and fit, like Jack, who he'd not have to pay as much as Dermot Murphy with all his experience? Mammy, too. She was a housekeeper and a cook, and just as there was no need for estate managers, there was scant need for cooks either.

Maybe they could all move to Dublin, or better still, to Cork, and get jobs in businesses, shops, or restaurants and the like. Eve had never been to Cork, but Jack told her it was a great city altogether. Leaving everything they'd ever known was sad and frightening, but maybe it was just the beginning of a whole new exciting chapter of their lives.

CHAPTER 11

*V*iolet wrung her hands in despair as Samuel slammed the drawing room door behind him. He was home for a few days' leave.

Austin really had left the most frightful mess, and it was most unfair that she now had to deal with the consequences. She sighed and sat down.

The news that Charlie Warren wasn't keeping the Murphys on seemed to have upset him disproportionally. Violet had merely pointed out that they would surely find work somewhere else, and he had rounded on her, accusing her of not caring. Which was utterly unfair. She did care, in as much as anyone would about their staff, but Samuel's interest in that family was, frankly, inappropriate.

SHE'D WAIT until he calmed down, and perhaps he'd see sense. He didn't even give her a chance to tell him that she had some good news for the Murphys. She gazed out at the fields, her daily view for so long, and wondered what it would be like to see city streets each morning. Part of her longed for the convenience, and of course to be back among one's own kind, and yes of course, she was a little sad, end of an era and all that, but it just had to be done. Why her son refused to see the reality of the situation confounded her. Still, at least she had some good news for Dermot; that would soften the blow.

She rang for tea; Isabella would be up to serve it, and she was expecting Dermot in for eleven, so she would tell them together.

At eleven on the dot, they appeared. She noticed how Dermot carried the tray for his wife, though she delivered it every other day by herself. He was just that sort of man, she supposed.

'Ah, Isabella and Dermot, too, good, so good that you're both here...' She tried to stop babbling. Though they worked for her, she was always slightly intimidated by them. She couldn't explain it; they were always polite and obliging, faultless servants, but still, she felt *judged* by them or something. It was hard to put into words.

She'd mentioned it to Austin once years ago, and he pooh-poohed the thought immediately. He'd told her she'd have to get used to the ways of the Irish, and that they didn't do deference in the way you could expect in England but that they were no less loyal.

'Now, ah, have a seat, both of you, and, ah... I want to discuss the future. Well, your future, I suppose, when I—well, actually, when we leave Robinswood.'

'Ah, we're fine standing, ma'am,' Dermot spoke for both of them. 'I'm in my work clothes.'

'Right, well, whatever you wish... Well, I have some news that may interest you. I recently received some correspondence from an old friend of mine. She and her husband live in Dublin—Thomas Hamilton-Brooks. You may have met him occasionally, Dermot; he did some business with Austin, and he came for a few hunts and suchlike.

'Anyway, Elena Hamilton-Brooks is in need of a housekeeper and someone to care for their children, and I daresay they could use a groundsman as well.' She smiled.

Dermot and Isabella's faces were settled in neutral; they really were a most infuriating pair. It was impossible to know what either of them was thinking.

'Now, I know it is only for the two of you, and you had hoped to secure a position where you could all stay together, but I believe the salaries are reasonable, bed and board and so on...' Violet's voice trailed off.

Dermot and Isabella stood before her, saying nothing. The silence was deafening. Violet felt the frustration rise within her. She had no obligation to these people whatsoever, and yet here she was using up favours with old friends in order to secure a future for them, and they had nothing to say about it? Admittedly, Elena had instigated it, having heard of the evacuation of Robinswood, and Violet was pleased to have someone so well connected as the Hamilton-Brooks in her debt, but still. Honestly, the sooner she was out of this ridiculous country, the better.

Eventually, Dermot spoke.

'Thank you for making those enquiries on our behalf, ma'am, but we won't be working for Mr Hamilton-Brooks.'

His voice was quiet, and the tone very final.

Violet wanted to scream. Now she would have to go back to Elena and say that she wasn't getting the staff she so desperately needed. Not only that, but it smacked of weakness. That she, Violet, had no control over her household.

'But that is silly,' she said evenly. 'Why ever not? It is a very good opportunity. Besides, they're expecting you now.' She hoped she sounded reasonable and not dictatorial, but their faces were inscrutable.

'Thank you, Lady Kenefick, for thinking of us,' Isabella spoke clearly, 'and I'm sorry if you've arranged something, but with respect, you should have asked us before making any definite decisions. We'll leave Robinswood at the appointed time, and we wish you all the best in your new life.'

Violet wanted to reprimand her for insolence. 'Should have asked' indeed. No wonder they found themselves destitute, when the offer of help was rejected so out of hand. But Violet managed to hold her temper in check; the last thing she needed was them storming off when there was so much to be done before the move.

'Well, I can't understand why you would reject such a generous offer, but it's your choice, obviously. I can't force you, but I would urge you to reconsider.'

Dermot fixed her with a steely gaze.

'We have given you our answer, ma'am. Now I need to go down. There's a man coming to buy the last of the yearlings.'

And without a further word of explanation, they both left.

Violet sat down heavily once more. First, a very unsatisfactory conversation with Samuel, who was being childish and unrealistic, and now this with the Murphys. To add to her stress, her daughter had written yet again from London, demanding funds. For the thousandth time, Violet cursed her dead husband for leaving her to cope with this mess.

How she longed for a nice, peaceful life in London, though how peaceful it would be with the war on was anybody's guess. Still, she was sure if she got a townhouse somewhere nice, then it would be safe. The Germans seemed to be focusing their attention in Norway these days, though she admitted to herself she should probably keep a closer eye on the news. Frankly, the whole dreary business bored her. The last time, Britain had been affected in the sense that so many young men had died, but the country itself was safe, and she had no reason to believe it would be different this time.

She hoped she had not mortally offended the Murphys, though goodness knows how she could have. She was only trying to help, and she'd had her generous offer thrown back in her face. It was unacceptable.

But she desperately needed the Murphys' help in the coming weeks. The prospect of packing up and leaving made her want to lie down in a darkened room. Samuel would be no help, and Lillian wouldn't dream of coming home to assist her mother. No, she was alone, and without the Murphys, she would have no help whatsoever.

She got up to look out the window, beyond the immaculately kept grounds to the fertile green hills undulating gently before reaching the azure sea. The lawns of the estate were emerald green, and they were separated from the farmland by dark-green privet hedging. She had hoped to have a flower garden in the early years—there was ample room for all sorts of beds in the lawns around the house—but Dermot wasn't interested in flowers when he could grow crops and grass for grazing, and nobody else seemed able to do it.

And when she'd told her husband they needed to employ a gardener, Austin had laughed and suggested if she was so interested in gardening she could go out with a hoe and a rake herself. She had flounced out in indignation. He really was an infuriating man, in life and in death.

CHAPTER 12

*K*ate was coming back from the square paddock where the new calves were cavorting when she spotted Samuel Kenefick. He was sitting on the old stone bridge over the Araghlin river that flowed through the estate. She was surprised to see him. Nobody had mentioned he was home. But there he was in his slate-blue uniform with the short, fitted jacket and perfectly creased trousers.

He wore a forage cap, which only sat on his head because of the vast amount of Brylcreem he used to keep his mahogany curls in check. Even the utilitarian military haircut could not fully tame Sam's curls. But he looked different, more grown up, in his uniform, and he also seemed to have filled out. His brown eyes were the same, though—deep and thoughtful.

Kate knew the girls were sick of her going on about him, but he was easily the best-looking lad in the whole place. She never told them how she really felt about him, though she knew Aisling suspected. Sam was unusual. He was sensitive and kind and funny, and her sisters would have laughed if she'd admitted it, but she'd loved him for as long as she could remember.

Dropping the bag of ration she was bringing back after feeding the remaining few calves, she crept up behind him and placed her hands over his eyes.

'What—' He jumped, startled to finally have company. He spun around and smiled when he saw Kate.

'Oh, it's you, Kate Murphy, and haven't you grown?' he teased as he always did.

"Ara, would you go on away, you big eejit! You're only gone six months, and no, I have not grown. Shove over.' She clamoured up onto the bridge beside him, and they sat in companionable silence for a few moments, as they'd done hundreds of times before. As children, they'd fished that river together, paddled in it, and if there was a summer storm, it was sometimes deep enough for a swim. Both Samuel and Kate kept the amount of time they'd spent together as children secret from their respective parents. Before they even knew why, exactly, they just knew neither the Murphys nor the Keneficks would approve.

Sam picked a stone off the top of the bridge and threw it into the shallow water below.

'So, am I going to have to guess, or are you going to tell me?' Kate never looked at him, watching instead the ripples created by the small splash.

'You know,' he said. 'I just thought Charlie Warren would keep you all on, but now, it feels like we're abandoning you.' His tone was dejected, and Kate could feel the sense of loss. She wondered at why she didn't feel the same. After all, Robinswood was the only home she'd ever known. But she just didn't.

Maybe because it had always been the Keneficks' property, not theirs, and so they didn't get attached. She could see it was a lovely estate, with woodlands, this river, fertile land, and then the sea beyond, but she'd walk out without a backward glance. Sam obviously felt differently.

'Yes, your mother told Daddy a few weeks ago,' Kate said. 'She did say you tried.'

'Not hard enough, obviously,' Sam said despondently.

'My idiotic father left such a mess. We've no choice, really. My father would joke about how bad things were, but I never believed it was as bad as all that. Seems the old codger was dead right to pop off when he did.' He gave a half laugh.

Kate realised that since she'd last seen Sam—last October—he'd changed his accent. He and Lillian were always much posher sounding than the Murphys and everyone else in Kilthomand, but not so lah-di-dah as their mother. But now he was all clipped and British.

Feeling sorry for him, Kate placed her hand on his shoulder.

'Well, Daddy has been saying it for years, that the place needed investment. So I suppose now that Lord Kenefick is gone, the reality of the situation is there for all to see. Though, I'm surprised your mother wants to go to London. I'd have thought the threat of Mr Hitler coming over would scare her off.' Kate could talk to Sam in a way that she never really talked to anyone else. She and he had been friends since they could walk, even though he was the same age as Eve. Once Eve was old enough, she was doing jobs for Mammy in the kitchen when she wasn't at school, so Kate was left to play with Lillian and Sam.

Kate had always known that someday their lives would part—she was an Irish Catholic girl from a working family, and he was gentry. They would never have the same life. But through all the years growing up in Robinswood, that didn't seem to matter.

'I think she thinks this time will be like that last war,' Sam explained. 'With the British government keeping the actual fighting in Europe, and though rationing and all of that would play a part, she thinks Britain itself will still be physically safe. And of course in the middle of this, my darling sister is having a marvellous time, with London full of servicemen of all kinds. She's flirting and dancing every night, and now she's broke. According to her letters, the good-will of cousins and friends is wearing thin. She writes daily to Mother, begging. My father would have given her short shrift, but my mother can't refuse her. Mother might have tried to stick it out until after the war and have me come back and take over, but for Lillian and her demands.'

Kate was used to Sam complaining about Lillian; it was the same as when they were children. Lillian had always been whiney and greedy and looked down her aquiline nose at everyone, but Lady Kenefick adored her and was made a total fool of, in the Murphys' opinion. They liked Sam better; he pitched in with the work some-times, and at least he wasn't haughty.

'And will it, do you think? Be like last time?' Kate longed for news of the war.

'No, I don't,' he said simply. 'It's going to be a war in the air, and the winner will be the one with the best trained pilots, the best tech-nology. The Luftwaffe are good, no doubt about it, but we're better.'

She smiled at the pride in his voice.

'Well, try not to get killed.' She nudged him playfully.

'Oh, I'll be fine, don't worry about me.' He grinned, his crooked front tooth revealed.

'And be careful of all those girls dying to get their hands on a man in uniform.' She was fishing now. There had never been any hint of romance between them. She was sure he saw himself more like a kind of brother to her. But seeing him in his uniform just melted her.

'Precious few girls wandering around the training centres,' he replied. 'They're determined to get as many of us trained up as fast as possible. My days are filled with mathematics and navigation, though I did get to fly a Tiger Moth on my own, which was amazing. When I go back, it's advanced training, so more charts and tests. It's not glam-orous, I can assure you.'

Kate took a breath. It was silly to be coy around him, he was just Sam, after all, but she felt the butterflies in her stomach all the same.

'Will I write to you?'

He turned his head to look at her. The weak March sun shone, but the air was cold. Involuntarily, she shivered.

The breeze danced around her head, and her curls blew across her face. She lifted her hand to tuck her hair behind her ear, but he beat her to it. His hand rested on her cheek, and she wished she wasn't blushing. His eyes never left hers.

'I'd love that.' The voice was deep and hoarse, nothing like his normal one, and now it was his turn to blush.

'Sam—' she began.

"Kate—' he said at the same time.

'You first,' she said with relief.

'Well, I don't know what I want to say—well, I do actually, but I just... I... I think about you a lot. I didn't realise how much I'd miss you when I went over. You are all I think about, Kate, and I know it's probably stupid, and we've known each other forever but I... I just hate being away from you. And now that you are all going to have to leave, I won't even have you to come home to...'

'Did you miss me like...the way you'd miss an old loyal servant?' Kate's eyes twinkled as she made the joke, but she was deadly serious. Was Sam really saying what she thought he was? Maybe he just meant he'd miss Robinswood and she was part of that. She didn't want to make a fool of herself.

'No, I don't mean that. I miss you the way a chap might miss his girl. I know you're not my girl or anything like it, and maybe it's just that I don't know any other girls... No, that's not true. I've met loads of girls in the last few months, but none of them are as funny or wild or kind and clever as you are. Not one of them holds a candle to you, Kate Murphy, and I can't bear to leave you, and that's the truth.'

Kate felt a thrill inside. Was she imagining it? Did Sam Kenefick actually want her to be his girl?

'I... I don't know what to say,' she stammered, wishing something better would have come out of her mouth.

'I'm sorry,' he said quickly. 'I've embarrassed you, and I should never have said anything. It was stupid of me... I'm just upset about everything here, and I...' He looked mortified as he stared at his polished RAF boots.

'You haven't embarrassed me,' Kate said. 'I feel the same way about you, but I never allow myself to even think it. You're the Lord of the

Manor, like, actually the Lord, and I'm just the servants' daughter, soon to be evicted. Nobody would accept us. Everyone would think I'm getting ideas above my station, and your mother would have a fit.'

'But leaving all those things aside for a moment,' he said, his face lit up with a hopeful smile, 'you do like me? You know...like that?'

'Yes, I do like you, like that.' She smiled shyly. She wasn't used to ever being shy around Sam before. It felt strange but also nice and a little unbelievable.

He looked down to where their hands were on the old stone bridge, so close but not touching, and he moved his hand to cover hers. She turned her hand and squeezed his.

He smiled.

'I don't care, not one single jot actually, what anyone thinks. If you can be my girl, then that's all I'll ever want.'

'You say that now, but, Sam, they'll never allow it,' Kate said earnestly. 'My father, your mother, the whole world. This sort of thing happens in films and books, not in real life, to real people. Aisling said you'd go over and find some horsey-faced one to marry who'd have a ton of money to fix up Robinswood, and even though it broke my heart every time, part of me believed she was right. I've nothing, not a bean, and neither do my family. How could it ever work—'

Sam leaned over and held her face in his hands. 'Shhhh,' he said and kissed her gently. 'We'll make it work. I love you, Kate. I don't care what anyone says, that I am who I am and you are who you are, or that we're too young, or anything. I love you, and I want to be with you. And once they all see we're serious about each other, no matter how long that takes, then they'll get used to the idea, and if they don't, well... Look, this war is not going to be over quickly, and I may not even survive—'

'Don't say that!' Kate hated to hear him voice the fear that had haunted her since the day he joined up.

'We have to be real here, Kate,' he said gently. 'I want to make it, of course I do. Knowing you have feelings for me makes me want to even more. But the odds are not great, and maybe before this, people would wait. And I know we're young, you more than me even, but we may not get another chance, so you have to grab life with both hands.'

He looked so earnest and sincere she smiled, though tears brimmed in her eyes.

'It's not me you need to convince, Lord Kenefick.' She giggled, and as she did, he kissed her.

CHAPTER 13

They walked for miles, talking and making plans, in around the hazel wood, through the orchard, and around the back of the house, where the ha-ha created a vertical barrier between the parkland and the house, while never interrupting the view of the landscape beyond. The sunlight glinted on the water-balanced panes of glass in the old sash windows of Robinswood, but they didn't linger where they could be seen from the house. Without conferring, they walked through the stables at the back of the house and down the ancient lane that led to a small stony beach, a favourite place of theirs for playing and swimming as children.

'You could come over,' Sam suggested. 'I mean, it would be dangerous, of course, and maybe your father would hate me more for encouraging you to come to England with everything that's happening, but I know you're adventurous, and I think you'd love it.' They sat on a big flat rock, the icy-cold but clear water lapping over the well-worn pebbles of the beach.

'Over to England? But what would I do?' Kate tried to keep the excitement out of her voice. Was Sam really asking her to go back to England with him?

'You could join up? They are recruiting WAAFs like crazy—telephonists, typists, cooks, drivers, all sorts of jobs really. Maybe you could get sent to Biggin Hill, and we'd be on the same base, and we could see each other on our days off, and go up the West End and all of that. You'd love London, Kate; it's so vibrant and busy with so much going on.'

'More than Kilthomand? Are you sure?' She nudged him playfully.

'I'd love to, Sam, but my parents would have a fit. I mean, Daddy would probably come over and drag me back by the hair. And the girls, well...' Kate sighed.

'I don't want to put any pressure on you, Kate. It has to be your decision. But, you'll be eighteen next month, and you're an adult. You can make your own choices. It's not up to your parents or anyone else what you do.'

Kate looked him directly in the eye.

'And you'd want me there? Not just as good old Kate Murphy, someone to have a bit of a laugh with, but actually Kate, your girl? Because if I'm going to alienate my whole family, it had better be for something worthwhile.' She knew she sounded fierce, but she needed to be sure.

'I would love it,' he said earnestly. 'Yes. But I don't want to be the reason your parents go mad. I mean, I want them to accept us, and maybe running away with me to a country at war isn't the wisest course of action. Maybe if we spoke to them together, I could explain that I would take care of you, and that—'

'Ah, Sam, did you come down in the last shower?' Kate interrupted. 'How will you look after me? My father would have an absolute canary if he thought I was going to Dungarvan with you, let alone over to England. I appreciate that you're trying to do the right thing and everything, but honestly, that won't work. Not with them. If I'm going to do this, then it has to be secretly. They can't know anything about it until we're there and it's too late.' The thought of being deliberately deceptive to her family broke her heart, but she wanted this—she wanted Sam—so much.

'Could you bear to leave them?' Sam's voice was quiet and sincere.

'I... I'm not saying it would be easy, or that I'd go without a backward glance… But we have to leave anyway. We're all going to be scattered to the four winds as soon as your mother goes, as the chances of us getting a place together are virtually nonexistent. Daddy pretends he's not worried, but I know he is, and I can hear him and Mammy talking late into the night every night. One fewer daughter to worry about might actually be a blessing. Eve is almost certain to wind up with Jack O'Neill; they are mad about each other. He'll be going home to Cork, and I wouldn't be one bit surprised if he took Eve with him. And that just leaves Ais. She'd be devastated, and I'd feel the worst about leaving her. Everyone else has someone, but since that eejit Sean Lacey made a laughing stock of her in front of the whole parish, she's been very low.'

Sam put his arm around her, and she allowed her head to rest on his shoulder. The action felt both strange and familiar simultaneously.

'Look, don't make a decision now,' he said. 'Just have a think about it. I'm here for a few more days. I'm helping Mother get everything packed away or sold, so you don't need to do anything for a while. I… I hate the rift it would cause, but the idea that we could be together, over there, well, it would be simply wonderful.' He coloured with embarrassment, still coming to terms with being soft and romantic with the girl he used to wrestle and chase.

He looked at his watch. 'Speaking of Mother, I'd better go back. I rather stormed out on her earlier, which was rather unfair, I suppose. But I was just so upset to hear you all wouldn't be kept on here.'

They stood up and Sam put out his hand to help her, something he would never have done before. She took it, feeling a bit silly. She was well able to get down herself, but it felt nice that he was taking care of her.

'See you tomorrow?' he asked.

She nodded. 'Here?'

'After breakfast?' He smiled, a different smile to his usual cheeky grin.

'I'll try to get away, but there's always jobs to be done.' Kate rolled her eyes.

'I'll wait for you.' His voice was barely audible as he slipped his arms around her slender waist.

'Til tomorrow morning?' She smiled.

'Forever. I'll wait for you forever, Kate Murphy.' He bent his head to kiss her.

* * *

KATE WALKED into the kitchen to find it deserted. She was relieved, sure that her news was written all over her face. Mammy was still up at Robinswood, making the tea for Lady Kenefick and now Sam probably, and of her sisters, there was no sign. Then, seeing the tape measure on the dresser, she remembered Aisling and Eve were in Dungarvan. Mammy had said they each needed a new dress if they were to go looking for work, so they were sent to buy material. They could have got it in Lacey's, but no Murphy would ever set foot in that drapery again after the disgraceful way the son of the house had treated Aisling.

Kate was glad she hadn't bumped into her father; he had an uncanny knack for sensing if she was hiding something. But it was almost milking time, and the few cattle that were left would be herded into the milking parlour shortly. Perhaps she should go and help him... She stopped. She rarely was in the house alone, and as the sun was setting, the kitchen was warm and inviting. The clock ticked on the dresser that held all their crockery, mismatched, as they were almost all cast-offs from Robinswood.

Little ornaments she and her sisters had made for their parents were there, as well, and the big old jug with the handle missing, filled with pencils and scissors and bits of string. The drawers contained sheets of used brown paper that Mammy always saved when anything was delivered, later to be used to make jam pot covers or cover their schoolbooks. The yellow-and-red oilcloth covered the scarred dining room table; Kate remembered the day Mammy bought it at the fair. She loved how bright it was and would go mad if they cut bread on it without using a bread board. All the meals, the jokes, the homework at the table... Mammy showing them how to polish shoes on a Saturday night to be ready for Mass on Sunday morning... The big old wireless on the table by the range... Were they really leaving all of it? Kate blinked back a tear.

As she was about to go out and help in the yard, Eve and Aisling arrived home, laden down with parcels.

'Well, don't help, whatever you do!' Eve sighed as Kate just watched them juggling bags and belongings.

'Sorry.' Kate sprang into action, holding the door and taking a large bag of brown flour from Aisling.

'Honestly, our mother thinks we're a pair of cart horses, the size of the list she sent us with,' Aisling grumbled. 'We were only going in for material, and suddenly we're dragging half of Dungarvan back with us. And on top of it, white flour is not to be got for love nor money. We tried three places, and they looked at us like we were mad. And the bus is reduced to one service a day because of the petrol crisis. Lucky Mrs Hanratty was coming back in the pony and trap and gave us a lift, but we had to walk from the creamery. Honestly, I can't stand Sean Lacey, but I think we might be going back to him for everything if this is to continue.' She examined the welts on her palms caused by carrying the heavy bags all the way.

Kate methodically put the shopping away in the larder and said nothing. Eve and Aisling prattled on about the lack of everything and how the British better hurry up and win the war because they were sick of having nothing to buy in the shops.

'Hey, Kate, don't you want to see the material we got for you?' Eve called.

Kate was pouring raisins from a paper bag into the big glass jar in the pantry.

She paused and walked over to the table, where the girls were admiring the material. Eve held up a lovely lemon-coloured fabric with tiny red flowers on it.

'Lemon is lovely on you, Kate,' Eve said. 'It makes me look like an egg with my red hair, but it's perfect for you. Do you like it?' She held the material out for her sister to examine.

Kate took it and tried to be enthusiastic, but it was an act; she had too much on her mind.

'What's wrong?' Aisling was very perceptive.

'Oh...nothing. I'm fine.' She smiled, anxious to divert any further interrogations.

'Well, by the look on your face, it doesn't seem like nothing! What have you done?' Eve was used to Kate's antics; she'd covered up for her enough times. Like the time Kate gave cheek to the nun and instead of going to the reverend mother's office for several hard slaps, she'd hid in the byre. Or the time she went to see Clark Gable in *Mutiny on the Bounty* when she was expressly forbidden by their parents.

'WE'LL HELP YOU,' Aisling said kindly, noting her younger sister's solemnity.

'I haven't done anything,' Kate insisted. 'I'm just sad about leaving this place, that's all.'

She watched as the words sank in with her sisters. Though all the family thought about it constantly, they were trying to remain upbeat for each other. So they rarely discussed the future, and never how they really felt about leaving the only home they'd ever known.

Eve drew her sister into an embrace, and Aisling joined them. Together, they stood, saying nothing, each girl feeling the same.

They broke apart as Jack entered the kitchen. He and Eve were going to the pictures.

'Is this a private hug, or can anyone join in?' he asked with a chuckle, but immediately stopped when he saw the tears shining in Eve's eyes. He crossed the room.

'I'm sorry, Eve, are you all right? Did something happen?'

'No, we're fine,' Eve said with a smile. 'I suppose the reality of leaving here just caught up with us. We're fine.' She wiped a tear away with the back of her hand. 'Come on, let's go, or we'll miss the picture.'

When they left, Kate went up to their room. She lay on the bed, mulling over everything that had happened. If they weren't leaving

Robinswood, she would never consider leaving the family to go to England, but since they had no future here, anyway... Round and round the various possibilities went, but each time, she came to the same conclusion. Her parents would be devastated.

Aisling came up a little later. 'Dinner is ready, Kate. Mam made too much above, so she brought down the rest for us. It smells lovely.' She saw her sister's solemn face and sat on the bed beside her.

'What's wrong, really, Kate? Are you sure it's just leaving here? You seem... I don't know...'

'Sam's asked me to go over to England, to join up and to be his girl.' Kate heard herself blurt it all out.

'What? Sam Kenefick asked you—'

'He loves me, Ais, he always has, and I love him. And I know you're going to say it's ridiculous and everything, but I just... I want to go, Ais.'

Aisling swallowed and tried to process what her younger sister was saying.

'Look, Kate, I don't know about you and Sam, like, if he says he loves you, then, well, I don't really know what to say about that... But you don't seriously want to go over to England, in the middle of a war? You think it's all tea dances and medals, but it's not.'

'I'm not stupid, Aisling,' Kate replied. 'I do know what the war is. But it's not like there are any better ideas here, anyway. And I know you probably think I'm such a child and don't know my own mind, but I really do, and I'm going. Please don't tell Mammy and Daddy, Aisling. I'm just going to go. I know if I asked them, they'd say no, and it would be so upsetting. So I'm just going to go either way.'

Kate knew she was taking a big risk telling her sister of her plans. She hadn't meant to blurt it out like that at all.

Aisling stared incredulously. Saying nothing.

Please don't let her go running downstairs this second, Kate begged silently, while maintaining what she hoped was a determined expression on her face.

Eventually, her older sister spoke.

'Kate, I know you think this is a great idea, and you love Sam and all of that, but think about what you're doing. Please, just for a minute. Leave Mammy and Daddy out of it for a moment; what would you do? How would you live?'

'I'm joining up.' Kate tried to infuse her voice with a confidence she didn't feel. 'The WAAFs, that's the Women's Auxiliary Air Force, and I'm going to work on the same base as Sam outside London.'

Aisling sighed deeply, knowing that to rant and rave at her impetuous younger sister would be pointless. Besides, she could hear voices downstairs; they'd have to leave it for now.

'Look,' she said in an urgent whisper, 'will you promise me you won't do anything rash, and we'll talk again? I won't tell anyone, if you promise me you won't go anywhere without talking to me first, all right?'

She looked sternly at Kate.

'I promise,' Kate sighed as they heard a footstep on the creaky stair.

'What's going on in here?' Their mother appeared at the bedroom door.

'Nothing,' both girls chorused. No matter what the argument, they didn't tell on each other, ever.

'Hmm.' Isabella looked sceptical. 'I don't know about that. The two of you are holed up here, whispering and looking guilty, so someone better start talking.'

'Honestly, Mammy, it was just an argument over material,' Aisling lied. 'We'll sort it out.'

CHAPTER 14

The weeks flew by, and Robinswood began to feel so empty. Lady Kenefick went up to Dublin a lot, sorting things out, and Sam had gone back to England last week. Eve thought Kate might be heartbroken, but she was remarkably upbeat, considering the situation. She was probably delighted to have less farm work to do. Though Mammy and Daddy were kept busy, there was very little to do compared with how their lives used to be.

Eve waited at the end of the lane that led up to the Warrens' property. She wanted to go up to the yard and find Jack, but she knew if she did that, it would get back to her parents and she'd be in big trouble. The Murphys were not the kind of girls who threw themselves at boys, no matter how nice the boy in question was. But Eve had finished all her jobs and was bored.

Jack had said he'd come over to their house after work, and he did it almost every night anyway, so hopefully he'd come out this way.

Eve mindlessly kicked a pebble across the lane, and a small rabbit scarpered out, its white bobtail disappearing as quickly as it appeared. She wondered for the millionth time what the future held for them. Mammy and Daddy were worried, she could tell, but they were trying to keep a brave face for her and her sisters.

She saw the cows being turned out into the field again after milking and knew Jack would soon be finishing up for the day.

She looked up the lane, and eventually, there he was. He ran to meet her when he saw her.

'Well, what's Waterford's answer to Maureen O'Hara doing at the end of Warren's lane?' He put his arms around her and hugged her tightly. Then he took her hand and tucked it in his as they walked along the quiet country road.

'Ah, I just had nothing to do. We're just making up jobs in Robinswood at this stage. It's hard to imagine leaving it all behind. I know Mammy and Daddy are trying to make out like it's all going to be fine, but the time to leave is getting closer and we've nowhere to go.' She sighed, and then coloured, realising what she'd said.

What if he thought she was angling for a proposal? And what if that was the furthest thing from his mind? They'd only been courting a short time; it was too soon for anything serious. She'd never even met his mother.

'I'm sure your dad will sort something,' Jack assured her. 'He's excellent at his job, anyplace would be lucky to get him, and your mam is the best cook for five counties, though don't ever tell my own mother I said that.' He winked and chuckled, and Eve sighed with relief. It felt good to be able to talk to him, tell him her worries. Everyone at home was so busy being optimistic there was no room for reality it seemed.

'I don't know,' she said honestly. 'It's not like a ton of job offers have been landing on the doormat, and Lady Kenefick isn't going to help us. Why couldn't she have found one of her lah-di-dah friends with a big house to take us on? I hate the thought of us all going our separate ways... Maybe I'm just an old stick in the mud, never wanting anything to change.'

'I'd be happy to be stuck in the mud with you.' Jack grinned and nudged her.

EVE PUNCHED HIM PLAYFULLY.

'I saw that Sean Lacey the other day,' Jack said, changing the subject, 'when Charlie asked me to go into town for extra feed. He looked very sheepish.'

Eve sighed. 'Well, if he looked sheepish with you, he's downright terrified of me, I'd say. He crossed the road after Mass last Sunday rather than pass me.'

'He's a right clown. I can't imagine how someone like him could get a girl as lovely as Aisling in the first place. You Murphy girls are outside almost everyone's league, but that eejit... I don't know.'

'We're not outside everyone's league.' Eve smiled and squeezed his arm.

He smiled and stopped walking. 'I...' He coloured with embarrassment. 'Are you serious about me, Eve? About us?'

'Ah, Jack, you know how I feel about you by now,' she said nervously, buying time, afraid to show her hand.

'Do I know how you feel about me?' Jack gave her a sidelong glance.

Eve was flustered. They'd spent almost every evening together since they met nearly two months ago, and they'd kissed and held hands and talked about everything. About families, his father, his mam, the fact that he'd missed out on having siblings—he loved to hear all the stories about her and her sisters growing up. And he really liked her parents, and they liked him. So what was he asking her?

Did he want more than kissing? Because if he did, then she would have to end it, much as it would probably kill her. She was not that sort of girl, and anyway, her parents, liking him or not, would have a fit if they thought even for a second she and Jack were doing something reserved for the sanctity of marriage. And she wasn't exactly sure of the whole mechanics of sex, if she was honest. It was never discussed, either at home or in school. She remembered barging into her parents' bedroom one night—because Aisling had accidentally cut a corner out of her good dress and she was so cross with her—and Daddy seemed to have no clothes on and was on top of Mammy, and he roared at her to get out. Moments later, Mammy had appeared in her dressing gown saying that Daddy had hurt his back carrying the plough and she was just giving it a rub for him, but even to a twelve-year-old, it all sounded a bit odd.

There was a mission in the church once a year when the Redemptorist Fathers would come, and the Wednesday night was just for men, and it was always packed to the rafters because it was the one about the evils of the flesh. She'd hear from girls in school whose brothers had attended, and it all seemed a bit of a mystery. It was all to do with not dancing too close or having bad thoughts. Eve knew her body reacted to Jack in a way she'd never experienced before with anyone else, and that his did too, but whenever things got to that stage with the kissing, they stopped. She assumed he was as scared of the mortal sin side of things as she was.

Regardless, she obviously was taking too long to answer.

'It's OK, you don't have to say it...' Jack was unusually serious. 'It was wrong of me to ask, but I suppose I wanted a bit of security before I laid myself bare.'

'Well... I...' Eve still thought he was suggesting they do it, and she was growing increasingly panicked.

'Eve, I'm trying—well, I've been trying for weeks now to tell you, that I'm in love with you, and the time is going to be up shortly with Warren's, all the setting and ploughing is almost finished and I'll have no more reason to stay around. And now your family are talking about moving away, it feels like life is pulling us apart. I know we're too young and we don't know each other that long, and I've nothing to offer you, but I just can't walk away and not say it. So, I love you, Eve Murphy, and I don't want to leave you, or for you to leave me, and I was thinking of asking your father if I could ask you to marry me.'

The words tumbled out of his mouth in one big long sentence. In his eagerness, he looked much younger than his twenty-four years.

Relief flooded Eve's mind—firstly, that he wasn't suggesting what she'd imagined he was suggesting, and secondly, at the dawning realisation that Jack was proposing to her.

She didn't know what to say, so she just stood there.

'Oh God, it's too soon, isn't it?' he said quickly. 'I've spoken out of turn, and I shouldn't have! Sure, you don't know me from a hole in the ground. Look, you're right, I don't know what came over me. We are too young, and we barely know each other, like, you haven't even met my mam yet, and you have no idea what kind of a setup I'm bringing you into or anything...' His voice trailed off, his pain at rejection masked by bluster.

'I'd love to marry you.' She only just managed to get the words out.

Jack stopped and looked intently at her, just to check she wasn't teasing him.

'Really, seriously, like? You'd marry *me*?' The way he said it made it sound like it was the daftest idea on earth. 'Like, I've no money or anything, and we've only a small house on Barrack Street...'

Eve grinned. 'Are you trying to talk me into it or out of it?'

'I don't know...' His face split into a wide grin. 'Both, I think?'

'Well, even with no money and a small house—we've **no** house by the way—I would love to be your wife, Jack O'Neill. But, yes, let's do it right. Why don't you ask Daddy, and then if he says yes, we can arrange a trip to meet your mam and you can show me this small house of yours.'

CHAPTER 15

*A*isling and Kate peeled potatoes in silence, each lost in her own thoughts. When Kate caught her mother's eye, she knew something was up. Her mother was like a terrier, their father often said, once she got an inkling of something, she would not let it go until she'd found out the truth. Neither Kate nor Aisling could withstand their mother's cross-examination, so they hoped Eve would appear soon.

'Is Jack coming for his tea tonight, do ye know?' Isabella asked, counting the number of potatoes she was putting on to boil to be served with the trout Dermot had caught earlier from the river. There were freshly dug carrots as well.

'I think so. He usually does, doesn't he?' Aisling tried to keep her voice light.

'Hmmm... He does, I suppose. I wonder how long more he'll be staying around? The ploughing and setting over in Warren's must be nearly finished by now. Will he go back to Cork then, I wonder?' Isabella's tone was conversational—the girls knew their mother wouldn't demand to know what went on straight out. She was better than that, she was digging.

'I don't know. I suppose he will...' Kate caught Aisling's eye behind their mother's back. They'd had no opportunity to discuss Kate's revelation about England and Sam and all of that; Kate had avoided the subject, as well as any alone time with Aisling. She'd made sure either one of their parents or Eve was always within earshot.

Sam had written to say he could make sure she would be at his base, if she was going to do it. She longed to write back and say she would. He'd even included a postal order for the fare, which Kate had cashed in Dungarvan a few days ago. She didn't dare do it in Kilthomand, because Mossy the postmaster would have the whole parish told by lunchtime.

'Poor Eve will be heartbroken,' Isabella said. 'She's really smitten with him, and he's a nice lad. I'm glad she met someone decent. Some of the lads you'd see knocking around in Kilthomand, well, they wouldn't be good enough for my girls, anyway.' She grinned at Aisling. Though the tone was jokey, they both knew their mother meant every word.

Isabella definitely smelled a rat. Normally, her two daughters would love nothing more than to speculate endlessly about what was going to happen with their sister's romance, but this evening, they were tight-lipped.

Just as she was about to go deeper with her questions, Dermot appeared, covered in mud and soaking wet.

'What on earth were you doing?' she asked her disgruntled husband.

'I was trying to load that bloody horse into the fancy horsebox Major Cotsworth sent over! He's taking the mare, and the cart horse as well, but that cantankerous animal didn't want to go, so she gave me a right job with her blackguarding. And eventually she reared up rather than be led, and I ended up in the trough. Put a drop of water on the stove there would you, to heat up, till I clean myself up a bit before we eat.'

Aisling busied herself getting some water, glad of the distraction. Kate used the opportunity to nip upstairs, thus avoiding any more work, as well as Aisling's interrogation.

Isabella followed Dermot into their bedroom and found him some dry clothes as he peeled off the wet and filthy work clothes and pulled on clean trousers and socks. It wasn't like him to have an accident, but he was tired. She knew he lay awake at night, not moving so as not to disturb her. But she wasn't sleeping either. This was their home. Leaving it seemed so horrible, but leave it they must.

Dermot racked his brain night after night for people who could help. He thought of his old comrades, not everyone was as black and white as Charlie Warren, but the only one he would really get in touch with was Oskar Metz, and he was in Germany. God alone knew what was going on in his life.

'Something's going on,' Isabella began. 'The girls have been in a right mood for the last week. Well, Kate and Aisling are, I don't know, they're plotting...'

'Sure, sounds normal, probably fighting over a frock or something...' Dermot was examining the beginnings of a bruise on his chest where the mare had butted him with her head.

'No, this is different,' Isabella insisted. 'They aren't letting on a thing. And it's not like Aisling to be so furtive. She's normally the reasonable one.'

'I don't know, sure with young ones, it could be anything.' Dermot winced as his wife examined a nasty scrape on his back where he'd hit the rough stone trough.

'I'll put a bit of disinfectant on that,' she said. 'You don't want it going septic, and God alone knows what's in that old trough.'

She went to the dressing table where she kept her potions and lotions, as Dermot called them, and extracted the pungent-smelling TCP. He winced again as she dabbed it on the cuts.

When she finished, she slipped her arms around his waist and laid her head on his bare chest. He cradled her and sighed heavily, kissing the top of her head. They stood together, and Isabella could hear his heart beating steadily. It made her feel safe. She closed the buttons on his shirt, and Dermot smiled that smile that was reserved only for her.

'We should talk about her offer, Der. I know you don't want to, but the time is passing, and we're desperate.' Isabella had been biding her time since Lady Kenefick's suggestion. It wasn't like Dermot to be so reticent, but he'd never raised the matter again once he turned Violet down. Isabella didn't want to nag him, and she wanted to wait and see if there was another way. She didn't know why, but she knew he didn't want to work for this Hamilton-Brooks man.

Dermot gratefully shrugged on the hand-knitted navy blue jumper Isabella knit him last winter; it was too warm to work in, but he felt cold to the bone after his dunking.

He sighed heavily and sat on the side of the bed. She sat beside him and held his hand.

'I know him, Thomas Hamilton-Brooks; he's a British agent. It's no accident that his wife came looking for us. He most likely knows who I am too. That's why I dismissed it.'

Isabella was shocked. 'But sure, what business has a British agent over here now we're independent?'

'He's here years, since back in The Troubles, and you may be sure he's keeping a close eye on this country now that Britain is at war with Germany. They don't want anyone sneaking in the back door. I met him, as Violet said; he used to come down supposedly to do business with Austin, but he was sniffing around. I think he knew I was involved. He never said anything, but it's too much of a coincidence now. We can't risk it.'

Isabella thought carefully. She loved Dermot with all her heart, but he could be very stubborn, and there was a way to handle him.

'But what danger are we in now? You've not been involved in anything for years and years, and he's keeping a low profile too. Maybe ye are old adversaries, but that's all over now. And I know it's not ideal, but the alternative is worse.'

He looked at her directly, his eyes searching her face. She knew if she asked him he'd do it, even if it was against his better judgement. It was a fact she'd never abused in all the years of their marriage. But she needed to use it now.

'Dermot, I never asked you to do anything you didn't want to do in all the years, but I want to take the offer. We have nowhere to go, nowhere for our girls to go, and I hate the fear. Please, can we take it, even short-term, until we get something else?'

'Bella, I—'

'I NEVER ONCE ASKED YOU for anything,' she interrupted. 'All those years, when you were out at night, I never questioned you, I never objected, though we were all in danger. I wanted to beg you to stop, I was so scared, but you believed in what you were doing, and I didn't want to stop you. But it was hard, Dermot, especially with a baby. I left my family for you, though I don't regret a single day of it, I could never have wished for another life. But now I'm asking you to do something for me.'

He gazed at her face for the longest time, and she remained still and silent.

Finally, he nodded. 'I'll tell herself I changed my mind in the morning.'

'Thank you.' Isabella felt her body relax for what felt like the first time in months.

Dermot sighed heavily and kissed her. Then he drew his head back, held her face gently in his huge calloused hands, and gazed intently into her eyes. 'I don't know what or who was looking down on me the day I saw you walking the beach in Salthill. Or what gave me the courage to go up and talk to you. I'd never done that before in my life. I'd face British soldiers with guns who were trying to kill me no bother, but walking up to a gorgeous girl was a whole other matter. But I am so glad I did. I'd follow you to the ends of the earth, my love, and if you want to go to Dublin and work for those people, then that's what we'll do.'

She smiled, turned her head, and kissed the palm of his hand.

They left their bedroom and went down to the kitchen, where dinner was almost ready. The table was set, and an unusual air of tranquillity prevailed. Of Kate there was no sign, but Eve and Jack were crossing the yard and Aisling was mashing potatoes.

'Kate!' Dermot called up the stairs. 'Come down for your dinner.'

There was no sound.

'Where is she?' her father asked.

'I don't know. I think she was going out to check on the chickens.' Aisling coloured. She hated lying, but the truth was Kate was avoiding her.

'She is in her eye worried about chickens,' Dermot snapped. 'She hates the bloody things.' He shrugged his big coat on once more and left the house to find his youngest daughter. He knew where she'd be —the same place she'd always gone since she could walk.

He was right. There she was on the bridge, dejectedly throwing stones into the stream. She looked up when she saw her father beside her.

'Your dinner's ready,' he said gently. 'Are you coming in?'

'I'm not hungry,' she said, never taking her eyes off the water.

Instead of admonishing her, Dermot sat beside her.

'Any word of young Sam?' he asked. He'd guessed how close they were.

'He's fine, working at the RAF base,' Kate said, knowing the very mention of the RAF would annoy her father.

Daddy refused to listen to the BBC news on the big old wireless, even though they could pick up the station. He knew everything about the war and its progress, but he got his information from Irish newspapers and radio. People in the village listened avidly for news of Hitler and the Nazis, but Daddy would only allow the deathly dull **Radio Eireann**, who either repeated the goings-on at the Eucharistic Congress of 1932 over and over, or played terrible programmes where fellas were playing fiddles and people were dancing. Irish dancing on the radio—it made the Murphy girls giggle every time it came on. Kate often wondered if it wasn't the presenter with a pair of shoes on his hands tapping away on the table. The only other thing on was farming programmes, going on about headage and roundworm and ringworm and sarcoptic mange mites. It was all disgusting and so mind-numbingly boring Kate would have rather watched paint dry. But it was hard to get the big old wireless back on the national station, so she dared not move it onto the BBC when her dad was out.

Dermot sighed.

'It's all happening again. Britain is getting itself into another war, and the last time out, they tried to conscript us Irish men to go as cannon fodder to the Western Front. We told them then, in no uncertain terms, that it was not going to happen. We are finished with them, thanks be to God, and it took long enough to be rid of them. That crowd aren't happy unless they're wreaking havoc.'

Daddy listened to all kinds of nonsense from the girls about the pictures or dresses or the goings-on in the village and never stopped them. In fact, he often joined in teasing them. But on the subject of England, he was resolute and hard. Even the day Sam left to join up, he didn't shake his hand or anything.

'Is that why you didn't even wish Sam well when he left? Kate asked sadly. 'Because you hate the British so much?' She was shivering; the evening wind was biting.

Dermot took off his coat and wrapped it around his youngest daughter lovingly. 'Kate, my love, I know this war seems so glamorous to you, and I suppose it's understandable, to an extent. You don't remember a time when British soldiers, Black and Tans and Auxiliaries, walked our streets here in Ireland by right of occupation.

'They were savage and cruel and held our people in disdain, and the only thing that got rid of them was to be resolute and strong and to meet their savagery with savagery of our own. It wasn't good, and I don't revel in the glory of it all like some do. There is nothing glorious about people being blown to bits, nothing honourable in a mother getting a letter saying her boy is dead. But I'm glad, in a way I can't describe to you, that they're gone, and gone for good. I have no gripe with the German people. In fact, before you were born, my best friend was a German chap, and 'tis them they'll be killing, not the top brass.'

'Now, I hope young Samuel comes back in one piece, he's a nice enough lad, but for as long as he wears that bloody uniform, then I don't have anything to say to him,' Dermot said sternly. 'It's not personal, but that's how it is. I'll tell you what, though, him and the rest of his majesty's pilots will have their work cut out for them. This will be a war of the air in a way the last one wasn't, not really. The Luftwaffe have amazing technology now, and the Brits have too—

fighter planes, bombers. And now that this is how it's going to be fought, I can't see them keeping the fighting over there.'

'I think a lot of Irish people will go over though,' Kate said. 'It would be a job, wouldn't it, for some people?'

Though she'd asked it quietly, Dermot heard the note of steel he'd come to recognise. Kate was by far the most determined of his daughters. He would have to be adamant about shutting down any discussion on the subject quickly and firmly.

'Kate, my love, I'm sure some will go, just like the last time, and come home in coffins, if they come home at all. Now, will we go back and have our dinner?'

He jumped down and offered her his hand, which she took. He then tucked her hand into the crook of his arm.

'Were you in the IRA, you know, during The Troubles?' Kate asked, the question popping into her head as the only possible explanation for the stance he was taking.

Dermot didn't reply for a few seconds. He'd been waiting for that question for a long time. He'd kept his republican past a secret from his daughters for a reason: they were growing up in a time of hard-won peace, and he believed the past should be left where it is, in the past. So, for the first time in her life, he lied to his daughter.

'Of course I wasn't. Sure, I was working for the Keneficks. But others around here were, and I'm glad they did what they did.'

They walked the rest of the way home in silence.

The meal was just being served as they entered the kitchen, to find Jack helping Isabella and the girls.

Eve looked flushed, and her mother thought perhaps it was the wind, which was really biting despite being well into spring. Eve went straight to helping bring dishes to the table, leaving Jack to talk to her parents. Once she'd placed the heavy bowl of mashed potatoes on the table,

Aisling asked, 'What has you looking like the cat that got the cream?' Kate gave a small smile but was unusually quiet.

Jack was in earnest chat with their parents by the range, and Eve wondered if he was using the moment of peace to ask for her hand in marriage. She'd suggested waiting, but Jack said it was best to ask now, especially since everything was up in the air anyway.

Eve's sisters looked at her expectantly. 'Well?' Aisling asked again.

'Jack proposed,' Eve whispered excitedly. 'But ye can't say a word until he asks Mammy and Daddy properly.'

'I don't believe it!' Aisling hissed, the delight in her voice obvious. 'We're getting a brother, Kate! I always wanted a brother...'

'Oh, Eve, he's so nice, not like that toad, Sean.'

Aisling was trying to be tough, but she was still very raw after her disappointment. Eve wondered if she ought to have told her about her exciting plans with Jack.

Since the incident at the dance, she and Kate made sure that any errands were done in Dungarvan—not one shilling of Murphy money would cross the counter of Sean Lacey's shop ever again. Aisling was worth a million Eleanor Conlons, and Sean knew it. He regretted his foolishness and had said as much to Eve only last Tuesday, when he'd bumped into her as she came out of the post office. Eve recalled the conversation as Aisling set out cutlery.

'How's Aisling?' he'd asked tentatively while his mother listened and watched with her beady eyes.

'Top of the world, Sean, just flying it, so she is. And yourself?' Eve had been bright and cheery; she wouldn't give it to the Laceys to know how much Sean's behaviour had upset them.

'Ah, grand, grand, you know yourself...' Sean had muttered, casting a glance at his mother as if to say, *I'm doing it*.

Honestly, she'd thought, Sean Lacey was such a lump of a mammy's boy, she didn't know what Aisling had seen in him in the first place. But she could tell by the sour look on Mrs Lacey's face that the prospect of her precious Sean's name being up with that trampy Conlan one was not going to do at all. The woman would have liked to see the match with Aisling, Eve knew. Aisling was a nice girl, and in Mrs Lacey's eyes, Ais would have to be grateful for the elevation in station a match with Sean would have brought, and therefore would be easily managed as a daughter-in-law. This new setup was most vexing to the old woman, clearly. Eve saw it as a narrow escape for her sister.

As she'd turned to go, Sean had stopped her. 'Like, I'm not with Eleanor Conlan or anyone,' he said. 'I never was. Will you tell Aisling that for me, Eve? Like, if she wanted to go out some day, for a spin maybe...'

His voice trailed off under Eve's cold stare.

'Oh, I don't think she'd have any interest in that now, Sean, do you? Not at this stage, after everything.' She said it loud enough for all the busybodies of the village who had gathered to hear. 'No, we're planning our next big move, so definitely not. A spin with you wouldn't be high on Aisling's priority list, I would think.' She gave him her brightest smile, though she wanted to punch him on the nose.

And she'd turned on her heel and walked imperiously out of the post office, the matrons of Kilthomand staring after her.

Eve felt such outrage on behalf of her sister, but she sincerely hoped she'd done the right thing in not mentioning the conversation to Aisling. The poor girl had been through enough.

CHAPTER 16

$\mathcal{K}$ate crept out of bed so slowly, trying to keep the bedsprings from creaking. The sun was rising and soon would flood the little bedroom with buttery light. The spring was giving way to summer now and Robinswood looked beautiful. Sam was back in England and every inch of the estate reminded her of him. Mammy and Daddy were doing their best to keep everyone's spirits up, and Eve and Jack's engagement a few weeks earlier had been very exciting, but nothing could take from the horrible sense of foreboding that hung over the whole place.

She'd stashed her bag in the shed outside under some old sacking because she wasn't going to risk dressing in the house. She didn't allow herself to even look at the sleeping forms of her sisters, in the same beds they'd slept in since they were small girls. She'd made sure she was last to bed the previous night and had left the door open a crack so the turning of the handle wouldn't disturb them. She stole out onto the landing.

Her parents' door was ajar as always, the gentle rhythm of Daddy's snores causing her to stop and allow herself a moment to look around one last time. Whatever happened, she would never again be in this house.

She went downstairs and slipped her feet into a pair of wellies inside the back door. Her coat was hanging on the nail, so she wrapped it around herself gratefully as she let herself out into the yard. It was still chilly in the pre-dawn air. She ran across the cobblestones to the shed and quickly retrieved her bag. On top, she had packed her warmest dress and jumper, stockings and her good shoes. She dressed quickly, shivering.

'I'm coming with you, and if you scream, you'll wake the whole house and we'll both be for it.'

Kate whipped around to find Aisling standing behind her, fully dressed, holding a small valise Kate recognised as one Lillian had discarded.

'I said you can't!' Kate hissed. 'Just go back in, Ais, please, don't ruin this for me.'

'No. I'm coming. There's nothing keeping me here. Eve is set up with Jack now, and Mammy and Daddy will get a job if they don't have us hanging out of them. I want to go, and I want us to stick together, so let's just do it and get going before someone wakes up. The bus is at seven from the village, so we better get going.' Kate recognised the rarely heard but unshakable note of steel in her sister's voice. This was happening.

'Fine.' She sighed. There was no time to argue. She had planned the whole escape down to the last second. She wanted to arrive for the bus exactly on time, not a moment before.

* * *

EVE WOKE as the sun streamed in the thin curtains. The other two beds were empty. Kate and Aisling must have gotten up already, so she had the room to herself, a most unusual occurrence. She and Jack were engaged officially, and the date was set. The move was next week, and as of yet, her family had nowhere to go.

The feeling of anxiety in the pit of her stomach had grown to a hard knot of tension that filled her thoughts every day. These should've been the happiest days of her life, planning her wedding, but the uncertainty of it all detracted from the joy. Kate and Ais had applied for jobs around the county, though Kate would no doubt have preferred to go abroad somewhere.

Any ideas Kate had of taking off somewhere exotic had been dismissed right away. Mammy had forty fits a day, and they didn't take a tack of notice. She'd always been threatening them with dire consequences since they were small but never followed through. But Daddy got cross about once a year, and when he did, everyone did as they were told. He'd never once slapped them or anything like that, but he had a way about him and when he issued a decree, then it was the law and there was no point in discussing it. This was one of those times.

Three weeks ago, Jack had taken Eve to Cork to visit his mother, and she seemed a nice woman, if a little overprotective of Jack. Eve felt she could have been warmer, but she was fine. She clearly adored Jack, and the thought of sharing him wasn't something she relished. Eve had come home and confided in her mother, who had given her great advice.

'All any mother wants in a partner for their child is someone who will love them, be kind to them, and treat them with respect,' she said. 'If you do that for Jack, and I know you will, then his mother won't see you as a threat, more like an ally. She loves Jack, and you love Jack, so it will all be fine.'

THE WEDDING WOULD BE in the summer, but in the meantime, Mrs O'Neill said Eve could have Jack's room and she'd make up a settle bed for him in the tiny front parlour, though she did remark that it was most unusual to have the girl move in before the wedding. Eve knew she would get a job when she got there, in a shop or something, but the happiness she felt at this exciting new phase of her life was overshadowed by fear for her family combined with a sense that Jack's mother would much rather her son came home alone.

Aisling had been quiet over the last few weeks, so Eve was glad to see, when she got back from Cork, that Ais seemed to have perked up a bit. The whole business with Sean had really hurt her, but the rage Eve felt for that snivelling little toad was never evident when she spoke to Aisling. For some reason, Aisling still didn't like to hear a word against him. Up until recently, Eve thought her sister secretly harboured hopes of a reconciliation—until she got the letter.

Aisling showed it to her as soon as she got home.

Eve took the envelope and extracted the single sheet.

Dear Aisling,

I just wanted to write to wish you and your family all the best in the future. I would have liked to speak to you in person, but since every time I've tried to get your attention you ignore me, I have no option but to write to you. I know you are upset about the night of the dance, but it wasn't as if we had any formal arrangement, and while Eleanor and I are just friends, I know how it must have looked. So for that I apologise.

Your sister Eve made her feelings quite clear when I bumped into her, that I was not 'high on your priority list,' as she put it, and since I've not heard anything to the contrary from you, I'll assume you feel the same. So it's best for both of us if we just move on. I have met a girl. She was staying at her holiday house in Tramore, but her family own a large hotel in Dublin, and we are getting along very well. I wanted you to hear it from me.

So, as I said, all the best, and I hope your future is bright.

Regards,

Sean (Lacey)

Aisling's eyes had shone with unshed tears as Eve handed her back the letter.

Eve felt awful. Sean Lacey was an eejit, but Aisling really liked him. 'Ais, I'm sorry. I must have made things worse when I met him. I shouldn't have said anything...'

'It's not your fault,' Aisling assured her. 'He didn't once make an effort to speak to me, not really. He knows where I live, but he didn't bother. And then this.' She waved the letter. 'I just feel so stupid for caring about him when, obviously, it was all one-sided. He was with Eleanor that night, and God alone knows who else, and now this rich one from Dublin. It's like he's rubbing my nose in it. I don't know which is worse, the humiliation or the heartache.'

Eve had hugged her sister, wishing she had something to say that would ease her sister's pain.

* * *

As Eve got up, she realised she must have overslept. She and Jack had sat at the kitchen table last night making plans and whispering quietly. Daddy had been reading, and the girls upstairs making a dress from a Vogue pattern Lillian had bought but never actually used. As if the young lady of Robinswood would actually have made her own clothes. The idea was laughable. Lady Kenefick had offered it to Aisling as she helped her clear out Lillian's bedroom. Lady Kenefick was leaving on Saturday, catching the boat from Dublin, and her things were being held in storage until she was settled. How easy life was when you were rich, Eve had remarked to Jack.

'Well, some things are easier, I suppose,' he'd whispered in her ear, 'but I'd not trade my life with hers for all the tea in China.'

Eve had held his hand under the table. Mammy turned a blind eye to their 'romancing,' as she called it, but Daddy had very strict rules about what was appropriate carry-on, and canoodling with a boy, even if he was your fiancé, was not something Eve would do in his sights, anyway. He'd never actually say anything, but you'd get a look, and that was enough.

Eve couldn't believe that in just a few short months she'd be a married woman, sharing everything with Jack. She wished it could be sooner, but very fast engagements and rushed weddings only meant one thing, and Eve didn't want the neighbours gossiping and watching her tummy for signs of swelling before nine months was up. It was so exciting, but she held most of her enthusiasm in check. There was little cause for celebration these days in the Murphy household.

She got up and had a quick wash at the sink before dressing quickly, pulling her dress over her head. She decided to leave her legs bare. The weather was getting warmer, and anyway, she was only packing up the library of Robinswood today.

'Girls! Time to get up!' Mammy called up the stairs.

Eve went out onto the landing and called down, 'It's just me. Aisling and Kate aren't here. I thought I must have slept in. What time is it?'

Her mother came to the bottom of the stairs.

'Not there? Sure, it's only half eight. That pair usually have to be dragged out. Where are they? Did you not hear them getting up?' A shadow of concern crossed Isabella's face. There was so much friction in the house these days, everyone was on edge and worried, that their normal conversations and the laughs they always had seemed to have become a thing of the past.

Dermot had spoken to Lady Kenefick about the job offer in Dublin, and she was making contact with her friends. Isabella knew how hard it had been for him to go back on his earlier word, but he'd done it for her. They'd decided not to say anything to the girls until it was settled.

Eve went back into their bedroom with a sense of foreboding. Yesterday, when she'd come into the kitchen after feeding the chickens for the last time—they were going to Pat Kelleher the butcher this morning—Kate had been taking some jam and bread and wrapping it in a tea towel. She'd looked very furtive, but Eve said nothing. Kate was distracted these days, and Eve spent so much time with Jack they didn't talk as much as they used to.

That had never happened before. They were all three of them thick as thieves normally, but things were a little strained and Eve also felt a bit guilty. Everything was working out great for her—she was moving to Cork, spending loads of time with Jack, who she just adored, and was going to get a new job in one of the fancy shops in the city, or so she hoped anyway. Meanwhile, the future for the rest of the family looked bleak. No wonder they were leaving her out of things.

Apprehensively, Eve opened the chest of drawers where they each had a drawer for their foldable clothes. Both Aisling's and Kate's drawers were empty. When Eve pulled back the curtain that hid the rail Daddy had put up for their dresses years ago, she saw those were gone as well.

Isabella came into the room and scanned it, quickly coming to the same sickening conclusion as Eve.

'They're gone.'

Eve watched helplessly as their mother sat on Kate's bed. Her normally upright posture slumped, and soon her shoulders were shaking silently. Eve wanted to comfort her, but perhaps if Daddy could get to the bus stop in Kilthomand, or even in Dungarvan before they left, he could stop them. She decided that was more important and went to call him.

His face was hard as she told him in the milking parlour. He swore, something she'd never heard him do before, and barrelled past her. He took the Keneficks' car, which was also being sold later in the week and drove down the avenue at speed.

* * *

DERMOT'S EYES scanned the people waiting at the bus stop in Kilthomand. No sign of Kate and Aisling.

He knew exactly where they were headed, his youngest, always the rebel child, leading the gentler Aisling behind her. He spotted that eejit Sean Lacey in the window of the draper's. This was his fault as well. If Aisling had not been so let down by him... Dermot fought the urge to go in there and wring his scrawny neck.

Still, Aisling would never have gone without Kate egging her on. Kate got her determination from him, and though she looked like her mother, with her dark curls and vivid eyes, she lacked Isabella's pragmatism and ability to weigh things up. When Dermot was younger, he was just as impetuous, just as rash, but he was a man. He could take care of himself. The idea of his two lovely girls, so innocent and unworldly, no matter what they might think, over there in England, with people ready to exploit them at every hand's turn... It made him nauseous with anxiety.

The square was as it always was, busy with people bustling about their business. Father MacIntyre was crossing from the chapel door to the convent, no doubt going in for the breakfast after early Mass. Mrs

Lacey was in the window of the draper's beside her son, putting the new men's shoes on display for the perusal of the wives and mothers of Kilthomand. Rory Sherrard was delivering milk to the creamery, and a few ladies were chatting outside O'Donovan's grocers.

Loathe as he was to admit to anyone that there might be a chink in the Murphy armour, he'd have to ask them if they'd seen the girls. The news that they were on the missing list would be the main topic at every dinner table in the village this lunchtime.

He parked the car and ran over to the ladies outside the grocer.

'Good morning, ladies, sorry to disturb you now, but you haven't seen my girls, Kate and Aisling, have you?'

All three stopped immediately and gave him their full attention. Dermot Murphy knew he was a bit of an enigma and any interaction with him would be seen as something out of the ordinary. He'd lived a double life for so long during The Troubles, keeping himself separate from others, and he knew he and his family were a source of interest because of it.

Joanie Boyle was the first to speak. For some bizarre reason, she wore bright red rouge on her cheeks and lips and drew her eyebrows on with a pencil, two perfect black semicircles. She looked like a permanently startled doll. Kate did a wicked impression of her sometimes, all snooty-nosed going up to receive at Mass.

'Oh, 'tis yourself, Dermot,' she said. 'We don't often see you in town. I suppose ye must be flat-out getting ready for the big move? Did we ever think we'd see the day that the Keneficks would be gone out of Robinswood? A sign of the times, I suppose....'

Dermot hid his frustration and tried to stay friendly.

'Well, to be honest, Miss Boyle, at the moment, I'm just trying to find my daughters...' He kept his voice light, but as she spoke he scoured the square.

'They got the seven o'clock bus,' May Courtney intervened. Clearly, she saw how worried he was. 'I saw them getting on when I put the cat out this morning.'

Dermot smiled gratefully at her, hiding his horror. He was too late. They'd be halfway to Dublin by now.

'Right. Thanks.' He turned to go.

'Is it the way they've gone shopping or what?' Joanie asked. ''Tis very strange for two young girls to go off like that, and May said they with a suitcase each as well? We did wonder, but we thought maybe they were after getting a job above in Dublin, now that ye have to quit Robinswood.' She was determined to get some titbit of gossip out of him. But she failed. Dermot turned and made his way back to the car, not even answering her.

Isabella and Eve were at the table when he returned, their faces drawn and pale. Eve had found a piece of paper in a novel Kate had just finished reading with the ferry times and prices on it. She had circled the one o'clock sailing for that day. Eve showed it to him, and he scanned it.

'They got the seven bus to Dublin,' he said. 'Even if I tore up the road after them, it would be too late. The ferry goes at one. It's eleven now.'

'Oh, Dermot, we have to do something!' The normally calm Isabella was distraught. 'We can't just sit here!'

'They're gone to England, Bella. Kate has been angling for it since Sam Kenefick turned up in that bloody uniform, and Aisling is sick of all the whispering here about herself and that waste of space Sean Lacey!' He was upset, but it came out as anger.

Eve looked at her father, knowing he was right. A part of her was worried for her sisters, but a bigger part of her felt a searing sharp pain of rejection. They were always so united, and yet they'd left and never said a word. Kate had been subdued of late, but Eve had assumed she was just mooning over Sam. And Aisling was upset about Sean, but Eve had never imagined they'd do this.

CHAPTER 17

$\mathcal{V}$ iolet thought the eggs were a little overcooked and the toast was not brown enough. She would normally have had a word with Isabella, but she supposed she had better not. Both she and Dermot were monosyllabic these days. Her departure couldn't come fast enough. The house was draughty at the best of times, but now, with everything gone or sold or dumped, it felt like a mausoleum.

She'd surprised herself. She'd thought she might have some last-minute qualms about moving away from her home of all these years, but oddly, she felt nothing but relief.

She had taken a tour of the house yesterday and collected whatever small knickknacks had sentimental value—a picture Samuel had painted for her birthday when he was a little boy, a vase the Viceroys' wife had given her for her twenty-first birthday in India. For form's sake more than sentiment, she took a photograph of Austin with a horse, goodness knows which horse, there were so many, probably another donkey on which he lost his shirt yet again. But he had his roguish smile in it, and it was small at least.

Violet had asked Lillian on the telephone what she wanted brought over from Robinswood, and she'd replied in that bored, clipped way she had developed of late, 'The proceeds, Mother, just the proceeds. I need a flat of my own with immediate effect. Leave the rest, it's only moth-eaten old tat anyway.'

Violet sighed as she dabbed her lips with a napkin.

Lillian was labouring under a considerable misapprehension, and Violet hadn't the strength to disavow her of it, fearing the onslaught of abuse that would no doubt ensue. There was no way Violet was going to be able to afford to buy Lillian a flat in London as well as a house for herself. They would need to buy a place for both of them, somewhere outside the city, and share it. She was dreading telling her daughter.

Totally indulged in every whim, Lillian was now an entitled, privileged young woman with no concept of reality or any sense that the world was anything other than some place for her to play. Lillian was passably pretty, though she did sometimes have the heavy florid look of the Kenefícks rather than the delicate features of Violet's side. Even so, Violet had hoped for an early match once she got to London, but there was nothing doing, as Austin might say. The longer Lillian was knocking about the social scene in London, the less likely it was that a wealthy prospective husband would show himself.

Also, Violet had heard, to her excruciating embarrassment, in a letter from an old school chum, that Lillian was getting a bit of a reputation as a 'good-time girl.' It had been the same during the last war—foolish young girls thinking that just because there was a war on, all the rules were null and void. London was flooded with officers, and they were after a good time, not commitment. Only the naive and the weak gave in to their carnal desires, and Violet feared her daughter may have been both.

Last night's telephone conversation had been most unsatisfactory. More demands for money, that Violet simply could not give in to because she did not have it to give, were followed by quite a bit of mention of a chap called Beau, of all things. Lillian was going dancing with this Beau, short for Beauregard, who was, inexplicably, an American. Violet had tried to point out that no nice English man she might meet in the future with a view to marriage would like to think of his girl having had previous interactions with any type of foreigner, let alone an American.

But Lillian had merely laughed, and that was another thing—the girl brayed like a donkey. Austin had dismissed and ridiculed every attempt Violet had made to curb that awful guffaw over the years, but Violet feared it was really going against her daughter now, as Violet knew it would, but who listened? Nobody. And now look where they were. Violet loved her daughter, but honestly, she could be very trying.

'Mother, you are ridiculous,' Lillian had told her. 'Daddy was right, you are simply bonkers. Now I have to go. Beau is picking me up in twenty minutes, and I have yet to dry my hair. And hurry up with that bloody money, will you?'

Violet thought fleetingly of the Murphy girls. How had Dermot and Isabella reared such girls with such a work ethic, and so respectful to their parents? Of course, the lower classes were trained from the cradle to be of service to their betters, but still, they were really very well behaved.

Just as she was musing on them, Eve Murphy knocked on the door.

'Your post, ma'am.' She carried a letter on a silver tray. It was probably silly, but it was nice to see that things were still being done properly even at this, the eleventh hour.

Violet took it. It was from Samuel, her darling boy. She felt her heart do a little leap. At least she had one child who was a success, who wasn't a wastrel or disrespectful to his mother.

Eve turned to go, but Violet was struck by the girl's demeanour. She seemed very subdued, possibly the loss of Robinswood, she guessed. Dermot and Isabella had come to their senses and accepted the offer from the Hamilton-Brookses. Violet had tried not to delight a little in Dermot's volte-face; he was clearly acting on his wife's orders. The younger two girls had left, apparently, goodness knows where, but Eve was still here.

Violet liked Eve, and Aisling, more than the youngest, Kate. That young woman had notions above her station.

'Eve, wait a moment please.' Violet always took care to address the staff politely. It was a sign of poor breeding not to.

Eve turned.

Violet was right, the girl looked wretched.

'Is everything all right, my dear?'

Eve thought for a moment. God, this woman could be so insensitive. Of course things were not all right.

Eve took a deep breath to steady herself. She was never comfortable talking to Lady Kenefick; something about the woman unnerved her.

'I know you're aware, ma'am, but my sisters Aisling and Kate are still missing,' she said. 'We're very worried, my parents and I, and I was wondering if there was any way to check if they had made contact with Lord Kenefick? He...em... He would be someone they would know in England and...em...maybe they might have...' Eve swallowed. As far as she was aware, Lady Violet knew nothing of Sam and Kate's friendship.

Indeed, Violet's face was like granite.

'Well, why on earth would they do that? Samuel is on an RAF base, and what could he do for them? Oh, I doubt very much they would have the audacity to prey on my son's good nature.'

Eve dug her nails into her palms as Violet went on, 'I was aware they had taken off. I could possibly believe Kate capable of such antics, but I must say, I am surprised at Aisling. She was always such a polite, sensible kind of a girl. Your parents must be very upset, though why you think they made contact with Samuel I cannot possibly imagine.'

Eve couldn't miss the ice in her voice.

'I suppose we are just trying to think of anyone they might know over there,' Eve lied convincingly.

'Well, with all due respect, my dear, they don't know my son, not really. I mean, their father worked for his father, that's not much of a basis for anything, now is it? They wouldn't mix in the same circles, so what he could do for them is rather a mystery.'

Eve took a deep breath to steady herself. 'I understand, and of course you are right, Your Ladyship, but I thought that if they were desperate, they might look him up. I realise we are grasping at straws, but my parents and I are so worried, we have to try everything. Could you give me his contact details?'

Eve felt the familiar frustration of dealing with Violet rise within her. There was nothing difficult about it. All she had to do was open her address book and give them his details. But of course Violet would make a meal out of it.

'I can't do that, Eve. I'm sure you understand.' Each word dripped with distaste.

Eve was not going to be fobbed off, though. This woman would leave Robinswood shortly, and she was the only link between Sam and the Murphys. She tried again, trying to look as subservient as she could, though it made her blood boil.

'Well, Your Ladyship, if there was any way *you* could contact him just to ask, then we, all of us, would be so grateful. We don't even know where to start, you see. They just got on the bus to Dublin a week ago, and we've heard nothing since.'

It worked. Violet softened slightly.

'Very well. If he calls, I will mention it to him. Now, tell me, Eve, what plans have you got, for when Robinswood is closed?'

Eve felt herself colour. She wasn't really comfortable talking to Violet at the best of times. The idea of explaining about Jack was excruciating for some reason.

'I... I am engaged to be married, to a lad, a man, I mean, from Cork, called Jack O'Neill. I'm going there with him. We are going to stay with his mother, and I hope to get a job, and then when we've saved up enough, we'll get married.'

Violet looked at her and smiled.

'Well, I hope you'll be happy, Eve. You've had a very good training in this house, so you should easily find a position as a domestic in some house in Cork. Do you want me to give you a reference?'

'Thank you, Your Ladyship, that would be very helpful.' Eve didn't bother to tell her that she was not going to go into service. She wanted to be with Jack, and if she lived in someplace, she would be bound by their rules.

All of the excitement of her engagement and planned move to Cork had had the air taken out of it by the girls' overnight flit. She'd lain in their room night after night for the past week, sometimes crying herself to sleep, other times seething with rage, but most nights just feeling so lost and alone. She still couldn't believe they did it. Whatever about not telling their parents, the fact that they said nothing to her hurt her so deeply it was a physical pain.

'Very well,' Violet said. 'Come tomorrow, and I shall have one prepared for you. In the meantime, I will try to make contact with Samuel, and we shall see if Kate and Aisling have been in touch with him, but I'm sure they haven't.' Violet's smile didn't reach her eyes.

Eve curtseyed and left.

Violet was seething. She could hardly contain her fury. How dare they? The Murphy parents began by refusing the best offer they were likely to get, out of hand and with such insolence, only to come crawling back a week later. And now that pair of... Unkind names for the Murphy girls flooded her mind... Well, they might just turn up on Samuel's doorstep, as if they were all the best of friends. It was outrageous to even suggest it. Samuel was perfectly polite to them when he was at home, she was sure, but the idea that they would impose upon him while he was defending his country was simply intolerable.

Later, she would telephone him, if possible, but not mention the Murphy girls. If they had contacted him, surely he would mention it? She remembered how upset he'd been when he'd heard Charlie Warren wasn't keeping the Murphy family on, and the memory unsettled her. The boy was just gullible enough to fall for their tale of woe.

* * *

EVE STOPPED at the bay window on the big winding staircase as she returned to her mother in the kitchen after her encounter with Lady

Kenefick. The rolling green fields, the river, and the stone courtyard surrounded by stables looked so beautiful it soothed her troubled soul. It was the only home she'd ever known, and her life had been idyllic up until recently.

It was hard to imagine how much everything had changed.

CHAPTER 18

*A*isling looked doubtfully at her sister as busy commuters milled around on the footpath. London was so huge and busy and noisy, and so far, she hated it. Her realisation that this was a terrible decision had dawned before they even got off the bus in Dublin. She should have gone back, just turned around and got the same bus back to Kilthomand, but Kate had said she was going either way. Their parents would go mad if they thought Aisling left Kate off on her own. She wasn't even eighteen yet.

'Come on then, if you're coming.' Kate grabbed Aisling's coat sleeve and pulled her into the recruitment station.

Aisling looked up at the sign over the door of the combined recruitment office. Apparently, Sam had given Kate instructions to go to this cricket ground that had been set up as a place people could sign up for either the army, the navy, or the air force, and Kate was determined to get into the Women's Auxiliary Air Force.

Samuel had explained all about the WAAF to Kate. Who they were, where you went to sign up, everything—and Kate was absolutely smitten with the idea. She could not get into a uniform fast enough. Aisling wondered how much of her enthusiasm was down to the fact that Sam was in the RAF and how much of it was because she thought she'd look gorgeous in the uniform. None of it, Aisling was sure, had anything to do with the reality of joining up to fight the war.

They entered a large area, where six tables were set up, with people in different uniforms milling around each table.

'This way.' Kate went off to the left, and Aisling reluctantly followed her. She could at least get the information. Maybe the reality of actually being in the British Air Force would dawn on Kate before they had to actually sign on the dotted line. Aisling was determined to talk some sense into her, but Kate just responded by telling her she didn't have to come and that it was her own choice, but now that she was here, she might as well get on with it.

The RAF table was busy, with young men all queuing up to join, and the women's, which was beside it, seemed to have as many if not more people gathering. The recruiting officers looked efficient and unfazed by the volumes of people they were attempting to process. Eventually, Aisling and Kate were beckoned forward.

A pleasant-looking woman in her forties sat in front of a plywood display featuring several posters, all depicting smiling women in the uniform of the WAAF and urging women to 'Serve in the WAAF with the men who fly,' or 'Take the road to Victory, join the WAAF.'

'NAME?' the woman asked, pen at the ready.

Kate smiled confidently. 'Kate Murphy, and this is my sister Aisling.'

'I'll just take you one at a time, please.' She indicated Aisling should return to the top of the queue with a shooing gesture.

She took down Kate's details and the address where they were staying. It was a nice house on the Tottenham Court Road that Sam had arranged for them.

Then the woman beckoned Aisling forward.

'So, your name?' She smiled briefly.

'Aisling Murphy.'

'Ashley?'

'No no, it's pronounced *Ash-ling*.'

'I'm afraid you're going to have to spell that for me, dear. I am a bit lost when it comes to those Irish names.'

'A-I-S-L-I-N-G.' She noted the woman's look of confusion when she was finished.

'My goodness, I would have said that was *Aysling* or something. Anyway, we must press on.'

She rapidly fired questions at Aisling: age, height, weight, work experience, level of education.

'You'll do very well, I should imagine,' she said at last. 'Report for duty at the RAF base in Biggin Hill. All further duties and so on will be explained to you and your sister at that stage. And can I just say how heartening it is to see women from Ireland joining up, after everything that's happened over there. It is good to see that some people at least can see the importance of what we are doing here.'

Aisling just smiled and nodded. All she could think about was her parents, and what they would say if they could see her now.

Within moments, she and Kate were back outside, standing there saying nothing.

Aisling spotted a Lyons Corner House café opposite them.

'Will we go over there and have a cup of tea?'

Kate looked uncertain for the first time since leaving Kilthomand.

'Fine, but if you're going to start again about us going home, Aisling, I'm telling you now, I don't want to hear it.'

'Just tea, all right?' Aisling smiled at her sister and saw her relax a little. Whatever fate had in store for them, they were in it together, and nothing would change that.

The cafe was almost full, probably down to the recruitment office, and they got in the queue. They had expected food to be worse in England than at home, but they'd had no idea how much worse. The landlady of the boarding house had told them that without a ration book for food, there was only going to be very basic meals available to them, so that was another reason they needed something more permanent. As Aisling watched orders of Welsh rarebit come out from the kitchen, which she gathered was what the English called cheese on toast, she realised she was starving.

'Could we stretch to two of those, do you think?' she asked Kate, nudging her to see the cheesy toast being delivered to another table.

'Well, we've got jobs now, so I suppose so?' Kate grinned and gave the order to the waitress.

They sat at a table for four, the only one left, and waited eagerly for their food.

'So, we've done it,' Kate ventured. The arguments of the previous days were now, she hoped, behind them.

Aisling bit her lip. 'Does this mean we're in? Like, I thought we were just going to get information or something.'

'No, we're signed up for the WAAFs,' Kate said confidently. 'Look, Ais, I know you're not as keen as I am, and I do wish you'd thought more about this before coming, but once we're settled we'll write home and tell them everything. You know if we'd contacted them before, when we were just staying at the boarding house, Daddy would've been on the doorstep dragging the two of us back to Kilthomand by the hair before we knew where we were. This way, it's all done, and he can't do anything.'

Kate saw the doubt on her sister's face.

'Think of it, Ais, being brought back there like a pair of bold children, with even more whispering behind their hands. *Oh, look at them now, the high and mighty Murphys. First she gets let down by Sean Lacey, then they get evicted, and then, God love them, they had to be brought back from England.'*

Aisling giggled at Kate's mimicking of the gossips of Kilthomand. She was right—going back was not an option.

'And what about all those gorgeous fellas we saw queueing up as well?' Kate nudged her sister. 'Imagine us all dolled up in our uniforms, going to dances whenever we want, meeting people from all over the world, and doing something really important and exciting. This is going to be great, Ais, I promise.'

The waitress delivered their food and tea, and they tucked in hungrily. The bread was so thin you could see through it and the cheese kind of tasteless, but it was the best thing they'd had since they arrived. It bore absolutely no resemblance to the lovely home-baked soda bread and salty churned butter they were used to.

'Maybe the grub will be better in this Biggin Hill place as well,' Aisling said with a sigh. She missed her mother's cooking already.

'Well, it couldn't be any worse than what we've had. They need to keep the forces well fed to see off nasty Mr Hitler, don't they?' Kate winked.

'Don't go mad now, Kate, but I need to talk about this. I feel awful about Mammy and Daddy—they must be going out of their minds—but I feel worse about Eve. Like, if you two went off and did something like this without telling me, I'd be devastated. Not just at ye leaving, but the fact that ye didn't trust me enough to tell me.'

'I know, Aisling. I'm not a totally heartless cow, you know.' Kate was bristling again, but Aisling wanted to say her piece.

'So, I propose we telephone Robinswood. Just give Violet a message if she answers, or talk to Mammy or Eve if it's one of them. We can tell them where we are, that we're all right, and what we are doing. It's only fair, and they could be told to ship out of Robinswood any day, and then what? Then we couldn't contact them at all because we don't know where they're going to go. So I'm doing it after this anyway, and I want you to be there too, but if you won't, then fine. But I am doing it.'

Kate glowered at her sister. Aisling was the sweetest-natured of the three of the Murphy girls, but right now, she seemed adamant.

'All right, we'll do it. But we are not being talked into coming home or going back on our plans. Agreed?'

Aisling sighed with relief. 'Agreed.'

CHAPTER 19

'*J* know I keep going on and on about this. You must be sick of listening to me.' Eve kicked a stone with her shoe as she and Jack walked along the road back from Kilthomand with some groceries.

'I could never get sick of listening to you, and anyway, I understand,' Jack said, tucking her hand into his arm. 'They're your sisters, and you're worried, but you're hurt as well. So would I be, if I was you.'

'And Mammy and Daddy are like briars, the atmosphere at home is awful.' Eve shook her head. 'Mammy started packing clothes and things yesterday, and she was up in our room, and I knew she was crying but I just couldn't go in to her. She and Daddy are going to some place up in Dublin, apparently, but once we leave Robinswood, how will Kate and Aisling even get in touch?'

Jack sighed. 'Look, I know you're worried, but you girls are the most capable people—let alone the fact ye're girls—that I've ever met. If I was stuck in a tight spot, I'd have any one of ye over most of the lads I know. Kate and Ais will be fine, I know they will, and so will your parents. And sure, we'll just be in Cork, so if it doesn't work out for either the girls or your parents, then they can always come to us, can't they?'

Eve stopped and kissed him right there on the road.

He grinned, his arms circling her waist. 'What was that for?'

'For being so kind, for listening to me banging on day after day, for trying to come up with a solution like it's your problem as much as mine… The list goes on.' Eve lay her head on his chest.

'You're going to be my wife; your problems *are* mine now.' He kissed her cheek and gave her a squeeze.

'Speaking of impending marriages, I'd say the Moriarty wedding was the last thing your mother and father wanted to go to today.' He chuckled. 'Your father had a face like thunder on him going out the door.'

'I know, but they had to go. Gerry Moriarty and Daddy have known each other for years, and Garrett is their only boy, so they had to be there. A night out might be just what they need anyway. I think the wedding party was going to be at the Moriartys' place, and they've a fine big house. Gerry's wife Lizzie has been baking since Christmas, and all her brothers are musicians, so it should be a good night.'

They arrived home to an empty house and put the groceries away in the kitchen, which was getting more and more bare. The place bore almost no resemblance to the busy, bustling house it had been all their lives. The big clear-out was well underway, and now only the essentials remained.

Jack took off his boots and stoked the range into life while Eve made tea.

'Look at us like an old married couple already.' She laughed.

'We should enjoy the time alone while we have it,' he said. 'It's going to be a tight squeeze in our place once we're both there, and all my aunts and neighbours will be finding reasons to call to get a look at you.'

'Well, I hope they're not expecting much.' She smiled ruefully, running her hands over her copper-coloured hair that had come dislodged from her ponytail during the walk.

Jack stood up and went to wash his hands of the turf dust. As she handed him a towel, she looked up into his eyes, and he put his arms around her waist. His dark hair and piercing blue eyes mesmerised her.

'What have I told you about that?' he whispered, his face close to hers.

'About what?' she asked. Her heart was beating loudly.

'About running yourself down? You are the most beautiful girl I've ever seen. Your hair is gorgeous, I feel like I could drown in your eyes, and as for your figure...' He ran his hand down over her bottom, and she inhaled and closed her eyes.

This was probably wrong, and if her parents or the priest walked in at this moment, they would both be in the height of trouble, but she never wanted him to stop touching her. She wound her arms around his neck, and he bent to kiss her. On and on they kissed, his tongue exploring her mouth as he pressed his body to hers. She arched her body to be closer to him, running her hands all over the muscles of his back.

He groaned, and she could feel his body react to her. The nuns had warned them often enough about avoiding any such situations, as men could not be trusted to control their carnal desires, but they never said how difficult that would be when the man was someone you loved and found so attractive.

'Let's go upstairs,' she heard herself whisper.

Jack held her close. 'Are you sure?'

Eve nodded. She wanted him, and this might be the only chance they would have. They couldn't get married for ages, as they needed to save up some money, and they'd be living with his mother. It was now or never.

'I've never...you know...before,' she began and felt her cheeks burn.

'Me neither,' he whispered and grinned.

She took his hand and led him up to the girls' bedroom. The three beds were made neatly, her sisters' clothes all folded and packed into boxes. Neither Eve nor their mother knew what to do with them.

The sun was setting outside, and though nobody could see in, Eve pulled the thin curtains. Suddenly, she was nervous. She was not married, and here she was in a bedroom with a man.

Then she looked up into his eyes again. This wasn't some man, this was her Jack, her future husband, and she wanted to share everything with him.

'We don't have to...if you don't want to.' With his normal confidence gone, he seemed vulnerable.

'I do want to.'

Suddenly, Eve felt brave. She slipped her cardigan and dress off and stood before him in her slip. He kissed her and ran his hands over her body before pulling off his braces and shirt. His chest was muscled, with a light covering of dark hair. She ran her hands over him and inhaled his scent.

Then she pulled her slip off, and they giggled as he struggled with the hooks of her bra.

'I can tack up a horse in two minutes flat, but these things are a mystery.' He chuckled as it finally came loose, and he dipped his head to kiss her breast. The stubble of his jaw sent electric shocks through her body. He led her to the small single bed, and together, they discovered each other.

Afterwards, they lay in each other's arms silently.

'Regrets?' he asked, his voice husky.

'Not one,' she whispered.

'I love you, Eve Murphy. I loved you before, but now...now you are my whole world. Let's get married soon. I know we said we'd wait until we had some money and all of that, but I can't cope with the idea of you being upstairs in my bed in Cork and me on the lumpy sofa downstairs...'

She leaned up on one elbow and looked down into his face, grinning mischievously.

'So you only want to marry me so you'll get to sleep in the soft bed, is it?'

Jack didn't joke back. Instead, he was deadly serious.

'I want to marry you so that I can sleep every night in a soft bed beside my beautiful wife. I want to make love to you every night, I want to have that to look forward to every day when I'm at work, and whenever the time is right, I want to make our babies with you in that bed. I want to worry about them with you beside me as they grow up. I want to talk about our victories and our troubles, I want to grow old with you, watch your hair go from copper to grey, and eventually, after years and years and years of a happy life with the most wonderful woman in Ireland, I want to die beside you in our bed.'

Tears filled Eve's eyes.

'I want that too,' she whispered.

'Good.' He drew her head back onto his chest. 'We'll go to the priest and go about getting the banns read tomorrow so. Who knows what the future holds for any of us, especially for your family, but at least if you and I are married, then that's some stability, isn't it? Like we can live with Mam for a while, but I'm a hard worker, Eve, I'll provide fine for us. And we'll have our own home before you know it. And not rented either. We'll buy someplace, even if its small, so we own it. When my father was shot, we were in a rented house. Of course, there was no money to pay the rent, so we were faced with being turfed out. Luckily, friends of my father's came to our rescue, and some money was found, so Mam bought our place. And at least whenever we had lean times, and believe me, we did, we knew we'd always have a roof over our heads anyway.'

Jack didn't talk much about his father. He'd died such a violent death, and under such bitter circumstances, those times were never raised in conversation. Now, though, things were different. They had no secrets.

'Do you remember him?' Eve asked.

'I do. Not very clearly. I was young, and he wasn't there much. He was in the IRA and went against Collins over the treaty, so he was on the run a lot of the time. But I do remember him, yeah. I look very like him, apparently.'

'Then he must have been very handsome.' Eve kissed his chest.

'Ah, go on outa that, you flatterer. I'm only a big lump of a farm-hand. I don't know what you see in me, to be totally honest. I ask myself every day how the hell someone like me got someone like you, but I don't want to question it too much for fear you might see the madness of it.'

'And you telling me to stop running myself down!' Eve snapped. 'We're both lucky, Jack O'Neill, the luckiest pair alive. But we better get up now and act natural since my parents will be home soon, I'd say, and I doubt either of us would be feeling very lucky if Dermot Murphy walked in on this cosy scene.'

Reluctantly, Jack sat up.

'I suppose you're right. Though I'd say Dermot had a job to keep his hands off Isabella too, back in the day.' He grinned.

'Urrggh! Stop that! Nobody wants to think of that. They did it three times, in the dark, and only to conceive me, Ais, and Kate. The end.'

'And if you believe that, my darling Eve, you'll believe anything.'

She swiped at him with her cardigan as they dressed. She was just brushing her hair when she heard the car pull into the yard.

'Quick, go down, quick quick!' She giggled as she half shoved Jack down the stairs.

CHAPTER 20

The last of her personal things were packed. Violet stood in the almost empty drawing room.

Dermot was going to drive her to Kingstown, where she was booked into The Royal Marine overnight before travelling by ship to Holyhead in Wales. Lillian had assured her that train transportation in England was awful these days—the trains were slow or late, and service personnel got priority—so Violet had arranged a car to collect her and take her to London, where she had rented a house in Sloane Square for six months.

Lillian had found the house, and while it seemed frightfully expensive, at least Violet would be back at home and ready to begin her new life. She didn't like to bother Samuel with the details of the sale of the contents, or the rental agreement of the land, so she was taking care of everything for him. She'd asked him about property and what they should do—after all, it was his estate—but he said she should do whatever she wanted with regard to where she and Lillian lived. He would be living on the base for the duration, and who knew what would happen. Violet hated that kind of talk. Sometimes he was so fatalistic. So she just changed the subject and rented a house. Surely the war couldn't go on much longer, and once it was over and Samuel was safe, they could make proper plans.

The peal of the telephone rent the air in the now hollow-sounding empty house.

It rang and rang, but nobody answered. Eve was around some-where, but Isabella was down at their farmhouse. It must be a difficult day for her, Violet imagined. But once again she soothed herself with the knowledge that she had, after all, found them an alternative.

But she would have to answer the dratted telephone herself.

She hurried into the hallway and lifted the receiver.

'A call from England, Lady Kenefick,' came the monotonous voice of Paddy O'Riordan from the Dungarvan exchange.

'Thank you. Put it through.'

A series of clicks and then:

'Hello?'

'Yes, hello, Lady Violet Kenefick speaking.'

'Oh, hello, Your Ladyship, it's Aisling Murphy here.'

'Aisling! Where on earth are you, girl? Your parents are very worried.'

'Yes, ma'am, please tell them that both Kate and I are fine and that we can be reached by writing to the WAAF section at Biggins Hill RAF base. That's just outside London.'

'I know perfectly well where it is, Aisling, Samuel is stationed there. The question is what are you two doing there?' Her voice was cold. Surely that foolish Kate had not decided to follow Samuel and made a total fool of herself and her sister into the bargain.

'Oh, we've joined up. We are in the WAAFs now, Kate and I.'

SILENCE.

Violet was furious. How dare they bother him? She considered for a moment not relaying the message to Dermot and Isabella. The audacity of the girls astounded her. But if anyone could get them home and away from Samuel, it was Dermot.

'You had no right to go off like that and upset your parents and

141

sister so. It was very inconsiderate of you. I will let your parents know that you have contacted me. Goodbye.' Violent hung up, seething.

Young people today had no sense of duty, no idea what was expected of them. And it was not just the Murphys; Lillian was refusing to find someone suitable, instead mucking about with Americans, for God's sake. And now this, it really was the last straw. It really was too much.

Utterly vexed, she went into the drawing room again and rang the bell for Isabella. Surely, she was back by now? The bell echoed in the empty house. Violet waited for the sound of feet, but there was nothing.

SHE LOOKED out the window and saw Dermot and Isabella strolling up the avenue as if they were on a Sunday afternoon outing, not the middle of a working day. They had taken advantage of her good nature once too often. She rapped on the window with the diamond of her engagement ring, not even caring if she cracked the glass. It was someone else's problem now.

They both looked up, and Violet beckoned them in. Isabella picked up her pace, but Dermot maintained his slow stroll, as if defying her. What Austin had seen in that man she simply could not imagine. He was arrogant and downright surly at times, and as for the due deference one is entitled to from staff, well, if your staff is Dermot Murphy, you can forget about that.

After what seemed like an interminably long wait, they appeared.

Without any preamble or niceties, Violet launched straight in.

'Your daughter Aisling telephoned earlier. She asked me to relay a message to you both that she and your other daughter Kate are well and in London. They have volunteered with the Women's Auxiliary Air Force, and you may write to them at Biggin Hill RAF base. That will be all.'

She turned, wishing there was something left in her writing bureau with which to busy herself. Perhaps she should have left the room, but it was her house. If anyone should leave, it was them. Instead, stubbornly, they both just stood there.

'I imagine you both have quite a bit to be getting on with,' Violet added, dripping ice into her voice. 'Don't let me stop you.'

'But, ma'am, is that all Aisling said? Did she give you any more information?' Isabella sounded both relieved and upset. 'Did she leave a telephone number where we can contact them?'

'I have relayed the message as it was given to me,' Violet replied. 'Now, as I said, you may go.'

Isabella opened her mouth to speak once more, but Dermot put his hand on her arm.

'Thank you for the message.' He did not afford her even a title. Honestly, the egotism of the man was infuriating.

He led his wife out of the room, closing the door after them. Violet wondered if there was any other way to get to Dublin besides a long car journey with Dermot Murphy, but she knew there wasn't. She would have to endure him.

The plan was to leave at midday, having had a light lunch to sustain her for the journey, but as she looked around, she realised she wanted to leave now, right this second. She wanted to get away from Robinswood and everything and everyone associated with it.

She rang the bell again, and moments later Isabella appeared, her face blotched from tears. The silly woman! They were only in England, not dead.

'You rang, ma'am?' Isabella's voice was choked.

Violet chose to ignore it.

'Have your husband bring the car round immediately. I am going to leave now.'

'But, Your Ladyship, I have almost finished making soup, and the bread is out of the oven. Do you not wish to dine before you depart?'

Violet fixed Isabella with a cold stare. 'If I wanted to stay to eat, I would do exactly that. Have him bring the car round. My things are in the hall; he should load them up quickly. I will be in my rooms. Come and fetch me when he has it all ready.'

'Yes, ma'am.' Isabella turned to go, but when she got to the door, she stopped, her hand on the doorknob.

'Lady Kenefick, is there something the matter? You seem very...em...very angry about something?'

Violet felt a surge of rage. The audacity of the woman! She was as bad as her husband.

Of course she was angry! She was furious that those Murphys, the offspring of her servants, would disrupt Samuel and make him feel responsible for them. They had no sense of their place, and Samuel was such a soft-hearted boy he would probably fall for their tale of woe and give them money or something.

But all she said to Isabella was, 'My mood is not of your concern.'

'I know that, ma'am, but I just wondered if there was something we could do to help. After all the years we've been together it seems wrong for you to leave with a cloud over us, when we may never see each other again. My family is intertwined with yours for so many years now, we shared so much, I just wanted to say—'

This was simply too much.

'Let me stop you there,' Violet interrupted. 'My family is not, as you put it, intertwined with yours. Your family are in my employ, and there the relationship begins and ends. Now, I wish to leave, and yes, you are correct, we will not see each other again.' She should probably have wished them all the best or at least said goodbye, but she didn't.

'Very well,' Isabella said quietly. 'Goodbye, Lady Kenefick, and I wish you all the best of luck in your new life in England.'

'Luck has nothing to do with it,' Violet spat, and she swept past Isabella as regally as she could.

Violet stood in her bedroom watching the exchange between Dermot and his wife outside on the driveway. He seemed frustrated at the news that he was to leave now. At least that's what Violet read from his body language. They didn't know she was watching them as Dermot held his wife's hand in a gesture of support and love. Violet had never had that with Austin, that sense that they were a team. Austin, and later the children under his influence, seemed to see her as vaguely ridiculous. It was hurtful, and she'd envied so many times over the years the closeness the Murphys seemed to enjoy. It was as if they had created this impenetrable alliance.

Isabella went back into the kitchen, and Dermot went to get the car. Violet would give him some time to load everything up, and then she would go down, sit into the car, and drive away from Robinswood without a backward glance.

She should probably have stayed until the house was shut up completely, but she was going to leave that to the Murphys. They were conscientious, she'd have to give them that, and so she knew they wouldn't walk away without securing the building properly. Besides, anything that could be sold had been already, so the remaining furniture would just stand there, probably forever. Violet didn't care a jot. The whole place could burn to the ground as far as she was concerned.

* * *

OUTSIDE, Dermot was strapping the last of her cases to the back of the car. He finished what he was doing and then slowly—too slowly, Violet thought—opened the door for her to get in. She did so without a word.

She had suggested to Austin years before that some sort of uniform would be nice for Dermot when he drove them, but that had earned her one of his scornful guffaws, the exact replica of which she heard infuriatingly frequently from Lillian.

She wondered if Eve or Isabella would come out. She recalled when they left India, how all of the staff lined the driveway, many with tears in their eyes. The Indians were so much better at everything than the Irish; they were grateful to get the opportunity to serve, and they took pride in it. But these Irish, even the ones who were not, on the face of it at least, insolent and ungrateful, like the Murphys, seemed to secretly resent those who employed them. One always got the impression they were secretly sneering at those they should consider their betters.

As she settled into the back seat of the Bentley, another luxury they could no longer afford, she wondered what her future held.

Neither of the Murphy women came out to wave her off, and so she gazed directly in front of her as they pulled away from the house that had been her home for almost thirty years.

As the car crunched over the gravel of the long avenue, she knew she should've been feeling something at her departure. It was the end of an era, and in many ways, all her memories of her marriage, her family life were here. But at the moment, all she felt was cross.

CHAPTER 21

*I*sabella lay beside her sleeping husband. Earlier, she'd told Eve the news of the girls, and they'd speculated about what they were doing. Then they'd both gone to bed, relieved the girls were safe but with a profound sense of sadness. Isabella had barely registered Dermot climbing into bed beside her when he got back from Dublin after dropping Lady Kenefick off at the hotel, but now she couldn't sleep. She wanted to wake him, to talk to him about the girls and the future and everything, but he was exhausted. She had never seen him so stressed and worried as he'd been these last weeks.

Even when he was playing that very dangerous game years ago—hiding guns and IRA men in the barns, passing on information he heard at the house, all of that during The Troubles—none of that had caused him the anxiety he felt now. His intention, when the country seemed such a dangerous place to be back in those days, had been to move on from Robinswood once everything settled down. But by then, Eve had been born and Aisling was on the way, and they'd stayed at the estate for the security his position offered them.

In truth, it was Isabella who had made the case for staying. So if this was anyone's fault, it was hers. If they'd found a place of their own, worked somewhere else, they wouldn't be in this predicament now. The girls would never have known the Keneficks, Kate would never have had her head turned by Sam, and their family might have been spared this horrible prospect.

Isabella knew this was an entirely futile way of thinking. As her father always said, 'If wishes were horses, beggars would ride.' But she couldn't help herself, and she couldn't say it to Dermot, in case it sounded like blaming him.

She stared at the ceiling as the dawn slowly crept across the sky. She tried to imagine where Kate and Aisling were. It was April now, the evenings were beginning to lengthen, and it was usually a time of life and regrowth. Yesterday, she'd looked out at the empty fields where the spring calves had always been kept. There were no hens in the hen house, the sheep and lambs all gone as well. There wasn't one animal left on the entire estate.

Violet was gone, and Isabella felt mostly relief, but also frustration. She knew full well the reason for Violet's venom yesterday. Violet thought the girls had a cheek to impose on Samuel. The woman obviously had no inkling that Kate might have notions of the young Lord Kenefick, because if she'd suspected it, she'd have had a fit. Isabella herself wasn't certain about Kate's intentions regarding Sam, but she could well have had romantic ideas. Their respective stations in life would have no impact on her youngest daughter's decisions, of that Isabella was sure. At least Kate and Aisling were together—that gave her some comfort. Aisling was more timid but much more sensible in many ways, so she might rein the maddest of Kate's ideas in.

Isabella and Dermot had had no opportunity to talk about the news that the girls were, on the one hand, safe and well, but on the other, now part of the British Air Force. They didn't know what their father was, what sacrifices he and others had made to ensure the British military had nothing to do with their lives. To know his own daughters were wearing the uniform of his sworn enemy must've been a bitter pill to swallow.

He stirred beside her.

'Are you awake?' he whispered, his deep voice rumbling in his chest.

WHAT ONCE WAS TRUE

'I have been for hours, to be honest. I can't sleep.'

He turned onto his back and stared at the ceiling just as she was.

'WHAT ARE we going to do, Der? I just can't believe they joined the British army. I'm still reeling.'

'I know. My girls in that uniform, saluting that flag...' Dermot's voice was tight, trying to keep his emotions in check.

'They don't know, though, that's the thing... Maybe we were wrong not to tell them.' Isabella reached for his hand beneath the blanket.

'IT's TOO LATE NOW ANYWAY.'

'What about Eve?' Isabella said quietly, so as not to wake their daughter. 'I was thinking, we should tell her at least, so one of them knows. Otherwise, we just look like we're being stubborn. I know Kate was so angry that we wouldn't even consider her going over to England; though she never said it outright, she dropped enough hints. Especially when things are so dire here. But if they knew, maybe things would be different.'

'WILL WE GET UP, go for a walk?' Dermot asked. 'There's no point in lying here looking at the ceiling.'

'Fine, I'll leave a note for Eve if she wakes, though she was out late with Jack last night so she probably will sleep on. It's not as if there's anything to get up for anyway.'

They dressed warmly and slipped quietly out of the house. Isabella tucked her hand into the crook of Dermot's arm, and they waited until they were well away from the house before they started to talk. Dermot opened the gate into the long meadow that led to the river and, by force of habit, securely closed it after them, though there was no need any longer.

'I'm glad Eve is sleeping on,' Isabella said as they walked in the fresh green meadow. 'She has done Trojan work clearing the house, despite her ladyship's snitty attitude. And now that she's just swanned off, I suppose it's up to us to do all the final work in closing it? Poor Eve's heartbroken over Kate and Aisling going without a word to her, but she just soldiers on.'

Dermot nodded. 'They were always thick as thieves, since they were small, the three of them. I can believe they never told us of their plans—I'd have done whatever it took to keep them from going. But leaving Eve out of it too... It's hard to take in.' He paused. 'On the subject of Eve, are you sure she's doing the right thing, marrying Jack so soon? It all seems a bit rushed. Would they not be better off waiting, till things are a bit more...I don't know, settled?' A while back, Jack and Eve had told them of their plans to marry as soon as they could.

Isabella never kept anything from her husband, but she wondered if she should now. In the end, she decided against it.

'They are young and in love, and they want to be together. He's a very nice boy and he's mad about her, and to be honest, I think marriage sooner rather than later is best, because we don't need a baby on the way and the dates not adding up.' She kept on walking but sensed her husband's reaction.

'Are you saying—'

'Dermot Murphy,' she interrupted, 'you were young once as well, remember, so don't consider getting up on your high horse. But, yes, Jack and Eve are sleeping together. Don't ask me how I know, call it mother's intuition, but they are, and so in the interests of their happiness and averting any scandals, the sooner they say *I do* the better, as far as I'm concerned.'

He looked horrified.

'But we were different.'

'Indeed, then we were not, we were exactly the same. And you know it well, so don't go rewriting history. They are like all young couples, and who can blame them? They want to be together in every way, just like we did, so I think it will all work out fine. Now, our other two lassies, that's another matter altogether.'

'Right.' He gave a hint of a smile at her admonishment. As usual, his wife was right. He went on, changing the uncomfortable subject of his little girl's relationship: 'I still can't believe Kate and Aisling are gone. Is it after Sam Kenefick Kate's gone, do you think?' Isabella knew everything regarding their girls. He never doubted or second-guessed her.

'Definitely,' Isabella said without pause. 'She and him are thick as thieves since they were babies on the rug. So a combination of him, and I suppose they just want a bit of adventure, and there was nothing to keep them here, so they took off. I'd say Aisling went to keep an eye on Kate, knowing that however worried we'd be about the two of them, the thought of Kate on her own would have given me a nervous breakdown. That girl is mad. She'd do anything. At least Ais has a hair of sense. That and the fact that poor Aisling is mortified and heart-broken about herself and that big mammy's boy Sean Lacey. And him flaunting that brash-looking one from Dublin every time she went into the village. They probably saw Eve as being set up with Jack, and thought you and I had a better chance of getting work if we were on our own.'

'I would have provided for us, I always have,' Dermot said, the hurt of their rejection in his voice.

'Ah but sure, Der, they're young. They know we'll always be here. The world is dangerous and terrifying to us adults at the moment, nobody knows what's going to happen, but for young girls all they see is romance and uniforms and travel and excitement, and they want to be part of it.'

'But we both know there's very little excitement in war, and a lot of death and destruction. War is a horrible, bloody waste, and some-times, it needs to be done, but I fought those bastards to get them out of my country and away from my family. To see my two darling girls only too eager to sign up with them, it makes me... I don't know, Bella. I'm so furious and worried and scared.'

She squeezed his arm. At least now he was talking, telling her about the pain of betrayal. She knew her husband nearly better than he knew himself, and he could let things simmer. He was inclined to brood. Better it was out in the open now. But she would need to tread carefully.

'In hindsight,' she ventured, 'I think we should have told them about what you did, the reasons we didn't want them to go to England. If they'd known everything, maybe they'd have thought twice.'

'Possibly you're right, but it hardly makes any difference at this stage anyway. And with the Keneficks, we needed to keep it to ourselves. The thing is, it will all come out once I make the pension application anyway. The government say it's confidential, but sure, nothing is confidential in this place. A secret is something you tell one person at a time.' He sat on a low wall, and Isabella sat beside him. He gazed at the grass between his boots, and she knew there was something else on his mind.

'There are things that I'll have to talk about to get the pension. Stuff I never even told you.' His voice was barely audible, and he wouldn't look at her.

She turned to face him and gently placed her hand on his face, turning him towards her. Her eyes never left his.

'You did what you had to do, Dermot. We all did. I was never anything but proud of you, nor would I ever be, no matter what you tell me now. But if the whole place is going to hear about it, you'd better tell me, so at least I know what I'm facing.'

He took a deep breath, as if he was preparing himself.

'It feels wrong, even now, here with you, to be talking about those times. In those days, having a big mouth would get you a bullet from someone. Like, if Violet had known I was in the IRA, everything I did, she'd have had us out on our ear. And Austin too, I suppose. I mean, he was all right as the gentry go, but he was one of them all the same. I often wondered if he had a clue, though.

'This fella, Thomas Hamilton-Brooks, who's offered us the job, he was supposed to be in business or something, but I got word from IRA command that he was from Dublin Castle. Apparently, he was a high-ranking British agent. He wasn't the worst as they went, but we were watching him, and I often wondered what his business with

Austin was. Old Austin had a lot of connections. He knew everyone, but I was never sure how much he knew about me.

'Well, one time your man Hamilton-Brooks came down here, ostensibly to shoot deer, but in reality, he was sniffing around for information on the attack on the Royal Irish Constabulary barracks in Kilmeaden. There were seven RIC men killed that night, and Dublin Castle was baying for blood. They wanted the culprits badly that time. Your man Hamilton-Brooks was very loose in his talk, sipping whiskey from a hip flask all day, and he was very talkative for a G-man, going on about the IRA and all of that—I was with them on the hunt. He kept offering me drink, trying to get a response out of me. Austin gave me a quare look that day, but he never said anything.'

Dermot cleared his throat. 'They arrested Charlie Warren and a few others for that, I remember. They gave him a right hammering, the poor man.'

Isabella looked at her husband. He had never said a word, on that night or any time in the intervening nineteen years, but on the night of the attack that left seven RIC men dead and the barracks relieved of all its weapons, Dermot had come home late. She'd run a bath for him and said nothing as he burned his clothes in a barrel while Eve and Aisling slept inside. Kate hadn't even been born yet. She'd never asked, and he had never said.

He turned and looked down into her eyes.

'I'm not proud of it, Bella, but it had to be done. Oskar was with me that night, and Charlie of course, and a few others, and there was only supposed to be two or three of them, but for some reason there were seven of them that night. 'Twas them or us, and that RIC sergeant was a dangerous man with a big mouth. He came outside to relieve himself and saw us. He drew his gun, and I had to shoot him first. The sound of gunfire brought the others hot on his heels. We managed between us to get them all.

'I never want to kill—even on the farm it sickens me putting an animal down—but it had to be done. The Tans, the Auxies, they'd have come in here, especially if they knew I was involved, and burned and raped and murdered with impunity. I had no choice. We had to make

153

sure there were no witnesses. We got a huge haul of weapons that night, but I felt no elation. Those men were sons, husbands, fathers, but we had to do it anyway. We had to get them out. They accused us of being vicious, but 'twas they brought that brutality over here to us, not the other way around.

Charlie and two other lads from Dungarvan were picked up after, and he was tortured and everything, but he never said a word about me and Oskar. Then, only two weeks later, the ceasefire was called. Charlie, and others—Mick O'Neill, young Jack's father, and plenty more—went against the treaty and, well, you know the rest. I was so sick of it all, I just bowed out, and Charlie never forgave me for accepting the treaty, flawed as it was. That's why he won't keep us on.'

A gentle breeze blew the lush meadow, grown long now without animals to graze it. Isabella said nothing; Dermot wasn't finished.

'There were others, men whose deaths are on my hands. Some where I pulled the trigger, some where I let others know about the actions or movements of the British that I heard about. I didn't tell you any of the details at the time because I wanted to keep you out of it as much as I could. And then, afterwards, well, there was no point. I suppose I didn't want you to think the man you married was a killer.'

The last words were barely a whisper.

Isabella put her arm around his shoulder.

'The man I married is a brave patriot who did what he had to do, and I cannot see it any other way, Dermot. As you said, there was no choice. What kind of way would our girls be if they were reared under the British? Terrified and downtrodden. Those people had to be sent back where they came from, and the only thing they understood was force. And those that had to do it, brave men like you, took no pleasure in it. You were only defending your country and your people.'

She held his big hand in her small one as they sat in the early-morning air.

'One thing always puzzled me though, and I never asked you. I knew you wouldn't tell me because, that way, if they questioned me, I genuinely wouldn't know. But do you remember a night not long after Aisling was born that you were out, and when you came back you had blood on your coat, and you said to me, "Don't worry, nothing bad happened"?'

Dermot nodded. 'I do.'

'Will you tell me now?'

He sighed and lit a cigarette, inhaling and then exhaling slowly before he spoke.

'IT WAS a raid on the RIC barracks at Ballinamult. Oskar, myself, Mick O'Neill, and Terence Galvin and Sonny O'Brien were there too. Mick was working in Warren's at the time. Anyway, we were waiting for them as they came out from the pub. It was St George's Day, and they were all on the rantan, most of them drunk as lords. Tans, Auxies, RIC, they were all there. Colonel Davis, the CO of the headquarters in Cappaquin, was with them, though he was sober. Anyway, we were watching them, and we followed them back to Ballinamult. The Tans and Auxiliaries were supposed to be billeted in the barracks in Dungarvan, and they were closing the smaller rural barracks. They reckoned it was too dangerous, we were attacking them every night and relieving them of their weapons. Anyway, there must have been a promise of more drink or something back in Ballinamult, so they all trooped back there, and when they were all inside, we surrounded it. Called them out, and petrol-bombed the end of the building, and took whatever weapons they had. They were all unarmed and plastered drunk.

'One of them made a grab for me, so Oskar hit him a clatter on the temple with the butt of his gun, and he went down like a bag of spuds. His pal then went for me, scratching my face. That's how I got blood on me, but Davis ordered him to stop. Sure, they were in no state to fight back anyway. We ordered them to strip off and took their uniforms as well. They used to come in handy. We lined them all up in their underwear, and your man Davis says, "Are you planning to shoot us?" just like that.

'I stepped forward and said I had no intention of doing anything of the kind, and that we'd be on our way once we had them locked into the barracks. They'd be found in the morning. So we marched them all into a cell, but as we were shoving them in,

Davis says to me, "What's your name?"'

"'YOU DON'T NEED to know that," I answered him, and I turned to go. But he says to me quietly, "

Thank you for sparing our lives. You could have shot us."

I stopped and looked at him. Oskar and Mick and the lads were locking the remainder up, but I brought Davis out to the old table and chairs outside. I don't know what came over me; it might have been a trick, but I kind of knew it wasn't. Oskar and I told the rest of the unit to head home, after they'd stashed the weapons. They probably thought we were going to kidnap the CO or torture him or something. Anyway, they did as they were told, and it was just me and Oskar and your man Davis.

'Oskar was for locking your man up with the rest of them, but something in me wanted to talk to one of them, try to get them to see what they were doing to us. I don't know, maybe it was because it had been going on so long, so much death and destruction. I was sick of it.

I gave him a cigarette.

"'I could have shot you all," I said, "but I'm not the kind of man who kills for no reason. I know who you are, even if you don't know me. And you're a decent man. You've showed kindness to our people when others of your kind were cruel just because they could be. You lifted young Benny McGrath, but you didn't allow those Tans to burn his mother's house. You questioned him, and when you realised he was only a kid, you let him go. You have no more interest in this bloody mayhem than I do, but we're thrown together here and we have to do our jobs. If only ye'd leave, just leave us in peace, go home to England where ye belong."

"'I'd love nothing better, mate," says he to me.

He told me all about his time over in France, in the trenches. How coming home was nearly worse than being there because nobody understood, and so many fellas never came back he nearly felt guilty about surviving and having all his limbs. Oskar told him he was half German, and Davis told us about meeting Germans out in France, realising they were just the same as the lads he fought alongside. Then Oskar talked about the effect the war had had on his family back in Germany. We commented on how the stories were the same—both sides losing hope, dignity, just the total waste of life of the whole bloody thing. We talked and talked, the three of us, about all of it, the whole mess, and Davis told me about his wife and the baby she was expecting, and I told him about you and the girls, and it was so... I don't know... It all seemed so stupid. I know it sounds mad, but in another lifetime, we could have been friends, you know?'

Dermot's eyes searched Isabella's face, desperate to see understanding there, fearing her revulsion at the revelations about what kind of a man he was, what he was capable of.

She rested her head on his shoulder.

'I do. Some of them were heartless, but most of them were just like us, stuck in a war not of their making and trying to survive.' She sighed. It all seemed so long ago now. 'I'm glad you told me, and I don't think anything less of you now that I know the full story. It was the time and the place.'

Dermot squeezed her hand. 'What would I have done if I never married you?'

She smiled. 'Oh, lived a life of utter misery with someone else, I'm sure.'

CHAPTER 22

*E*ve tried not to cry as she saw her reflection in the mirror. Her mother's wedding dress fitted her perfectly, and while she was so happy to be marrying Jack, her special day was sad. She wanted her sisters here with her more than anything. She'd written several long, angry letters, all of which ended up in the bin, telling them just how hurt and betrayed she felt, but eventually, she did write, telling them she missed them terribly and asking if they could come back for her wedding.

They waited for a reply—their parents had written, as well, and it had felt so wrong addressing the envelope to Aisling and Kate Murphy at an RAF base in England. They'd tried telephoning, even went into Dungarvan to make the call, in case the whole village turned up in the post office in Kilthomand to listen in, but there was no way of contacting them like that. The snooty-sounding woman just told Mammy she would have to write and that the telephone lines were for emergencies only.

The letter finally came, on thin blue paper.

Kate and Aisling had both written it, and in it they apologised for everything they'd put the family through, but the rest was full of news about training and complaints about food. They could hear Kate's voice as Mammy read the letter aloud in the kitchen.

The main point was that there was no way they would be released so soon after joining up to come home. Eve had considered putting the wedding off, but she wanted to marry Jack, and what with all the uncertainty about the future, marrying Jack was one of the few definite things.

She glanced around the bedroom she'd shared with her sisters since they were babies. If they came back, they'd hardly recognise the house. Eve had always imagined what it would be like if one of them got married, but it was never this. Almost everything was gone, sold or returned to the main house, their personal things packed away in boxes. Neither she nor her parents knew when or if they would ever be opened again. It was like packing up their whole family, all the memories, all the things that meant something only to them. They were trying, all three of them, not to be too woebegone, but Eve had walked in on Daddy boxing up all the Christmas decorations they'd made over the years, and when he saw her, he couldn't speak for a second or two.

They were due to leave next week; Violet's early departure changed nothing. They were leaving on the appointed date, not a moment before. The wedding had been organised with haste, what Kilthomand no doubt considered indecent haste, and her belly would have been watched with eagle eyes in the coming months if she had been staying. Thankfully, she wasn't. She and Jack were going to Cork after the wedding, and her parents were taking up their new position in Dublin.

'Well, are you ready? We'd better go.' Isabella's eyes were bright with unshed tears. 'Your dad is picking Jack's mother up from the bus, so he'll be back for us then, and you know Father MacIntyre hates to be kept waiting.'

'Ah, Mam, don't cry. You'll set *me* off again. It's sad enough without that. The whole place will think I'm the most reluctant bride ever to be bawling up the aisle.' Eve tried a watery smile.

'I know, and I'm happy you're marrying Jack. He's such a lovely

JEAN GRAINGER

lad, we love him like one of our own already, you know that. But it's just without the girls, and leaving this place, and we can't even give you a proper wedding... You deserve so much better, Eve.'

'I miss Ais and Kate too, more than I can say, but the wedding business means nothing to Jack and me,' Eve said. 'All we want is to be married and live happily ever after, which we will. Now, let's go down and give the village something to talk about. As if being evicted wasn't enough for them, now they'll have my hasty wedding to add to the gossip menu.'

Eve was anxious to get away, afraid her mother would try to give her the 'what to expect on your wedding night' speech. She could think of nothing worse, and she was sure that if her mother started, her face would betray the fact that she and Jack had used every opportunity they'd had in the recent weeks to make love.

'Eve, there's something I want to say to you, before we go.'

Eve felt herself redden before her mother even started talking.

'Ah, Mam, look at the time...'

Isabella gave her daughter a knowing smile.

'It's not what you think. That ship has sailed, I would imagine.'

Eve stared studiously at the freshly swept floorboards.

'Don't worry,' Isabella said gently, 'I'm not judging you. In fact, you were on the way when your father and I got married, so we're in no position to throw stones.'

Eve looked up in shock, her mother's revelation sinking in.

Isabella smiled at her daughter's expression.

'There now, and you thought you knew everything, didn't you?' She grinned and gave her daughter a wink. 'What I wanted to tell you is that marriage is not always easy. Today, you're going to marry this man you love, and he loves you, and you can't ever imagine the hard times. But they will come, my love, no matter how much I wish they wouldn't. So my advice is this: Stay loyal to each other, keep talking, and when you fall out, as you will, remember he is your home and you're his.

'Your Dad and I have had a wonderful marriage, but there were times when I was so frustrated with him, so angry. There were times

160

when other men caught my eye, and other women his, I have no doubt, but we are united, and nothing but death will ever divide us. We talk, even when it's hard to do it, and at night in bed, we share everything. All our joys and fears and anger—everything. I wish for you, not riches or a comfortable life, though I hope it happens, but I wish that you and Jack enjoy a marriage like we have. Jack has never known a father, not since he was small, so when the children come, please God, you'll have to show him how to be a father. And you can, because you've had a great one. But do it without undermining him.'

'I will, Mam.' But Eve was still wondering how her mother knew about her and Jack. They'd been so careful. Then another horrific thought occurred to her. 'Daddy doesn't know, does he? About...you know?' Surely not, or he'd have murdered Jack by now.

Though, in light of her mother's revelation...possibly not.

'Your daddy is not as blind to what goes on here as you might think,' her mother said, 'and I knew because of the way you look at Jack and he at you. Now, I'm not going to ask you if you're sure, I know you are, and he's right for you. We all wish Aisling and Kate could be here, and I'm sure they are thinking of us today. So let's go and have a lovely day and let tomorrow take care of itself.'

Eve hugged her mother. She really was an extraordinary woman, and Eve knew how lucky she was to have her.

* * *

STANDING at the back of St Declan's Church in Kilthomand, her hand linking her to her father's arm, Eve waited for Mrs Barry to start up the bridal march on the organ. It seemed a big fanfare for such a small gathering of people, but she didn't care. They'd only asked a few of the neighbours and one or two old school friends. Jack's friend Billy had come from Cork, as well as his mother. Afterwards, they were going to the Granville Hotel in Dungarvan for the wedding celebrations.

Eve and Jack had tried to insist that they just went home for sandwiches and cake—it was too expensive to go to the hotel—but Eve's parents had insisted, so they were hosting a small gathering after the

Mass. Eve knew her dad wanted her to have a bigger day, but she honestly didn't care. Without Aisling and Kate, it wasn't a proper family party anyway, so she was happy to let it go with a minimum of fuss.

She could see Jack standing in his good suit at the top of the aisle, with Billy beside him as best man. They were like chalk and cheese. Jack was dark and slim while Billy was red-haired and huge. Jack often entertained her with all of the antics he and Billy had gotten up to when they were growing up. They seemed very close and Eve almost envied him. She had no close friend because Aisling and Kate were her friends. Their parents had always encouraged their closeness, and the girls had followed their lead in staying somewhat aloof from the village.

Eve glanced at her father, who was staring straight ahead, a serious look on his face. She knew people in Kilthomand thought he was handsome but dour, but she and her sisters, and of course Mammy, knew what he was really like. It seemed like only a short time ago he was cavorting around the kitchen floor being a horse, with all three of his daughters on his back, or showing them how to tickle trout, or how to identify all the different butterflies. Their dad was great fun, and he adored them, but that was not the image he showed to the world.

He looked down at her as they waited and smiled.

'You all right?'

She nodded.

'I love you, Eve,' he said quietly. Though nobody in the family doubted it, he didn't often actually say the words.

'I love you too, Daddy,' she whispered. 'Thanks for everything.'

He squeezed her hand in close to his body as Mrs Barry began to play. As Eve walked up the aisle on her father's arm, all she could see was Jack's smiling face. She thought her heart would burst with joy.

The Mass went by in a blur, but the exchange of vows meant everything. She gazed deeply into Jack's eyes as she repeated after Father MacIntyre her promises to love, honour, and obey her husband. They had laughed about the obey bit when they had practiced their vows at home, and Jack had said he doubted he'd manage to get her to stick by that one. She assured him of her love and even her honour, but on the obey front she had to agree it was unlikely.

Jack's mother wept quietly in the front row, and Eve hoped it was tears of happiness. She'd only met the woman once, when she'd visited Cork, and she seemed nice, but she was very protective of her son. Eve supposed it was only to be expected. They had been just the two of them since her husband died.

Kate and Aisling had sent a telegram saying how much they wanted to be there and wishing Eve and Jack all the love in the world. Eve caught her mother's eye, shining with tears, as Billy read that one. The lunch went well, and they were very surprised to be told by the manager that the wine was being supplied by the Kenefick family. Eve suspected the hand of Samuel rather than Violet, and certainly not Lillian. Kate must have told him. Still, it was a nice gesture. She had never had wine before, and to be honest, it was a little bitter. But she felt very grown up and sophisticated.

Mammy and Daddy were treating them to a night in the hotel for their wedding night, and Eve couldn't wait to have her husband all to herself. She glanced over at Mrs O'Neill, her new mother-in-law. She still looked fairly sorrowful, but Jack and Billy seemed oblivious as they recounted funny stories to each other.

Every so often, Jack caught her hand under the table and gave it a squeeze.

Eventually, the lunch drew to a close, and Dermot offered to drive Mrs O'Neill and Billy to the bus. The Keneficks' old Bentley wasn't being collected until the weekend.

Jack's friend thumped him playfully on the shoulder and gave him a wink while his mother clung to him like he was going off to war or emigrating. Isabella and Eve exchanged a glance over Jack's shoulder, silently concurring that she was being a bit dramatic. He wasn't going to America, like so many of his friends, he was only getting married, and they'd be in Cork by the weekend.

'You'll have your work cut out for you there then, Miss Eve,' Billy murmured in her ear.

Eve looked up at him.

'How do you mean?' she asked quietly.

'Mrs O put the run on any young one who took a shine to Jack over the years. She'd have managed to give you your marching orders, too, if she knew about ye. By the time he brought you home, she could see there was no point in going against you; she could see if he was forced to choose between you and his mammy, he'd pick you every time. And he'd be dead right to, too. 'Twas a lucky day for himself that he came down here.' Billy put his arm around her shoulder and gave her a friendly squeeze. 'Ye are both lucky, and I wish ye all the best. And sure, we'll see you up in the real capital soon.'

Though Billy had confirmed what Eve suspected, at least her new husband's best friend was on her side. That was something, she supposed.

Jack's mother reluctantly released him from her embrace with a face that reminded Eve of the pictures the nuns used to show them of medieval saints, all drawn and miserable looking.

'You'll mind my lad, won't you?' she asked, her voice trembling with emotion.

'We'll both mind him, together, Mrs O'Neill,' Eve promised. 'Sure, won't we be living under your roof till we can get a place of our own? I don't know the first thing about being a wife, and my mother won't be there, so you'll have to show me the ropes.'

Isabella smiled at her husband. Eve knew how to handle Jack's mother. The woman clearly needed to feel needed, and Eve would make sure she wasn't left out. Though, she hoped, for the young couple's sake, that they got their own place sooner rather than later.

CHAPTER 23

*A*s she sipped her morning tea in the bedroom of her suite at Claridge's, Violet opened the letter from Elena Hamilton-Brooks thanking her for organising the Murphys to go to work for their family. Violet was moving into her rented house on Sloane Square shortly, but since she'd arrived in London earlier than expected, the agent had explained that the property was not yet ready to be occupied. It was an inconvenience, but she had to admit she was rather enjoying it.

She had planned to visit the Hamilton-Brooks family before she left Ireland, as she was very fond of Elena and Thomas, but the humour she was in upon hearing of the Murphy girls' audacity in contacting Samuel had made her less than convivial company. She'd sent a telegram, apologising and giving the Hamilton-Brookses the details of where she could be contacted in London. At least someone cared where she was.

She extracted the cream embossed paper—such lovely things were what made life worth living, she thought—and began to read.

Dear Violet,

I hope this letter finds you well and settling into life back in London. I imagine it must be quite a change, but hopefully one that you are enjoying, despite the dreadful war. Thomas sends his regards, and as you know he was very fond of you both. I think he misses his jaunts with Austin very much. He wanted me to reiterate his offer of any help you might need, please just get in touch.

How are Lillian and Samuel? Well, I hope. It must be nicer for you to be closer to them as you come to terms with the loss of darling Austin.

Life here in Dublin is busy, well, chaotic is probably a better word, so I am anxiously awaiting the arrival of the Murphys. The latest housekeeper has just resigned, and by that I mean simply walked out the door one morning at eleven fifteen and has not been seen since. She and Thomas had words, apparently, but he refuses to tell me what about. Either way, she is gone, and I am left dealing with the house, the children, and everything else.

We have often discussed the matter of staff, and I agree with you, these Irish are unfathomable, to say the least. But I got a very nice letter from Dermot and Isabella, and they will be here by the 15th so I am counting down the days. I cannot ever thank you enough, dear Violet. The children are adorable but very naughty, and they totally ignore me.

I'll be in London next month so perhaps we could meet for tea and a chat?
All my love,
Your friend,
Elena.

VIOLET FOLDED the letter and replaced it as the maid came to clear the morning tray. The tea was weak, the bread dry, and the little pat of butter was microscopic, but there was a war on, and one had to manage and not complain. She missed Isabella's soda bread and scones, though.

She drew her writing pad towards her and began,
Dear Elena,
Life in London is fine, though the rationing does make it a bit trying. Samuel and Lillian are doing well, and yes, it is nicer to be near them.
She paused. *Should she say something about how lonely life was without Austin when it was simply not the case? In lots of ways, life was easier—not*

worrying what he was doing, how much he was spending... Still, she reasoned, one must play the game.

I am coming to terms with life without Austin, though it is lonely.

Regarding Dermot and Isabella, I hope it all works out. They are wonderful servants, and Isabella is very well able to manage children, so I'm confident it will be a success.

Yes, please do get in touch when you come to London. I would very much enjoy meeting you again.

Fond regards,

Violet

She sealed the letter and rang for the maid. The girl appeared promptly.

'Please post this.' The girl bobbed respectfully and took the letter.

SHE WOULD RISE and bathe and perhaps meet Lillian for lunch. In lots of ways, she was dreading it. She would have to explain that funds could not permit Lillian to buy a place in London just for her.

Violet decided there and then to arrange to meet her daughter somewhere public—less chance of her making a fuss.

* * *

THREE DAYS AFTER THE WEDDING, Dermot and Isabella stood in their bedroom, their bags waiting at the front door. Without speaking, each knew the despondency of the other. Their happy home, their girls, their livelihood, all gone. They faced a very uncertain future, but they were trying to be strong for each other. The weeks had been spent in preparation for the wedding and boarding up all the windows and securing Robinswood against intruders in as much as was possible. It was hard to imagine the big old house empty and dark, and Isabella shed a few tears as she closed the door on her empty kitchen for the last time.

'Eve will be well on the way to Cork by now, I suppose,' Dermot said, looking at the back of the pantry door, where he had marked the girls' heights as they grew.

'She will, and at least we know where the other two are.' Isabella was trying to see the bright side of her daughters enlisting.

'For now we do anyway, until Churchill has them driving around London dodging bombs.' Dermot's worry always came out as anger.

'Look, there's nothing we can do,' Isabella said, determined to stay positive. 'They're there now, and they'll probably just be typists or something on the base. We'll drive ourselves daft if we start imagining all sorts.'

'And where do you think Hitler will want to drop his bombs, Bella?' He stared at her intently, daring her to contradict him. 'Where can he do the most damage?'

He interpreted her silence accurately.

'You see, you know just as well as me: a bloody great big RAF base is where. I could strangle them, I swear I could.'

'Let's just go,' Isabella said. 'We'll miss the bus at this rate.' She didn't want to think about her girls on a RAF base, let alone talk about it.

They walked out and pulled the door behind them, throwing the key back through the letterbox. The bulk of their stuff was in one of the outbuildings, and they could send for it whenever they got settled. The Bentley was being collected this afternoon. They could have arranged for someone of the neighbours to leave them into Kilthomand for the bus to Dublin, but they decided they wanted to walk. Leaving was hard enough without having to make small talk with someone on the mile-and-a-half drive.

The sun was doing its best to break through the clouds, but there was a mist and it reflected their mood.

As they waited for the bus outside the post office, Mossy Flanagan, the postmaster, gave them a sympathetic smile.

Isabella could feel the eyes of the village on her from behind their lace curtains. She smiled a radiant beam and chatted animatedly to Dermot. She would not give it to them to say that they were sad leaving.

As she spoke, the bus pulled in. Thankfully, there were not too many passengers, so they sat together near the back and could speak without being overheard.

In Dublin, the bus left them off at the quays before O'Connell Bridge, and they stood for a moment and got their bearings. It was still bright, so they walked in the direction of the General Post Office, the site of the Easter Rising of 1916. They passed the exact spot where Dermot had been arrested after the week-long battle and marched with his comrades to Arbour Hill prison and subsequently to Frongoch Internment Camp in Wales. It seemed to him like another lifetime.

They planned to take a tram to the station near the Hamilton-Brooks house and walk from there.

As they walked, carrying their bags, Isabella stopped and asked, 'I know you said this man was an agent back during The Troubles, but surely not still? I mean, we're an independent country. Why would the British have agents working over here?'

Dermot smiled. 'Ah, come on, Bella, you're not that naïve, surely? Mr Hitler is doing his damnedest to blow the United Kingdom to kingdom come so they need to make sure there's no way anyone can sneak in the back door. There's talk that the Nazis are in cahoots with the IRA, promising them all colours of independence and to get the North back in return for cooperation. No, you can be sure there are plenty of British agents operating over here still. He was all right, though, reasonable enough, I always found. I remember he had plenty of money anyway, and as I said, a nice man. I remember I helped him stalk a deer for five hours one time, but once we had the beast in range, he didn't shoot. Said there was enough senseless killing going on.' He shrugged.

They stopped for a cup of tea and a bun at Bewley's, and Isabella went to the ladies' to freshen up. When she emerged, she was dressed impeccably, in a dark-green dress and jacket she had made herself, her jet-black curls pinned up demurely under a hat she'd got as a Christmas present from the girls last year. She grinned when she caught her husband's admiring glance.

'You look like a girl,' he said, 'not a woman with three grown-up daughters.'

'I don't know about that, but hopefully they'll be happy with a fine, respectable pair like us.' She straightened his tie, brushed a bit of fluff off his jacket, and fixed his hat at a better angle.

'Thank you for agreeing to this,' she added as the waitress left, having served them tea. 'I know you're only doing it for me.'

'Look, this way at least the girls have some place they can contact us, and as I said, he wasn't the worst. I still think it's a bit odd, that he suddenly has a vacancy for me, but as you said, we haven't too many options. It will do till we get somewhere better. I want to get a job, and I'll apply for the IRA pension, and maybe we can buy a place. I don't ever again want to be beholden to someone like we were to the Keneficks. I should have done it years ago, I realise that now, but it's not too late.'

'I KNOW,' Isabella sighed, 'I've had enough of service as well. At least with a job, you left it in the evenings. I felt like we were at the beck and call of the Keneficks all the time, and this place will probably be no different.'

Dermot leaned over and placed his hand on hers. 'I should have provided better for you and the girls, Bella. I'm sorry.'

'Don't let me ever hear that talk from you again, Dermot. We are in this together, and we'll get out of it together too. It's up to both of us to care for each other and our family, and we'll be fine. Now, let's go and meet these people.' She stood up and grinned. 'This Mrs Hamilton-Brooks can't be any worse than bloody Violet with her notions, anyway.'

Dermot chuckled, picked up their bags, and followed his wife into the spring sunshine.

They waited for the tram opposite the big old post office, which still bore the scars of the bloody revolution.

* * *

THEY ARRIVED to Dun Laoghaire and walked up a leafy road with substantial houses either side. When they came to the one indicated on the telegram they'd received from Thomas Hamilton-Brooks confirming their arrival date, they opened the gate and walked up the short gravel driveway.

They knocked on the door, and a young girl in a maid's outfit opened it. She had clearly been crying.

Dermot let Isabella do the talking.

'Good afternoon. We have an appointment with Mr Hamilton-Brooks?'

The girl seemed to pull herself together and replied quite tartly,

'What is it in connection with? He is not at home at the moment, but perhaps I can give him a message?'

Just as she finished her sentence, a short, slim woman in a biscuit-coloured skirt, cream blouse, and a beige cardigan with a string of pearls round her neck came to the door.

'Oh, hello.' She smiled broadly. She seemed to know who they were.

'It's Dermot, and you must be Isabella?'

Dermot nodded and offered his hand to shake.

'Yes, we are.'

'Marvellous, I'm so happy you found us! Simply marvellous. Come in, come in.' She ushered them inside. '

I am Elena Hamilton-Brooks... I believe you know my husband, Thomas?'

A boy of about five years old ran from behind her and viciously stamped on the foot of the girl who had opened the door, causing her to shriek.

'Arthur! Please behave yourself!' Elena sounded exasperated, and the boy scowled, sticking his tongue out at Isabella and Dermot.

The woman looked embarrassed but said nothing further to reprimand the child.

· · ·

171

'Now, please tell me you're here to stay and that you are a housekeeper and a nanny and a zoo-keeper all rolled into one?' Elena smiled apologetically.

'Well, I am a very experienced housekeeper, and I've reared our three girls and took care of the Kenefick children, so I'm no stranger to little ones.' Isabella smiled, wanting to put the other woman at ease.

'Well, Violet has spoken so highly of you, you two are like a pair of miracle workers by all accounts, and that's exactly what you'll need to be to manage this house and these children. Our housekeeper has left, in rather unpleasant circumstances, and Nancy here is finding it all rather too much. Arthur and Georgina, our children, are... Well, you can see.'

A little girl appeared, and she was completely covered in lipstick. Both children gazed at Isabella and Dermot, fascinated.

'I am very busy as secretary of the Protestant Orphan Society,' Elena went on, 'and therefore am out much of the time. They will have a governess just as soon as I get around to hiring one, but in the interim, things have rather been let slide.' She glanced in Nancy's direction. The girl was dramatically nursing her foot.

'So, please come in, sit down, tell me about yourselves.' She led them into a lovely sitting room that was badly in need of dusting.

'Please sit.'

Isabella and Dermot sat beside each other on the chintz-covered sofa while Mrs Hamilton-Brooks took a seat opposite. Isabella dared not look at Dermot, but years of being married to him meant she knew what he was thinking. That this woman would be better off staying at home and teaching her own kids manners rather than spending all her time on a charity while her own house was falling asunder.

'So... I'm so glad you could come...?'

She seemed a little unsure of what to ask, so Isabella and Dermot explained what they had done for the Keneficks, and Mrs Hamilton-Brooks seemed impressed.

'Well, that sounds absolutely splendid. Now, since he is notable by his absence yet again, I think we can dispense with any more formalities. I definitely need a housekeeper, and my children, and Nancy too if I'm honest, need to be firmly taken in hand. It is not a position for the faint-hearted. As for the outside work, well, the garden is gone rather to seed, so perhaps you, Mr Murphy, could start there?'

Isabella felt a profound sense of relief.

'Now, as for pay and such, my husband will have to speak to you about that, but I'm sure it will be fine. You will take your meals in the kitchen, and there is a room on the top floor where Mrs Collins— that's our old housekeeper—used to live. I'm not sure what state it's in, as I've not been up there of late, but it has its own bathroom and a small sitting room off the bedroom. You are welcome to move in, unless you'd rather live locally?'

'Thank you, Mrs Hamilton-Brooks,' Isabella replied. 'We would be happy to live in.'

'Very well. Now, Nancy will have to show you around. She lives with her sister not far from here, so she comes in every day at seven and works until six. She has one and a half days off per month and does not work on Sunday mornings. I know it is irregular to ask you to start now, but perhaps you could? I have an important meeting in town, and I am already late. The children have not eaten as far as I am aware. Nancy tried to make something for them, but they... Well, it ended in tears. Theirs, Nancy's, and at one point, almost mine.' She seemed unperturbed by the fact that she was essentially allowing two total strangers into her house to care for her children.

Isabella glanced at Dermot. He seemed happy to do as suggested.

'Yes, that will be fine, ma'am.' He rose. 'We'll drop our things upstairs and begin right away.'

Elena Hamilton-Brooks gave him her full attention, measuring him up. Isabella glanced at him, hoping his tone hadn't made her reconsider. He was used to dealing with upper-class women, and while he was polite, they seemed to sense a proud belligerence in him. Nothing they could put their finger on as such. He was always courteous, but he just didn't kowtow to them. Isabella loved that about him, but she knew it didn't endear him to employers who were used to more deference.

But Elena's face broke into a smile.

'Oh, splendid. Thomas should be home later, so you'll see him then and you can discuss money and so on. Now, I really must dash. Nancy will show you where everything is and the routine of the children such as it is. I am eating out this evening, but when my husband appears, I'm sure you'll manage to find something to feed him down there.'

And without further explanation, she was gone, and Isabella and Dermot stood alone in the living room.

CHAPTER 24

'Lady Kenefick, how nice to see you. Your son is waiting in the Palm Court. May I take your coat?' The beautifully liveried waiter escorted Violet into the sumptuously decorated salon of The Ritz Hotel. Palm trees grew out of huge urns, reminiscent of her youth in India, and in each alcove, a gold statue lounged. The crisp linen and sparkling silver serving bowls gave the impression of the utmost decadence, and she absolutely loved it.

Samuel had called on her and Lillian once she had settled in, and Violet had never been happier to see him. He looked so handsome, dazzlingly so, in his RAF officers' uniform, and it made such a pleasant change from listening to Lillian complain endlessly that the house they were renting was too small. The wretched girl simply refused to accept that they were not as wealthy as she would wish and that her lifestyle as a good-time girl, quaffing champagne at all the best places till dawn and then sleeping all day in a perfectly proportioned, ideally located flat all of her own, was simply way beyond the family's means.

Lillian refused to bring any of her friends home to what she called 'the hovel,' though it was a nice little house, with only three bedrooms, admittedly, but it was in Sloane Square. Once the debts and duties had been paid with the profits of the sale of the furniture and assets of Robinswood, they'd been left with very little. Violet was as disappointed as Lillian, but she could accept it. The rent from the land would be paid four times per annum, and while it was going to be enough to live on, it didn't allow for extravagance.

Violet toyed with the idea of returning to India. She was still a relatively attractive woman, she reasoned, and her days there had been filled with suitors. Perhaps she could remarry, someone better than Austin. Things were improving even more now that she was back in civilisation with decent hairdressers, beauty rooms, and couturiers. At first, she'd been fearful that rationing had removed all of the niceties of life, but she soon learned that if one had the means and the connections, most things were possible, even in these troubled times.

Surely there were some single men who would enjoy her company? Admittedly, they may not be as handsome as her suitors once were, but it was better than living in penury here, with the constant threat of that nasty little Austrian coming and blowing them all to bits. She planned to ask Samuel's opinion over afternoon tea. He was such a wonderful son. He knew she needed a little pick-me-up after all the stress of moving and so on, and when he'd invited her, she'd been over the moon. She also needed to talk to him about their finances, and that was impossible to do with Lillian around.

She followed the waiter's lead and soon spotted Samuel's handsome head as he rose to greet her. No sooner had she registered her son did she notice he was not alone.

She tried to disguise the horror on her face as Kate Murphy rose and extended her hand.

'Hello, Lady Kenefick. It's nice to see you again.' Kate's smile seemed genuine, but Violet just looked down at her outstretched hand in horror.

Kate withdrew her hand, but Samuel didn't seem to notice.

'I knew you wouldn't mind, Mother,' he said, 'and I have been promising Kate lunch at the Ritz since we were children, so I thought why not entertain two of my favourite ladies at once?' Samuel smiled broadly, as if this was the best idea he'd ever had.

As they took their seats, Violet tried to steady herself. The Murphy girl was a servant, who had no business whatsoever in a place like this, but apart from that, what on earth was going on with her and Samuel to say he brought her to Afternoon Tea at the Ritz? Aisling and Kate turning up, begging from him, manipulating his good nature, was one thing, but this? She tried to swallow down panic.

The tea sommelier appeared and explained all the different teas to them. In a daze, Violet chose one.

'So, Mother, how is being back in London suiting you?' Samuel smiled. 'Are you missing Robinswood yet?'

Violet swallowed and tried to sound natural.

'Very well, I'm enjoying it. Reuniting with friends and acquaintances is most diverting, but of course there is the business of trying to find staff. That is most trying, as everyone is caught up in the war effort.' She hoped her reference to staff was not lost on the Murphy girl. She had the same insolent look in her eyes that her father did, though she had that wild European look of her mother, all black curls and a full mouth.

'As they should be,' Samuel said. 'We all need to pull together, and sacrifices must be made. Look at Kate and Aisling. They didn't have to lift a finger, but they did and came over and signed up. That's bloody brave in my book.'

His eyes rested on Kate, and Violet's heart sank. She knew her son better than anyone, and she could hardly believe her eyes. That was not a look from a benevolent employer to his young servant. Samuel seemed to be besotted with the Murphy girl. Surely this could not be happening?

'Yes, well,' Violet said, 'I suppose with the sale of Robinswood, the servants had choices...'

She was interrupted by the waiter pouring tea while another placed a large tiered tray containing all sorts of delicious cakes and sandwiches in the centre of the table.

'My goodness, what a spread!' Kate announced gleefully. 'The food on the base would make you want to give up on life completely. I really miss my mother's cooking. So much! I bet you do too, Lady Kenefick?'

Violet felt the stain of red indignation creep up her neck into her face. The cheek of the girl, addressing her as if they were equals. She was about to retort something cutting to restore the balance of power, but she thought she got a warning glance from her son. If he was infatuated with this little urchin who used to run around Robinswood in her bare feet with a dirty face, then making an enemy of her risked alienating Samuel as well. And he was all Violet had left, apart from the exasperating Lillian. She would have to play this cleverly.

'Yes, I certainly do.' She managed to smile. 'Your mother is a wonderful cook.'

Samuel physically relaxed. Clearly, he thought the moment of tension had passed. Violet drew on whatever strength she had and nailed a smile on her face. This highly unsuitable arrangement would have to be stopped, but it would require subtlety and resourcefulness.

The afternoon unfolded with Kate telling stories of her exploits on the RAF base, and Samuel seemed to find her hysterically funny, frequently wiping his eyes at her witty observations of life in the British Air Force. Violet thought the Murphy girl sounded disrespectful of her elders and betters, and that Irish accent of hers was particularly grating on the nerves, but after years of marriage to Austin, Violet knew she was nothing if not an actress, so she smiled along indulgently.

Of course, she never got to raise the issues she had intended to raise with Samuel, and when the horrible experience finally drew to a close, her son called her a taxi. As it pulled away from the kerb, she saw Kate Murphy sneakily slip her hand into his.

Violet fumed in the back seat as the driver attempted to make conversation. He had picked up a lady from the Ritz; surely, the buffoon did not think such people made random conversation with taxi drivers? She sighed. The world had gone mad. The prospect of returning to India, where people knew their place, seemed even more appealing.

* * *

'NICE FOR SOME!' Lillian drawled from the sofa as Violet entered the drawing room. 'Afternoon Tea at the Ritz! I thought we were supposed to be broke?'

Violet had to hang up her own coat, as they still had no staff, and there, she saw her daughter, who was not alone.

She had a man with her. Not just any man, either, but a large, negro man in an American uniform. Violet felt faint.

'Mother, this is Beau,' Lillian said. 'He has ventured out to visit me since you are clearly punishing me for something by insisting we inhabit this hovel. But, Mother Dearest, if I hear one more syllable from you about poverty, I shall simply reply with, "Afternoon *Tea* at the Ritz."'

She gave her braying donkey laugh, and this Beau man at least had the grace to look embarrassed.

An American was one thing, a barely tolerable reality, but a negro? No wonder Lillian had never mentioned that fact about the person with whom she spent most of her time. The man stood up and politely extended his hand. He was absolutely enormous, and his frame seemed to take up the entire room.

'It's a pleasure to meet you, Lady Kenefick,' he said. 'I apologise for calling in your absence, but Lillian telephoned me, and I assumed you would be at home.'

His voice was deep and rumbling, and Violet gazed for a second at his outstretched brown hand. She had known brown people—well, Indians, not Africans—all her life, but she had never shaken the hand of one. For the second time in a day, she found herself swallowing her true feelings and smiling.

She allowed him to hold the tips of her gloved fingers before she withdrew as quickly as was possible within the confines of politeness.

'Good afternoon, Mr...?' She raised a questioning eyebrow. On the floor beside the sofa where Lillian remained stretched was a bottle of gin, and the room stank of cigarette smoke.

'Lane, ma'am. Beauregard Lane.'

'And your rank?' she asked.

His face registered surprise at the question, though she thought it a perfectly straightforward one. Military men of her acquaintance throughout her life had introduced themselves as Major So-and-So or Lance Corporal or Group Captain. This man was in uniform, therefore, he should use his rank for introductory purposes. How else was one to know how to behave?

'Em... Staff Sergeant, ma'am.'

Was Lillian trying to scandalise her mother and everyone in their social circle? Was that the girl's purpose? Perhaps she and Samuel were playing an elaborate joke on her? A negro NCO lounging in her home, a servant sipping tea with her son in the Ritz—it was all a prank. It must be!

Violet thought for a moment. She had to be clever with Samuel—he was necessary for her future protection—but Lillian was a liability. Violet owed her daughter nothing, and now that they were marooned together in relative poverty, she saw her daughter for what she truly was: a grasping alcoholic of dubious morals, who mistakenly thought her dear departed papa had made provision for her to continue in the vacuous life she had adopted for herself. On the contrary, the paltry sum remaining from the sale of the house contents and animals would have to stretch, and if Lillian was to have her way, she would ensure they were in the poor house by the end of the year from bar bills alone.

Violet had hoped to convince Samuel to have a word with his sister, try to knock some sense into her, but that was clearly not going to happen. As usual, if something needed to be done, Violet had to do it herself. A few home truths were going to be necessary. After all, the girl was drunk and still in her nightclothes. At least the American was dressed.

'Well, Sergeant Lane, please don't assume me rude, but would you mind leaving?' Violet's tone, while light, brooked no argument. 'I need to have a conversation with my daughter in private.'

He gazed at her for a long second, his liquid brown eyes seemingly summing her up.

'Certainly, ma'am. It was a pleasure to meet you. Bye, Lillian.' He took his hat from the coffee table and left.

'GET UP,' Violet told her daughter coldly. 'Get dressed and be back down here in five minutes.'

'If you think you can speak to my friends...' Lillian slurred slightly.

Violet stood over her.

'Get up. Get dressed. Now.'

Something about the way she spoke had the desired effect, and Lillian stood up and left the room, slamming the door. Honestly, the woman was ridiculous! She behaved like she was fourteen, not twenty-five. She should have been married by now, and somebody else's problem.

In truth, Violet had hoped they would become close, that Lillian would marry someone wonderful and wealthy and they would have children, for whom Violet would be a doting grandmamma and adored by her family. But that was clearly not to be, and she needed to make the best of the situation.

The door opened, and Lillian reappeared, in a dress more suitable for a dance than a night in with her mother.

'I'm going out.' She picked up her cigarettes.

'If you leave this house before I am finished speaking to you, then I will have the locks changed in your absence and you will no longer have access.' Violet could not, of course, change the locks on a rented house, but that small detail did not seem to register with Lillian.

'What are you talking about?' she snapped.

'Sit.'

'I said I'm go—'

'And I said sit.' Violet enunciated each word slowly.

'Oh, for God's sake, what on earth is wrong now?' Lillian sighed and lit up a cigarette.

Violet calmly removed it from her lips, stubbed it out, and threw it in the fire.

Before Lillian could object, she began.

'Do not interrupt me, and listen carefully. This will not continue. I don't know what life you envisaged for yourself, and frankly, I don't care any longer what you do, but what I do know is that we will not fund it.'

'Is this because Beau is black?' Lillian began. 'It is, isn't it? You are such a bigot, Mother... He's over here fighting for us, for people like you, actually, and all you can do is—'

'I said let me finish.' Violet remained composed.

'For the record, I have no issue with Sergeant Lane. He is, at least, doing something productive, which is more than can be said for you. Your father died in chronic debt. He did not provide for you, nor me, nor Samuel. He cared nothing for the future of his family, and he dedicated his life, and all of our family money, to his own base desires. That is the fact. We have no money because your father drank it, gave it away, gambled it, and so on. So the first myth you need to disavow yourself of is that he has left you anything. He hasn't. We have paid his many debts, through the sale of all of the house contents and the live-stock. What remains, and the rent for the land, is essentially Samuel's, as he is the heir.

'Now, I do not believe that my son would see me destitute, so I will live frugally and I will survive, but you, well, you don't really feature. Your father left you nothing. I exist on the goodwill of my son, but, well, you and he are not exactly close. It is not my meanness, as you often claim, that is stopping you swanning around the hot spots of London, but the fact that you have no money. Nor do you have any skills or talents that could be converted into an income. Frankly, the company you are currently keeping is damaging your already slim prospects of making a decent marriage. You're on the shelf, you drink too much, your behaviour is promiscuous, and everyone knows about it. It would seem these factors combined have made you an unsuitable match for anyone of any value. You are soiled goods, Lillian, and you have neither face nor fortune with which to redeem yourself.'

Lillian took this home truth with incredulity.

'Have you gone stark staring mad? Is that it?' she demanded. 'Daddy always said you were ridiculous, but this... Look, we don't get along, Mother, we never have, and it was Daddy I loved. So I don't believe there is nothing for me. You're lying, and I know it, so just give me my share of the inheritance, and we'll part company. I don't think I want to have anything to do with you after those mean things you just said to me.'

Violet laughed.

'You are just like him. Head in the sand, refusing to face reality. Are you deaf? You don't get a share. His estate goes to Samuel; he made no provision for you. But I am not a heartless woman. This house is rented for six months, after which time I will leave England for India, where I will live out the rest of my life. If you can find someone to take you on in that time, then well and good, and I wish you the best of luck. If not, well, as I say, I am going to India and I won't be returning—or answering calls or letters demanding money.'

Lillian looked stricken.

'But, Mummy—'

'I'm Mummy now, am I?' Violet smiled. 'No, Lillian, let's not do that. You loved your father, and in his own stupid, selfish way, he loved you too, just not enough to ensure you were provided for, and that is the truth of the matter. Even if I were a wealthy woman, I would not continue to support this self-destructive lifestyle you have embarked upon. You drink too much, you are slovenly in your habits, and as for the American, well, I don't know what to say about that.'

'Did you speak to Sam about me?' Lillian asked.

'Samuel is busy being useful and serving his country, so no, I did not bother him with trivialities.'

Violet saw a malicious gleam in her daughter's eye.

'Ah, precious Samuel. You always adored him. But what if I told you, Mother dear, that the company he was keeping these days was also less than suitable?'

'Do you mean Kate Murphy? If so, it was she, Samuel and I had afternoon tea with today. A very hardworking girl, and I really admire her stance, coming over to defend our country.' Despite her horror at the relationship between Samuel and the Murphy girl, it felt good to have one up on Lillian.

'Oh, that's just priceless, and so typical of you. You hate the idea of me having a black boyfriend, but it's fine for precious Sam to be having it off with one of the servants! Good grief, Mother, how can you bear to live with yourself?'

Violet used every ounce of her inner strength not to retaliate.

'So we are clear: I will provide you with bed and board in the short term. During that time, you will not entertain here, and you will not give cause for scandal. You will behave with decorum and dignity, and while by now I don't care whether or not you marry, I would suggest for your own sake you apply yourself most studiously to the task of becoming engaged, as once the term of our arrangement is up, I will be leaving and taking what remains of my money with me.'

'Back to the glorious days of the Raj, Mother?' Lillian sneered. 'How foolish you are! Nothing is like it was, can't you see that? You will not be able to travel to India, you stupid woman! There is a war on, if you hadn't noticed! All non-essential travel is strictly forbidden.'

'Well, Lillian, getting away from you is essential for my mental well-being, so I think I will manage. Now, my plans are not your concern, but yours are. So I suggest you take your future seriously. London is not kind to those down on their luck, and I believe you have exhausted all lines of hospitality.'

Violet turned and left her daughter aghast at her new reality.

CHAPTER 25

*E*ve picked up the post from the mat, delighted to see a pair of letters from her sisters. Jack was gone to work. He had secured a foreman's position in the dockyard in the city. The money was better than labouring, and he was excited to tell her that they would soon have a deposit saved for a place of their own. Living with Mrs O'Neill was bearable, but Eve couldn't wait to get her own house. Her mother-in-law was still resentful of her son's marriage.

Eve tried her best to warm to the woman, try to understand things from her point of view, but it was very difficult. The woman wouldn't eat anything Eve cooked, and if Eve cleaned, then Mrs O'Neill did it again the same day. She was careful to never do these things in front of Jack, though, and Eve knew he was working as hard as he could, and her complaining wasn't going to help. When Jack was home, Mrs O'Neill doted on him and treated him like a little prince. It got on Eve's nerves, but it was Mrs O'Neill's house and he was her son. A fact that was made abundantly clear to her every single day in so many subtle ways.

She was so happy with Jack, and she loved snuggling up with him every night, but he left so early in the mornings and he took all the overtime he could to earn more money. She felt like she never saw him. She was trying to get a job, but so far nothing. One man had kindly explained he didn't take on newlyweds, as he had learned to his cost how he trained them up and then they were pregnant. She coloured when he said it, and he apologised for being so blunt, but he had a policy of only employing single girls or women past child-bearing years. Each place was the same, and Eve's days were long and lonely. She longed for the days in Robinswood. She missed her sisters and her parents.

Mam wrote every few days, and they seemed to be settling in to a mad house in Dublin where the children were absolute brats and the mother and father always out. Eve had laughed out loud at her mother's descriptions of her inventive methods of getting the children to behave. Funnily enough, both children had taken to her father, though he took none of their nonsense, and he had them digging and planting all day so they were too tired for tantrums in the evenings. She had a girl helping her, called Nancy, and she seemed nice, and sometimes Eve felt a pang of jealousy as she read about her, immediately berating herself for thinking their mother could ever replace them.

Kate and Aisling wrote less frequently, as stamps and paper were hard to come by, and by the sounds of it, they were so busy as well. So she was delighted to have a pair of letters from them today. Seeing the flimsy blue envelopes from her sisters landing on the mat every few weeks was a highlight in an otherwise long day.

She waved her mother-in-law off to Mass with relief, made herself a cup of tea, and sat at the kitchen table in the little terraced house with the letters from her sisters. Mrs O'Neill had remarked only this morning how Eve made the tea very strong and that if the rationing came in because of the Emergency she'd have to get used to much weaker tea.

She poured hot water on the leaves and took a bun out of the tin, relishing the hour alone.

She opened the first letter from Aisling.

Dear Eve,

Or should I call you Mrs O'Neill now? I still can't believe you're really married. Imagine, my sister a married woman, and I missed it. How are you and Jack? Good, I hope. No news as of yet, I assume? You know what I mean by news...

Life here is fine, exhausting though, and the food is vile, but the other girls are good craic and we have a laugh. I'm in the -------- which I really like, --------------------------- and all of that. It is tricky but very rewarding.

Eve hated when the censor scratched out so much of the letter. It was like trying to read in code. And so random, as well, allowing things in one letter, chopping them out in the next.

Kate is ------------------------- and wreaking her usual brand of havoc, I hear. You'd think I'd see her all the time, but I don't. We are billeted according to department, so she is in a different hut to me and the base is ----
--
----------------.

I'll let her tell you her big news, as I don't know which of our letters will reach you first. We'll post them together, but that doesn't mean anything. My news is that I've met someone. Well, it's early days, but he's very nice. He's from Bristol and has a really funny accent, but he grew up on a farm as well, so we have lots in common. His name is Mark, and he's a -------------------- which basically means he -----------------------

Eve groaned in frustration.

Anyway, we've gone out a few times, and he's good company and certainly treats me better than a stupid draper's son I could mention, though that wouldn't be hard.

Mam and Dad seem to be all right, do you think they are? It's hard to tell if they really are or if they're just saying it not to worry us. I wish more than anything we were all in our big cosy kitchen drinking tea and eating one of Mammy's fruitcakes. I swear I dream about food.

I'll write again next week. Be sure to tell me everything in your next letter. I tell Mark about you and Mammy and Daddy so much he says he feels like he knows you all.

Lots and lots of love,

Ais xxxx

Eve folded the letter and wiped a tear from her eye with the back of her hand. She wished they could be back in Robinswood too. Jack knew how much she missed her family and her home, but she didn't like to go on about it in case he thought she regretted marrying him or something, which she definitely didn't.

She'd got her period ten days ago, as well—four days late—and she had really hoped she was pregnant. She and Jack were married for nine months now, and month after month, nothing was happening. He told her not to worry, once they had their own place, it would all be fine, but she wondered what the problem was.

When she opened Kate's most recent letter, she saw to her dismay once again that most of it was censored. She tried to read it, but it was almost impossible. She felt like screaming. Kate wasn't going to give away any war secrets in a letter to her sister, for goodness sake!

She lay the page flat on the table and did her best.

Dear Eve,

I'm writing this ---------------------------- Even though its ----------
-------------------- because everywhere is so busy. I'm due back -----------
------------------------- and ------------------------------------- just
to tell you. Ais is threatening to blurt it out if I don't, but I don't want you
thinking it was the reason --

Anyway, the thing is, me ---
---he is -------------
--- and I don't get to see
him much -- in case
of ---

Are you shocked? I hope not. I know you liked him. Went to the Ritz for
afternoon tea with ----------------------------- and that was an experi-
ence, I can tell you. I thought she was going to explode when she saw me.
Anyway, Ais is also all loved up, a big hunky fella from ----------- called
Mark, but he's very nice. He's ---

I love you and I miss you.
Write back soon,
Kate xxx

. . .

EVE TRIED to piece together the words. It sounded like Kate had a boyfriend as well. Surely Kate didn't mean Samuel Kenefick? She reread the letter. That must be who she meant. And if the person they met in the Ritz was Lady Violet, then Eve could just picture her, fit to be tied with horror! Wait till she told Jack that! He'd roar with laughter. He loved her sisters, and while he appreciated Aisling's gentleness, he thought Kate was hilarious.

It wasn't that much of a surprise, if she thought about it. Kate and Sam had always had a special bond, and he was a thoughtful and sweet little boy. He had none of his mother's snobbishness, nor was he as spoiled as his sister. He was like a nicer version of the father, Austin. People said the Great War had changed how the world worked, that the social order was upset, never to be restored, but that wasn't really true in Ireland. The gentry still lived up in their ivory towers, and the ordinary people slaved for them and were supposed to feel grateful for the opportunity. But maybe this war would be the one to change it.

The idea that Kate and Samuel Kenefick, well, Lord Kenefick, if he were to have his proper title, would get together would have been inconceivable if the war hadn't happened and everyone was still at Robinswood. It explained why Kate had left. Eve felt the familiar pang of pain that her sister hadn't felt she could confide in her.

Lady Violet wouldn't like it, though, that was for sure. Eve wondered if their mother knew. Kate would be worried telling her, and as for Daddy, he'd surely be appalled.

EVE WAS GOING to write to them this morning, but she'd say nothing. It was Kate's story to tell, and anyway, she wasn't even completely sure that was who Kate meant, since so much of the letter was chopped.

She sipped her tea and started when she heard a key in the front door. Mass had only just started, so it couldn't be Jack's mother. Within seconds, she was swept up in a hug.

'Jack? I thought you were working! What are you doing home?' She giggled as he nuzzled her neck.

'I just had to see you. I was taking delivery of a load of coal, and I was taken by an overwhelming urge to see my wife, so I told the lads I needed to go up to the depot for some paperwork and jumped on Frankie Twohig's bike, and here I am.' He grinned, as if dossing off work in the middle of the morning was a perfectly reasonable thing to do.

'But what if they notice?' Eve asked. 'Won't you get in trouble?' Jack was so impetuous sometimes.

'Nah, they're all gone racing for the day. I'm the boss. Anyway, the coal is all that's due in, coal, coal, and more coal... It's exciting stuff. The boys will be sitting around playing cards until the next boat arrives later on. Anyway,' he murmured in her ear, 'enough dock chat. How about we go upstairs for a while, now that we have the place to ourselves?' He held her in his arms, and she melted into him.

'If your mother came back...' Eve really wanted to, but the idea of Jack's mother finding them in bed at ten in the morning, when Jack was supposed to be at work, made her blush to the roots of her hair.

'She won't. It's a first Friday, and there's a parish flower-arranging meeting after. She'll be ages. Come on, Eve, please?' His blue eyes twinkled with merriment, and his hair flopped over his forehead. He wore it longer than most men, and his friends teased him, but she told him she thought he looked gorgeous so he let it grow.

She grinned and allowed him to lead her by the hand up to their small bedroom.

They made love with abandon, without the terror of Mrs O'Neill overhearing. Afterwards, they lay in each other's arms, happy. Eve told him all about the letters from the girls, and he was delighted Aisling had met someone, even if he was English.

'Ais is so kind, she deserved so much better than that eejit Sean Lacey. But if you're right about Kate and the Lord of the Manor, that will cause some sparks to fly right enough.' He chuckled. 'Between your dad and his mam, they'll have their work cut out for them.'

They chatted for a while, and Eve admitted how much she missed her sisters.

Jack leaned up on one elbow.

'How about this: we nearly have a deposit saved, so I was thinking maybe by summer we'd have our own place. But we could dip into it and take a trip over to see them? Go by Dublin, and we could call to your mam and dad as well. I know it will mean we won't get a house of our own until the autumn, but we've lasted here nearly a year, and I know my mother drives you up the walls, I'm not blind, but you never complain, so what do you think? Would you rather keep on saving like mad and get our own home sooner, or will we take a little trip over to England? I don't mind, it's up to you.'

Eve's heart almost burst with love for him. He was the kindest, most generous man she'd ever met. Her immediate response was yes, she would love to see her family, but maybe that was being foolish.

'Talk to me, Eve, what's going on in there?' he whispered and kissed her temple.

'Well, I would give anything to see Mam and Daddy and the girls, but I also think that if we get our own place then maybe I'll get pregnant. Like, I know we, you know, here, but I don't know what the problem is...' Tears came unbidden, and all her fears poured out.

'Ah, Eve, don't cry, sweetheart, please. I don't mind at all. I have you, and you're all I need. And if we are destined to be parents, then we will be, and if not, then we'll make each other happy anyway.' He cradled her in his arms, kissing the top of her head.

'I'm sorry. I can't get a job, I can't get pregnant, I miss my family, and you are so good, and I love you so much, I feel terrible complaining.'

'That's it, I'm deciding.' He smiled. 'I'm going down to the Isisfallen office on Saturday and booking us two tickets over to England. I'll get a week's holidays from the yard, it will be quiet anyway, and we'll go up to Dublin and see your parents and then hop on the boat like a pair of international jetsetters and see what all the fuss is about over there.

And then we'll come home, and I'll work night and day if needs be to get us enough for our own place. And when we do, you'll be so busy making it lovely for us and attending to my every need'—he gave her a quick squeeze, and she smiled—'maybe God will send us a baby and maybe he won't, but either way, we are going to have the happiest life, and we'll be an old pair shuffling along the road when we're eighty, still in love. Right?'

She laughed at his enthusiasm. 'Right.'

'Now, I have to get back because Frankie goes for a pint at lunchtime and he doesn't know I took his bike, so I'll see you tonight, my darling girl. Don't worry about the baby thing. Sure, think of the craic we'll have trying.' He winked as he pulled on his clothes. He kissed her quickly once more, and then he was gone.

CHAPTER 26

*E*ve sat in the freezing-cold church, Jack's mother on one side of her, her parents on the other. A steady stream of people trooped past them, each one shaking her hand, saying they were sorry for her troubles. It was as if she was watching it all happen from underwater. She heard them, but she didn't register who they were.

Eventually, the stream of people stopped, and the altar boy rang the bell to start the Mass.

The priest, a kind man who had said soothing, meaningless words to her the night before in the small parlour of Mrs O'Neill's house, began.

'Dear Father in heaven, we are gathered here today to beseech of you to accept our brother Jack into the arms of your heavenly kingdom...'

Mam held her hand so tight it hurt, and Mrs O'Neill was cocooned in her own private grief.

The crowd answered the responses to the Mass, and Eve thought she probably should too, but no sound came out. She couldn't perform that most basic function. Three days since Jack died, three short days, and in some ways if felt like a lifetime ago.

The whole thing was a blur.

The policeman at the door, his cap in his hand, saying there had been an accident.

The dockyard owner, saying how very sorry he was, how Jack was the best foreman he ever had, how the chain snapped on the hoist, which caused the pallet of coal to fall, how it was nobody's fault, just a terrible accident.

The doctor saying Jack would have died instantly, there would have been no pain.

The endless streams of people coming to the house with food.

Billy was there, too big for the small front room. He'd loved Jack too, and his heart was breaking, but Eve couldn't help him. She was empty.

Mrs O'Neill had railed at her in her grief, screaming into Eve's face. If only he wasn't working so hard! He was exhausted, but he was trying to save up for a deposit—it was Eve's fault! Jack's aunt had pulled his mother away as Eve just stood there, frozen to the spot.

Afterwards, someone, she couldn't remember who, said she didn't mean it, it was the shock, but Eve just nodded. She couldn't respond.

The only thing that was real to her was her parents' arrival, her father's arms around her as she cried for the first time. He said nothing, no words of consolation or explanation, he just stood, like a huge oak tree, and held her as she wept. Her mother made her eat and put her into bed, then lay beside her in the dark, rubbing her hair just like she used to do when she was a little girl.

It happened the day he came home in the morning to make love to her. The day they lay in bed, talking about their future, about visiting Aisling and Kate. She never saw him again.

Jack is gone, he's gone, I won't ever see him again. The words thundered around in her brain like a train on a track, never going anywhere except in circles.

The priest droned on. There were prayers and hymns, and then Daddy and Billy and some of his friends went up and they lifted Jack's coffin onto their shoulders.

Eve and Mrs O'Neill and Mammy walked behind, and Eve knew

all eyes were on her, but she didn't care. She felt nothing but a burning in the pit of her stomach, like acid was eating her up.

It was less than a year since she'd walked up the aisle in Kilthomand church and promised to love Jack for the rest of her life. How could she now be walking down an aisle after his coffin?

She could not do this—she just could not allow them to put her Jack, her lovely, lively Jack into a dark hole in the ground and leave him there. All the religion she learned as a child in school, that it's only a body, a shell, that our souls go home to God in heaven, none of that seemed relevant to her, or to Jack. She wanted to be with him, wherever he was, she wanted to be there. Not here, surrounded by people who didn't understand.

She wanted to scream, to drag him away from all of them in their black clothes and solemn faces. He shouldn't be here! He was funny and light-hearted and all this misery and cloud would have made him run a mile! She looked up, into the faces of the congregation who watched in silence as they followed the coffin out of the church. She didn't know most of them.

The graveyard was cold and windy on the February day. Eve felt so cold she could not imagine ever feeling warm again. Her parents stood on either side of her as the priest began again, with more prayers, sprinkling holy water all over the coffin, into the grave. Eve stared straight ahead of her. She could not look down into the hole where they planned to put Jack.

Mrs O'Neill broke down, sobbing and howling like an animal in pain. She cared nothing for what those around her thought. When Jack's father had been shot, she'd clung to her boy like a lifeline, and now he was gone. She could not cope with the pain.

Eve watched the older woman being led from her son's final resting place by her relatives and wondered if she had the right to be the chief mourner. She had only had Jack for such a short time compared to his mother. There were no tears now. She was numb. Freezing cold, empty, hollowed out.

Then they were back in the house, with people calling all day, offering their condolences. Mrs O'Neill was up in bed. She had been given something by the doctor to help her sleep, and Isabella managed the food and drinks for the visitors. Dermot never left his daughter's side, managing conversations, answering for her.

Eventually, it was night, and the last of the callers went home. Jack's aunt Catherine told them Mrs O'Neill was asleep and that she would be back in the morning to check on her. Then it was just Eve and her parents.

'Will you try to have a bowl of soup, pet?' Isabella asked her.

'I can't, Mam, I can't swallow,' Eve whispered. Even the effort of talking was too much.

'You should try, Eve.' Her father was gentle. 'You need to keep your strength up.'

'Why, Daddy? Why do I need strength?' She twisted her handkerchief around in her hands. 'I don't want to be strong, I want to be with Jack. I want to be above in that cold grave beside him. I...'

Dermot got down on his hunkers in front of her and held both her hands in his, locking eyes with his daughter.

'My darling Eve, Jack would want you to live. He loved you with all his heart, I know he did, and he would want you to live. To go on without him, and make a life for yourself. It's not going to be easy, it is going to be torture for the first while, and every day will feel like hell on earth. But it will get easier, and you will never forget him, never stop loving him, that won't change, but you'll find a way to go on without him, and please God, you'll meet him again, when it's your turn to go to heaven.'

'How do you know?' she asked, her eyes fixed on his. 'I don't think I'll be able to breathe again, let alone live a life.'

Dermot sighed and tucked a stray strand of her hair behind her ear.

'I know because I've seen a lot of heartache, a lot of death, back during the war, especially of young people like Jack. And I was there watching as their loved ones carried on. That's how I know.

'Eve, I have never lied to you in your whole life, not once, so trust me now. You will survive his loss. It will hurt like hell for so long, and you'll wonder if you'll ever smile again, but I swear to you, just ride it out, and me and your mother will be right beside you as you do. For now, don't think about the future, just manage each minute, each hour. Nobody expects anything more of you. Just breathe in and out, eat and drink what your mother puts in front of you, sleep as much as you can, and don't worry about anything else. These coming weeks and months will be like a dream, or a nightmare, but we're here, and you'll be all right. And one day, we'll all see that beautiful smile of yours again, the one that made Jack fall in love with you.'

'I don't think I can, Daddy,' she whispered.

'You can, my love, I know you can. And when you can't, I'll be here, and you can fall into my arms just as you've done since you were born, and I'll carry you.'

Isabella stood at the door, watching Dermot with Eve, and she had never loved him more. He was their rock, strong, silent sometimes, but unwaveringly loyal.

An hour later, Eve was sleeping in the bed she'd shared with Jack, the blankets pulled up to her chin. Isabella watched her, thinking she looked so young and so vulnerable.

'Will we go down and make a cup of tea, and then you can lie down with her and I'll sit here on the chair?' Dermot whispered.

Isabella nodded and crept downstairs behind her husband. It felt odd to sit quietly in the O'Neills' kitchen, but they had nowhere else to go, and besides, they were not going to leave Eve. Elena and Thomas had been very nice about them taking off with no notice once they knew the circumstances. Thomas had lent them a car, and they had even offered Eve a home with them until she got herself sorted out. Dermot had admitted to Isabella that his worries about Thomas having an ulterior motive were way off the mark. They genuinely just needed household staff, and it was working out well.

Dermot moved quietly around the tiny kitchen, gathering cups and a jug of milk. He made tea and handed Isabella a cup.

'I suppose we'll bring her back to Dublin with us?' Isabella asked as she sipped her tea. 'The Hamilton-Brookses won't mind, and she can't stay here. I daresay they would employ her if we asked.'

Dermot sighed. They sat at either side of the kitchen table. 'I don't know, Bella, she may not want to come. All her memories of Jack are here, and his mother...'

'Well, she can't stay here with her. I mean, I know the poor woman's heartbroken, and who can blame her, but Eve can't be around that day in day out. She blames Eve. She makes out like she's the only one grieving. And it's not like Eve is deserting her. She has loads of family. No, I think we take Eve back with us tomorrow. We can't stay here, and the Hamilton-Brooks' were good to let us go, but God knows what kind of havoc is being wreaked while we're gone. Eve needs us, and we have to go back, so she'll just have to come with us, where she will be minded and safe. Though, since the Germans tried to bomb Dublin last month, it's hard to know where is safe these days.'

Dermot sipped his tea. 'I suppose you're right. I wish we could have spoken to Aisling or Kate. She needs them as well now. We all need to be together. It's not right that they're over there.'

'I know, I wrote to them as soon as we heard, and Nancy said she'd post it right away, so they should have it soon, but I agree, she needs them as much as us now. Maybe they could come home, now that we're settled kind of in Dublin. Maybe we could organise jobs for them, get a house—'

'Bella, love, you know they can't do that. That's not how the British army works. They are signed up for the duration now, come what may. No, they may be allowed back on compassionate leave or something, for a visit, but to be honest with you, I doubt even that will happen.'

'Oh, Der, this is such a mess. The girls gone, Jack too, and poor Eve, she is so broken. My darling girl, I hate to see that pain in her eyes.'

Dermot leaned over and put his hand on hers.

'I know, but we have to keep it together for her sake. At least there is space at the Hamilton-Brookses'. She can have that little room off ours, and we'll take it from there, I suppose.'

* * *

THE FOLLOWING MORNING, Eve sat in a trance-like state as her mother packed her things.

'Are you sure you're all right to come up to Dublin with us, Eve?' Dermot asked. He wasn't as sure as Bella that they were doing the right thing.

'I don't know, I...I need to be with ye, so maybe I'll go up for a while...' Eve seemed incapable of making any decisions.

They left as Mrs O'Neill was being attended once more by the doctor. She raised no objection to Eve's departure, and it was an awkward and tense moment as the two women said goodbye. Each was stricken by her own anguish and sorrow, but it was as if neither of them could intrude on the other's heartache.

As her parents walked her down the street towards the car, Eve stopped.

'Can we go to the grave before we go?' she asked quietly.

Dermot nodded.

'Of course we can, pet.'

They walked up to the cemetery, only a stone's throw from where Jack had lived.

At the gates, Eve turned to her parents.

'Can I do this alone, please? I just want to talk to him on my own.'

Isabella held Dermot's hand, and her heart broke as she watched her little girl walk in the direction of the newly filled in grave.

Eve stood at the foot of the grave and just stared at the rich brown soil. Some flowers were laid on top, and a wooden cross with *Jack O'Neill, Died 24th February 1941* on a small brass plaque. She remembered Billy telling her he had done it. Poor Billy. He'd loved Jack too and had been so happy to have his friend home when they moved to Cork. He even understood that Jack was a married man now and didn't complain when Jack couldn't go out with him like they used to do. He often called to Eve and Mrs O'Neill in the evenings when Jack was doing overtime, and he always made them smile.

Eve touched the little cross. She would organise a proper headstone later. She could use the deposit money they'd saved.

Eventually, she spoke, her voice sounding raspy to her own ears.

'Jack, it's me. I don't know what to say except I wish I could talk to you properly. I wish none of this ever happened, that you were not under that stupid hoist. I wish I'd begged you to stay at home with me instead of letting you go back to deliver Frankie Twohig's bike to him. I wish we had all the time in the world, time to get old together and walk arm in arm when we're eighty like you said we would, but we won't have that. Because you're gone and I'm here and I don't know how I'm going to do this without you, Jack. I know we're not even married a year, but you were the other half of me. I feel like I'm cut in half, blood pouring out of me, without you.'

'Mam and Dad are taking me back to Dublin with them. I don't want to leave you, but I can't stay. Your mother is in such pain, and I can't help her, and having me there is not what she wants, so I'll go with them to Dublin. To be honest, I can't really think straight. All I know is I'll have to go on without you and I don't want to.'

Eve would have given anything just to lie down on the cold earth and to sink down, down into the deep grave beside him, but she glanced over to the gate and there were her parents, loving and strong and doing their best, and she knew they were worried about her. Daddy was right, she would just have to try.

'Bye, my darling. If you are up in heaven, please help me to survive this. Be with me in whatever way you can, and I'll try to keep going. I love you, and I always will.'

She rested her hand on the cross and ran her fingers along the brass plaque before turning and walking away to join her parents.

CHAPTER 27

'We'll have to go home. They'll have to let us go when we explain what happened.' Kate looked forlorn as she held the letter from her mother.

Kate, Aisling, Mark and Sam were sitting in a Lyons Corner House sipping weak tea. Sam had bought buns, but they sat untouched. Jack was dead over three weeks, but they'd only gotten the letter that morning. It had arrived at the base earlier, but some mix-up meant it didn't get delivered to their hut. They had planned for weeks to have all four of them off for an afternoon to the pictures, but the letter changed everything.

The two men exchanged a glance.

'Kate, sweetheart, they won't let you,' Sam said gently. 'I already asked my CO, he's a good old sort, and I explained what happened, but they said since last month all WAAFs are subject to RAF discipline and that means leave when you're given it and not before. Compassionate leave will only be considered for the death of a parent or spouse or child, and even then, they might not grant it. I'll keep trying, of course I will, someone of my father's old circle might help us out, but it could be a while.'

Mark held Aisling's hand as she sat, pale and stricken.

'I just can't believe it. Jack. Dead. It just doesn't make any sense.'

'What if we just go? Just leave anyway without their stupid permission! We're Irish, not English, so what can they do?' Kate was lashing out in her frustration, and other diners were starting to look in her direction. The Blitz was raging every single night, so people were exhausted and nerves fraught. The city was almost in ruins, reduced to piles of rubble where once magnificent buildings stood.

Biggin Hill base had been the subject of a bombing mission the previous August, and both Aisling and Kate were lucky not to have been on the base that day. The WAAFery, the cookhouses, and several of the mess areas were destroyed, but Kate was a driver and had been taking her CO to a meeting at Whitehall at the time, while Aisling had been in the underground map room. They'd written and told their parents they were fine without ever mentioning the raid. It would have been censored out even if they did. But after that, they both knew for sure this was a very serious thing they'd gotten themselves into.

Any talk that was deemed unpatriotic from anyone, especially someone in uniform, would be dealt with most severely, but Sam had many years' experience of the fiery Kate and knew he could talk her down.

'You know you won't do that, Kate, desert, not now,' Sam said quietly.

She sighed. 'I know, I know, but I just need to go home. We both do. We need to be with Eve. You don't understand what it's like; we're, like, triplets or something we're so close, and it's my fault we are over here. I dragged Ais along, but it was my idea, and now, when our family need us, we can't be with them.'

Aisling looked up. 'Stop that, Kate. I came over here of my own accord. I'm not some kind of imbecile being dragged around anywhere—'

Kate glared at her sister. 'I didn't mean that, I just meant—'

'Girls, if I may,' Mark's soft west-country accent interrupted, and Sam shot him a look of gratitude. 'Can we just think about this rationally?' He cleared his throat.

'How or why you two got here is sort of beside the point now. The air force won't let you go back to Ireland—that's a fact about which we can do nothing. Even if you took off, went Absent Without Leave, then you'd both be in all sorts of hot water. And anyway, you have no travel permits, so you'd be lucky to get beyond Hammersmith, let alone all the way to Ireland. Now, you need to see your sister, of course you do. So, if it's impossible for you two to go there, maybe she could come here?'

All three of them stared at him.

'But, Mark, Eve is distraught, why on earth would she want to come over here, where Hitler is bombing us every night, where we have nowhere for her to stay?' Kate asked. 'She's not going to join up, and I don't think she'd be able for any work, even if she did want to come...'

'I think he means for a visit, just to get a break,' Aisling said slowly. 'And we could at least see her when we were off. Doesn't Vera—you know the girl in the officers' mess, her sister runs a boarding house near Farleigh. That's only on the other side of the base. Maybe Eve could stay there if we could get her over?'

'I think that's a great idea,' Sam announced. 'I would say my mother and Lillian could put her up, but less stress is what she needs, not more.' He gave half a smile, and Kate reciprocated weakly.

'Well, given how horrified she was to discover you and I are together, I don't think landing another Murphy on her doorstep would be ideal, no,' Kate agreed. 'I don't know how Mam and Daddy would feel about it though. Well, I do—Dad will go mad and say absolutely not under any circumstances, and Mam will try to talk him around if Eve wants to come.'

'But Eve is a grown woman, a widow now, the poor thing, surely, she can decide for herself?' Mark asked.

Kate and Aisling exchanged a sad little smile.

'You don't know our dad,' Kate said. 'He's just very protective, and I can't imagine how he'll be now. Poor Eve, I still can't take it in.' Her eyes shone with unshed tears for her funny, handsome brother-in-law.

'Look,' Sam interrupted, 'why don't you both write, this minute? We'll catch the last post if we're quick. Invite her, and your parents too, if they want. No arguments, tell her I'm paying for the tickets.'

Kate looked up. 'We can't let you do that—'

Sam raised his hand to stop her objections.

'You can, and you will. Not because I love you, which I do, hopelessly, but because my family owe yours. You've taken care of us and our home for so long, it's what my father would have done, and I want to do it now, in his memory. So please, let's send the fare along with the letter. I'll run along ahead to the post office and get a postal order. We can enclose it in the letter.'

Mark stood up as well.

'I'll go with you, let the girls write their letter in peace.'

Aisling looked up at him, with his reddish-blond hair and ruddy complexion, and realised this is what it was like when you were in a relationship with someone who cared about you. Despite the war and destruction, the fear all around them day and night, how was it possible that both she and Kate had met men that made them so happy?

To add to it, they got along really well, Mark and Sam, so all four of them palled around together, and it was effortless. Aisling had almost forgotten that Kate's Sam was actually Lord Kenefick, and that she and Kate were only the servants' kids. The war changed all of that. Everyone, no matter who you were, was pulling in the same direction.

Aisling even felt a patriotic duty to the WAAFs now. She'd do her job and see it out and make sure Hitler and the rest of the Nazis got what was coming to them. Her job was in the map room, plotting coordinates and delivering reports of enemy and Allied movement, and it was a very responsible position. Meanwhile, Kate was in the driving pool—she could be called upon at any moment to drive the top brass around the city. In true Kate style, she'd lied on her application and said she could drive, when all she'd ever driven was the ancient old tractor at Robinswood. Sam had borrowed a car from a pal of his when he'd heard she was assigned to the driving pool and taught her in one afternoon. Aisling had had her doubts about Sam and Kate, but time had proved her wrong. All four of them were united in their determination to do whatever they could to defeat Hitler. And, if anything, the Blitz reinforced that resolve. Mr Churchill was so honest and blunt, but he believed it could be done, and so did everyone in uniform and out. Aisling knew her father would never understand it, but it was how she felt and she knew Kate did too. It felt good to be useful, to feel like what you were doing was actually achieving something. Even with the bombing and the rationing and the exhaustion, life had been good—up to the arrival of today's letter.

The two men left, and Kate rooted in her handbag for a notebook and pen.

'You write it, you've got better writing,' she said as she pushed the dog-eared notebook at Aisling. 'The nuns always said I was terrible at writing.'

'All right, what will we say? I just don't know what to write, Kate. How do we express our sadness?' Aisling felt the tears well up, and Kate sighed and took the notepad back.

She wiped her eyes almost angrily with the back of her hand and began writing.

Darling Eve,

We are heartbroken. That's all we can say. Me and Ais are sitting here in a cafe in London, and we would give anything, literally anything to be there with you. We can't bring our darling Jack back, we wish we could, but we could stand beside you, our darling sister, and help you. He adored you, and you him. Anyone that looked at you two together could see it.

There are no words we can say to make this hurt less, I know, but we could just talk or go for a walk or something. We are including a postal order for a ticket for you to come over here for a visit. The Air Force won't give us leave, so if you are anyway able, even if you can only barely manage it, please visit us. Come alone or bring Mammy and Daddy, whichever is better for you. A girl we know, her sister runs a nice boarding house near our base, and between me and Ais and of course Sam and Mark, who really want to help as well, we'll take really good care of you. Please come. We want to see you.

Ps. Don't worry. Sam gave us the money for the ticket so we didn't rob a bank or anything

We love you.

Kate and Ais xxx

KATE HANDED it to Aisling for her to check, and Aisling just nodded and gave her younger sister an encouraging smile.

'That's exactly what we wanted to say. Those nuns hadn't a clue.'

They stood and put their coats on and went to the post office, where the boys were waiting. Sam handed Kate an envelope that already contained the postal order for far more money than the cost of three tickets.

She said nothing but placed the letter inside, licked the envelope, and put it in the postbox.

They walked away, hand in hand, down the street, Aisling and Mark behind.

'Thanks for doing that,' Kate said, looking up at Sam.

'You're welcome. I hate to think of Eve so sad. She was always such a kind person. And I met Jack that time I came home on leave, and he seemed like such a nice chap.'

'He was, great craic, you know? Always up to a bit of mischief, no more than myself. He was cracked about Eve the minute he laid eyes on her. She was really hurt when we took off without her—she wrote and told us. But Jack was the reason we never told her. If we had, she would have had to choose us or him, and knowing Eve as we do, and with her being the eldest, she'd have felt like she should go with us, to take care of us. We didn't want to make her change her life, and she loved Jack so much. I think, reading between the lines, she was a bit lonely in Cork, stuck in the house all day with his mother, who was a bit of a trial by all accounts, and him out working so hard to get them a place of their own. Eve is fiercely independent and would have hated to be the little housewife. Over here, you learn not to think too far ahead, but back at home, everything seemed so mapped out, you know? I just thought Jack and Eve would live happily ever after, and she'd have a few babies, all of that. But look how much has happened in a year. We could never have guessed when we were all at home how things would go.'

'All because we left Robinswood.'

Kate knew Sam felt awful about how her family had been made homeless by their departure.

'Ye had to, though, with the debts and everything, didn't ye?' Kate asked. In general, they didn't discuss his inheritance or Robinswood, apart from reminiscing. That conversation would inevitably bring them to Violet, and they both knew how she felt about Kate. Of course, it hurt Sam to admit it, so Kate never brought up the topic.

'Yes, I suppose we did, but maybe if I'd stepped in sooner or something...' Sam shook his head. 'I don't know. My mother wittering on about my father's debts just bored me. She is kind of irritating. It was like she resented my father for their entire marriage for taking her away from her perfect life in India. She never liked Ireland, never saw it as home the way my father and I did—and I still do, actually. I love Robinswood. I wish I'd fought harder now—for your family, if not for mine.'

Kate squeezed his hand.

'Well, it's not sold. I mean, you could always go back, you know, after the war.'

'On my own?' he asked.

Kate got flustered. She would hate him to think she was angling. Enough people would think she was a gold digger as it was, without Sam thinking it too.

'Well, you are Lord Kenefick, and it is your place. Why wouldn't you go back?' She deliberately skirted round the question.

'Robinswood wouldn't be Robinswood without the Murphys,' Sam said. 'Your family is as much a part of that place as mine is. You are Robinswood for me, always have been. You know, Kate, when I came home and first saw you, there on the bridge where we always sat, you took my breath away.'

'What do you mean came home and first saw me? You've known me your whole life.'

'I know, but you were just a wild kid all those years. But that time I came home in uniform, well, you were different, more grown up. I hadn't been home for a year or more, and all of a sudden, the girl I used to play with, the one with the cut knees and the tangled hair, she was gone, and in her place was this beautiful woman. Look, I know my mother isn't thrilled about you and I, and your father will probably try to murder me, but you are the best thing to ever happen to me, Kate. When I'm flying, and I get panicked, I just picture your face and it calms me, reminds me that I need to do my job and get back to you. I know the world will look at us and think they know what's going on, but we know the truth. This isn't a fling for me, Kate, or a wartime romance. This is, for me at least, the real thing.' He coloured, embarrassed at his outpouring of emotion.

It felt strange to have their relationship go from constant joking and teasing, as they'd done their whole lives, to something more sincere.

'I think I love you, Samuel Kenefick.'

She'd never said those words to him, though he had often proclaimed his love for her. But a part of her didn't believe someone like him would be allowed to fall in love with someone like her. And meeting his mother that day at the Ritz had confirmed it.

But Jack's death changed everything. Nobody was guaranteed a tomorrow, and in London, during the Blitz, this being anyone's last day was a distinct possibility.

He stopped and turned to face her, a look she'd never seen on his face.

'I KNOW I never said it before,' she went on. 'I was afraid, I suppose, that your mother or your sister would talk you out of it, but now, it feels like we have no time to waste. Anything can happen to anyone at any time. Look at poor Jack. And you, flying night after night. I look up and think, is tonight the night one of them is going to get you? And I try to be brave, but sometimes...' To her horror, she started to cry, right there in the street.

He drew her into his arms, her face pressed to the coarse fabric of his uniform.

'I love you too, Kate Murphy, I always have. When we were making dams with logs when we were children, when I taught you how to ride a bike, each summer I came home from school, you were there, and everything was more fun when you were involved. I can't picture my life without you.'

He released her a little and tilted her chin up to look her in the eyes.

'Marry me,' he whispered.

Everything—her parents, Eve, Jack, Robinswood, his mother, all the reasons why marrying Sam was a bad idea—disappeared.

'I will,' she said.

CHAPTER 28

'*A* telegram for Mr D Murphy.' The telegram boy stood at the kitchen door, knowing from experience there was a chance of a bun and a drink after his long cycle if Isabella met him.

'I'll take it, Jamsie. Will you have a drink of squash and a slice of brack?' Isabella asked as she took two loaves of soda bread out of the oven.

'Thanks, Mrs M, I'd love it.' He sat down, delighted.

Dermot appeared and took the telegram from his wife, scanning the short message.

Am in Dublin for a day or two. Pint in Hennessy's 8pm tonight?
Marlene Dietrich

Dermot grinned. Isabella looked over his shoulder as she delivered the snack to the boy.

'Who is Marlene Dietrich?' she asked.

The telegram boy was tucking into his cake and drink, so Dermot led Isabella to the pantry off the kitchen.

'It's Oskar. I wrote to him when we didn't have a plan for after Robinswood, asking if he had any ideas. I didn't expect him to come over, though it will be great to see him again.'

Her face said it all.

'Oskar Metz? And we were only talking about him! How do you know it's him, though?'

Dermot chuckled, and Isabella realised she hadn't heard him laugh in so long.

'One night, in the winter of 1921, we were out on a job, freezing cold and wet, a horrible dirty night, and we were laughing about which woman would warm a man up better, Greta Garbo or Marlene Dietrich. Of course, he said Marlene Dietrich, but I said that was his German side saying that, and anyway we had a good laugh about it.

'We had a lot of code words, Oskar and I, and it saved our skins on several occasions. Like, if either of us was suspicious of the company we were in, IRA or civilian, we used to say, *'Tis only a night for the fire.* One night, we were in a pub, meeting someone, and Oskar overheard a fella in there talking to someone outside, so immediately he says the code phrase, though 'twas a lovely summer's evening. We both burst out laughing like it was a joke, but the message was clear. I wonder, though, how would he know to find me here?'

'Well, I suppose if he went to Robinswood looking for you, they have our forwarding address. They might have told him?'

'I suppose so.' Dermot smiled. 'Anyway, I'll get all his news tonight. I wonder what has him back here? Especially now, getting travel papers and all of that is really difficult with the Emergency. But he must have managed it.'

Isabella smiled, glad to see her husband so happy.

'From what I remember about him, he could charm the birds out of the trees, so I'm not one bit surprised the normal rules don't apply to him.'

The day went quickly, and Dermot jumped on the tram into town that evening. It was the first time he'd been away from Eve since Jack died, but Isabella assured him she would keep her busy darning that evening. It felt good to get out of the house.

Dermot rarely drank in pubs, so much of his work with the IRA was done in them, listening and gathering intelligence. He had no interest now. In lots of ways, it felt like another lifetime, like something that had happened to someone else.

He and Oskar had gone on many missions together, trusted each other completely. Oskar was committed to Irish independence; he wanted his country free, so badly. Apart from his surname, there was no way anyone would know he was half German.

Dermot got off the tram and made for the bar. Hennessy's lit up the street. It looked so warm and welcoming, the yellow light spilling out onto the street.

When he

reached the bar, he scanned the place and ordered a pint of stout. He was about to sit at the bar when he spotted Oskar in a booth. He looked older, but apart from that, he hadn't changed much. He was shorter than Dermot but stocky and well-built—just as Dermot remembered him—and impeccably dressed in a double-breasted charcoal suit. His hair was still blond, though with more silver in it than Dermot remembered, and brushed back off his high forehead. His blue eyes twinkled with merriment.

Dermot brought his pint over, Oskar stood up, and they embraced.

'Well, there you are, like a bad penny, I thought we'd seen the last of you.' Dermot grinned.

'It's great to see you, Dermot, my old friend! I can't believe it's been —what? Seventeen years? You look the same.'

'It was 1923 you took off for Germany, I suppose. My God, we're old men, Oskar. Who'd have given us odds on getting to this age at all? Tell me, how are things with you?'

'Oh, good—well, apart from this bloody war of course, but good enough. How about you, and Isabella and the girls?' Oskar took a sip of his drink. 'I went to Robinswood, but they told me you were here.'

'That's right.' Dermot shook his head. 'The Keneficks left, so we had to move on. Charlie Warren is renting the place, but he'd rather rot than give me work, and old Austin died, remember him?'

'I do. I lived on his food and drink for many years, unbeknownst to him.' Oskar winked.

'That's right. Yerra, he was all right. I always thought he was kind of on our side. Not like some of the English landlords, he was happy enough for us to take over, so long as he got his whiskey and a few days out at the races. He wasn't the worst. But anyway, his son Samuel is the new lord, and he's saddled with a load of debts. Old Austin liked the high life, drinks for the house and all of that, and he frittered every shilling of his money away. So they had to close up the house, sell everything, and rent the land to settle his accounts. And now Lady Kenefick is back in England, along with the daughter, and the boy is in the RAF.'

'And you and the girls without a home?' Oskar shook his head sympathetically. Dermot noticed a slight German accent to his English that had never been there before.

'More or less,' Dermot said. 'My eldest girl, Eve, sure, she was only small when you left, she got married last year, but her husband was killed a few weeks back. She's in an awful state, the poor girl, so myself and Isabella are working here in a house and they said she could come and stay. It tears the heart out of my chest to see her so miserable.'

'Poor Eve, that's terrible.' Oskar shook his head. 'What happened to him?'

'An accident at work. Actually, you knew his father, Mick O'Neill, from Cork. He was shot in 1923 by the Free Staters...'

'I do, of course I remember him. My God, and Eve married his boy?'

'She did, and he was a grand lad altogether. The poor divil, a pallet of coal broke loose and landed on him.'

'That is dreadful. Maybe I can see her before I leave. I would love to meet her and her sisters and Isabella again. I bet they grew up into beautiful young ladies, if they take after their mother.' He winked again.

'They certainly did, with minds of their own too.' Dermot paused. He felt ashamed to tell his friend, the man with whom he had fought bitterly for Irish independence, about Aisling and Kate. When they joined up, he'd suppressed his hurt and disappointment and kept telling himself that they didn't know. They took Irish independence for granted, they had no idea what had to be done to free their country, the unspeakable lengths people like him and Oskar had to go to.

Still, how easily they put on a British uniform tore at his soul. He'd tried to hide his frustration and regret from Isabella, she had enough to deal with worrying about them, but the thought of admitting where the girls were to his friend was hard.

'And Aisling and Kate?' Oskar asked. 'They are not married surely?'

'No, not yet. They... Well, there's no way to say this...' Dermot took a sip of his drink. 'They joined the British Air Force, took off in the middle of the night. Myself and Isabella knew nothing about their plans. Kate has a romance going with young Samuel Kenefick, Austin's boy, and he's a wing commander in the RAF, and Aisling was kind of disappointed in love as they say, by a total eejit back in Kilthomand, so she followed her sister, and next thing we knew, they were signed up.'

Oskar smiled slowly at his old friend.

'Life is so strange, isn't it? Who would have thought we'd have made it through those years? We had some scrapes, some near misses, but here we are. And you know, Dermot, we were young once, full of adventure and fun, and yes, it was hard, but we loved it. That's the truth, and God himself could not have convinced us to stop. You and Isabella are strong people, so of course you reared strong-willed children. Your girls don't know what it was like for us—they just see adventure and romance and medals. It is the same in Germany. They cannot wait to sign up, follow Herr Hitler to the death, but they don't know. Their fathers and mothers do. They saw it all the last time. But you cannot explain that to young people. They don't want to hear it.'

Dermot nodded, glad his friend wasn't horrified.

'What about you? Did you marry? Have children?'

A shadow crossed Oskar's face, and Dermot immediately regretted asking.

After a pause, Oskar said, 'Yes, I married. Brigitta, she was killed last year in Berlin. An RAF bomb, direct hit on the library where she worked. We didn't have any children.'

'Oskar, I'm so sorry to hear that... I...' Irrational as it was, Dermot felt in some way responsible. The very organisation that employed his daughters had killed his friend's wife.

Oskar shrugged. 'It is war, terrible things happen in war, and nobody is immune. You and I know that better than most. But my Brigitta, she was wonderful. I always told her I would bring her home, to meet you and Isabella and my mother's family. She laughed because I always called Ireland home. That day, she wasn't even supposed to be working, she was covering for a friend whose son was getting married. It was just really bad luck. Some people are lucky, others not. It's just how it is.' Though his words were logical and circumspect, the pain of her loss was in his eyes.

'That's true,' Dermot said. 'I wouldn't be sitting here now if it wasn't for you. You saved my skin more than once.'

Oskar chuckled. 'Well, you did the same for me. Those were the times we lived through. But I am glad you are alive and well, my friend, I'm glad you are.' He raised his glass in a silent toast.

'So, what has you in Ireland?' Dermot asked. 'I thought you couldn't get travel papers for love nor money?'

'I did not come by, shall we say, traditional routes.' Oskar winked. 'Though, I have an Irish passport. I got one of the first ones in 1923, saying I was a citizen of the Irish Free State, and then I applied for one in 1939, on that first day that you could, for the new ones that have no reference whatsoever to the King of England. That was a happy day when I got that. Brigitta and I went to the park, had a picnic, and I got drunk of course and started singing rebel songs, and she had to bundle me in a taxi. But seeing it there in black and white, a nation of our own, not answerable to anyone, it meant something, you know?' Oskar flagged down the barman and ordered two more drinks.

'I do.' Dermot nodded. 'Every time I see a green pillar box, or a guard, or the harp on a letter, symbols of our nation, it moves me. Though, Churchill is putting savage pressure on Dev to get us to join the Allies.'

'He is a wily old goat, that Churchill, but he is mad if he thinks the Irish would ever throw their lot in with them, after everything they did to us. It won't ever happen.'

'I hope not, anyway.' Dermot shook his head. 'I mean, what did we fight for if we are just going to go running to back them the minute they crook their finger? No, this is their mess, and they may solve it themselves. Anyway, you never said, what are you doing here?'

The barman delivered their drinks to the table, and Oskar waited for him to leave before answering Dermot in a hushed voice.

'I'M HERE to do a job. I seem to have spent my life fighting the English, and here I am again. This war must be brought to an end, it cannot drag on and on like the last time. We believe that there are people here who can help us bring about the end, quickly and with minimum bloodshed. That's why I'm here. To deliver weapons to them in return for their assistance. I'm overseeing the operation.' Oskar's eyes never left Dermot's face.

Dermot was shocked. Oskar was working for the Germans. He'd heard rumours of contacts between them and the IRA, but the Germans would be very foolish to trust the IRA to deliver anything in their current state. Dev was doing everything in his power to crush them after their bombing campaigns on the British mainland, and they were in disarray.

'You... You're a spy?' Dermot asked quietly.

'I work with the Abwehr, yes. Look, Dermot, I don't like Hitler any more than anyone else, but he talks a lot of sense, you know? Germany was brought to its knees after the last war, blamed for it, though we were not the only ones. And then someone like Hitler comes along, he fixes the economy, puts everyone back to work. Suddenly, we have cars and holidays, and we get to hold our heads up again. It's not surprising he is so popular. Anyway, we need to make decent contacts within the IRA, not hothead kids, but smart men who know what they're doing. The truth is we have no interest in invading Ireland. Ireland staying neutral suits us just fine, but we do need some intelligence from here—weather, observations, to bring agents in and out. And I said I knew just the man. So, I'm asking, will you step into the breech, as Shakespeare said, with your old comrade one more time, so we can hopefully end this nonsense, then both retire and live a life of peace?'

Dermot was acutely aware of the fact that Oskar had saved his life many times, and that his wife had died because of an RAF bomb, the organisation that employed his daughters. Dermot was also a republican through and through and would never really forgive the British for what they did to his country and people.

But this was too much. His days of fighting were over, and he wanted no part of it. He had no issues with the German people, but if even half the things the world was saying about Hitler were true, then he was a very nasty piece of work indeed.

People escaping from occupied areas of Europe were coming back with horrific stories of people being rounded up—Jews, gypsies, and others. It was hard to imagine such a cultured and educated society as Germany being led by someone like him, but as Oskar said, they were so beaten down. Every day, Dermot and Isabella read the news with ever increasing dismay.

So Dermot knew what he had to do, though letting his old friend down would be hard.

'I'm sorry, Oskar, I won't.' He looked him in the eye. 'I owe you my life, I know I do, and if you're ever in trouble, I swear to you, I'll be there to help. But I just can't help a man like Hitler. I have no love of the British, as you well know, but Hitler, he's in a league of his own. What he's doing, its horrific, and I can't support him in any way. I'm sorry.'

There was silence for long seconds before Oskar spoke.

'I'm sorry too. I need you, but I accept no as no.' He shrugged. 'I'll have to try elsewhere, I suppose, my old friend.'

'Have you someplace to stay? Do you need money?' Dermot wanted to help, but he couldn't go so far as to assist the Nazis.

'No, I don't want to draw attention to myself, checking into hotels and so on. The British have spies everywhere, and I am, as we used to say, *known to the authorities.*' He gave a small smile.

'Look, where we are living isn't safe—the man who owns the place is OK, but he's English,' Dermot said, keeping Thomas's exact role to himself. 'But Robinswood is still there. It's all locked up, but I have a key for the back door. I just forgot to hand it over when we left.' He took out his keys and removed a small key from the ring, placing it on the table.

'Now, in the loft over the first stable, there's a Webley, and some bullets in the chest in the corner. In case you need it. I don't know when it was last fired, but I wrapped it well and hid it under some sacking so it should be all right. I'm sorry I can't do more, but I just can't. Apart from anything else, I promised Isabella all that stuff was over, and I can't go back on my word. She's been through enough.'

Oskar leaned over and took the key, placing his hand on his friend's shoulder.

'I understand, Dermot. We all have choices. There are ones we can live with, and ones we can't, and I respect your decision. I would have felt happier with you beside me, no doubt about it, but I think I might be more afraid of Isabella than the British anyway.' He grinned to show there were no hard feelings. Then he stood up and put his coat on.

'Now, I must go. Take care, my friend, and I hope your girls come home safely. Maybe we'll meet again sometime, when all of this is over?'

'I hope so, Oskar, I really do. Be careful, all right?'

Oskar patted his back and was gone.

CHAPTER 29

*D*ermot stood up from the breakfast table in the kitchen of the Hamilton-Brooks house as Isabella scoured the paper and Eve read a letter from her sisters, delivered just minutes ago. Arthur and Georgina were playing out on the newly cut lawn, where Isabella could keep a close eye on them.

He'd lied to his wife about the reason for Oskar's appearance in Ireland, one of the very few lies he'd ever told her, and he felt guilty, but it was better that way. Dermot looked at the children outside, oblivious to the dangers of the world. Over in Germany, in England, the same scene would be there, innocent children playing in the sun. He sighed.

The Hamilton-Brooks children really were little scamps, and while Isabella had managed to get some kind of order into their lives by enforcing a strict daytime and bedtime routine, they were still liable to do anything. Thomas and Elena loved their children, but they had absolutely no control over them. They were both from very well-to-do backgrounds, where nannies and governesses reared children, and Isabella soon realised it was not a lack of love on the part of the children's parents, but a lack of any idea how to do it. That, combined, of course, with the fact that they were absent so much of the time.

But things were improving. Thomas had played football with Arthur and Georgina last Sunday on the lawn, and they were in ecstasy to have their daddy's attention. Of course, it had all been carefully choreographed by Isabella. She had asked both Elena and Thomas when would suit them for Arthurs's birthday tea, and while they had both looked a little dismayed that their presence would even be necessary, they agreed that Sunday at three would be fine. Isabella had even invited some of the other children who lived locally. It would do the children good to have other little ones to play with. They were still naughty, no doubt about it, but they loved Isabella and Dermot, who spent far more time with them than their parents did. Isabella only had to give them one of her looks, and they immediately stopped whatever devilment they were up to. Arthur was going to be six on Friday, and she'd been using the withdrawal of the making of the birthday cake as bribery for weeks. They loved to bake with her, and the kitchen usually looked like a flour bomb had exploded afterwards, but it was worth it to see their little faces. Four-year-old Georgina adored her brother and did whatever he told her to.

Dermot looked out at them playing and chuckled.

'They're a right pair, aren't they? Georgina reminds me of Kate when she was small, traipsing around after the other two, doing their bidding.'

'Except it was Kate making all the rules,' Eve interjected with a weak smile.

'True enough.' Dermot winked at his daughter. She had lost so much weight she looked like a gust of wind would knock her down. It had been two months since Jack's death, and she was still in the darkest of mourning. She helped her mother in the house and played with the children sometimes, she'd even shown Nancy how to hem the new sheets, but she was just going through the motions of living. That was all she could do for now.

Elena and Thomas had been so kind, paying Eve when there was really no need. But they saw the pain in the young woman's eyes and wanted to help. Dermot felt grateful to them for that. It struck him how odd it was that he could like a man such as Thomas Hamilton-

Brooks. He knew Thomas was an agent for the British crown, he had been for years, and had stayed here, despite Irish independence, his business merely a front.

The IRA were still alive and kicking, though they were a different generation from the IRA Dermot was in. Now, it was all youngsters who never saw a real war but were full of big ideas. They were being very foolish if they thought for one second that Hitler would make good on his promises in return for help attacking Britain from Ireland. Dermot wondered if Oskar knew that, but then, his friend was a shrewd man for all his joking around, and he knew the Irish. He wouldn't be easily duped or taken in.

One night, after he and Isabella had first arrived in Dublin, Dermot had met up with a few of his other old comrades for a pint, men he'd served with during the Easter Rising and the War of Independence. They had alluded to the plans of these young bucks, and of course Dermot

never mentioned where he was working now. Hamilton-Brooks was well known. Not as a brutal man, like many of those who came over here to carry out the King's orders, but he was one of them no less. Dermot wouldn't have been able to explain to his old friends how he'd come to the man out of desperation but was staying because he truly liked him and his wife and they needed the help.

The house was lovely, but even it was badly in need of a little attention. By his own admission, Thomas couldn't drive a nail, nor would he, so Dermot had been kept busy fixing things and tending to the garden. He had even slung a rope over a thick bough of an oak tree to make a swing, and dug out a sand pit for the children to play in. The fact that the family had welcomed his poor, devastated Eve had made him respect them even more.

He saw she'd just folded the letter from her sisters back into its envelope.

'How're Kate and Aisling?' he asked.

'Fine.'

Dermot was used to Eve answering in one word these days. It was as if even talking was an effort.

And he already knew a bit about his other girls' activities.

Kate had written to tell them about her relationship with Sam Kenefick, and while they weren't altogether surprised—the two had been close since childhood—they weren't exactly pleased. Not because they didn't like Sam, but more because they knew what Lady Violet would make of it and the way Kate would be treated by her and Lillian. They were happier to hear from Aisling that she had met a nice man, even if he was English. Unlike her sister's choice, Mark sounded like an ordinary lad from a background they could relate to, and they looked forward to meeting him.

Dermot was used to Eve answering in one word these days. It was as if even talking was an effort.

'Had they any news?' Dermot pressed gently.

'Well, anything about the war is blacked out as usual,' Eve said quietly.

'It says here that the night bombing on London seems to have stopped,' Isabella piped up. 'There hasn't been a raid now since the tenth of May, a full week, so maybe he's giving up. I wish they weren't so vague. They don't give any details in the news.' She put the paper down in frustration.

'Well, you can't blame them,' Dermot pointed out, 'and our papers are being fair enough by not reporting too much either. War is as much about intelligence as it is about guns and bullets.'

Isabella rankled at his logic. 'I just want to know my girls are safe.'

'And they are,' Dermot soothed. 'Didn't Eve just get a letter from them?'

'They want me to visit,' Eve said.

Her parents stared at her.

'What?' Isabella gasped. 'Visit them where? Over there? But there's a war on! You can't just go wandering off to England...' She was clearly trying not to panic, but the very last thing Eve needed was an arduous journey to a city being bombed.

'I won't go,' Eve said. 'Sam Kenefick sent the money for the fare and everything, but I...I just can't go without Jack. We had a trip planned. The day he died, he said we'd dip into our savings a bit and go over to see the girls...' Her voice cracked.

Relief flooded through Isabella.

'It's all right, pet, they'll understand.' She leaned over and covered Eve's hand with her own. The girl had been so crushed by his death, and then she had hoped she might be pregnant. So when she found out a few weeks after Jack's death that she wasn't, she was so upset. In some ways, Isabella was relieved at that, though she would never admit it to Eve. But the girl had been through so much, having a baby alone would have been too hard. Still, she understood her daughter's pain. She wanted to have something of Jack to cling to. But she would recover. She might even meet someone else. She was a young girl, and the chances of it happening were greater if she didn't have a child.

Dermot had remained silent during this whole exchange. He was still trying to come to terms with the idea that Kate and Sam Kenefick were together. The boy was all right, there was definitely more of Austin than Violet in him, but Dermot still wasn't happy about it. He knew young men and what they were after, and if young Sam thought he was going to use Kate and then discard her... Even if he didn't, the whole thing was a disaster waiting to happen. His daughter would never fit in that world. During a war, things were different. It had been the same the last time, and even during the Anglo-Irish wars, society's conventions had meant less. But once peace came, those class walls went right back up again, and there was no way that Violet Kenefick, or Lillian or any of their like, would accept Kate then. It was not what Dermot wanted for her. Still, he had to admit it was kind of Sam to send Eve the fare.

'I'd better get up and fix that guttering, there's rain forecast, and it's only going to get worse.' He crossed the room, kissed his wife and daughter on the cheek, and left.

All day, as he worked, he thought about his daughters. Life had been so easy when they were small. He and Bella knew what was best, and they loved and fed and clothed them. But now, things were much less certain. In the short term, he wanted Kate and Aisling to be safe from Hitler's bombs and bullets, and for poor little Eve to find her smile again, but long term, it was hard to know. Still, if Sam Kenefick was taking care of the girls, then that must be a good thing—at least someone was. The Keneficks would have connections, so it was a comfort to know they weren't alone over there.

Later that night, with the house asleep, Dermot sat at the kitchen table and drew the writing pad towards him. He wasn't much of a writer, leaving it to Bella to keep in touch with the girls. She always read aloud to him what she wrote, and he added a scrawl to the end. This letter, though, he was writing without his wife's involvement.

Dear Samuel,

I hope this letter finds you well and in good spirits. I wanted to contact you

He paused. Why was he writing to Samuel Kenefick? He tried to compose his words to convey the feelings he was having. Really, he wanted to say that if Sam had any notions of sleeping with his lovely daughter and then leaving her high and dry, then he could think again. But Dermot knew he'd have to temper his language. After all, he couldn't go around accusing the lad with no evidence.

He continued:

to ask you what your intentions are regarding my daughter Kate. I apologise if this is blunt but I see no point in beating around the bush. If I could speak to you face to face, I would, but circumstances will not allow that. She wrote to her mother and me explaining that you two were now in a relationship and I have to admit to being less than happy about it. It is not personal, I always liked you as a boy around Robinswood. But war means that things that were not acceptable can become so, by virtue of the circumstances people find themselves in. I will assume your intentions are honourable and that you are not merely toying with her. And if that is the case then you and I are both acutely aware of the difference in class between Kate and you, and I do not wish my daughter to be consigned to a lifetime of being made to feel inferior by virtue of what some people will consider her lowly rank in life compared with yours.

In addition, I thank you for the kind gesture regarding Eve. It was a generous thing to do. You are like your father in that respect. But neither Isabella nor I think Eve travelling anywhere, let alone to war-torn England, is a good idea at the moment. She is very fragile and still in deep mourning for her husband, which is understandable, so please do not be offended, but we will decline your offer.

I would appreciate a response from you to my question, and of course all correspondence between us remains strictly confidential.

Regards,

Dermot Murphy

HE ADDRESSED THE ENVELOPE. Kate had said he was at Biggin Hill RAF base along with her and Aisling, so it should get to him. He stuck a stamp on it, and there and then, despite the lateness of the hour, he decided to walk to the end of the street to post it.

CHAPTER 30

*T*he lights from the harbour twinkled, and the gentle *ting ting* of masts and rigging were the only sound in the early summer's night air. Dermot posted his letter and strolled back to the house. As he approached the kitchen entrance, he noticed the light on in Thomas Hamilton-Brooks's study. The man kept odd hours, so Dermot took no notice and was just about to creep upstairs when the study door opened, flooding the dark hallway with light.

Thomas appeared.

He was in his shirtsleeves, and he looked tired. Though he was about ten years younger than Dermot, Isabella said he looked older.

'Dermot,' he whispered. 'Have you a minute?'

Dermot turned. He and Thomas got along fine as employer and employee, but they were not friendly. Early on, when Dermot had called him Mr Hamilton-Brooks, Thomas had stopped him and asked him to call him Thomas, which he now did.

'I've known you since I was a young apprentice, dealing with Lord Kenefick's accounts,' the Englishman had explained. 'It seems ridiculous for you to call me Mister anything.' Isabella always called him Mr Hamilton-Brooks, and

Dermot always addressed the man's wife as Mrs Hamilton-Brooks, but between the men, they were Dermot and Thomas. Still, that was the extent of their friendliness.

'Of course,' Dermot said quietly and walked into the study.

'Please have a seat. Can I get you one?' He poured whiskey into a cut-glass tumbler and offered it to Dermot, who accepted it.

Unlike the rest of the house, which was full of the detritus of family life, despite Bella's best efforts to keep it tidy, the study was clinical. There was a large oak desk with a leather insert, and on it stood an inkpot, a foolscap pad, and two fountain pens in a small glass jar. There were two chairs, one either side of the desk, and against one wall was a large, beautifully ornate filing cabinet, mahogany inlaid with rosewood.

'An oasis of calm in a sea of chaos,' Thomas joked as he saw Dermot take the room in. 'Before I married, the whole house was like this, but since the arrival of hurricane Elena and then the two mini tornados, I have given up. At least everywhere but here.'

Dermot nodded. 'I know what you mean. It must be nice to have a retreat.'

'It is. Though, since Isabella and yourself arrived, I can't tell you how much better everything is. I am so grateful, truly. Poor old Austin Kenefick's demise and Lady Violet's decision to move back to England has been the saving of my family.' Thomas raised his tumbler in a toast.

'Well, you got us out of a hole too, so everyone benefitted,' Dermot said, his voice low. He didn't want to disturb anyone, and Elena and Thomas's bedroom was directly overhead. 'And thank you for taking Eve in as well. We really appreciate it.'

'Of course, the poor girl. How is she doing?'

Dermot looked across the table at this unremarkable-looking man. He was slim with thinning brown hair and a pleasant enough face. He could have been anything, a banker, a solicitor, something like that, but he wasn't. He was one of the most astute and clever British agents to ever set foot on Irish soil. There was a time when either one of them would have put a bullet in the other without compunction. How times had changed.

'She's all right,' Dermot said. 'It just takes time, nothing else for it. She misses her sisters, as well. It would be easier, I think, if they were here, but since they're over in England...'

Thomas nodded. 'Indeed. I hope you don't mind me saying, but I was surprised when I learned your daughters were in the WAAFs.'

The tone was light, a simple enquiry, but the hair on Dermot's neck stood on end. immediately suspected there was more to the questioning. Years of dealing with the British meant he was sensitive to the way they spoke and when there was more to a line of questioning.

'I was surprised myself,' he said, revealing nothing further.

'Well, it was a brave thing to do,' Thomas said with a slight smile. 'You must be very proud of them. Though, what with the bombing here again last week, it seems nowhere is safe. Irish neutrality may not hold on too much longer if the Germans make another raid like that one. The old adage of *my enemy's enemy is my friend* seems to be fueling the thought processes in republican quarters. That's the gossip around town, anyway, that the IRA are in bed with the Germans. But, in wartime, rumours and counter-rumours abound.'

Dermot sat, saying nothing, for a few seconds. Thomas was fishing, no doubt about it, trying to gauge his reaction. But why was he saying this now? It was likely Thomas knew about his past, but still... Could he know that Dermot had met with Oskar? It was possible, not much happened in Dublin that the British didn't know about by fair means or foul.

But that also meant if Thomas had been watching him, then he'd know that Dermot had no interest in the modern incarnation of the organisation he had spent so many years fighting for. He'd promised Isabella once the treaty was signed that he was out, and out he'd stayed. At no time was he ever tempted to go back on his word, not even when asked by an old friend to whom he owed his life. He thought the IRA were foolish to trust the Germans, and the Germans equally foolish getting involved with what was left of the IRA, but he would not interfere.

'I've been proud of them since the day they were placed in my arms, Thomas,' Dermot said carefully. 'Nothing would ever change that.' And he would never admit to anyone but Bella how much their joining the British hurt him.

'Indeed, indeed.' Thomas took a sip of his drink. 'I've had a letter from Lady Kenefick, as luck would have it.'

Dermot waited for Thomas to go on.

'She and Elena used to meet occasionally, in later years, if Austin had business in Dublin. And I helped her with the move. It's so tricky nowadays, shipping, what with the war and so on. So she just wrote to let me know she had settled. She knew you two were here and asked after you both.'

Dermot nodded, unsure how to respond.

Thomas was suppressing a smile. 'She mentioned there was some sort of a friendship developing between your daughter and her son.'

Dermot could just imagine the tone of the words expressing Violet's horror at her precious boy and the servants' child. This was precisely why he was against the match.

'So it would seem,' he said simply.

'Violet seemed a little, em...surprised,' Thomas said tactfully.

'I could imagine she is. They've been close since they were children.' Dermot fixed him with a stare. 'Did she ask you to speak to me?'

'She did,' Thomas admitted, 'but as I wrote back to her, it is none of my business. I just wanted to warn you that she's not happy. And reading between the lines, or even on the lines, she's determined to put a stop to it. You have helped my family, so I wanted to help yours, or at least put you in the picture.'

Dermot took him at his word. That was what this conversation was all about. He thought for a moment.

'Is there a way of getting leave for my girls? I know through normal channels they wouldn't be allowed to come home, just for a visit, but is there a way, would you think?'

Thomas exhaled slowly. 'Well, with the right connections, anybody can do anything, but you'd need the right connections.'

The two men watched each other in the dimly lit room. Dermot was not certain, but something told him Thomas was issuing an offer.

'And how would you go about getting the right connections?' Dermot asked.

Thomas exhaled again. 'Usually, such matters would be dealt with by the commanding officer, but these are not usual times. So, occasionally, when desperate needs call for desperate measures, and I'm speaking in general terms here, it would be an exchange of some sort. If you wanted someone to do something for you, such as having family members temporarily released from military service, for example...then you would in return do something for them.'

'Something like what?' Dermot knew the conversation had wandered out of the conversational and into much murkier waters. Neither man was willing to lay his cards on the table yet.

Thomas sat back and paused, his eyes never leaving Dermot's face.

'Well, the government needs all the intelligence it can get, from whatever quarter it can come. Valuable information is what wins wars, not tanks and guns, contrary to popular opinion. So, if someone was in a position to offer assistance to them, with something like information, then they would usually be happy to show their appreciation in whatever manner was deemed appropriate by both parties.'

'What sort of information?'

Thomas gazed out over the rim of his glass.

'Well, for example, if someone had connections with certain people who might be on the German side, or were in possession of information about any such persons, and they were willing to share that information.'

Dermot remained passive, his face giving nothing away.

Thomas went on,

'Like or loathe the British, Dermot, Hitler must be stopped, and anyone who was offering him assistance for whatever reason, and no matter what was promised, would have to be stopped. There are German agents operating here, with the assistance of certain factions within the republican movement. If someone could lead us to one of them, for example, then I think something like leave, or possibly a release, if that was what they wanted, could be arranged.'

Dermot sat back. So that was what the man wanted. For Dermot to hand Oskar over in return for the release of his daughters. It all made sense. He thought back to Lady Kenefick telling them of the job, Thomas letting the previous housekeeper go with no explanation… Thomas had employed him for this. He'd been playing a long game. And Dermot had been right to be suspicious his first day.

Of course, he wasn't surprised they knew about Oskar, he had learned to never underestimate the British, but if Thomas thought he would do a thing like betray his friend, then he was very much mistaken.

The clock ticked on the mantelpiece. The conversation was much more candid now. But it still didn't feel threatening or anything like that. Dermot trusted his instincts.

'I want to get my girls back,' he said, preparing to lay his cards on the table, 'even for a visit, but I'm not naive enough to think I can lure them away from Mr Churchill at this stage. But Bella is worried about them. She hasn't seen them in over a year, and Eve needs her sisters. While I would love to see them, of course, they have been reared to know right from wrong, allies from foes, and above all else, to have the courage of their convictions, their principles. They were reared with emphasis on the attributes of bravery and loyalty, so if it means sacrificing that, then I don't think I'll be seeing them anytime soon.'

Though nothing explicit had been suggested or rejected, both men knew exactly where they stood.

'I hear what you're saying, Dermot. Anyway, if your daughter is seeing a wing commander in the RAF, she should be able to get him to pull a few strings. Try that, and if that fails, get back to me. The door is always open.' Thomas poured another whiskey and again offered it to Dermot.

Dermot held his glass out. 'Just a drop.'

The two men sat in companionable silence for a minute, and then the conversation moved to Elena's plans for a garden party to raise money for her charity. They chatted and joked gently for a few minutes.

'Now, I better get to bed.' He stood and handed Thomas the glass. 'Thanks for the drink.'

'You're welcome. And think about what I said.'

Dermot nodded, and as he went upstairs, he thought about Oskar and hoped he was all right. He was still at large, if Thomas wanted Dermot to help them find him, so that was good. Hopefully, he was on his way back to Germany.

Dermot thought about warning him, but there was no way to reach him from here without alerting the whole of Kilthomand to his whereabouts. It was safer to leave him be.

Dermot thought of what Thomas had said about Sam pulling strings and considered writing again, but decided against it. He would wait to hear what he had to say in response to his first letter.

* * *

SAM MUST HAVE WRITTEN by return, because six days later, Isabella entered the kitchen and handed Dermot a letter as he was having his breakfast. He took it and put it in his pocket.

Immediately, she was suspicious.

'Who is that from?'

'I don't know, I haven't opened it,' he replied, buttering a slice of soda bread.

'Well, would you not open it now?' she asked.

'No, because now, I'm trying to eat my breakfast in peace.' He concentrated on spreading marmalade on his bread.

'Well, you're being very furtive.' She sat down. They were alone for once. 'Please tell me,' she whispered, 'you're not getting into anything...anything with those hoodlums trying to cosy up to the Germans.' The worry was clear in her eyes. Fighting for Irish independence twenty years ago was one thing—they'd been young and idealistic, and anyway, it needed to be done. Bella had understood that, even though she was terrified all the time. But this was different. Rumours were going around republican circles about a rise in the IRA's activity, the old adage coming to the fore once more: *England's difficulty is Ireland's opportunity.*

Dermot stopped, turned to face her, and took her hands in his.

'Bella, I swear to you, I've nothing to do with them anymore. Not in any active way. I'm a republican at heart, nothing will change that, and I think Sean MacBride was right to get all the IRA who were interned out of jail, of course I do. Dev had no business putting them there in the first place. And I supported those volunteers on hunger strike when they got rearrested. But as for the bombing of Dublin Castle, and assassination of Irish policemen, and all the other stuff they did last year, I want no part of that. Most of them are interned now in the Curragh or have left the country. Only the odd cell of fanatics is left, and they are being well monitored, you can be sure. Honestly, my love, I won't ever put you in danger like that again. Those days are long behind us.'

She relaxed visibly. Dermot went back to his breakfast. Helping Oskar could have been seen as getting involved again, he knew, but he wouldn't worry her with it. It was over, and he'd said no, so there was no point in bringing it up.

'A woman down in the butchers was saying how some lad who joined up came home on leave,' Isabella said, shaking her head. 'He went down to the pub in his British army uniform, and he was jumped on the way home. He's almost dead, she said.' Isabella sighed. 'Will it ever end, Dermot? All the hatred?'

He drew her onto his lap. 'I know these things happen, and it's very sad, but what kind of a clown swans around Ireland in his British uniform? Like, that's only looking for trouble. It will get better, but just now, with the war raging and showing no signs of being on the turn yet anyway, any Irishman who joins the British army would be well advised to stay over there, till the bloody thing is over anyway.'

'Maybe Kate and Aisling are better off over there. If they came back, and someone knew what they were doing, maybe...'

Dermot was spared having to reply by the arrival of Arthur and Georgina, who burst into the kitchen.

'Lellabella, did you cut your knee?' Georgina asked, her blond curls escaping her pigtails, her china-blue eyes innocent.

'No, darling, I didn't, why?' Isabella asked, jumping up from Dermot's lap.

'Well, when we cut our knees we go on your lap, so I thought you might have cut your knee.'

Dermot chuckled. 'I'll leave you to deal with that one.' He gave his wife a kiss on the cheek and pulled Arthur's cap down over his eyes as he went outside with his letter.

Once he was sure he was alone, he went into the small potting shed at the bottom of the garden and took the letter out of his pocket, slit it open and extracted a single thin blue sheet.

Dear Mr Murphy,

Thank you for your letter, and I do appreciate you being straight with me. I understand your position totally, and so I hope you will allow me to be equally straightforward. I love Kate, and I want very much to marry her. I would like to ask for your blessing on our union, in person, if possible, but current circumstances will not permit that. As far as my relationship with her is concerned, I know you are right. There are some who will not accept it, my mother and sister most notably, but I don't care and neither does Kate. I would never allow anybody, my family or anyone else, to treat Kate with anything but the upmost respect, please be assured of that.

With regard to the matter of Eve visiting the UK, I understand. The girls are desperate to see her and they thought it might be a break for her, but as you say, it is probably too soon after her bereavement. Please be assured of my respect and affection not just for Kate, but for the entire Murphy family.

Yours faithfully,
Samuel Kenefick

So, Kate was to be Lady Kenefick. That was a turn-up for the books.

Young Sam seemed sincere, but it would have been better to get the opportunity to talk to the man face to face. Then Dermot would have known for sure if the lad loved his darling Kate enough to weather the problems they would inevitably face. He was still hoping it all came to nothing, but he knew when two young people decided they wanted to be together, then all heaven and earth wouldn't stop them. In fact, Bella's family had never thought Dermot good enough for her, but nothing would ever have dissuaded them from getting married. The same with Eve and young Jack, God rest him. And so Dermot reluctantly accepted that Sam and Kate deserved a shot if it was what they both wanted.

* * *

FOUR DAYS LATER, a telegram arrived.

Mr Murphy.

Got *a 48-hour pass for Kate and Aisling.* Taking *night boat Thurs, arr Dublin* 6pm Fri *20 June. Gresham* booked. *Eve* welcome stay too.

YOURS,

Samuel Kenefick

Dermot sat and smoked a cigarette. Was this a coincidence? The boy couldn't organise it before, then Dermot has a conversation with Thomas, and all of a sudden they can come? He dismissed his qualms. He was probably being overly suspicious. Sam would of course have a lot of high-ranking contacts, through his father, so one of them probably came good. Dermot wasn't one to look a gift horse in the mouth anyway.

He waited until the evening, when the children were in bed and both Elena and Thomas were out. Isabella was mending one of Dermot's socks, new ones were almost impossible to buy, and Eve was reading a book, but more often than not, when he looked over at her, she was lost in her thoughts. The wireless was on in the corner of the cosy kitchen, and it smelled pleasantly of warmth and baking. It wasn't Robinswood, but it wasn't too bad.

'I've a bit of news,' he said, putting down the paper.

Both his wife and daughter looked at him expectantly. It was not his way to be full of surprises.

'Well, what is it?' Isabella asked. 'Don't keep us in suspense.'

'Kate and Aisling are coming to Dublin for a night. They only got a 48-hour pass, but they are coming to see us next Friday. They are getting the night boat from Wales and will dock here on Friday morning. They take the boat again early Saturday morning, but at least we'll see them.'

Isabella squealed with delight, while Eve just hugged her dad and cried.

'I can't believe we're going to see them,' Isabella cried through her tears. 'How did they manage to get a pass?'

'Samuel Kenefick arranged it. I got the impression he had to pull quite a few strings.'

'But how come *you're* organising...?' Isabella asked. Generally, family arrangements were her domain.

'I wrote to Sam, and I asked him what his plans were,' Dermot explained, still holding a tearful Eve. 'I knew Violet would be furious at the romance between him and Kate, and I wanted to see if this was just a bit of a fling for him or if he knew what the hell he was getting into. I also thanked him for the gesture of the ticket for Eve but declined it. He wrote back to say he loved Kate and he wanted to get over here to ask our permission to marry her, but it was impossible.'

'Married?' Isabella was stunned. 'Kate and Sam Kenefick? Are you serious?'

'I think it will be all right, Bella.' Dermot drew her into the hug as well, and all three of them stood there, delighted with some good news at last.

CHAPTER 31

*V*iolet was seething inside but managed to keep her emotions in check. Samuel stood before her, looking so handsome in his RAF blues. She was so proud of him, and he could have had anyone, anyone at all, if only he'd looked properly instead of cavorting around with that wanton brat of the Murphys.

He'd dropped the bombshell of his plans to marry her just as Violet was about to explain why she needed to go back to Dublin to finalise some legal matters regarding the auction of the contents of the house. Ideally, Samuel would go himself, after all, it was his money, but she'd explained to them that he was too busy and that she would act on her son's behalf. Initially, she had mentioned to Lillian that it might be nice for all three of them to go, but her daughter had responded with her usual disdain.

'Oh, for God's sake, Mother,' she'd snapped, 'I have no interest whatsoever in returning to Ireland ever again, if I can help it. And in case you hadn't noticed, Sam is a pilot for the RAF, and the Nazis are doing their best to blow us all to kingdom come, so I think our pilots might have more things on their minds than squiring their old maters around Dublin.'

Lillian was probably right, but did she have to be so conde-
scending?

Violet put all her energy into Samuel, such a sweet boy, and so
handsome. He looked just like her father, she always thought, but now
he was throwing his whole future away, on a servant child. Where was
this ever going to end? Other people had nice children who married
well and took care of their parents. Why had she drawn the short
straw?

Kate Murphy had snared him, probably made him feel guilty about
leaving Robinswood, and then ran after him when he got away from
her. Men are weak and think with a part of their anatomy not
designed for rational reasoning.

Samuel's impatient voice cut through her reverie.

'So, Mother, I'm asking for your blessing. I hope you'll be happy
for me, for us, and welcome Kate into the family.' His tone was
measured, but there was a steely determination there.

The tea Violet had ordered from the imbecile woman she had
employed to do the housework lay untouched.

'Do you hear anything about Lillian, about town?' she asked, trying
to steer the conversation away from his revelation of a few moments
ago.

'What?' Samuel was taken aback.

'Lillian, your sister, do you hear anything of her about town, in
clubs, that sort of thing?' Violet tried to paint a pleasant smile on her
face.

'In clubs? Mother, what are you going on about? I don't go to
clubs; I work on the base, I fly planes, and when I can, I see Kate.'
Samuel was exasperated. 'So, no, I don't hear anything about Lillian.
Why would I?'

When Violet had no answer, Samuel went on,

'Look, Lillian is a grown woman. I know you two have had some
sort of falling out. She wrote to me asking for money, which I refused.
I don't know what went on between you two, and frankly, I don't care.
I've not seen her for months. She's too old to be so dependent, in my

opinion anyway, and she should be doing something for the war effort. Kate and Aisling aren't even British, but there they are doing their bit, and then there's Lillian swanning around all night drinking and dancing and sleeping all day. She is ridiculous, Mother, and if you've told her so, then good for you. Now back to the subject of Kate and me...'

'Tea?' Violet asked, picking up the china pot to pour.

Samuel fixed her with a steely stare.

'Mother, I don't want tea, and I don't want to talk about Lillian. I want to hear your opinion on me marrying Kate Murphy. Let me warn you, though, I will propose to Kate, and if her father agrees, we will be married, and soon. I would like very much for you to be there, to be happy for me that I've found someone to love who loves me in return. You and Lillian are all the family I've got, and to be frank, Lillian and I are not close, as you know. So really it's just you. Please, Mother, be happy for me. Kate is a wonderful girl, so kind and funny and loyal. She could bring great things to our family if you'll let her.'

Violet looked at her son. He was so lovely but so easily led. He'd adored Austin, of course he did, Austin was the parent who let him ride wild horses and gave him whiskey when he was thirteen. But, unlike his sister, he didn't seem to feel like it was a choice of *which* parent to love. No, Sam loved Violet too and always sought out her advice and support. Lillian didn't give a hoot what her mother thought about anything; she only saw her as a meal ticket, and not a very good one at that.

This sweet boy was different.

In some ways, he could be determined. He had that streak in him from his father. Once Austin set his mind to something, no matter how ill-conceived and frequently downright foolish, he was not for changing. Violet saw the same resolve in her son's eyes now. But a servant! Violet could not imagine how on earth it would work. It was like breeding two different species of creature. Kate would not be welcome in his world, nor presumably would he be in hers. No, it was a folly.

'Samuel, my dear, I know you think you have feelings for this girl, and she is nice enough, and certainly very pretty, I can see that, but do you really think it's a good idea to marry so far beneath your social class? You are Lord Kenefick. You have a certain position within society, and it never augurs well to deviate too far from that place we occupy. People fit into their own social strata, among their own people...'

'Oh, for God's sake, would you listen to yourself, Mother?' Samuel scoffed. 'Lord Kenefick, indeed! Ha! My estate is rented, my ancestral home is locked up and empty—God knows if anyone will ever live there again, we'd have sold it if anyone would buy it—I earn my salary from the RAF, and you are constantly telling us how our father squandered all the family fortune. So I have very little else. I could not care less for what you deem to be our class of people. Our class don't want to know us, Mother, because we are in that most appalling of conditions: poor. Have many of your so-called friends been by, or invited you to their lavish parties or country houses since you've been here? No, they haven't, because they don't see you as one of them. Poverty embarrasses them. Lillian said you had some plan to go back to India, and good luck to you if you do, but the India you left does not exist anymore either. You can't turn the clock back, Mother, you simply can't.

'And I'm not like you, I'm not a snob. I take people as I find them, and I love Kate, and I like her family very much, and they will accept me, I know they will, and do you know why that is so, Mother? Because they love Kate, and they will see that I make her happy, and that is what they care about—making their daughter happy. This is the turning point. You either accept Kate and be kind and welcoming to her and her family, or we are finished.'

SAMUEL WAS QUITE flushed and very worked up. Violet wondered what to say.

Perhaps she should pretend to be happy. But then, no, Samuel could not have meant what he said. That if he was forced to choose between the Murphys and his own mother he would pick them. He didn't mean it. He was just emotional.

'Samuel, I love you,' she said. 'I want you to be happy, of course I do.'

'So does that mean you will give our marriage your blessing, with a full and open heart?'

'Have you asked her father yet?' Violet deflected the question.

'No. I wrote to him explaining my intentions and that I've managed to get a 48-hour pass for both Kate and Aisling to go over to Dublin next week. I would have liked to ask him face to face, but I can't do that.' Violet thought she heard a note of doubt creep into her son's voice.

'And you're so sure he will approve? Remember, Samuel, I know Dermot Murphy and his wife of old. They are, well, shall we say, they do not approve of how we live. And they—well, Dermot—was always a little insolent. He may not give his consent.'

Samuel walked to the window, his shoulders stiff with frustration, and dug his hands into his trouser pockets. He spoke to his mother with his back to her.

'That's as may be, but I have asked, and we will take it from there. Kate and I will be together, regardless of what either of you has to say.'

Aha, thought Violet. *He's not as sure of Murphy as he is letting on.* Violet knew that no matter how wild the Murphy girl was, she would not defy her father.

Violet calculated quickly.

'Well, in that case, I wish you all the best, my dear. Do let me know how it goes. And give Kate my best wishes.'

He turned, the relief evident on his face.

'Thank you, Mother.' He kissed her proffered cheek. 'Now, I must get on, I'm due back on duty in two hours.'

'What's it like?' she asked suddenly.

Samuel stopped on his way to the door. 'What?'

'Flying, over enemy territory? Are you frightened?'

He walked back towards her and led her to the sofa, where he sat beside her and held her hands.

'Sometimes yes, but not when on a raid, more just before. When I'm actually airborne, I have several flight commanders reporting to me, and under them, the men of each squadron, so the thing I fear most is not being killed myself, but more leading these men into death.'

There was a few seconds of silence, and Violet's voice, when she spoke, was trembling.

'I worry about you. I look up at the sky at night and worry that you are safe.'

'You and every mother of every man all across the services. That's why all this nonsense about class and where people fit is so silly. We are united in the face of adversity, and Hitler cares nothing for whether his bullets hit Lord Kenefick or Joe Bloggs.'

Violet nodded and raised her hand to rub his head just as she'd done when he was a boy at her knee.

'Now, Mother, I really must go.'

'Very well, my dear. Stay safe.'

And he was gone.

Violet rang for the maid, who came shuffling in. She really was the most unsatisfactory servant, but she was all that was available. People did not want jobs in service anymore, it seemed. There were other, better, more interesting ways of earning a living.

'Take those away and bring me a notepad and a pen,' Violet ordered.

'I don't know where anything like that is kept, missus,' the woman replied.

'Oh, for goodness sake, you will address me as ma'am or Lady Kenefick, and it is your job to know where things are kept,' Violet snapped.

'No, it ain't. The agency said you needed a cook and a bit o' houskeepin', and that's wot I'm doin'. But if it's not good enough, then I can get work elsewhere no problem.'

Violet was shocked at the woman's tone. She was in her fifties and very heavy set and far more common than Violet would have liked, but she surely did not think this level of insubordination was acceptable?

'Please adjust your tone,' Violet said carefully, remembering how difficult it was to find anyone, especially for what she was willing to pay. 'But I will, on this occasion only, overlook your outburst and forgive it. You may go.'

The woman put the tea tray she was carrying back down on the table with a clatter.

'Y'know what? Stuff it! I don't need this. My daughter is workin' in a munitions factory in West Ham, and she's earnin' more than I am here, and it's a bit of a lark, singin' all day and goin' to the pub for a gin in the evenings after work!' She removed her apron and hat, the frilly one Violet had insisted she wear, and dumped it unceremoniously on the sofa. 'My girl, she says I'm mad to work for you, but I felt sorry for you, over from Ireland and all that. Thought I'd help an old lady out. But you wouldn't talk to a dog the way you talk to me, so I'm off!' With that, she turned on her heel and slammed the door behind her.

Violet stood, stunned. She hated this new world, where nobody knew their place. It was an alien country to her, and London was not the glittering city with parties and balls she remembered. It was bleak, cold, destroyed by that dratted man Hitler and his horrid bombs. But worse than that, Samuel was right: she had no friends, and he was probably correct about India as well. Her title meant nothing, and it was all she had left.

There was nothing for it. Her only hope lay in Samuel. He would need to be dissuaded from his current course. He was a peer of the realm, a flying ace, and a good-looking chap to boot. He could easily marry well, if only the Murphy girl was out of the picture. Clearly, asking Thomas Hamilton-Brooks to intervene with Dermot had been a waste of breath. No, Violet would have to orchestrate it another way. But Samuel must never know.

She went to her desk and extracted her notepad and pen.

Dear Dermot,

I hope this letter finds you well. I understand that you and Isabella have found work with our friends the Hamilton-Brookses. That must have been a relief. I am glad your connections with us proved useful. Dear Thomas has written to say you are both settling in well and are a tremendous help, so I am pleased you were both well trained in Robinswood.

Firstly, let me offer my condolences to Eve on the sudden and tragic death of her husband. The poor girl must be devastated. The loss of such a young man, and I understand a good one, is a terrible burden for her to bear.

The main reason for my letter, however, is to discuss with you the burgeoning romance between your daughter Kate and my son Samuel. I trust that, like myself, you have reservations. Though we come from different worlds, we both understand how things work. Our children are young and impetuous and think they are in love, but I must urge you to reject any entreaties my son might make to you with regard to your daughter's hand in marriage. They are too different, and it can only end in heartbreak.

Violet thought for a moment, wondering if she should write the next line. She decided to do as Austin would and put her last farthing on the nag, in the hope of turning the whole mess around.

Should you find it difficult to do as I ask, I would urge you to think again. Thomas and Elena Hamilton-Brooks are good friends of mine, as you know, and I'm sure they would be most disappointed to know that some of your activities in the past were less than savoury. Lord Kenefick knew more than he revealed to you, Dermot, and whiskey, as you know, had quite a tongue-loosening effect on my late husband. I think we'll both agree that the past is best left in the past, and I would hate to think that new information could come to light that would damage your position within the Hamilton-Brooks home. Especially with Eve as fragile as she no doubt is.

She paused again. Would he heed her threat? Should she say more? The thing was she didn't know any more, just that Austin, once, when drunk of course, told her there was no fear of Robinswood being burned by the IRA as so many of the other big houses were because Dermot Murphy would see to it that it wasn't. When she tried to interrogate him as to what he meant, he'd just tapped the side of his nose and grinned inanely, as was his wont, before whispering, 'Sometimes it is good to keep the enemy close.' Then he fell asleep.

She had her suspicions but nothing solid. She'd tried questioning her husband when he was sober, but he had dismissed her out of hand.

No, she decided, it was best to leave the letter at that. It was a gamble. If Murphy showed the letter to Samuel, he would be furious and may cut her out entirely, but she hoped Dermot's need to maintain his position with Thomas and Elena would prevent him from telling her son. It was a wager she hoped would pay off, and the stakes were too high to do anything by half measures.

She took a stamp and moistened it on the sponge, affixing it to the envelope. She addressed it to Dermot alone and went to ring the bell to get the maid to come and take it for posting, when she remembered there was no maid.

She sighed. She had never posted a letter in her entire life, but she would have to do it now. All over London were posters urging people to *Make do and mend* and talking about how *Loose lips sink ships*. Everyone was having to do things they were not used to, and Violet would be no exception. She squared her shoulders and put on her coat. On the way out, she extracted another letter she had written earlier to her solicitor in Dublin, confirming their appointment for Friday morning the twentieth of June. She wasn't looking forward to going back to Ireland, but it would hopefully be the last time, and all of Austin's debts and the sale of Robinswood would be settled for once and for all.

As Violet walked to the end of the street, all around her were the signs of war. The Blitz had been terrifying. Samuel had tried to convince her to go down to the Tube station, but she'd refused. Goodness knew who would be down there. Instead, she got under the bed each night and listened as the bombs exploded and the fires raged all over the city. Miraculously, they'd survived on Sloane Square. She liked to think it was because the government made sure people like her were protected. Of course, Lillian had brayed that awful laugh when she heard her mother's theory.

'Oh, of course, Mother,' she'd laughed, 'Mr Churchill and the King have asked nasty Herr Hitler to bomb all the poor people in the East End, but for God's sake, stay away from the nicer parts of London.

Are you mad? They bombed Buckingham Palace, for God's sake! And what about Belgravia and Park Lane, and even the Sloane Square Tube station took a direct hit. You really do take the biscuit sometimes.'

Beau had been waiting for Lillian outside as she said all that, and Violet had been shocked when she heard him say,

'Lillian, that is no way to speak to your mother. If I spoke to my mama like that, big as I am, I would regret it. I think you should apologise.'

Violet and Lillian had both stood in the hallway, neither knowing what to do or say. Beau had never entered the house since the day Violet dismissed him, but he and Lillian still spent a lot of time together and Violet had to admit her daughter's behaviour had improved. Lillian was volunteering at a dressing station now, and the drinking and partying had ground to a slow trickle. Now, she and Beau went to the pictures or out for tea. Apparently, he didn't drink alcohol and was very religious.

Beau fixed Lillian with a look that brooked no argument, and to Violet's amazement, her daughter did as he asked.

'I'm sorry, Mother, I shouldn't have spoken so harshly.'

Violet had been embarrassed and once again sorry she'd aired her opinions to Lillian, of all people. Of course the West End got bombed! She just meant it didn't get the same battering as the east end of the city, where the poorer people lived.

'Well...em, very well,' she'd stuttered. 'Run along, or you'll miss the start of the film.' And before she could consider what she was saying, she added,

'I got some cake from Fortnums. It's in the larder, help yourselves when you get back, if Sergeant Lane has time.'

Beau had come in that night, had a cup of tea and some cake, which he complimented, and then left, giving Lillian a respectful peck on the cheek. Though every fibre of her being had resisted their relationship, Violet had to admit that Beau seemed good for Lillian. He didn't put up with any of her nonsense, and she seemed to genuinely crave his respect.

Since that evening months ago, he'd even taken it upon himself to do some odd jobs around the house as well, never accepting any payment. There was a quiet dignity to him that Violet found soothing. She had almost come round to the idea of Lillian and Beau, odd as it was, and anyway, she wasn't going to be given a choice in the matter. But she could in no way consider the same for Kate Murphy. Not for Samuel. It was just totally unsuitable.

She hesitated for a moment before putting the letters in the post-box. Perhaps she was making a huge mistake. Perhaps Murphy would see her threat as a challenge and react badly. But it was the only option. Samuel would have to be stopped, and she could not do it. She'd tried to be rational, supposing he did marry the wretched girl. They would not want to have Violet live with them. Of course, Kate Murphy was not used to much, so it wouldn't bother her not to have staff, and gardeners, and a place in town and another in the country... But it wasn't the future Violet had envisaged for either Samuel or herself. Houses, cars, staff were normal things that normal people like them needed. She let go of the letters and turned around and walked back to the house.

She was startled to find Beau there on the doorstep.

'Oh, Sergeant Lane, Lillian is at the dressing station, I believe. She isn't due to finish until at least six this evening.'

'I know, ma'am,' he said. 'I had the afternoon free, and I noticed the windows of the house weren't taped. I thought I might do it now for you, if that would help?' He held up a large roll of grey tape. It was very difficult to get things like that in the shops, but the Americans seemed to have whatever they wanted. Violet had been very worried about the windows smashing to smithereens in the event of a bomb. One heard awful stories of people being injured or even killed by flying glass.

'Well, if you can spare the time, Sergeant,' she said, 'that would be most welcome, thank you. Please, come in.' She extracted the key from her purse.

'Allow me, ma'am,' he said, taking the key and opening the door. Just as he did, an elderly woman walked by and stopped right in front of Beau.

'Thank you, son, for coming over and helping out. We don't know what we'd do without the Yanks. You lot will have Hitler turning tail in no time, God bless you. I pray for you all.'

Beau smiled a rare smile. 'Thank you, ma'am. I appreciate your prayers very much. It means a lot to me. God bless you too.'

Violet entered the hallway, relieved the exchange was a cordial one. When people saw negros, one never knew how to react. There had been very few dark-skinned people before the war, but now the place was flooded with them, it was most disconcerting in many ways.

Beau set about his task and soon tapped gently on the drawing room door.

'I've finished, ma'am, so I'll bid you good day.'

'Thank you, Sergeant, I really do appreciate it. I was worried. Can I interest you in a cup of tea?'

He smiled. 'I don't drink tea or coffee, ma'am, but I'd like a glass of milk if you had some?'

How extraordinary. No adult she'd ever met drank milk. But then, Beauregard Lane was not like anyone she'd ever met.

'Of course.' She went to ring the bell to summon the maid when she remembered. 'Oh dear.' She blushed. 'I...I don't actually have staff just now. The woman I hired found another position closer to home, so I...' She was flustered and hated being caught out like this.

'How about we go to the kitchen and figure it out ourselves?' Beau suggested. 'I'm sure between the two of us we can manage.' He gave one of his slow smiles to reveal gleaming white teeth.

Her initial reaction was to refuse, but she didn't want to appear churlish. She'd never actually made a cup of tea herself, but it couldn't be that difficult, surely?

She followed Beau down the corridor to the kitchen, and immediately he took charge. He found cups and side plates and searched the tin for some cake, and within moments, she had tea and he had a glass of milk. To her amazement, he seemed to think they should have it in the kitchen.

'Lillian was describing your place in Ireland, it sounds so beautiful.' He spoke slowly, with an American drawl, and his voice was so deep he seemed to rumble rather than talk.

'Robinswood, yes, it was rather lovely, very different to here.' She sipped her tea and cut them two slices of cake. It had cost a small fortune in Harrods, but she bought it in case any of her friends called. They hadn't, and it was a shame to waste it.

'So what part of the United States are you from, Sergeant?'

'Ma'am, if you don't mind, could you call me Beau?'

'Of course, Beau.' She smiled. 'Is that a popular name where you come from?'

'I'm the only Beau I know. My great grandfather was a slave, and his owner was Beauregard Lane Esquire, of Savannah Georgia, but he was a good man in as much as any of them were, so he named my grandfather after him, and he named my father, and then my father named me.'

Violet swallowed her cake. She found she was horrified and fascinated in equal measure.

'And so are your family from Georgia?'

'Yes, ma'am, my daddy died of tuberculosis when I was only six, and my mama raised me and my four brothers on her own. We live just outside of Savannah.'

'That must have been very difficult for her. I presume there is some sort of support, financially, I mean?' Violet realised she was thinking out loud. It was audacious to ask such a delicate question.

'I'm sorry, I shouldn't—'

'It's OK, ma'am. To answer your question, no, there wasn't. The Social Security bill didn't come in until 1935, and even then, it excluded farmworkers and maids, all the work coloured people did, so no. She worked, and the neighbours took care of us until we were old enough to work too. I went to work in a factory at the age of twelve, and my brothers all got farm work. I remember being jealous because they could walk, but I had to take the bus, and when it was busy the drivers wouldn't stop at our bus stop, so I'd have to walk a long way.' He shrugged.

Violet had heard from Lillian about the segregation of the US armed forces, how the white soldiers treated the black ones terribly and how often English people intervened in the defence of the negro soldiers.

'Is it as bad as it is portrayed?' she asked. Normally, she would never have been so forthright, but then she had never drunk tea in a kitchen with a black man before.

'Yes. People like me get lynched; white people are the police, the city hall, the courts, everything. Nothing can be done. We have no protection. We retaliate, and we are beaten, arrested, jailed. You learn just to keep your head down and your mouth shut. We stay out of their way. We have our own churches, schools, everything. If white marines found out Lillian and I were friends... Well, it would be bad for me. But the English are different. I can't believe it, they see me as a person, not a useless nigger.'

Violet winced at his use of the uncouth word.

'I'm sorry to offend you, ma'am, but that's what they call us. I ain't never in my life before been treated with the kind of respect I've seen over here. That lady outside? Thanking me? My mama wouldn't believe it! Some of the guys in my unit say they hope the war goes on and on, they don't ever want to go back there.'

'Well, I'm glad to hear it,' Violet said. 'Your country is helping us, and the least we can do is be welcoming and generous. I'm shocked to hear the way your fellow countrymen treat you.'

Something occurred to Violet, and since they were being so frank, she decided to ask.

'What do you see in my daughter, Beau?'

He smiled. 'Lillian sure likes to party, and she doesn't welcome Jesus into her heart, but I'm working on that. I guess I like her because she sees me for me, not the colour of my skin. I met her when a bunch of us were trying to go into a tea room and some of our own marines, white guys, stopped us. One of them threw a punch at one of my friends, and then they all jumped on us. Lillian ran out of the cafe and shouted at them to stop or she would call the police. I was on the ground, and one of them was kicking me. I didn't dare hit them back, none of us would, and those guys were mean, they were looking for a fight. But Lillian standing between us and them, brave as a lion, that was the moment. I'd never seen anyone like her.'

Violet sipped her tea. 'Well, she is certainly unique.'

CHAPTER 32

*K*ate and Aisling made the laborious journey from London by train. They sat in a carriage full of soldiers presumably going home on leave, so the atmosphere was jubilant. But despite the boys' efforts to flirt with them, they kept to themselves.

'I can't believe we're actually going to see Mam and Dad and Eve, I have to pinch myself,' Aisling said as she opened a parcel of sandwiches she'd made for them for the journey. 'I don't know what Sam did to pull it off, because Daphne, you know the one who works in the Officers' Mess, she applied for leave to go to her grandmother's funeral and it was denied. I felt a bit awkward telling her that we had a pass actually, and when I did, she looked jolly peeved.'

Kate chuckled.

'Aisling Murphy, our father will have a stroke if he hears you saying anyone was *jolly peeved* about anything. You better lose that British accent before we land.' Kate took a fish paste sandwich and winced.

'Ah, Ais, was this the best we could do? This bread is stale, and that smear of disgusting paste isn't doing anything to improve the situation.'

'Well, don't eat them if you don't want them. It was all that was there.' Aisling looked at her own sandwich without enthusiasm.

'What will we order in the Gresham?' Kate asked. She was almost salivating at the thought of some lovely Irish food.

'It's such a pity there wasn't room for us at the Hamilton-Brooks house,' Aisling said. 'I'd have loved a big bowl of Mammy's home-made soup and a slice of soda bread with proper butter. Followed by a lovely roast dinner, chicken maybe, and roasted spuds and carrots and parsnips mashed together with cream and salt. Oh, and then a huge slice of apple tart with custard.'

'Ooohh,' Kate groaned, gingerly nibbling the horrible sandwich. 'We better change the subject, dreaming is only making it worse.'

A conductor came through checking tickets, and Kate asked,

'How long more before we get to Holyhead?'

The man checked his watch.

'About half an hour, I should say, but this train don't go all the way to the port, just to the town, so you'll have to walk from there. I assume you're going home for a break?' He smiled. He must have recognised Kate's Irish accent.

'We are,' Aisling confirmed.

'Well, mind how you go, and maybe change out of those uniforms before you land. Some of your countrymen obviously can't tell right from wrong and are making life hard for lads and lassies like your-selves who were brave enough to join up, no matter what your Mr deValera says.' He clipped their tickets and moved on.

Kate bristled, but

Aisling put her hand on her sister's arm. 'Just leave it, Kate, they don't understand and they never will. They don't know what it was like for us being under their jackboot for centuries. I wish they could understand too, but they can't. I even had to explain it to Mark when we started going out. They just think we won't join out of selfishness or cowardice or something. But they don't learn in school what they did to us. You'll never change their minds, so just let it go.'

Kate sighed. 'You're probably right, but I can't believe they don't teach history in English schools! It's just so hard to listen to, you know?'

'I do, but Mark says they never learned anything about Ireland in school, so they genuinely don't know.'

As the train pulled into the station at Holyhead, the girls gathered their bags from the rack overhead. They had civvies to dress in once they were on the boat, but since military personnel got priority on transport, wearing their uniforms to the port was a good idea. As they stepped down, they realised it was teeming with rain.

'Oh, bloody hell, we'll be soaked!' Kate had got one of the WAAFs who was a hairdresser in civilian life to do her hair in a victory roll, and she loved it. 'My hair will be ruined!'

Ignoring her sister, Aisling pulled on her WAAF greatcoat with its king's-crown brass buttons.

'Ais, if these coats get wet, we won't dry them for a month,' Kate grumbled as she put hers on.

'Well, it's either that or go out in this weather in our tunics, and we'll be soaked to the skin. Come on, there's no other way.'

The two girls left the station carrying their holdalls. It wasn't cold, but the rain was relentless and the ferry port was two miles away.

As they crossed a road, a car slowed down beside them, and the back window opened.

'Good afternoon, girls. Please let us give you a lift?'

Aisling and Kate stared in disbelief.

'Lady Kenefick.' Aisling recovered first. 'Em... Thank you... We are—'

'Going to the port, I imagine? Yes, so am I. Now do come along, you'll catch your deaths out there.'

Aisling half dragged Kate into the car.

The tension was palpable, but since Kate seemed to have been rendered speechless, Aisling tried to be polite.

'Thank you very much, ma'am, for the lift. The train only went as far as Holyhead town...'

'Yes, I know, I was on that train, that's why I asked the conductor to arrange this taxi for me.' She nodded and tapped the silver head of her cane on the glass separating the driver from them. He pulled away from the kerb once more into the torrential rain.

The silence only lasted seconds, but to Kate it felt like an hour. Sam had told her his mother's reaction to the news that they wanted to marry, and she could not think of anything to say.

Aisling prattled on about England and how different it was, desperately trying to fill in the awkward gaps, and Lady Kenefick was her usual stuck-up self, making no effort to be nice. Sam never came up in conversation, and Kate decided she would have preferred to walk in the rain than endure this.

'So are you going back to Robinswood, Lady Kenefick?' Aisling asked politely.

'No, Aisling, just to Dublin. I have some legal matters I must attend to on my son's behalf. So, tell me, how are you girls enjoying being in the WAAFs?'

'Very well indeed, ma'am,' Aisling replied. 'The work is tiring but very rewarding. It's nice to feel that we are doing everything possible to protect the pilots and the civilian population.' Aisling emphasised the word *pilots* slightly, to let Violet know that they worked all the hours to keep her son and so many others in the RAF safe.

'Indeed. I'm glad you are doing your bit.' Violet looked out the window, and Aisling cast a sidelong glance at Kate, who rolled her eyes irreverently.

Kate was tempted to disavow her of the notion that they, as Irish citizens, had 'a bit' to do, but instead held her tongue. The idea that Violet was going to be her mother-in-law filled her with dread, but then the thought of not being with Sam was worse, and she was sure he would always defend her if it came to it.

The taxi pulled up on the quayside, where a weary-looking purser stood at the gangway checking tickets as a small group of people boarded the *Irish Poplar*. It was essentially a cargo ship with space for a few passengers. Most non-essential travel between the islands had stopped. Once the group were aboard, the whole quayside was deserted but for the purser.

. . .

'LET us help with your bags, Lady Kenefick,' Aisling said as the disgruntled taxi driver dumped everything on the quayside after getting the exact fare down to the last penny with no tip. He drove off, splashing Kate by driving into a huge puddle.

As they gathered their bags to walk the fifty yards to where the purser was standing, the man turned and walked in the opposite direction, towards a hut on the quayside.

'Oh, for Goodness sake!' exclaimed Lady Kenefick. 'Where on earth is he going? We'll get soaked in this rain.'

Kate felt something sharp in her back, and a voice in her ear said, 'Just come with us quietly, Ms Murphy.'

A large black car appeared beside them.

There was another man behind Aisling. He was skinny with longish, greasy hair and a lot of acne on his face; he looked no older than them.

Lady Kenefick spun around indignantly.

'I say, do you know who I am? Get away from us at once!' She'd had enough lately of being pushed around by the working classes. 'My son is a wing commander in the RAF, and you would do well to leave us alone this minute! How dare you?'

The older man, who was clearly in charge, took her walking cane, an elaborate thing with a silver fox for a handle. She'd slipped a week earlier on a loose bit of carpet, and her ankle was very painful. Beau had checked it wasn't broken and then dressed it in a bandage, and Lillian had found the cane in a shop and bought it for her. They had actually been very kind.

'I need my cane,' Violet announced. 'Give it to me immediately.'

The man ignored her and turned to the girls. His gapped teeth and severe halitosis made them recoil. He was fat and wore a stained jacket and a collarless shirt. 'Just get in the car, all of you,' he said in a strong Welsh accent. 'I don't know who you are, nor do I care, but I've a job to do...'

The one behind Aisling shoved her roughly into the car, followed by Kate, who received an equally forceful push.

'Allow these girls to go free at once!' Violet shrilled from outside the car. 'They are employees of my husband, Lord Kenefick!'

The two men looked at each other and made a swift decision. Before they knew what was happening, Violet was lifted bodily and thrown in on top of the girls, her cane following her. The men appeared in the front, and the car sped away from the quayside.

'I'll see to it that you both hang for this!' Violet was incensed. 'Kidnapping is a capital offense, and as for kidnapping the wife of a peer of the realm, well, you shall soon see who is judge, jury, and executioner when you are brought to justice!'

As the older man drove, the younger one turned around. 'Listen to me, you old bat!' He too had a Welsh accent, which Kate recognised from Taffy, one of the girls on the base. '

I've had just about enough of you carping in my ear, all right? So unless you want me to shut that whiney trap of yours permanently, then I'd suggest you zip it, all right?'

He cocked his gun and pointed it at the three of them. The older man kept his eyes on the road.

Grinning, the young one swept his greasy, floppy hair back on his head. It was so unusual to see men with hair longer than regulation these days. Most men his age had joined up.

The older man kept his eyes on the road.

'You will not get away with this...' Lady Kenefick struggled to right herself and sit beside Aisling. Her hat had come off, and her hair was dishevelled. The girls had never seen her looking anything but pristine.

'Ha! You're joking, aren't you?' the younger one barked. 'Nobody's comin' to rescue you, Lady Muck, or you two Paddies, either! Nobody knows where you are, so just shut up, do what you're told, and there's a slim chance you'll get out of this alive, right?'

Kate held Aisling's hand tightly as they sped down country lanes.

Eventually, the car stopped at an old farmhouse. They were ordered out of the back seat and in the door of the house. The room was sunny and bright, with a bunch of flowers, and some bread, cheese, and milk on the table.

'We don't want anyone to get hurt,' the older man said in a surprisingly soft voice. He had none of the swagger or bravado of the other one, but he was more frightening because of that. His voice was emotionless, as if kidnapping women was a daily occurrence for him.

'Our orders are to look after you, but if you try to escape, we will shoot, so don't bother.'

'I demand to know why we've been incarcerated like this! This is an outrage, and my son—'

The man turned and punched Violet in the face. Blood gushed from her nose, and Aisling and Kate were stunned for a moment but then immediately went to her side, offering her a handkerchief.

'You bully, do you feel like a big man hitting a lady?' Kate snapped at him.

'Oh, you'd know how to make me feel like a big man, love.' He rubbed his crotch, and Kate shuddered. He moved forward and pulled her close to him. She was revolted at his foul breath.

'Let her go immediately!' Aisling screamed as the younger man came inside.

'Dai, let them go,' the younger one said urgently, casting him a warning glance loaded with meaning.

The older man released Kate reluctantly. He gave her a lecherous grin and allowed his eyes to rest on her breasts.

The younger one watched the situation, a half-smoked cigarette dangling from his lips.

'Look, I think you have the wrong people,' Aisling said, 'we're not involved in anything...'

'No, we've the right people all right.' The younger one seemed to have relaxed a bit, though they got the impression he was a bit nervous about what his partner might do. 'Now, there are three bedrooms here, and there's food.' He pointed at the table. 'You can say we took care of you, right?' He glanced at Dai, who was still staring at Kate.

'There's nobody for miles, so don't bother trying to get anyone's attention or anything silly like that,' the young man said. 'And me and him will be here all the time as well.' He was trying to sound reassuring, but his colleague spoke again.

'So you know, we might get lonely during the night...' He gave a lecherous gap-toothed grin.

'I demand to know what is going on.' Violet was not going to be intimidated by these thugs, despite the fact that her face was swelling. Kate had at least managed to stem the flow of blood.

'And Lady Kenefick needs a doctor,' Aisling tried. 'When we are released, we will give a good account of you, but you need to get her medical attention immediately.'

'You can demand all you like, love, but we don't got to tell you nothing, see?' The younger man crossed the room and got right up in Aisling's face, suffocating her with his disgusting cigarette breath. He pulled his pistol from his trousers and shoved the barrel roughly under her chin, forcing her head back painfully.

'DON'T GIVE us any trouble, and everything will be fine,' he said.

CHAPTER 33

*E*ve sat in the lobby of the Gresham. Isabella and Dermot needed to get the children ready for a day with Nancy, and then they would join their daughters at eleven o'clock. Eve felt something like joy for the first time in months; she was going to see her sisters. She wondered if they'd changed much. She felt like a totally different person since she last saw them. Gone was the carefree girl, to be replaced by this woman with such sadness in her eyes she couldn't bear to look in the mirror. She felt so guilty as she thought how she wished it was Jack she was about to see. Life without him just seemed so pointless. She hated the mornings the most because for a brief few seconds before she woke, Jack wasn't dead, he was beside her. Each morning, the realisation of her new reality came crashing over her like an icy wave.

Eve tried to force down the bitter bile of jealousy for her sisters and their loves. Their letters, though sensitive to her situation, were full of stories of Sam and Mark and the fun they had over in England. She even thought about joining them, for the want of something to do, but she couldn't do that to her parents. And anyway, all she wanted was to bring Jack back. Running away wasn't going to change anything.

Of course, she wanted Kate and Aisling to be happy. She loved them and trusted them to choose good men. But she was still so consumed by pain and grief and shock that sometimes she wondered if she could stand it for another second. She went through the motions for her parents—eating, cleaning, helping with the children— but it still felt unreal. She had nightmares, that Jack was alive but stuck in a box under all that earth, and in the dream, she was kneeling and scraping the earth with her fingers but she couldn't move it. So often she woke, screaming, to find her mother or her father holding her tight, shushing her back to sleep.

She should really go to Cork, visit the grave, and see Mrs O'Neill, but she just could not summon up the energy. She checked the large clock over the fireplace in the ornate lobby of the hotel. It was seven fifteen. Kate and Ais had sent a telegram saying that the boat was docking at six and that they would be at the Gresham by seven. Perhaps the boat had been delayed. She wondered if there was a way of finding out. They would be there as soon as she could, she told herself, and she sat and nursed the cup of tea she'd bought.

Across the room was a large ornate mirror, and Eve got a shock when she really saw herself. Mrs Hamilton-Brooks had very kindly given her a dusty-pink summer coat and a pink-and-green cloche hat. She said she had grown too fat for the coat, but it was swimming on Eve. She recalled how Jack used to joke about her curvy figure. He claimed true Irishwomen never got rail-thin because something in their heart knew they'd need to be plump as a partridge in order to survive famine and torture by the murderous Brits. For all his joking, though, she knew he loved her curves. He'd hardly recognise her now, she'd lost so much weight. She just had no interest in food. Her auburn hair was pinned up under the hat, and Mammy, who was normally against makeup, had even urged her to put a little colour on her face.

Eve watched her reflection like she was someone else. She looked nothing like the girl she once was, the one who ran around Robinswood, who fell in love with Jack O'Neill.

The time ticked on, and still there was no sign of the girls. Eve wondered if she should telephone to the Hamilton-Brooks house, in case they had made contact there, but she decided she was being silly. It was only seven thirty. She'd just wait.

At ten to eight, she approached the lady on the reception desk.

'Em, I'm sorry to disturb you, but my sisters were to check in this morning, and they haven't turned up yet. Have they contacted you to say they'd be delayed by any chance?'

The middle-aged woman looked kindly at her.

'What was the name, dear?'

'Aisling and Kate Murphy. They had a triple room booked for tonight, I believe.'

The woman consulted the checking-in book, a large, leather-bound tome.

'Yes, we have the booking and are expecting them also, but I'm sorry there has been no contact apart from the original booking. Where are they coming from?'

'England.'

Eve spoke quietly.

'England.'

Despite several thousand Irishmen enlisting in various regiments, and women going to work on the land or in the munitions factories in England, people did not broadcast the fact. Independence was still young, and eight hundred years of British occupation of Ireland was not going to be forgotten in a few short decades. Anyone either going to or coming from England these days kept their mouths shut on the subject, as there were many who saw it as treason, siding with the old enemy.

'Well, I can check if the boat has been delayed, if you like?' The woman smiled warmly.

'Thank you, that would be very kind,' Eve replied.

The woman picked up the large black receiver of the telephone and asked to be connected to the Port of Dublin.

After a minute or two, she spoke.

'Good morning. Ms Sexton here from the Gresham Hotel. We are expecting some guests travelling aboard the *Irish Poplar*. It was due to dock at six o'clock this morning?'

Eve waited as the woman listened.

'Thank you, I'm sure they have just been delayed. Good day to you.' She replaced the receiver.

'The ship docked on time, I'm afraid, my dear. There were not many passengers, but the person I spoke to assured me that all passengers disembarked and left the port building over an hour ago. I assume they would have taken a taxi directly here, which should have taken no more than twenty minutes. Unless they took a detour, or met someone. They could not have gone shopping, as none of the shops are open yet.'

Eve tried to suppress her panic. There was probably a very simple explanation and Kate and Aisling would walk in the door any minute now.

'Can I get you some more tea, dear? Or would you like to go and leave a message for your sisters?'

'Thank you, I'll wait. But could I make a telephone call, please?' Eve opened her purse to get the change for the call.

The woman must have felt sorry for her.

'Is it a local call? If so, I'll dial it here for you, no charge.'

Eve smiled gratefully and gave her the Hamilton-Brookses' number. She made the connection and handed Eve the receiver.

'Hello, Nancy, it's Eve. Is either of my parents there please?'

Nancy ran to get Isabella.

'Eve? Is everything all right?' Her mother sounded worried.

'They never turned up,' Eve said desperately. 'The lady here at the hotel rang the port and everything. The ship docked on time, but they haven't arrived here at the hotel. What should I do?'

Isabella thought for a moment. If they had missed the boat, they would surely have sent a telegram, but with the war, communications were not as reliable as they once were. She tried to keep the concern from her voice.

'I'm sure there's a reasonable explanation. The postman is just arriving here now, he might have a telegram. Look, why don't you come back here, and if they turn up, ask the lady there to tell the girls to call us at this number.'

Eve finished the call and thanked the woman, doing as her mother instructed with the number for the Hamilton-Brooks house.

'I'm sure they will turn up shortly, my dear,' the woman said as she noted the number.

Eve walked back down the street. People were in a flurry of activity, still in shock from the Luftwaffe air raid on Dublin the last month that killed thirty-four people. And then the following week, Arklow in County Wicklow was bombed, showing the Dublin attack was not an accident. People were putting tape on their windows and preparing sandbags in case of another raid. Eve tried not to worry about the girls. They must have missed the boat and never got to send a telegram or something. Still, she was so disappointed. She wanted to see her sisters so badly.

She took the tram back to Dun Laoghaire, and when she arrived into the kitchen, she found her mother and father poring over a letter, their faces like thunder.

'What is it? Are they all right?' Eve feared the worst. 'Is it from them?'

'No, not from them, it's from Violet Bloody Kenefick.' Isabella was barely keeping her temper in check, muttering the 'bloody' so the children didn't hear.

'What does she say?' Eve asked.

'Nothing worth repeating,' Dermot said, folding the letter and placing it in his pocket.

'The cheek of her!' Isabella began, but Dermot shot her a warning glance, and she stopped.

'Now, that pair never appeared, did they not?' Dermot tried to sound light-hearted, but Eve could tell he was worried.

The kitchen door opened, and Thomas appeared, looking grave.

'Could I have a word, Dermot?' he asked, with no greeting to anyone, not even Arthur and Georgina, who were munching bread and jam happily at the kitchen table.

'Of course.' Dermot glanced at his wife, then followed Thomas to his study. Until the door was firmly shut both men stayed silent.

'Please, have a seat.' Thomas gestured to the chair before his desk, and Dermot sat down and waited for the other man to speak.

'Look, Dermot, something has happened. The girls are all right, I must stress that—'

'What? What's happened?' Dermot panicked.

Thomas sighed.

'Look, Dermot, I wish there was another way to do this, I truly do.'

Dermot was very uneasy now. 'Just tell me.'

'We know a large shipment of weapons for the Irish Republican Army is due to be landed somewhere on the south coast tonight. It's a German payment in return for the IRA's assistance in getting their agents into Britain. We have to intercept it.'

'What has this got to do with my girls?' Dermot asked. This must have been what Oskar was talking about.

'Well, if you'll just allow me to explain. We have reason to believe that a senior Abwehr agent is operating here, but he is proving very difficult to catch. We believe he must have a way of blending in, and so we need you to help us find him. I know I asked in a roundabout way recently, which you refused, but—'

'And I still would refuse, even if I knew what the hell you were on about, which I don't.' Dermot interrupted. 'All that has nothing whatsoever to do with me or my—'

'Well, yes, but, actually, it does,' Thomas said grimly. 'Perhaps this information will change your mind. You see, we have Kate and Aisling, and we will hold them until you cooperate.' He never lost his measured tone. 'I know this is not fair, and believe me when I say I wish there was another way, but there isn't. You're the only one who can lead us to this German. I suspect he was an old comrade of yours, and I think you two have been in touch of late...'

'What? You have kidnapped my daughters?' Dermot was incredulous. 'I don't believe for one second that the British government would sanction the kidnapping of two of their servicewomen in return for my help in tracking someone down!' He paused and fixed Thomas with an icy stare.

'You're bluffing. I've been dealing with you people all my life, and I know what you're capable of, I've seen it firsthand, but there is no way they would sanction this. Kidnapping two innocent girls, Irish citizens, and WAAFs to boot—the papers would go mad. And if I don't help you, are you telling me that someone somewhere will order to have my girls shot?' Dermot barked a cynical laugh. 'You must think I'm a right eejit if you think I'd fall for that.'

Thomas sat down at his desk.

'I don't think anything of the sort, and you're right, the government hasn't sanctioned it and they probably wouldn't, either. Though, if the girls' father was proven to be a Nazi sympathiser and a former IRA ringleader, then they just might. For the time being, however, this is what you might call a solo mission on my part. I am under considerable pressure from London to deliver this agent, and all other avenues have proved fruitless. I am left with no choice. My problem is the Germans are infiltrating the UK via Ireland, and I am not doing my job effectively if this is allowed to continue. If I can't manage it, then my superiors were quite clear, they will appoint someone who they think can.

'So you see, Dermot, I need you to do this. I'm not willing to give up my life, be demoted as a failure to some miserable clerk's position in the Ministry of Transport or something. I've been in my position for a long time, back when things were very fraught over here, and I've executed my duties well. If they recall me, it will be to London, and the children would have to be evacuated to go live with God knows who. Elena would be out of her mind with worry. My family love it here, they are safe and well-fed and cared for so well by you and Isabella, I won't upset that for the sake of one bloody Nazi. There are young guns who think it's time someone like me was put out to pasture, and I'm damned if I'm going to let that happen. So I have to do this, and you have to help me.'

·   ·   ·

ALL PRETENCE that Thomas wasn't a British agent or that Dermot was not an IRA man was gone.

'How long have you known who I am?' Dermot asked.

Thomas smiled. 'Since shortly before Austin's death. Austin was, if not fully aware of your activities, certainly suspecting of it. But he turned a blind eye. He was more Irish than he let on, you know. He called me to visit him last year, he must have known the end was in sight, and he told me that if I ever needed help with the IRA you would be a good man to call. So, when things were heating up in London, and they were demanding answers from me, I engineered it for you to come here, knowing that eventually I would need your help. I have to get to that German, I simply have to, and when you wouldn't help, well...needs must and all of that.'

'I've known who you are for a long time too, Thomas,' Dermot said quietly. 'And so do the IRA.'

Thomas smiled. 'Is that a threat? Because let me warn you, I am not easily intimidated.'

Dermot moved quickly, dragging Thomas to his feet and pinning him to the wall. Dermot was taller and stronger of hand; he was able to almost lift Thomas off his feet. The other man gasped for breath as Dermot squeezed his throat.

'Where are my girls? I'm warning you, you have five seconds to tell me, or I swear I'll make sure you never see another day.'

As Thomas struggled to free himself from Dermot's grasp, Dermot just slightly loosened his grip on the man's throat, so he could talk.

'IF ANYTHING HAPPENS TO ME,' Thomas wheezed, 'I have issued instructions to the men I have employed that they are to do what they wish with your daughters, but that they are to be found dead. They are being held by former Black and Tans who cannot get work because of their brutality and criminal records. They know that you are IRA, so there's no love lost there. They feel they lost many of their best to your bombs and bullets over the years, so they see your daughters as a bit of payback, regardless of the fact that I'm paying them.

They would be only too happy to settle some old scores. Trust me, Dermot, these are not nice people to deal with.'

Stunned, Dermot released him and stared into his face.

'Look, Dermot,' Thomas went on, rubbing his neck. 'I know this compromises you. Your history is one of fierce resistance and defiance of British rule in your country, I understand that, and the idea of joining forces with the old enemy to face down people with whom you're politically aligned is going to be difficult. But please believe me when I tell you that there is no other way. Either you give the agent to me, so I can tell my employers that I have caught a high-ranking Abwehr agent, or Kate and Aisling get hurt—or worse. You would be very foolish to underestimate me, Dermot. I'm desperate, and we both know there are no lengths to which a desperate man won't go. You're not a foolish man, I know that.'

CHAPTER 34

*D*ermot stared out of the window as Thomas quickly drove south, in the direction of Robinswood, racking his brain. He'd had to tell him where Oskar was, or at least where he thought he was, to buy himself some time, but he would not sacrifice his friend if it was in any way possible. If only there was a way he and Oskar could combine forces to torture the information out of Thomas—where he had the girls—before shooting him. No police would look for him, as he wasn't supposed to be operating in Ireland in the first place. The British could not make a big issue of it without having to answer some very awkward questions from the Irish government.

'Give the order to let my girls go,' Dermot said, speaking for the first time on the journey. 'I want to find a telephone, speak to them, and know they are safe before I do anything.'

'That won't be possible,' Thomas replied. 'Where they are, there is no telephone. But once you lead me to the agent, I'll give the order. They will be expecting a telegram, which I'll send the moment you hand the German over, you have my word.'

'That's not good enough. I don't believe a single word that comes out of your mouth.'

'Well, that's a pity, but what I say is true. As soon as Oskar Metz is in custody, the girls will be freed. If those who hold them do not hear from me by tomorrow night, they will assume I am dead and carry out their contingency orders.'

'What the hell is wrong with you?' Dermot thundered. 'Have you even thought this through? Aisling and Kate are my children! Can you imagine someone doing this to Arthur or Georgina?' A fleeting thought crossed his mind, to hold those small children as a kind of insurance, but it was too late now. And besides, Thomas knew any threat Dermot made would be empty—he could never hurt them.

'I'm sorry, Dermot. As I said, I'm desperate, and desperate people do desperate things. Look, it needn't come to that. You just hand over Metz, and we all carry on as before. The girls get released, no harm done.'

Dermot watched him as he drove. Surely Thomas couldn't think this was going to be solved so neatly, with everyone going back to being friends after? The man was mad. Despite his calm exterior, there was something manic about him. None of this made any sense. He couldn't possibly think he'd get away with it! But he apparently did.

For the moment, Dermot couldn't take any chances. He'd kill the man with his bare hands if necessary, but not before he knew the girls were safe.

They reached Robinswood and drove around to the far entrance, the one used for deliveries and farm business, rather than draw attention by going up the main avenue. There was no sign of life anyway, no lights on or vehicles to be seen anywhere.

'Stop here.'

Thomas did as he was told and took a gun from the glove compartment. 'I must say, I thought you'd hide him here, but I've been down twice already and there was no sign of anyone. I hope for your girls' sake you're not leading me on a wild goose chase. Lead on.'

Dermot realised then that capturing Oskar was not going to be enough for Thomas. The British authorities would want to question him, and there was no way Thomas could risk Oskar giving away under interrogation the circumstances of his arrest. If he was taken into custody, it would leave Thomas facing some awkward questions. No, Thomas intended to kill Oskar, there and then. He would tell his superiors that there was no way of taking the agent alive, and a dead Nazi was better than one who managed to get back to Germany.

Dermot walked in the direction of the back of the big house. The old kitchen where he and Isabella had come in and out of the house a thousand times was invisible behind old sheets they had hung in the floor-length windows to stop nosey locals peering in. The cobbles of the courtyard outside were mossy underfoot since nobody had walked there for so long.

The door was locked, but Dermot knew where there was another key. A spare was always hidden behind a loose brick in the courtyard wall, and luckily for him, it was still there. He opened the door, the wood scratching the tiles as it had expanded over the winter.

'Oskar,' he called as they entered. 'Oskar, it's me, Dermot! Where the hell are you? 'Tis only a night for the fire!' He tried to insert some cheeriness into his voice and prayed fervently that his old friend remembered the code phrase.

THERE WAS NO ANSWER, so Dermot moved out into the passage that linked the kitchen with the main entranceway of the house. The shutters were closed, so the whole house was in murky gloom and smelled of damp and mouse droppings.

Dermot moved gingerly in the semi darkness, Thomas behind him, his Webley cocked and ready.

He prayed that Oskar not only heard and remembered the code phrase, but that he didn't shoot Thomas outright. They needed to learn where the girls were.

Dermot didn't risk repeating the phrase, as it would alert Thomas.

'Have you a match?' Dermot asked Thomas, surprised at how calm he was.

'No, just carry on,' Thomas whispered, nudging Dermot in the back with the gun. He pushed Dermot along the passage, into the main entranceway with its cantilever staircase.

'Oskar?' Dermot called again. He looked into the breakfast room, to the right of the front door, but it was empty. He crossed the hallway into Austin's study, and again, all that was left was a battered old desk and a mouldy-smelling rug. There was an ominous scurrying sound from the fireplace.

They climbed the stairs, Dermot in front, Thomas behind him, the revolver in Dermot's back. At the corner of the stairs, there was a landing and small alcove, designed for servants to jump into in case they met one of the householders on the stairs.

As they passed it, a voice came from the shadows.

'Now then, what have we here? Drop your weapon, Mr Hamilton-Brooks.'

Dermot turned to see Oskar standing beside them. He had been concealed by the alcove, and the barrel of his gun was now resting behind Thomas's ear. Thomas froze.

'I said, drop your weapon.' Oskar's voice was cold.

'I must warn—'

A shot rang out, followed by a piercing cry as Thomas fell to the ground. Dermot panicked, but Oskar had only shot Thomas in the foot. Blood pumped from the wound, and Thomas writhed on the small landing in agony. Instantly, Dermot grabbed the gun that had fallen from the Englishman's hands.

'He has my girls!' he shouted to Oskar. 'Don't kill him.'

Oskar threw him a strange look but said only,

'Let's take him up where we can see what we're doing.'

'I'm not sure we weren't followed,' Dermot replied.

'You weren't, at least not by the British, anyway.' That was all Oskar said.

Oskar and Dermot half dragged Thomas up the remaining steps to the next floor and into what was once a bedroom, him howling in agony all the way. There was one iron bedstead without a mattress in the room. Dermot held the Englishman's gun in his spare hand and kept it pointed at Thomas's head.

Oskar opened the shutters, flooding the room with dusky sunlight, and their eyes took a moment to adjust.

Then, using twine he had in his pocket, Oskar tied Thomas to a leg of the bed.

'Please,' Thomas begged. 'I—'

Oskar turned and hit him forcefully in the temple with the butt of his pistol. The man grunted, and then his head hung, by now only semi-conscious.

'I need him awake to tell me what he's done with my girls, Oskar,' Dermot protested.

'We'll get to that,' Oskar snapped, 'but first, would you tell me, old *friend*, how you managed to decide you would sacrifice me for the sake of your children, bearing in mind that without my intervention, as you pointed out when I met you in Dublin, you yourself would be dead many times over?'

Dermot looked into his old friend's eyes and saw something there he'd never seen before. There was a deadness there, a coldness. This man was not the Oskar he knew.

'I wasn't going to sacrifice you,' Dermot replied, desperate for his friend to know it was never his intention to hand him over to the British. 'You surely don't think I would do that! I used our old code to warn you, didn't I? I knew we could take him together, but I couldn't on my own. Not when he had a gun, and I didn't. I decided we could work together, like we used to do.'

Oskar listened, unflinching, as Thomas left an odd groan out of him.

'Ah, Dermot,' Oskar murmured, though they were far enough away from Thomas for him not to hear. 'Nothing is like it was, nothing at all. What once was true is no longer the case. When we were young, everything was so clear-cut, black and white, right and wrong. But as you get older, things become a little greyer, until, I am sure, by the time you become an old man, everything is grey. Still, I suppose it doesn't matter, not really. In two hours, I will be rowed out to sea, where I will get on a U-boat, one that is delivering weapons to our former comrades, and go back to the whole stupid thing again. I'm tired, Dermot, so tired. I feel like an old, old man who has seen too much.'

'I would never have betrayed you,' Dermot said.

'Yes, you would not, I know. I'm... I don't know... This war has made me suspect everyone. And anyway, I don't have children. I would have killed for my Brigitta, but now... Look, it doesn't matter. Go and do what you have to.' Oskar sighed and wearily took out a cigarette.

Dermot didn't waste a second. He ran downstairs. Thankfully, the water was still connected in the kitchen. He took an old saucepan, filled it from the tap, then ran upstairs and threw the cold water over Thomas. The shock of it brought the man back to consciousness. He groaned.

Dermot grabbed him by his hair and pulled his head back.

'Now, Thomas, listen very carefully. You are going to tell me where my girls are, and you are going to order that they be released immediately. What you need to decide is if we'll do it the hard way or the easy way. Myself and Oskar here learned well from you lot all those years ago, pulling out fingernails with plyers, water torture, beatings to within an inch of death, so we're fairly adept at it. Now, I'm not a violent man anymore, Thomas, you know that, but you threatened my family and that changes everything. You won't be the first Englishman I've killed, but then you know that, don't you? So here's what I'm proposing. We go to the post office now, you and I and Oskar, and we send the telegram. We then wait until my daughters make contact, and then you're free to go. I should kill you, but for the sake of Elena and your children, I'm willing to spare you, provided my girls are safe. But, if that's going to be a problem for you, then we'll just have to find another way.'

The Englishman didn't respond so Dermot stood on his injured foot, and the shriek was bloodcurdling.

'All right, all right! I'll do it,' he rasped.

'And how do you propose we do this?' Oskar looked bemused. 'This place doesn't get too much action, so we'll be the talk of five parishes if we take him out bleeding into the post office.'

'Is there a code word?' Dermot asked Thomas, who was by now

sweating profusely and moaning. Dermot nudged him and rested his foot on Thomas's.

'No...' Thomas groaned.

But Dermot was smarter than that. 'So is there a code word?' he repeated, exerting a little pressure on the foot.

'Firebird—it's firebird,' Thomas managed to get out through gritted teeth.

'Give me the address.'

Thomas was drifting into unconsciousness again, so Dermot rifled through the man's pockets. Nothing.

He grabbed Thomas by the hair, yanking his head back. 'Give me the address.'

'It's...my shoe.'

Dermot looked down at the man's bloody foot. The shoe had disintegrated with the bullet.

'It had better be in the good shoe,' Oskar said with a wry smile as Dermot leaned down to remove the shoe from the uninjured foot.

Luckily, it was, and Dermot extracted the piece of paper from under the insole. Sure enough, it was an address in Wales.

'So? Are we off?' Oskar asked pleasantly, as if they were going on a Sunday drive. He stamped out his cigarette on the floor, and they dragged Thomas down to the car. Dermot took the keys from Thomas's pocket and threw them to Oskar, who sat into the driver's seat while Dermot shoved Thomas into the back and sat beside him.

Oskar drove in silence into the village of Kilthomand. A few of the locals who were out and about noticed the strange car and stopped to stare.

'Stay here with him. I'll be back.' Dermot got out of the car and crossed the square to the post office. He could feel all the eyes of the village burning into his neck as he walked, saluting nobody.

'Ah, Dermot, is it yourself?' Mossy Flanagan, the postmaster, opened with a smile.

But Dermot had no time for small talk. 'I need to send a telegram, Mossy, please, it's an emergency.'

'Right so, if it's an emergency, I suppose I can't say no. Have you it written?' he asked patiently.

'No, I'll just dictate it to you,' Dermot said, his patience thin.

'I can't do that, I'm afraid, Dermot. You must write it, and I must read it back to you, otherwise you could say I got it wrong and refuse to pay, d'you see? Them's the rules. Not my rules now then, no indeed, but the rules of the Posts and Telegraphs bosses above in Dublin.' Mossy's slow delivery and painstaking attention to detail meant Dermot was fit to lash out, but he knew of old there was no way of hurrying Mossy. 'So now, here's a card, let you write whatever you want to say on it there'—he pointed to the blank space in the centre of the card—'and write the address there'—he pointed to the space clearly marked *address*—'and then I'll send it for you.'

'Fine.' Dermot grabbed the card.

He copied the address from the piece of paper he'd found in Thomas's shoe.

Brick House, Cylch-y-garn, Anglesey, Wales.
Firebird. Release immediately. Confirm by return.

He handed the telegram card back to Mossy, who read it aloud. Thankfully, there was nobody else in the post office.

Mossy raised his eyebrows, but when he saw no explanation was forthcoming, he simply said,

'Don't you want to sign it, Dermot?'

'No, it will be too expensive. They'll know it's from me.'

Mossy shrugged. 'Fair enough so. Now that will be....' He counted out the words. 'Two shillings.'

Dermot handed over the money, and only when that was placed in the till drawer, and an entry made on a ledger, did Mossy sit down at the telegraph machine and began to tap out the message.

'How soon before it is delivered?' Dermot asked.

Mossy looked up. 'Well, the post office in that place will get it straightaway, I should think. So it depends on how far that house is from the post office. I have no idea, I was never there. I suppose you'll just have to wait? But sure, if you wanted to go over to Keoghs to wet the whistle, I'll call you when it gets here?'

Dermot thought about Thomas bleeding in the car.

He knew instinctively that he had the right address—Thomas was in no position to try to double-cross him; all he would be thinking about was the pain. So the girls were going to be all right. Dermot thought about Elena and Arthur and Georgina. In the old days, he and Oskar would have shot someone like Thomas, buried him in the bog, but those days were gone. He didn't want to make a widow of Elena or take Georgina and Arthur's father from them. Suddenly, like Oskar, Dermot felt weary and very old.

He went outside, to talk to Oskar about how they could get Thomas to the hospital, but when he got out, he realised the car was gone.

'Your friend left without you, did he?' Mrs Lacey from the draper's shop remarked. She had never gotten over the way Eve had shown her precious Sean up at the dance. That all seemed like years ago to Dermot now.

'It certainly looks that way, Mrs Lacey.' Dermot sighed as he shoved his hands into his pockets. 'Which way did he go?'

'Well, I don't know now,' she began, 'I'm not one for taking much notice of people's comings and goings—'

'All right,' Dermot said wearily and walked back in the direction of the post office.

Not to be outdone in the knowledge stakes, however, she followed him. 'But I do think I remember him going out the coast road because I said to myself, surely he's going back to Dublin in a big fancy car like that, but no, out the coast road he went, and like the clappers too, I might add. Who was he at all that was driving? I didn't recognise him.'

Dermot sighed and turned to face her. 'He's a very old friend of mine, Mrs Lacey, but I don't think I'll be seeing him again.'

He turned on his heel and went back into the post office.

Mossy was now painstakingly selling stamps to Sister Teresita from the convent, and Joanie O'Leary was behind the nun. He'd have to wait.

He should have guessed what Oskar was going to do. Dermot mused that he was losing his edge. Once Oskar was sure Dermot had

277

all he needed to free his daughters, it was back to business. A British agent would be too good a prize for the *Abwehr* to give up, and hard as it was to accept or imagine, his old comrade was a Nazi now, and so served that man Hitler.

Yes, Thomas would be halfway to a U-boat by now, and after that, well, Dermot didn't like to think. He hoped Thomas survived, but knowing what he did about Oskar, he doubted the Englishman would ever see his wife and children again. Still, he thought, if you play dangerous games, then the consequences can be very serious. Thomas would have known that. The fact that he survived for so long as a British spy in Ireland was, in itself, a miracle.

Eventually, the women ahead of him completed their business.

'Any answer, Mossy?' Dermot asked.

'Nothing yet, Dermot, but as I say... It could be miles away, or they might not have been able to deliver it. There could be any number of reasons. If you want, you could head on home, wherever that is these days, and you could pay me now for a confirmation telegram, and I'll send it as soon as I hear?'

Dermot nodded. 'Thanks, Mossy. But I'll just wait, if you don't mind.'

CHAPTER 35

*A*isling and Kate sat on the single beds facing each other in one of the bedrooms upstairs. Lady Kenefick was lying down next door. They had cleaned her face up as much as possible, but she probably needed a stitch or two on her lip. She was shaken but surprisingly calm.

'What's this all about?' Aisling whispered. 'Who are these people, and what do they want?'

'Why are you looking at me like that? I have no idea!' Kate responded testily. 'Do you think I know something about this... Seriously?'

Aisling sighed. 'No, of course I don't, sorry. I just... It must be Lady Kenefick they were after, and we just happened to be in the wrong place at the wrong time.'

'Well, if they're kidnapping her for a ransom, they're in for a rude awakening. Sure, she's skint!' Kate exclaimed, and Aisling hushed her.

'She's just next door,' Aisling whispered.

'So what? Stupid old witch getting us caught up in her...' Kate was furious and would have launched into a loud rant about Sam's mother if they were not interrupted by a rap on their bedroom door.

'May I come in?' Lady Violet stood in the doorway. The bruising on her face was livid looking, and dried blood had congealed on her face.

'Yes, yes, of course.' Aisling pulled the chair out from the dressing table for Violet to sit on.

'Now, do either of you know what this is about?' she whispered.

Kate stared and said nothing. 'No, we don't,' Aisling answered.

'Well, I had a look out of the window, and we are in a very desolate place indeed. I can only assume they want a ransom for me, but since that will not be paid and I fear for our safety, we need to find a way to escape.'

The two girls looked at her as if she was insane.

'They have guns,' Kate said, trying to keep her voice steady. 'If we try anything, they'll shoot us.' She deliberately didn't use Sam's mother's title, as the woman would expect. 'Nobody knows we're here, so nobody will even know where to look for us.'

'Well, I don't know about you two, but I am certainly not remaining here,' Violet announced. 'I'll take my chances, but I will not be incarcerated by hoodlums. I say we wait until they fall asleep, then get out one of the windows, and make a run for it.'

Kate smiled. 'To where? This isn't some game. They'll hardly toddle off to bed and just leave us to our own devices. And even if we did manage to get out of this house, all around us for miles is this kind of moor, and they have a car...'

Violet looked down her nose at Kate. 'You saw how he looked at you,' she said in withering tones. 'We are not safe here. For goodness' sake, girl, have a little gumption. This is not the Kate Murphy I knew from Robinswood who could climb walls and shoot and fight as well as any boy.'

Aisling knew Kate would react to that remark, though in what way it was impossible to tell. Kate was volatile and headstrong, but she, like Aisling, was genuinely frightened now.

'This is different, though,' Kate began.

'Yes, but your father and mother brought you girls up to be brave, so it's time to show that bravery now.'

The mention of their parents made both Kate and Aisling realise that Lady Kenefick was right.

'Fine, let's give it a go.' Kate sighed. 'What's the plan?'

'How about we go downstairs, say we wanted to make something to eat, and take a few knives or scissors or something as weapons?' Aisling suggested. 'I noticed when we arrived they left the keys in the ignition. Maybe we could distract them and jump in the car? Kate's a good driver.'

'Good idea, Aisling,' Violet praised her. 'Let's go down, see what the lie of the land is, and we'll take it from there.'

The unlikely leader of the three turned and made her way to the top of the stairs. Before she stood on the first tread, she looked back.

'We *will* get out of this, girls.'

Kate and Aisling exchanged glances before following Lady Kenefick, who regally descended the stairs, her cane with the silver fox head keeping time as she banged it loudly on each step.

'We require sustenance,' she proclaimed as they entered the room, and if the situation were not so serious, Aisling and Kate might have giggled at her audacity.

'What?' The younger man seemed to be alone, thrown on a chair, reading what looked like the racing pages. Aisling scanned the area for the older one, but there was no sign.

'Food,' Kate explained. 'We're hungry.'

'Well, you can see what's there, make yourself something.' He returned to his paper and

lit up a cigarette.

Lady Kenefick started coughing dramatically.

'Extinguish that at once!' she spluttered.

The man seemed taken aback by the coughing, and despite trying not to be intimidated by Violet's tone, the girls could see that he was.

'Listen here,' he began, but his words were lost in yet another bout of wheezing and coughing.

'She's allergic to cigarettes,' Aisling said, sensing where Violet was going with this. 'Can you take it outside please?'

He hesitated.

'Look, if you don't, she could end up having an asthma attack, and then we'll need an ambulance!' Kate snapped. 'Whoever's put you up to this won't be happy if she dies, now, will they?'

Three bossy women proved to be too much for him. He grabbed his paper and went outside, slamming the door behind him.

'Quick, girls, gather anything you can that we can use as a weapon,' Lady Kenefick ordered quietly.

'He's here alone,' Kate hissed. 'The other one is gone somewhere. What should we do?'

Suddenly, Aisling's eyes shone. She quickly crossed the room to the chair where the man had been sitting. On the ground beside the chair was his gun. In his hurry to get out, he must have forgotten to take it. She picked it up and checked the barrel—it was loaded.

'Can you fire it?' Lady Kenefick whispered.

'Of course,' she said. 'Daddy showed us when we were twelve.'

'Right,' Kate said. 'He'll be back in any second! What's the plan?'

'Shoot him and run?' Lady Kenefick suggested.

'Now now, ladies, what's going on here?'

The older man walked in the door. Aisling shoved the gun in the waistband of her skirt, shielded by the other two, and hurriedly turned around.

'We are hungry,' Lady Kenefick said, 'and when we told the other one we required sustenance, he lit up one of his vile cigarettes and almost gave me an asthma attack. I am allergic to cigarette smoke, and so we asked him to leave. Now, as we still have had nothing to eat, please permit us to go about our business unimpeded.'

He looked amused, if anything, and stepped backward. With a sweep of his hand in the direction of the sideboard, he said, 'Be my guest.'

Aisling and Kate brought the bread and cheese to the table and set about cutting slices off the loaf, watched by the man. Lady Kenefick, much to their surprise, filled the kettle from the very noisy tap. The noise caused the man to look in that direction, so Kate took the opportunity to take a sharp chopping knife from the table and hide it under her cardigan.

But she didn't know what to do from there. The younger one would be back any second, and he'd surely notice his gun missing.

Suddenly, Aisling winked at Kate.

'I...I'm sorry,' Aisling said to the man, 'but I need the toilet... I couldn't see one upstairs.' She wrung her hands and tried to look embarrassed.

'There isn't one,' the man barked, annoyed to be interrupted as he found more kindling for the fire. 'The privy is outside, bottom of the garden.'

'Oh... Oh, right...' Aisling went to leave, and Kate and Lady Kenefick followed.

'No, you don't,' he snapped, turning from where he was kneeling down to stoke the fire. 'One at a time... You two wait here. You can go when she gets back.'

Once he had turned his back again, giving the fire his attention, Lady Kenefick gave the girls a nod, and quick as a flash, she crossed the room and swung her silver-handled cane like a cricket bat, hitting the man hard on the head.

He slumped, dazed for a moment, and Kate took her chance. She took the knife from where she had secreted it and stuck into the man's ribs. She looked horrified at what she'd just done, but Lady Kenefick and Aisling grabbed her and pulled her away. The knife was still in him as they ran out the door.

When they got outside, they scanned the yard for the other man. He had his back to them, relieving himself against the wall, and Aisling showed no hesitation. She reached into her waistband and drew the pistol.

She cocked it and aimed. One shot, and he was down.

'You bitch!' The older one had managed to drag himself outside, his shirt soaked in blood. Aisling spun and shot him, the bullet piercing his chest. He looked surprised for one second, then fell forward.

Aisling was stunned, trembling with the pistol in her hands. Violet stepped forward and took the gun from her, and then led her quickly to the car.

Luckily, the keys were still in the ignition, as before, so Kate jumped into the driver's seat as Violet shepherded Aisling into the back seat.

Kate drove as fast as she could. She had no idea where they were, and since the war began, all road signage had been removed to impede the enemy in the event of an invasion. Through miles and miles of open countryside, none of them spoke.

At one point, Aisling looked down and realised she was holding Lady Kenefick's hand. They both came to that realisation at the same time, but instead of letting go, Lady Kenefick squeezed hers.

'That was very brave, my dear.' Her voice had none of its usual imperious tone.

'Do you think they're dead?' Kate could barely get the words out.

'I...I don't know. I doubt it. Aisling shot the younger one quite low down, I think....' Violet realised Aisling was shaking. She took off her coat and put it over the girl.

'You'll be fine. It's just shock. Whatever their fate, they brought it on themselves. You have nothing to feel guilty about.'

Tears of relief and fear took Kate by surprise as Lady Kenefick spotted her tears in the rearview mirror. She leaned forward and patted her on the shoulder as she drove.

'You both were magnificent,' she said. 'Your parents are right to be as proud of you as they are.'

'But what if I murdered someone?' Aisling turned to Violet, and suddenly, she looked so young.

'I wish Sam was here,' Kate whispered.

Lady Kenefick caught Kate's eye in the rearview mirror and nodded in agreement. 'So do I, my dear, so do I.'

They never even noticed the telegram boy as he cycled furiously towards them.

Eventually, they arrived at a small village. Kate stopped the car and got out. There were a few people standing around, wondering whose was the strange car, no doubt. In many ways, it reminded her of Kilthomand.

Two ladies stood in a doorway, mid-chat, and she approached them nervously.

'Excuse me, is there a police station here?' she asked.

'No, dearie, not in Llanfaethlu, not since before the war, you see. But there is an LDF branch. Perhaps they can help you?'

'Yes, yes, please, where would I find them?' The Local Defence Force would have to do.

'Oh, Captain Weston should be in his house, I would think. It's that one over there, with the red door. You go on over there and knock and tell him what your problem is, and I'm sure he'll help you.'

Kate thanked her and went back to get Aisling and Lady Kenefick.

Together, the three women crossed the street and knocked on the red door.

A tall, broad man in his seventies answered. He had a most incredible handlebar moustache and the hairiest eyebrows they had ever seen.

'Yes, can I help you?' he asked, his voice surprisingly gentle for such a bear of a man.

'May we come in? We need to give you some information, and it is of a confidential nature.' Violet had a way of commanding respect.

Kate and Aisling did allow themselves a small smile this time, as the man seemed taken aback by Lady Kenefick's haughty demeanour.

'Certainly, madam.' He stood aside, and the three of them walked in.

She told the story quickly and without emotion, making sure that the man understood that all actions they had taken were entirely self-defence. She explained how Aisling was so brave, and the way she spoke about both the Murphy girls was quite incredible to them, knowing Violet as they did. She seemed convinced she was the target of the kidnapping, that there was probably some kind of ransom demand made to Samuel or Lillian.

Captain Weston waited until she had finished and then sprung into action. He assured them that he would place a call to the police and they would send someone as soon as possible.

Within moments, a tiny, bird-like woman, presumably Mrs

Weston, arrived with tea and sandwiches, and an order was sent to Holyhead docks to retrieve the ladies' luggage, while a section of the LDF were dispatched to the farmhouse.

'I wonder if there's any way we could telephone home, to let them know we're all right?' Kate asked. 'They'll be worried sick if we don't turn up. We were supposed to be on the boat to Ireland early this morning.'

'Oh, dearie, I'm not sure,' the tiny woman said. 'We do have a telephone, but it is only for military use. Perhaps when Captain Weston comes back? Or there is a post office up the street, perhaps you could send a telegram?'

AISLING STOOD UP. 'Fine, I'll find the post office. I need some air anyway. Kate, you'd better stay here with Lady Kenefick. The doctor is on the way, apparently. I'll get a message to Mammy and Daddy.'

'And to Sam.' Both Kate and Lady Kenefick spoke at exactly the same time.

They realised, in that instant, that they had more in common than divided them. A day previously, the idea that they would have been thrown together would have been an appalling prospect for both of them, but now there seemed to be an understanding between them, though how long it would last Kate couldn't begin to guess.

'I can now see why Samuel is very taken with you,' Lady Kenefick said.

Kate saw her chance, possibly the only chance she'd ever get, to make things right with her future mother-in-law.

'Lady Kenefick, I know I'm not the kind of girl you had in mind for Samuel to marry.'

She never called him Samuel, but his mother always did, so she decided to default to the name the woman had given him. '

But I really do love him. In fact, I think I've always loved him, even as a child. And he loves me. And this war, it will be a miracle if any of us make it through alive, but I know he cares a lot about what you think, and it hurts him so much that you don't approve of us. He wants your blessing so badly, just as I would if my parents didn't like him. I know you and Lillian aren't that close...' She was on thin ice here, she knew it, but she carried on, 'But you and Samuel are, and if you could bring yourself to support us, I promise you, you would always have a home with us. It won't be what you're used to, nothing like it, but if this war has taught us anything it's that material things can be replaced, people are what matter. I want to marry your son, and I want to be the mother of your grandchildren, please God, in the future. So can you please consider it and not cut us out?'

The old Kate could never have envisaged herself going cap in hand to Violet Kenefick, but the events of the last day had changed her irrevocably. She just wanted to go home, to live a life of peace and happiness surrounded by her family and Sam.

The brass carriage clock, the only decoration in the whole room, ticked rhythmically in the silence.

Lady Kenefick put down her teacup and sat back in the chair. She fixed Kate with an intent gaze, as if seeing her for the first time.

'YOU ARE RIGHT. I didn't think you were a good match for my son, and I know both you and Samuel saw that as snobbery on my part. I will admit, I do not approve of classes intermingling, but there was more to it. I just imagined how difficult life would be for both of you, neither really fitting in the other's world. Marriage is a great cure for love, Kate, and it is not all roses and champagne, I may as well tell you. But, as you say, you love him and he loves you. I underestimated you, Kate. You showed such bravery back there. If they'd captured me on my own, which was their intention I'm sure, I doubt very much that I would be here now. Though they clearly did not do their homework, assuming that because I'm titled that I am wealthy. The war is changing everything, you're right.'

She sighed wearily, but Kate didn't dare interrupt. 'The old ways,' Violet went on, 'where who you were meant something, seem to be gone forever, and the world is a place I no longer recognise. Lillian and I have had our problems, as you rightly point out, but, in a peculiar twist of fate, this man she is seeing, Beau, seems to be actually having a positive influence on her. He is a negro, and an American, and goodness knows what the future holds for them, but I must admit I like him. And he is good for her. I don't understand this new world —it's like a foreign country where I don't speak the language—and while initially I was fearful and resentful of it, I'm actually starting to see the potential. I raised two children, and I realise now I was preparing them for a world that no longer exists. I can see now the benefit of raising children to be productive, as your parents did. We, people of my background, didn't need to be able to do anything, really, except marry well, produce an heir, and that was more or less it.

'I didn't even manage to do that particularly successfully. Lord Kenefick was a gambler and a drinker, and he lost all of our money. When we were kidnapped, I was en route to Dublin to settle the last of his debts, which will more or less clean us out financially, so I will be dependent on my son for my care. It's not a pleasant position to be in, coming from where I was, but I don't know what else to do.'

Kate looked at her, amazed she was being so open.

'You could get a job?' she suggested gently.

Violet's face registered what Kate took to be horror at such a prospect, but Kate had already started so she might as well finish.

'I just mean, with the war and everything,' she explained, 'there's a huge shortage of staff everywhere. And even Princess Elizabeth has a job. You could drive an ambulance or work at a nursing station or even in an office. Lord Kenefick is gone, God rest him, and so is Robinswood, for now at least, and you said yourself everything is different now. Why not embrace it? Lillian with Beau, me and Sam, we might not be what you imagined, but maybe that's all right? You could make a new life for yourself, with your family around you— servants, Americans, whatever—a future where you earn your own money and you aren't relying on any man to support you. And you could do some good at the same time. You talk like you're eighty, but you're a young woman, not much older than my mam, and she's definitely not ready for the scrapheap. You can make a new life, a better one, if you'll let go of all the old stuff.'

The older woman smiled, the first genuine smile Kate had ever seen from her.

'The idea that you believe someone would employ me is flattering, Kate dear, but even if I could do it, I have no skills, nothing to offer, I'm afraid. I am like the dodo, extinct and obsolete.'

She looked much smaller than Kate ever remembered her, and suddenly, Kate couldn't believe how frightened she'd been of this woman at one time.

'I don't know,' Kate said with a shrug, 'you're fairly handy with a cane. Maybe you should join the home guard.' Kate chuckled, and Lady Kenefick looked horrified for a moment before joining in.

When Aisling came back in, she found, to her amazement, the two of them laughing together.

CHAPTER 36

*D*ermot stood in the centre of Kilthomand wondering what he should do next. He'd waited for over two hours, but there was no response to the telegram. Without a way of knowing how far the address was from the post office, there was little point in waiting, but he couldn't go back to Isabella with no news of the girls. He would have to do something.

He would make his way back to Dublin and take it from there. He could go to Wales, see if he could find them. After all, he had the address. He wondered if he should go to the guards. It was the obvious thing to do, but he was inherently mistrustful of them, being made up as they were of Free Staters. He didn't dislike them, he just gave them a wide berth. He had spent a lifetime avoiding answering questions, so it went against the grain to volunteer information to the authorities. Maybe he could contact Sam Kenefick, see if he knew anything.

He checked once more with Mossy for a return telegram, but nothing. Eventually, he went out to the square in time for the bus.

On the way back, he went over and over it. He had no options; he would have to go to the guards. Thomas had said that if the kidnappers had not heard from him by tomorrow morning, they were to kill the girls. That still gave Dermot time, but maybe not long enough to get back to Dublin, catch a boat, and find the house. No, he'd have to go to the guards, give them the information, and ask them to contact the British police.

Then he had another idea. He need not contact the Irish guards at all. He could just telephone the British police in Holyhead directly, give them the address, and tell them to go out there. But could he trust them not to mess it up? He looked at his watch. What if he caught the boat to Holyhead, went over and rescued the girls himself? Maybe that was the best thing. But would there be time?

The journey back to Dublin seemed interminable, but eventually the bus pulled into the stop on Bachelors Quay. Dermot got off and was about to make his way to the B&I Ferry office when he passed a public telephone. A pang of guilt overtook him. He should contact Isabella, even if he had no news. She would be out of her mind with worry by now. He wanted to be able to tell her it was alright, but if he was going to have to go over to Wales, then she would need to know.

He stepped into the box and dialled the Hamilton-Brookses' number. It was answered on the first ring. By Elena.

'Hello?' Dermot could hear the panic in her voice.

'Elena, it's me,' he said. 'Can I speak to Isabella, please, quickly?' He did not want to have any conversation with Elena. He knew he would have to tell her the truth eventually, the woman was owed that much, but not now.

'Dermot! Oh, Dermot, everything is all right. They sent a telegram —they are fine. Apparently, it's a long story. I'll call Isabella now...'

Dermot leaned against the wall of the call box for support. The relief was incredible. Kate and Aisling were all right.

'Dermot!' Isabella cried. 'Oh thank goodness, are you all right?'

'I'm fine Bella, fine. Are the girls all right?'

'They are grand,' she assured him. 'They sent a telegram, just a short one to say they were fine and that they will ring soon. And you'll never guess who's with them.'

'Sam?' Dermot guessed.

'No, only Lady Muck herself, Violet. Don't ask me how, but they are all together. Oh, Der, I thought today would never end. I was convinced something terrible was going to happen...' Isabella's voice was muffled by tears. 'Where are you now?'

'I'm on Bachelors Quay. I'm on the way back. I'll see you soon.' He was about to hang up when he heard himself say, 'I love you, Bella.'

'I love you too.' She hung up.

All the way back, Dermot wondered what he was going to say to Elena. She'd seen him leave with her husband, though she had no idea why, and he was returning without him. She would demand an explanation, and he would have to be the one to give it to her. No matter how many times he went around it in his head, the only thing he could come up with was the truth.

When he walked up the gravel driveway and went in the kitchen door, Isabella threw herself on him, embracing him tightly. Tears streamed down her face. Eve joined them, and for a few moments, he just stood with both of them in his arms.

Then he stepped back and said,

'Can you take Georgina and Arthur? I have to talk to Elena.'

Isabella knew by his face what that meant, and her hand went to her mouth in involuntary horror.

'Not...'

He just nodded and

went out into the hallway. From there, he could hear Elena with the children. She had become so much better with them since Isabella began her gentle instruction in parenting.

Within seconds, the children came running down the stairs. 'Dermot!' Georgina cried excitedly. 'We found a baby rabbit in the garden, and it's so furry, and we don't know where its mummy is, and Bella said you could make a house for him and we could keep him as a pet...'

Before he had a chance to answer, Eve appeared at his shoulder.

'Come on, you two, I think the bunny is awake now. Let's go and see...' They scampered off happily.

Elena smiled when she saw him. 'You must be so relieved...'

Something in his face stopped her in her tracks.

'What?' she asked.

'Come in here...' Dermot led her into Thomas's office. 'Sit down.'

Without protest, she allowed him to lead her to the desk and sit her down in Thomas's chair.

There, Dermot told her everything.

When he'd finished talking, she just sat in the chair, stunned.

'And he's now on his way to Germany, to be...what...interrogated?' She looked incredulous.

'I believe so.'

'And you're absolutely sure Thomas arranged the kidnap of your daughters...and threatened to have them killed...? I just...I can't believe it... It's like some kind of a nightmare... I don't think he is capable...' She looked suddenly very young and vulnerable. Dermot hated having to do this to her, to her children.

He sighed, walked around the desk, went down on his knees in front of her, so his eyes were level with hers, and held both her hands in his.

'Elena, this is horrific, all of it, but I swear I'm telling you the whole truth. Thomas was under enormous pressure to stop the flow of German agents into Britain through Ireland, and those in charge, in London, told him that if he couldn't, then they would appoint someone who could and he would be recalled. What he did, well, those were the actions of a man terrified of losing everything. He knew you and the children were happy here, and he knew if he was recalled to London, Georgina and Arthur would have to be evacuated. He did it for you all, and while I don't condone it, I do understand.

'I am a private man,' Dermot went on. 'I keep myself to myself, and there's a reason for that. I was an active member of the IRA back in the twenties. Thomas knew that, and he also knew that an old friend of mine was now a high-profile German agent. He arranged for Isabella and me to come here, to use me as leverage with my friend Oskar. He thought he could force my hand to lead him to Oskar and that would get everyone off his back. The plan backfired badly, and now, well, now he will, I'm afraid, pay a high price.'

Tears shone, as yet unshed, in Elena's eyes.

'Do you think I'll ever see him again?'

Dermot longed to give her some hope, to take a fraction of the awfulness away from her, but that would not serve her in the long run.

'No, Elena, I don't,' he said, though each word hurt him.

* * *

LIFE in the house went on. The children were told that their Daddy had to go away, and though they were very sad, they were young and resilient and clung even more than before to Elena and the Murphys.

Elena's sister and mother were coming over from England for a visit next week, as she needed their support. His solicitor had made contact, Thomas had transferred everything into his wife's name a few days before so Elena was financially secure and the home in Dublin was safe. Thomas must have had a strong sense of foreboding; education funds for the children, all the paperwork regarding investments, bonds, stocks, and all matters financial were perfectly in order. The solicitor also delivered a letter for Elena, which she showed to Dermot and Isabella.

Looking pale and tired, as she had since the whole terrible business started, Elena walked into the kitchen one morning as they were having breakfast and placed the opened letter in front of them. Dermot picked it up, and Isabella read over his shoulder.

Dear Elena,

If you're reading this then things have not worked out as I hoped. I was playing a dangerous game, but the stakes were very high. I lost, clearly. I am sorry to leave you my darling.

Bertie has all the paperwork, so whatever else happens, you and the children are taken care of financially. Elena, I am so sorry.

Please allow Arthur and Georgina to grow up knowing how much I loved them, and you, my darling, I am so sorry. I couldn't bring you all back to London, separate us from the children, risk a bomb falling on your precious head. It's no consolation at this point, I imagine, but I did what I did for you and our children. Dermot and Isabella have shown us the wonder of being a

proper family, something we were not excelling at before they arrived, and
you're all so precious to me, I wanted to protect you.
    It was only ever you, Elena.
    Your husband,
    Thomas

DERMOT FINISHED READING AND STOOD. Thomas was clever enough to make it sound like a suicide note, so at least that would satisfy anyone that came looking for him. He and Isabella held Elena in their arms, where she sobbed like a baby for the first time since the whole wretched business happened. She was shattered with grief and hurt, and fear for the future, and while Isabella felt sorry for her, she still burned with resentment for Thomas Hamilton-Brooks, for putting her girls in danger like that. Dermot said Thomas would never have given the order, but Isabella didn't care. The man didn't know what would happen, and Isabella would never forgive him.

    She had thought Elena might ask them to leave, considering everything that had happened, but thankfully, she was most adamant that she needed them to stay, especially now, and they were happy to. Eve was doing all right, and though it would take her years to get over the loss of Jack, for now, she was managing.

EPILOGUE

*T*he journey to England was long and slow, but Isabella was so happy to be reunited with her girls, she didn't mind. She had never left Ireland before, but when Dermot suggested they go see the girls and then Kate and Sam announced they were getting married, it seemed sensible to do it all at the same time.

Isabella smiled inwardly at what horror must be on the faces of the busybodies of Kilthomand. They'd hear soon enough that Kate Murphy was marrying young Lord Kenefick, in a registry office no less. They would nod at each other knowingly—those Murphys always had notions of themselves, ideas above their station and all the rest of it. Isabella couldn't care less.

THEY HAD PLANNED on staying in a hotel, but Lady Violet insisted on putting them up, much to Isabella and Dermot's reluctance. Kate had assured them by letter that she had changed, and that it would be fine, but all three Murphys were filled with trepidation as they made their way across bombed-out England. But, true to her word, Lady Violet was waiting at the arrivals area of Paddington Station, and she was, as Kate said, entirely different.

She was dressed in a very ordinary skirt and cardigan, and she waved excitedly when she saw them.

'Isabella, Dermot, and Eve...I am so happy you could come. Kate and Aisling have spoken of nothing but your visit for weeks. Come, come, follow me. I'm so glad you don't have too much luggage, for we shall have to take the bus, and the crowds are rather tiresome.'

Dermot shot Isabella a glance. Was this stuck-up Lady Kenefick? Dressed like an ordinary woman and actually getting on a bus?

Her house was relatively small, compared to Robinswood, though still a nice house by any standards, off Hampstead Heath. She welcomed them inside and, to their amazement, offered them tea, which she proceeded to make herself.

'I know, it is a change from how things were at Robinswood,' she acknowledged, 'and I will not say the transition was simple. But none-theless, I must say I am enjoying my life so much more now. Kate has been wonderful, truly wonderful. She and Samuel and Lillian and Beau helped me move here, and I must say, I love it. I can walk on the heath, and while I've had to learn how to cook and take care of the house, it's impossible to get staff and even if I could nobody would hold a candle to you, so I've decided to become a modern woman. It's actually been very rewarding. I've even got a part-time job with the council, helping those who have been displaced by the bombing to be rehoused, and though I'm hopeless really, I can't type or anything, I have proved useful in encouraging those in society who are better off to loosen their purse strings a little. Some people seem to respond to the Lady Kenefick moniker, though goodness knows why! An old friend of Austin's, for example, has agreed to allow twenty temporary dwellings to be placed on his grounds, which will provide a home for so many needy families. So, the title Austin left me has been useful for something.'

Dermot had taken the bags upstairs, and Eve and Isabella stood in the kitchen, not knowing what to say.

'Well, the house is really lovely, Lady Kenefick, really homely,' Eve managed.

'Please, Eve dear, let's dispense with all of that nonsense. Call me

Violet. After all, we are about to be family. I know it is a shock, seeing me like this, but honestly, this new life is so much more fulfilling. Kate and Sam are a great support, and Lillian is happy with Beau. Though I will be honest, when I first met him and realised my daughter was in a relationship with a dark-skinned man, I was horrified. But do you know, he is such a good influence on her, and he's really a lovely man. I told her to find someone to marry, to settle down and put an end to the drinking and dancing every night, and she has. Not as I imagined she would, but she and Beau are very happy. He told me terrible things about the way his people are treated in America, but he always speaks highly of the British and their sense of fair play. It seems he experiences less discrimination here than he does at home. Lillian says he plans to come and live here once the war is over.'

Isabella tried not to react to the irony of Violet's new take on things. There wasn't much British fair play displayed by the British in Ireland down through the centuries, she thought, but kept her own council. Still, she struggled with each new revelation. The girls had mentioned in their letters that Lillian was going out with a negro American GI, but the idea that Violet liked him was incredible.

'I've never met a dark-skinned person before,' Isabella said. 'Kate and Aisling have met him, and they say he is very nice. But is he not being sent to Europe?'

'I don't believe so, he's a mechanic or some such like that so he services the machinery and so on over here. I do hope he is kept out of harm's way, worrying about Samuel is bad enough.'

Isabella was astounded. Was this really Lady Violet Kenefick and her snobbish ways?

'Oh and he is so gentlemanly, and he has pulled Lillian up on more than one occasion about the way she speaks to me. He helped me move in here. The neighbours' eyes were out on sticks, to see Sam and Beau lifting furniture, but let them talk. I've been through so much by now, I care nothing for people's opinion anymore.'

Isabella smiled. Samuel had become Sam, and Violet was actually a normal person.

'Can I help?' she asked, as Violet opened cupboards and took out some meagre provisions. 'We brought some ham and eggs and some tomatoes and vegetables from the garden.'

Violet's eyes lit up. 'Did you really? Oh, how kind! I can't remember when I last had food like we used to enjoy back in Ireland. Everything here is thin and tasteless.'

'Will I get them?' Eve asked. They had been worried that such a gift might seem a little unsophisticated, despite Kate and Aisling's protestations that food from home would be the best present ever. And Kate had mentioned Violet was holding a lunch after the wedding but there was very little food to be got so anything her parents could contribute to the feast would be most welcome. So they'd packed a suitcase full and were happy to share with Violet. 'Will I get them?' Eve asked.

'Do, Eve, please,' Isabella answered, and when she returned and opened the suitcase with the carefully wrapped butter and cake and meat and vegetables, they couldn't believe how Violet's eyes welled up.

'I THOUGHT we could make sandwiches or cold plates for after the wedding tomorrow?' Isabella suggested. 'Kate said you were kindly hosting a little party.' Isabella was warming to this new and improved Violet.

'Oh, this is wonderful, simply wonderful!' Violet crooned. 'However did you manage it? You two are so clever, so resourceful, I can't believe my eyes! We shall have a feast fit for a king. Actually, I was hoping at some stage in the visit that, Dermot, maybe you could start me off growing some vegetables? I haven't a clue, but I'd like to try. The food on the base is dreadful, according to the girls and Sam, but Beau does get some marvellous stuff from the Americans. I try to have them all for dinner once a week, and to have some fresh vegetables would be super.' She took each item out of the case and gasped as if it was all precious jewels, not butter and cheese. 'Oh, Isabella, you even have cake. How splendid. Here, they rent out iced boxes just for the occasion, but nobody has real cake anymore. Oh, thank you so much! I was despairing as to what we could feed people. There is nothing available, and Sam said he would try to get some things from the mess, but you know men...'

'I do.' Isabella chuckled. 'Dermot thought I was mad bringing all of this, but I'm glad now that we did. So, how about we have that cup of tea and maybe a slice of cake, and then we can start the preparations for the big day?'

Kate and Aisling arrived to Violet's house that evening when their shift finished, and Dermot went out for a drink with Sam, Mark and Beau. The girls pitched in and were delighted to see Violet intently watching Isabella as she made a trifle. Lillian even appeared, and while the transformation wasn't as stark as her mother's, she certainly was more pleasant.

Violet produced two bottles of champagne—she'd had the contents of Robinswood's cellar taken out of storage for the occasion—and the night before the wedding really was a very jolly affair.

* * *

THE NEXT MORNING, Isabella sat in the registry office between Eve, Aisling and Mark. She gave Eve's hand a quick squeeze, imagining how hard this must be for her without Jack and her eldest daughter squeezed back and gave a reassuring smile. Today was about Kate and Sam. Dermot was outside with the bride, and Sam stood in his uniform at the desk at the top of the room, looking handsome and nervous. Isabella allowed herself a glance across the tiny aisle to where Lady Violet Kenefick sat, Lillian and Beau beside her. Lillian was still haughty and a bit standoffish but she did seem to be reined in considerable by the amazing looking Beau. She tried not to stare, but he really was handsome. He filled any room with his huge presence, but his voice was gentle, he was interested in everyone and so polite and helpful. Wherever he was raised, they did it right. She wondered what Austin would have made of it all, and said as much to Violet as they companionably made the sandwiches last night and Isabella had laughed at the other woman's reply.

'As long as there was whiskey and someone to blather on about horses or the war with I would imagine he would be in his element.' Her smile showed there was no bitterness, just a fond memory of a jovial, if useless man.

The registrar stood up, and Kate entered on her father's arm. She looked radiant and winked at her mother and sisters as Dermot shook hands with Sam.

The ceremony was short and had no frills, but the room was filled with love.

'I CALL upon these persons here present,' Kate said, her voice strong and clear, 'to witness that I, Kate Theresa Murphy, do take thee, Samuel Austin George Kenefick, to be my lawfully wedded husband, to love, honour and obey, as long as we both shall live.'

Dermot shot Isabella a glance when she said obey. They had joked in bed last night how Sam, just like Jack, God rest him, need not expect full compliance on that one either.

Sam then took Kate's hands and repeated the same words after the registrar.

The small balding man then congratulated them, and Kate and Sam kissed, and before they knew it they were all back out in the sunshine, laughing and joking happily.

Violet's house wasn't far, and Dermot, with his beloved wife on one arm, offered Violet his other, which she gratefully took. He smiled down at her, and together, they led their family into their future.

The End

THE BEAUTIFUL HOUSE featured on the cover of this series is in County Sligo and is called Temple House. It's a spectacular place complete with lake and Knight's Templar castle on the grounds. It is the family home of friends of mine and is a fabulous place to stay, host a party or even a wedding. If you ever get the chance you should visit and walk among my imaginings of the Keneficks and the Murphys, you'd love it.

www.templehouse.ie

THE SEQUEL TO THIS BOOK, which follows the story of the Murphys and the Keneficks into the future is called *Return to Robinswood* and can be purchased here:

https://geni.us/ReturnToRobinswoodAL

HERE IS a sneak preview to get you started,

Return To Robinswood

Brighton, England, 1946

DERMOT MURPHY SAT opposite his son-in-law and said nothing.

'Well? What do you think?' Sam Kenefick asked, trying to figure out what was going on behind Dermot's inscrutable face. Kate's father had hardly changed a bit in the war years. He was tall and as strong as an ox, and his dark copper hair was thick with very little grey. Kate and Aisling looked nothing like him – they were Mediterranean-looking, all dark and curvy like their mother – but Eve, Kate's other sister, was his spitting image.

The murmur of conversation, the occasional burst of laughter, the general hum of a busy Brighton pub all around them seemed a million miles away. The euphoria of the war being over at long last was wearing off, and life was still hard for people. But the old-world pub with its brass fittings and dark wood interior seemed to help melt people's cares away, and there was a general air of bonhomie.

'What do I think?' He repeated the question.

Sam swallowed. Dermot Murphy was a man he admired immensely, and he had done so all his life, but his father-in-law didn't suffer fools gladly. Sam needed to convince him to return to Robinswood.

'Look, Dermot, it's a good offer – well, it's the best offer I can make you at any rate. Kate wants to go home, and for her, home has always been and will always be Robinswood.'

'With all due respect, Sam, the fact that Robinswood was my family's home didn't seem to bother you too much in 1940 when we were thrown out by your mother. I know it was she who did the evicting, but you'd inherited it by then, and you did nothing.'

Sam knew Dermot's lifelong mistrust of the English had not melted away when his daughter became the new Lady Kenefick. British titles did not impress him. He decided honesty was best. 'You're right. And I'm deeply ashamed of that. I should have taken more of a role, but I just wanted to fly, and I was caught up in the excitement of the war. I should not have left the management of Robinswood to my mother, nor should I have allowed her to leave you all homeless. Your family and mine have worked together for a very long time, and it was shabbily done. My father would have been appalled.'

Dermot took a sip of his pint and grimaced. Warm British beer was no match for a creamy pint of Guinness in the pub in Kilthomand. 'My family worked *for* yours, Sam, not *with*. I worked for your father, God rest him, and Isabella and the girls worked for your mother. So let's not sugarcoat this. Also – and I don't mean any offence – but what in the name of God do you know about farming? You're not an outdoor man, and you look like a gust of wind would knock you over.' He winked to show he wasn't being unkind.

Sam always felt like a schoolboy around Dermot, and the man was right – he was slight and boyish looking. But he desperately wanted to go home, to put everything right. He really believed things were different now; the class structures of the past were just as demolished as the buildings of London, and it was a new era.

He grinned. 'I am actually tougher than I look. And you're right, I don't know much about farming, but I'll learn. And who better to teach me than the best groundskeeper Robinswood ever had? And now that we have Jack to consider, it's for him as well. I've inherited the title and not much else, as you know, but I really think if we went back together, we could make a go of it. There's nothing you don't know about running the estate. Goodness knows, you did it all single-handedly when my father was distracted by whiskey and horses. The point is, none of us thought we'd make it through the war, but here we are, in one piece, and it feels like another chance, an opportunity to put things right. Not just for our generation, but for little Jack as well. I know he's only tiny, but one day he'll be Lord Kenefick, and I want that to mean something.' Sam knew he sounded like an overenthusiastic schoolboy, but he and Kate really wanted to go back to Robinswood, and the only way it would work would be if Dermot and Isabella came as well.

Dermot smiled at the mention of his first grandson, though the idea that Kate's son was going to be a peer of the British realm, the country Dermot and so many others had fought tooth and nail to remove from Irish soil, was odd to say the least.

'Well, it is certainly something to think about. I'll talk to Isabella, see what she thinks. As you've no doubt come to realise, the women are the decision-makers in this family.' He smiled and took another sip of his pint.

Isabella had insisted on coming over to Brighton for the birth of Kate's baby. The whole thing had gone smoothly, and little Jack Kenefick was a lovely little lad who was thriving under his mother and grandmother's devotion. They were due to go back to Dublin tomorrow.

'The ladies' rule is something I am well aware of.' Sam smiled. 'But Kate and I are in complete agreement on this. The only way we can do it and not end up in the poorhouse is if you and Isabella are in on it with us.'

'Right, so explain to me again – and in detail this time – what you have in mind.' Dermot sat back.

Sam, encouraged, went on. 'So, our plan is to return to Robinswood and not open all of the house yet. It was in terrible condition when we left, and that was six years ago, so I can only imagine the state of it now. But Kate thinks we could open the small back wing – remember where Father had his study and sitting room? We could manage in that section for a while until we got the house back into some kind of habitable condition.'

Dermot said nothing, but he thought they were being overly optimistic at best and, at worst, positively delusional.

'Meanwhile, we take the land back from Charlie Warren – he's on a rolling year-to-year lease – get it into full production and start producing food for export. I gave him twelve months' notice six months ago.'

Dermot was impressed. At least the lad had been thinking it through; it wasn't some mad notion.

'The whole of the United Kingdom is crying out for food, and we can make a killing supplying it to them. I haven't a clue of how we'd do it, I'll be honest. But you do, and I am willing to work day and night if need be.'

'Go on.'

'Well, we are living, as you know, off my RAF salary and the rent of the land, but since Mother has remarried, she is no longer my responsibility, financially speaking. Perry Goodall has quite enough money for both of them. She sends her love, by the way, and is very sorry she wasn't here when Jack was born, but Perry needed her to play hostess for some business contacts of his in Nice. They are all British, but he's entertaining them on his new yacht, I believe. Now that the war is over, people can't get enough of travel and the good things in life, I suppose.' Sam shrugged.

'Is he good to her, that Perry Goodall?' Dermot asked.

Sam smiled, and Dermot knew why. The idea that he would come to care about Sam's snobby upper-crust mother was an odd one. But life was strange, and over time, resentment had turned to grudging respect and now, after all these years, was bordering on affection.

'Lord Goodall, as she refers to him when he's not there – Perry darling when he is – is actually besotted with her. They make an odd couple, no doubt about it. He's about a foot shorter than her for starters, but he is loaded, and he knows everyone, and he's thrilled to bits to have my mother on his arm, so it's all working out fine. Kate gets a great kick out of him, and he really enjoys her – he thinks she's hilarious.'

'I'm glad. Give her our regards when you speak to her. By the way, have you mentioned your harebrained scheme to her?' He grinned to take the sting out of his words.

'Actually, I have. In fact, when we spoke about it, she was the one who said the only way it could be done is if you and Isabella were in on it with us. She's even given over all her entitlements to my father's estate to me to help out financially, her only proviso being she never has to go back there.' Sam chuckled.

'She was never happy there anyway, that's for sure.'

'No indeed.' Sam nodded. 'She has no love of Ireland, and she remembers Robinswood as draughty, cold and damp. She was endlessly trying to make ends meet while maintaining a façade of wealth and attempting to manage my father as part of the bargain.'

Dermot chuckled at the memory of the previous Lord Kenefick. 'Old Austin was a great man for the horses and the bottle, and he was known all over Munster for his generosity, but he didn't want to face the facts. He left your mother in a right old mess. I did try to warn him, but he wouldn't listen, so I can't say I blame her for never wanting to darken the door of that place again.'

Sam paused, then asked the question he had debated about as he prepared for today's pitch. 'And you? Can you go back in there, after everything?'

His father-in-law shrugged. 'I could, I suppose. It's just a house. And to be honest with you, I saw so much during the Troubles with the British in the twenties to haunt a man, that what happened in Robinswood was nothing by comparison. So no, if I refuse this, it's not because I'm too scared or upset to go into that house again.'

'All right. So here's my offer in a nutshell. You and Isabella move back into your old farmhouse, which I will sign over legally to you. That is your home, you should never have been forced to leave it, and now you never will be. Charlie Warren's lease of the land will be up in the time it will take us to get organised. I have three months left on my commission before I'm discharged. We work the estate together, and we split the profits fifty-fifty.'

Dermot held his hand up. 'That's generous, Sam, but I don't need your charity. We're fine and settled at the Hamilton-Brooks place. Eve is with us, and we've a home there for as long as we want, so we don't need handouts.'

Sam cursed inwardly. He'd overdone it. Dermot Murphy was a proud man, and it had hurt him deeply to leave Robinswood six years ago.

'It's not charity, it's a plea. I want this so badly, and so does Kate. Whatever terms you dictate will be fine with us.'

Dermot gazed at him, saying nothing. Sam held his nerve. Eventually, the older man spoke. 'If I do it – and it's a big if – I'll have to talk to Isabella, and she may not want to. She likes it in Dublin, and she loves Georgie and Arthur. If she agrees, I'll take the house, but it's a seventy-thirty split to you. It's your land, for God's sake.'

'Fine, fine, whatever you say. This could be fantastic. The harder we work, the more we make. Then as we make money, and I'm sure we will, you can either keep your share or you have the option to buy some land from me at half of the market value. The only other thing I'll ask in return is that you help me get Robinswood habitable again. Kate has an idea that we open it up as a kind of country house hotel, Isabella doing the cooking – just a restaurant to begin with, but converting the rooms into guest bedrooms eventually.'

'Your mother would have a canary at the idea of riff-raff wandering the corridors of Robinswood.' Dermot chuckled.

'She doesn't care. She has Perry's very plush mansion to swan about in. And anyway, it's not hers, it's mine, and I just want to find a way we can live there. That house is too big for Kate and me, and everything has changed now. All that nonsense about class and position is a thing of the past.'

Dermot raised one eyebrow sceptically. 'It has and it hasn't changed, then, young Sam. It has and it hasn't.'

To read on, click here:
https://geni.us/ReturnToRobinswoodAL

ABOUT THE AUTHOR

Jean Grainger is a USA Today bestselling Irish author. She writes historical and contemporary Irish fiction and her work has very flatteringly been compared to the late great Maeve Binchy.

She lives in a stone cottage in Cork with her husband Diarmuid and the youngest two of her four children. The older two show up occasionally with laundry and to raid the fridge. There are a variety of animals there too, all led by two cute but clueless micro-dogs called Scrappy and Scoobi.

To download a free book, go to her website www.jean grainger.com and join the readers club. It's 100% free and always will be.

ALSO BY JEAN GRAINGER

To get a free novel and to join my readers club (100% free and always will be)

Go to www.jeangrainger.com

The Tour Series

The Tour

Safe at the Edge of the World

The Story of Grenville King

The Homecoming of Bubbles O'Leary

Finding Billie Romano

Kayla's Trick

The Carmel Sheehan Story

Letters of Freedom

The Future's Not Ours To See

What Will Be

The Robinswood Story

What Once Was True

Return To Robinswood

Trials and Tribulations

The Star and the Shamrock Series

The Star and the Shamrock

The Emerald Horizon

The Hard Way Home

The World Starts Anew

Made in the USA
Monee, IL
15 August 2022

11703818R00184